P9-BBU-964

Praise for the Novels of C.A. Belmond

A Rather Curious Engagement

"Lilting . . . it's fluffy and fun, even if you don't have your own yacht."
—*Publishers Weekly*

"Bound to charm romantic suspense fans." —*Booklist*

"What's not to like about C.A. Belmond's new novel? I was hooked by the end of the first page . . . *A Rather Curious Engagement* is delightful . . . something you can pass through the generations."
—*Story Circle Book Review*

"An entertaining and witty story, *A Rather Curious Engagement* displays the author's flair for keeping the reader attached to the spellbinding story and adventurous, enchanting characters."
—*Affaire de Coeur*

"*A Rather Curious Engagement* is narrated by Penny from her own insightful perspective . . . and is as well crafted as its predecessor. I highly recommend them both and look forward to any sequels to come starring this likable couple." —*Romance Reviews Today*

continued . . .

"*A Rather Curious Engagement* is a high-seas adventure with a wonderful little mystery and some nice laughs as Penny and Jeremy try to outwit some thieves . . . I found Penny and Jeremy to be a very endearing and sweet couple that I wouldn't mind reading more about in future books to come." —*Ramblings on Romance*

"Five stars! Excellent writing . . . I look forward to more books with these wonderful characters." —*Night Owl Review*

A Rather Lovely Inheritance

"A spirited heroine." —*Publishers Weekly*

"An entertaining yarn with family drama and intrigue aplenty."
—*Booklist*

"Utterly charming . . . excellent characterization and dialogue [with] a sweet touch of romance. If a novel can be both gentle and lively, surely this is one . . . *A Rather Lovely Inheritance* tantalizes and entertains with its mystery and skullduggery . . . Penny [is] a perfectly lovable heroine. It's a rare gem of a book that leaves behind a feeling of pure pleasure." —*Romance Reviews Today*

"I haven't read anything like it in quite a while, and I thoroughly enjoyed myself . . . Penny is a delightful heroine . . . Who wouldn't enjoy the unexpected chance to rattle around London and then fly off to the sunny Côte d'Azur?" —*DearAuthor.com*

"Combines suspense, romance, and crafty wit. The protagonist is a character to cheer for, and the mystery subplot will keep readers turning the pages." —*Romantic Times*

"[Penny] hooks everyone . . . with her klutzy optimism . . . Fans will enjoy the lighthearted breezy story line as the Yank takes England, France, and Italy." —*Midwest Book Review*

"[Has] everything—mystery, romance, [and] a whirlwind tour of Europe's hot spots." —*Kirkus Reviews*

"A return to the golden age of romantic suspense! *A Rather Lovely Inheritance* weds old-style glamour to chick-lit flair. You just want to move into the novel yourself—on a long-term lease, with hero and snazzy sports car included (villains sold separately)."

—Lauren Willig, author of *The Temptation of the Night Jasmine*

Other Novels by C.A. Belmond

A Rather Lovely Inheritance

A Rather Curious Engagement

A Rather Charming Invitation

C.A. Belmond

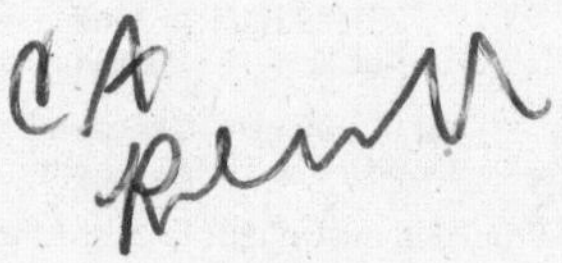

NAL NEW AMERICAN LIBRARY

New American Library
Published by New American Library, a division of
Penguin Group (USA) Inc., 375 Hudson Street,
New York, New York 10014, USA
Penguin Group (Canada), 90 Eglinton Avenue East, Suite 700, Toronto,
Ontario M4P 2Y3, Canada (a division of Pearson Penguin Canada Inc.)
Penguin Books Ltd., 80 Strand, London WC2R 0RL, England
Penguin Ireland, 25 St. Stephen's Green, Dublin 2,
Ireland (a division of Penguin Books Ltd.)
Penguin Group (Australia), 250 Camberwell Road, Camberwell, Victoria 3124,
Australia (a division of Pearson Australia Group Pty. Ltd.)
Penguin Books India Pvt. Ltd., 11 Community Centre, Panchsheel Park,
New Delhi – 110 017, India
Penguin Group (NZ), 67 Apollo Drive, Rosedale, North Shore 0632,
New Zealand (a division of Pearson New Zealand Ltd.)
Penguin Books (South Africa) (Pty.) Ltd., 24 Sturdee Avenue,
Rosebank, Johannesburg 2196, South Africa

Penguin Books Ltd., Registered Offices:
80 Strand, London WC2R 0RL, England

First published by New American Library,
a division of Penguin Group (USA) Inc.

First Printing, February 2010
10 9 8 7 6 5 4 3 2 1

Copyright © C.A. Belmond, 2010
Readers Guide copyright © C.A. Belmond, 2010
All rights reserved

NAL REGISTERED TRADEMARK—MARCA REGISTRADA

LIBRARY OF CONGRESS CATALOGING-IN-PUBLICATION DATA:

Belmond, C.A.
A rather charming invitation / C.A. Belmond.
p. cm.
ISBN 978-0-451-22908-3
1. Americans—Europe—Fiction. 2. Weddings—Fiction. I. Title.
PS3602.E46R35 2010
813'.6—dc22 2009031739

Set in Simoncini Garamond
Designed by Ginger Legato

Printed in the United States of America

Without limiting the rights under copyright reserved above, no part of this publication may be reproduced, stored in or introduced into a retrieval system, or transmitted, in any form, or by any means (electronic, mechanical, photocopying, recording, or otherwise), without the prior written permission of both the copyright owner and the above publisher of this book.

PUBLISHER'S NOTE
This is a work of fiction. Names, characters, places, and incidents either are the product of the author's imagination or are used fictitiously, and any resemblance to actual persons, living or dead, business establishments, events, or locales is entirely coincidental.
The publisher does not have any control over and does not assume any responsibility for author or third-party Web sites or their content.

The scanning, uploading, and distribution of this book via the Internet or via any other means without the permission of the publisher is illegal and punishable by law. Please purchase only authorized electronic editions, and do not participate in or encourage electronic piracy of copyrighted materials. Your support of the author's rights is appreciated.

For my hero

A Rather Charming Invitation

Part One

Chapter One

I must admit that my life—and my wedding day—might have been completely different, if, months earlier, I hadn't answered that telephone call. It was late spring, and the London days were warmer than anyone dared hope, but the nights still had a damp chill. We'd just lit a fire in the fireplace of the first-floor study at the back of the townhouse. One door in the study opened into Jeremy's office, and, on the opposite side of the room, another door opened into mine, so it was the ideal place to meet at the end of a busy workday.

Jeremy and I had finally arranged our schedules so that we could do something we'd always wistfully dreamed of: take time out to just sit there together, relaxing over a glass of wine before dinner; he in his favorite chair of caramel-colored leather, and me in my paisley wing chair. His leather ottoman was between us so that we could both put our feet up, and a low table stood beside us, with two glasses of burgundy.

"Bit more wine, old girl?" Jeremy said waggishly.

We were playing at being an old English couple. We kept grinning at each other like two happy fools. It was the first time in two years that we were actually sitting still, without being on some mad chase. It was quiet, very quiet. If I had a clock, you'd have heard it tick. As it was, the only sound was the rustle of *The Yachting Gazette* (Jeremy), the scratch of a pencil (me, with the final sketches for my wedding dress), the crackle of the fire, and the occasional sudden slump of a log. And just as I looked up surreptitiously at Jeremy to see if I could imagine him agreeing to wear a grey morning coat at our wedding, with perhaps a maroon silk scarf in his pocket to match the roses I would carry . . . *Bri-i-i-ing!* The telephone at my elbow broke the spell.

"I'm not expecting any calls," I said, hoping he'd get it.

"Nor I," said Jeremy firmly. "Let's toss a coin. Call it."

"Heads," I said. He flipped the coin. I lost. I sighed, and picked up the phone.

"Hello?"

"Bonjour, *chère* Penn-ee," said the voice on the other end—female, light, slightly high-pitched, and a bit agitated. "I am Honorine, your *cousine* from Mougins. Sorry for the inconvenience, but I need your help. I think I'm under arrest!"

"Who—what—?" I stammered. The one thing I didn't ask was, *where*? But that's what she chose to tell me.

"I am calling from my mobile phone and I am in ze police car!" she cried. "We are coming soon. The policeman, he does not *comprend* that I am innocent!"

"Good God," I said involuntarily, flabbergasted. This girl knew my name, but, after all, it had been printed recently in all the newspapers: *American Heiress Uncovers Another Priceless Treasure*. So, we'd had our share of strangers skulking on our doorstep—usually looking to engage us on some far-fetched quest for dubious fortune. I'd never heard of a cousin Honorine. Yet there was something authentic in her attitude that made me pause.

"Who is it?" Jeremy asked, startled by the comical look on my face.

"Er, well," I said, covering the mouthpiece, "she says she's my cousin, and she's under arrest."

Jeremy gave me a reproachful nod. "It's because of that brass plaque you put next to the front door. *Nichols and Laidley, Ltd. Discretion guaranteed. Inquire within.* You *will* keep pretending we live in a 1930s movie!" he chided affectionately.

"I hardly think you can lay the blame for this on my whimsical little sign," I objected. "Our new agency is bound to attract eccentric clients. This only proves that we've got to hire someone to field all the phone calls and letters." Just then, I heard a car pull up in front of the house.

"I think we are here now," said the girl on the phone. I repeated this to Jeremy.

"Oh, hell," he said resignedly, lifting his feet off the ottoman, rising from his chair, and going down the hallway to the little reception room at the front of the house. I followed him, and we peered out the window. Sure enough, a police car was parked at the curb. No siren, thankfully, but a few flashing lights. Jeremy studied the driver, who was getting out of the car.

"Hey," Jeremy said, "that's Danny."

Danny is the cop who keeps an eye on our corner of Belgravia, and he helped us out when this townhouse was burgled by cousin Rollo. Which gives you an idea of the kind of relatives I already have. So I think I can be forgiven for not having "the more, the merrier" as a family motto.

"I'd better see what this is all about," Jeremy said, going to the front door.

I remained at the window, transfixed. "*Allô, allô?*" said the voice in my ear, still on the phone, as the girl got out of the passenger side of the police car, her mobile phone clapped to her ear, while Danny escorted her toward our steps.

"Yes, we're coming to meet you at the door," I said hastily. The girl clicked off. I figured I'd better talk to my folks *tout de suite*, so I quickly made a long-distance call to the States. As soon as I heard my father's rich Burgundian drawl, I blurted out quite unceremoniously, "Hey, Dad, there's a French girl on my doorstep who says she's a cousin. Do we know somebody named Honorine?"

There was a brief pause as my father absorbed this.

"Honorine," I repeated helpfully. "Cousin. Do we know her? Is she for real?"

"*Bien sûr!*" he said. "She's actually the daughter of *ma cousine* Leonora. Is some-zing wrong? What's she doing in London?"

"Getting herself arrested," I cried. "She showed up here with a cop. What am I to do with her?"

"Let her in," my father advised quickly. "Help her if you can. Find out what's the trouble and call me back. Meanwhile, I'll phone Leonora to see what she can tell us."

I hung up, and now heard voices at the front door, so I went out to face the music. Jeremy was standing in the vestibule, holding the door open, talking to our visitors, but not inviting them in. Danny, with his policeman's expression of I've-seen-everything, stood on the front stoop, with the girl beside him.

Now I got a closer look at her. She was pretty in a schoolgirl kind of way, with shiny chestnut brown hair smoothed back from a clear, pale complexion and wide, bright dark eyes. I guessed her to be in her early twenties; she was wearing torn jeans and a chic jacket, with a student-style backpack slung behind her. She seemed frightened and affronted, but when she saw me peer around Jeremy, her face lit up with touching relief and trust.

Danny was in the midst of explaining to Jeremy that Honorine had been picked up with a bunch of drunken kids outside a bar not far from here. "She doesn't appear to have been drinking, and she insists she didn't even know the other kids on the street who were causing a ruckus—says she just happened to be there when the trouble broke out," Danny was saying in a low voice.

"Why'd you bring her here?" Jeremy asked, eyeing Honorine to see if she was conning us.

"She hasn't got an address in London, so I asked if she had any family in town, and she says you're it," Danny replied.

"She does. I mean, we are," I said. Jeremy gave me an astonished look. "I just spoke to my folks," I said hurriedly.

"When I heard this address, I knew it was you guys, so I thought I'd run her over here, but I'm sticking my neck out," Danny warned. "Can you vouch for her?"

I looked at Honorine. I realized we'd all been talking about her as if she were deaf, dumb, and blind . . . instead of merely French. "What happened?" I asked her gently.

With injured dignity, Honorine explained that she never meant to inconvenience us; she had planned to "crash" with some of her older ex-pat university chums who'd been working and living in London. Her pals had left her a standing invitation to join them whenever she could. But when she arrived, she discovered that her friends' group in London had recently split up, some married and some transferred to far-flung places like America and Japan.

So Honorine was left stranded. The landlord told her that only one of her friends was still in town, but had moved with no forwarding address. He gave her the name of the pub that her crowd favored. But when Honorine went there, the bartender told her she'd just missed her friend. And while she was out on the street trying to figure out her next move, she got swept up with that rowdy crowd outside the pub. Her voice went up in a slight wail at the mention of the pub, and she glanced apprehensively at Danny.

"How did you get my address?" I asked her.

"My mother sent you an invitation, weeks ago," Honorine said matter-of-factly. "She made me write out the address on the envelope for her. Did you not receive it?" she asked curiously, without recrimination.

"We've been just swamped with mail," I said apologetically, stepping back so that they could enter the vestibule. "We're only now catching up. . . ."

I glanced guiltily at the floor, where today's multitude of letters and courier envelopes were scattered in a corner, having been slipped through the slot. Neither of us had picked up the day's haul, because it would require carrying it into the adjacent reception room, and thereby facing up to the great big bin of unopened, unsolicited mail that just keeps stacking up with alarming regularity. When your inheritance is written up in the press, you start to feel like someone who won the lottery, because suddenly, everyone's your "best friend" and wants a piece of the action, including people you barely knew in school . . . or, relatives you never even knew you had.

Jeremy, aware of what all this mail on the floor must look like to outsiders, scooped it up and tried to offhandedly pitch it into the reception-room bin before anyone noticed. But Honorine and Danny, intrigued, followed him to the little room to see if the letter from her mother was there.

Honorine gazed at the overstuffed bin; then, like a hunting spaniel who'd spied its prey, she reached into the chaos, and pulled out a violet-colored envelope, lightly scented with violet sachet, addressed in a perfect, beautiful schoolgirl handwriting.

"Voilà!" she said triumphantly, handing it to me.

It was really quite lovely stationery, elegant and artful, as if from a bygone European era. While everyone watched, I opened the envelope carefully, unfolding the matching note inside:

We are so delighted to hear of your upcoming marriage, and wish to invite you and your fiancé to dine with us at our country cottage.

It was signed by Leonora. The invitation, indeed sent weeks ago, was for this upcoming weekend. "So sorry!" I said, deeply embarrassed. Honorine shrugged.

"Thank you, Danny," Jeremy said in his lawyer's voice. "We can take it from here."

"Just keep her off the streets and out of the pubs, hey?" Danny said as he departed.

"Won't you come in and sit down?" I asked Honorine, leading her through the hallway. She followed more shyly, now that the danger of being arrested was past, and she realized she was entering our little sanctuary.

Jeremy, ever observant, and with that quiet English reserve of his that goes a long way toward calming people down, said, "Honorine, when's the last time you've eaten?"

She was well-brought-up enough to deny the necessity of feeding her, so she answered very casually, "Oh, in Paris, just before I boarded the train."

"That must have been ages ago," I commented.

Honorine admitted that, upon her arrival in London, she had walked all the way from the station to the house where she expected to find her friend, and then spent the whole day searching for her. We insisted she come into the kitchen and share our supper. Jeremy and I had dined out at lunchtime rather significantly with law colleagues of his, so I'd planned to have only soup tonight. But I managed to add some tasty cold sandwiches on a nice fresh baguette, with olives and a green salad, all of which Honorine ate very gratefully. Despite her genteel manners, it was obvious that she was really quite hungry.

Between her French delicacy and Jeremy's reserve, the conversation would have been quiet and tactful, with huge gaps of unspoken questions. However, although my bloodline is both French and English, I am an American, and we have no qualms about cutting to the chase.

"So, what's up, Honorine? Did you run away from home?" I asked, half-teasing and half-serious. Her startled, then sheepish expression made it clear that she had indeed flown the coop.

But all she said was, "What must you think of me!" She sighed, glancing down in embarrassment at her own dusty, disheveled state. "*Normalement*, I would not choose this foolish way to introduce myself to my famous *cousine*, Penny Nichols, 'the international, adventuring American heiress'!" she exclaimed with a smile as she quoted the papers. "I wonder," she murmured, "if I might impose upon you further, to allow me to wash up a bit? Then I will look for a student hostel or something—"

I saw the fatigued look in her eyes. "You can stay overnight," I said promptly. "We have a guest suite upstairs, so you'll have a bath and bed to yourself. Tomorrow we'll sort this all out."

"*Merci*," she said, following me up the staircase. We passed the second floor, which had belonged to Great-Aunt Penelope, with its library, two bedrooms, dining room and little kitchen; these were now our living quarters. Jeremy and I had managed to pool some of our unexpected windfall to buy the other two apartments from elderly residents eager to retire to warmer climes. We'd converted the first level into our offices. The third-floor flat was a one-bedroom version of the second, perfect for guests.

"You'll have plenty of privacy here," I assured Honorine. She gave me a grateful smile as I left, closing the door behind me.

When I came back downstairs, Jeremy had already tidied up the last of the dishes in the big kitchen where we prefer to cook at the end of a busy workday. We returned to our study, and he said wryly, "Well, Honorine got out of telling us the rest of her story rather gracefully. And I must say, you aided and abetted her. Sleep-over, indeed. What will you do if she's brought drugs or other problems to this little slumber party of yours?"

"Oh, stop it," I said. "Are you joking? That kid?"

The phone rang, and this time Jeremy picked it up, but when he heard it was my father, he switched to speaker mode, so we could all take part in the conversation. Dad announced that Leonora was absolutely livid with Honorine, who, after a mother-daughter quarrel, departed without so much as a by-your-leave, and had now disgraced the family by nearly getting arrested in London.

"Leonora says she cannot think what possessed her wayward daughter to trouble you two in this way," my father said, having been instructed to deliver this message, "so she apologizes deeply for the inconvenience."

"Well, we owe her an apology as well," I confessed. "We never answered the nice invitation that she sent us, weeks ago. Don't tell Mom."

"I heard that," came my mother's crisp English reprimand, as she picked up the extension. "You are wasting your time, swearing your father to secrecy. We tell each other everything, don't we, darling?"

"Everything I can remember," my father replied, playfully exaggerating his age.

Jeremy just grinned at me. He's fascinated by my parents, whom he sees as a wonderful pair of eccentric hermits with a mystifying synchronicity between them. From my father, I inherited my brown eyes and a fascination with tales from the past. From my mother, I got my copper-colored hair and a fairly unexpected way of occasionally blurting out my thoughts to clear the air.

"Dad, what's the story with Leonora?" I inquired. "Do you know her well? How come I never met her?"

"Ah, *oui*," he sighed. "Leonora is my younger cousin. Her mother and mine were sisters. We grew up together in Burgundy."

Now it was starting to make sense, although I knew so little about my French relatives, apart from the kind of family lore that gets repeated, like heirloom silver being polished again and again. I was aware that my Grandmother Aimée had died in France when Dad was twenty years old and unmarried, before he came to the States to pursue his career as a chef. His father, an American sent overseas as a soldier, had died even earlier, when my dad was only fourteen. So, in coming to New York, Dad was really looking to leave France behind, and have the new experience of exploring his American roots.

It was in New York that he met up with my mother, who was deliriously happy on her own, released from being under her English family's thumb. I'm the only one in the family with a nostalgia for Europe and a hankering for a glamorous past I never had . . . well, until now. Life, these days, has exceeded even my wildest expectations. And now, finding out about our French relations was, to me, a bit like opening presents on Christmas morning.

My mother interjected, "Leonora married into a very old, influential French family. So, that makes hers the most illustrious branch of your father's family tree! She lives in Mougins, an elegant town not far from Cannes."

"Did *you* ever meet them, Mom?" I asked curiously.

"Oh, yes. I met cousin Leonora and her husband Philippe once, before your father and I got married. It is actually a great honor that she has invited you to come to her home. They are really quite charming, very proper, with beautiful manners, and they're very generous people. They gave us a gift of a beautiful Sèvres soup tureen as a wedding present. Go, you'll have a nice time, as your French relatives are fond of doing things *en famille.*"

"Besides," my father said pragmatically, giving me a hint of what was to come, "it is best to do what Leonora asks, because in the end she always prevails anyway. Even when she was a little girl she was *très formidable.*"

"A real bossy-boots," Jeremy translated.

"*C'est vrai!*" my father chuckled.

"Anyway, you *should* meet your French relations," my mother said positively.

"Besides, if you and Jeremy go to Mougins, you can make sure that Honorine returns home as her mother wishes," my father added meaningfully.

"Er, that raises an uncomfortable question," I pointed out. "If we go there and accept a wedding gift, does it mean we have to invite all our French relatives to the wedding?" The idea of a huge guest list, filled with people I didn't know, gave me a strange feeling of stage-fright.

"Yes, invite them all," my mother said serenely, "but bear in mind that they may have asked you to visit them so that you won't be offended if they don't show up for your wedding, especially if you decide to have it in England—and by the way, dear, when *will* you decide? We must make plans, you know; caterers and florists can be beastly. Have you even set a date yet?"

"We think maybe September," I said hurriedly.

"September? You're quite mad, you know," my mother exclaimed. "An autumn wedding when spring is already on the wane? How do you think this will come about, by waving a magic wand?" she added incredulously. I knew this tone well. She was on the verge of telling me that she can't believe I'm her daughter, so disorganized and impractical.

"Yes, I *have* been putting off a lot of decisions," I said, since there was no point in denying this. I glanced at the wedding-dress sketches still lying on the ottoman where I'd left them. They'd been sent to me by that nice Monsieur Lombard, whose atelier was busy enough without getting last-minute notes from the bride. A strange feeling of panic arose in me, and I turned resolutely away from the sketches.

My father, sensing two females about to—well, I guess females don't exactly lock horns, but anyway, Dad cleared his throat and said, "Let's take one zing at a time. Yes, you should experience Mougins—it's a great capital of *gastronomie* restaurants that attracts connoisseurs from all over the world—even the Parisians will go out of their way to eat the cuisine of the great chefs there. And," he added, "although Leonora is a distant cousin to you, you'd better call her '*Tante* Leonora'. It's more respectful, and it's what we do in our family."

"Okay," I said, delighted to have a newly-minted French "auntie," and grateful to my dad for bailing me out of the wedding talk.

"Meanwhile, you might ask Honorine to give her mother a call," Mom suggested.

After we hung up, Jeremy and I just looked at each other. I said, "Well, I guess we're going to Mougins."

"Seems like an enormous spot of bother just to go and pick up a soup bowl," Jeremy groused jokingly, indicating that he'd already made up his mind to grin and bear it. I hugged him for this.

"Tureen," I corrected. "It's beautiful, I remember it. It always had pride of place on the sideboard of my parents' dining room. Besides, it's not about the gift. It's about family."

"Right," said Jeremy. "But don't you wonder why your father, in all these years, hasn't gone back to visit?"

"Well, it looks like we're about to find out," I said.

Chapter Two

The next morning, when I came down to breakfast, Jeremy had already made coffee and toast; then he'd disappeared into his office, from which I heard various curses and growls. Eventually, when he returned for a second cup of coffee, he announced, "We're having incredible computer problems—the whole bloody system crashed, probably under the sheer weight of all these junk e-mails. If I can't fix it myself, I'll have to get someone to take a look at it. Meanwhile, you'd best stay off your computer."

And he drifted right back out again. The computer glitch gave me an excuse to linger over my coffee and have a little tête-à-tête with Honorine when she came down to breakfast, sleepy-eyed. She was a bit disoriented, which I shamelessly exploited by peppering her with questions. I couldn't help it, I was bursting with curiosity.

Stirring in her sugar and milk, she confided that this was the first time she'd impulsively strayed from her home and country. As she chattered on, I soon discovered that, while Honorine had a certain sophistication, which came from being raised in a "good" family, she was also a bit innocent, having led a fairly sheltered life. The dreams she had in her head were intellectual, not born of a wide experience of the world; and I saw that there was something girlish about the way she'd secretly plotted her escape, in theory, not really making concrete plans, not even stopping to alert her friends of her imminent arrival, as if she feared that doing so would give fate a chance to stop her. So, one day when the family pressure got to be too much, she just impulsively got on the train, and *voilà*!

"But—what is it about your family that's so . . . difficult?" I quizzed delicately. She blurted out that her mother and big brother were trying to marry her off. "Wow," I said. "Marriage already? Aren't you just out of school?"

Honorine nodded vigorously. "Can you believe it?" she demanded. "They are from another century, my parents. And my brother David, well, he's a big bore!"

I was still admiring her thick, curling dark eyelashes and pale skin. She was as pretty as a doll, but now her eyes flashed with vitality and fierce intelligence. "So, who's the guy?" I asked, pouring her more coffee so she'd keep talking.

Honorine said, "His name is Charles. *Alors,* we've known each other since we were little kids, but really, now that he's out of school, he is turning out to be a *bourgeois fou*. Does exactly what his parents tell him to do. It is not at all romantic. All the parents are arranging this, just because it's good for both family businesses. He studied law, and might go into politics, so what he really wants is a politician's wife. It has nothing to do with me. Frankly, I would rather kiss a pig than marry a lawyer!"

Jeremy entered now, just in time to hear this insult to his profession, but he chose to ignore it. However, I saw that it registered. "The computer guy says he can't tell what's wrong with it from our phone conversation," he announced, having abandoned the DIY approach. "He'll stop by on Friday to have a go." He glanced at Honorine, then at me.

"So," he said meaningfully, "did you tell Honorine about our upcoming weekend in Mougins?"

I shook my head at him warningly, then quickly turned to her, and said as casually as I could, "We'd love to take your folks up on their invitation, if it still stands."

"But of course, I'm sure it does," Honorine said somewhat absently.

"Great," I said heartily. "Why don't you come along with us?"

At the aghast look on her face, I felt just terrible, for I'd practically told her that she wasn't welcome here, which normally I would never do. It was all Jeremy's fault. Rushing me into this phony ruse to get her to join us this weekend. And my father, too, who had come up with this scheme. Men. Always in such a hurry to dispense with a problem, before you've even figured it out.

"I don't want to go home!" Honorine cried. "I want to travel, and see the world, and find my one true love, just like you, Penny! Don't worry, I won't impose on you any longer. I will have a career and get an apartment of my own."

Now I gave Jeremy a dirty look. She'd be back out on the street in no time, after very nearly getting arrested. And it would be on our heads.

"In London?" Jeremy said to her incredulously. "Honorine, do you have any money?" She mumbled that she'd brought a little, but not enough to put down on a flat and pay monthly rent all by herself. "Then," Jeremy said sternly, "how can you be independent?"

"*The money you have gives you freedom; the money you pursue enslaves you,*" Honorine quoted loftily.

"What wise person said that?" I whispered to her conspiratorially.

She looked at me as if it were obvious. "Why, Rousseau, of course," she said.

"Philosophy major," Jeremy guessed. She nodded triumphantly. I was impressed. Jeremy wasn't.

"In France, philosophy majors are extremely respectable," I reminded him.

"Yes, well, she's in London-town now," Jeremy said, not ungently. "So it's not exactly a ticket into a high-paying job in this vast, competitive metropolis full of kids with connections, is it?"

I couldn't deny it, but I didn't want to say outright that Honorine didn't have a hope in hell. But she got it, of course, and appeared so crestfallen that Jeremy looked immediately contrite.

"Actually, we're asking you to come with us to Mougins for purely selfish reasons," he said, more in the protective tone of an older brother now. "You can help us out with your mum, and explain how hopeless we are with our mail system."

Honorine smiled, but turned to me, seeking my opinion trustfully. "Yes, we need you to help us with your family, so we don't commit another faux pas," I agreed. I was shuffling through my scrawled, disorganized "organizer", and I now said involuntarily, "Holy smokes! Jeremy, we're supposed to have dinner with your mother on Saturday!"

"Never mind that," Jeremy said firmly, having decided that the only way to get rid of Honorine was to personally escort her back home this weekend. "Mum won't mind rescheduling."

Dubiously, I picked up the phone. Jeremy's mother answered it and, to my surprise, although she was perfectly willing to change the date, she insisted that she really had to see us before we went off to France. Something was clearly up. She never insisted on anything. But now here she was, mysteriously saying, "Darling, let's at least meet for drinks and a curry on Thursday night? All right?"

"Tomorrow? Okay," I said meekly. This was, after all, my future mother-in-law. I wondered if I'd ever learn to stop calling her "Aunt Sheila", since she'd been married to my mother's brother, Uncle Peter, who was Jeremy's stepfather. The world is a complicated place. At least, my world was, more and more each passing day.

Chapter Three

So the next evening, we got dressed up to meet Jeremy's mum for dinner. I put on a nice pale green knit dress to celebrate spring, after a long winter of black-clad city folk. When I came downstairs, Honorine gave me a quick glance of approval, smiling in that appreciative way that Europeans do when you make an effort to look good.

"That color is *magnifique* with your red hair," she noted. Then she asked daringly, in a low voice so Jeremy wouldn't hear in the next room, "Is it true that you and Jeremy were raised as cousins, even though, technically, you are not related?"

"Yes, we first met many years ago, as kids. But he grew up in London, and I grew up in America, so we didn't meet again until just recently, when my Great-Aunt Penelope died," I explained.

"And you were both heirs to her fortune?" Honorine prompted. I realized that she, and perhaps her entire family, had heard quite a lot about it, but surely not from my parents, who never volunteered personal information. She still seemed to be quoting the international press. When I nodded, she sighed and said, "And when you met again you fell in love? How *romantique*!"

She wasn't really prying; it was more as if she wanted confirmation that life could be more exciting than the usual path which her elders told her she must take. This I understood perfectly. Still, I felt suddenly self-conscious, and I changed the subject, saying, "Honorine, will you be okay alone here tonight? There's roast chicken in the refrigerator, and lots of take-out menus in the drawer."

What I wanted to say was, *So stay put and don't go out and get yourself arrested again*. She sensed this, and made it easy for me.

"Yes, perfect, you mustn't worry," she said, opening a book. "I'll stay in tonight. It's fine."

"Great," I said, relieved. "Maybe you could call your mother, just to let her know you're all right," I added, mindful of my father's suggestion.

"I guess so," she sighed.

"Please do, otherwise I'll get a scolding from *my* mom," I explained with a grin. She nodded.

As Jeremy closed the door behind us, I still had misgivings. "I really hope she doesn't bolt," I said with some trepidation.

"Well," Jeremy replied cheerfully, "we can hardly be responsible if she does."

"Oh, cut it out," I said. "We can't turn her loose in London. She's like the kid sister I always wanted. Something about her brings out the maternal instinct in me. I didn't even know I had one."

"You're just a kid yourself," Jeremy teased. "Newly born." He gazed at me. I gazed back. He looked so nice tonight, as always—that dark wavy hair, blue eyes, and the confident way he has of navigating the world, with a teasing humor that invites you to enjoy the small absurdities of life. Jeremy's the kind of guy who, when his attention is focused on you, well . . . it makes you feel as if today is your lucky day.

"You're only four years older than me," I flirted back, "but, I *suppose* that entitles you to talk to me like Old Father Time."

"Someone has to look after you," he said. "Might as well be me." In such moments, the warmth in his voice actually does makes me want to swoon. Dope that I am. I wondered if this feeling could possibly last if—when, I mean—we got married. A chill of fear ran through me. Of course it could. No reason to pay any attention to those fatalistic articles and statistics about the thrill going out of marriage after a couple of years . . . right?

London was in a good mood tonight. Like any important city, its daily vibe has an immediate effect. On bad days, when it's hostile and defeating, every move you make seems to be an uphill battle. But on nights like this, the air positively pulsed with a collective jubilance that instantly put spring in my step. There were birds flitting in the venerable old green trees that ringed the small parks we passed, and the scent of the earth made my nostrils twitch with pleasure like a colt who wants to kick up its heels. Other people on the street must have felt it tonight, too, for they were laughing and hurrying in and out of taxicabs and Tube terminals, as if eager to collectively celebrate having survived another winter.

When we arrived at the elegant Indian restaurant that Aunt Sheila had selected "for a curry", and the hostess took our coats, Jeremy said, "There's Mum . . . looks like she's got a friend with her . . . ?"

I glanced across the dining area, which was decorated all in red, with pretty textured red wallpaper and draperies, and a red-and-gold bar, and red leathery seats. One wall was mirrored, and the brass lighting fixtures twinkled in its reflection. In a far corner, a man was playing sitar music, his bare feet covered with a cloth so as not to offend the Raj. The waiters all wore black pants and gold-and-white embroidered shirts with full sleeves. It was a festive atmosphere, yet a calm, dignified place.

Aunt Sheila was seated at a nice corner table with a curved banquette that faced the door, so she'd be able to spot us when we came in. She looked very chic, as always, with her slim figure, and blonde hair cut in that timeless bob with bangs that emphasized her green eyes and slightly pouty lips. But there was a new pink flush to her face tonight, and her smile was less guarded. Right next to her, with his arm around the back of her seat, was a man whom she quickly introduced to us as Guy Ansley. In a flash I saw that he was her new beau.

He was old-fashioned enough to rise when I approached the table and took my seat opposite him, and he kissed my hand, which I could see struck Jeremy as a pretentious thing for an Englishman to do. Guy was dressed in an expensive, tailored grey suit with a bright yellow sweater, a silk ascot, a neon blue handkerchief, yellow socks and conspicuously new shiny shoes. He was beefy, genial and laughed easily . . . and loudly. As we exchanged pleasantries about the weather and the traffic and all that harmless stuff people say to start a conversation, I noticed that Guy kept one arm around Aunt Sheila the whole time, even as we began to eat the little appetizers that started appearing at our table.

"Well, shall we break 'nan' together?" he asked, nodding at the arrival of the Indian bread.

I grinned, and Aunt Sheila caught my eye and smiled wryly. If every man in the entire restaurant had been assembled at the bar so that I could guess which one was her date, it's quite possible that this is the last fellow I would have picked. And she knew it, too, but it didn't dampen her spirits one little bit. She seemed to be in on the joke, and was nonetheless aglow in a way that I'd never seen her before, making her look years younger. Not once had Aunt Sheila felt the need to identify Guy as "my friend" or anything else, but it was pretty clear that he was indeed someone very special.

"Shall we order the main course now?" Guy beamed. I stole a look at poor Jeremy, whose shocked expression was the same as if, say, he'd suddenly swallowed an olive with the pit still in it. I knew this must be difficult for him, and I wondered why Aunt Sheila hadn't warned him in advance. But perhaps she knew her son even better than I.

"They do a nice chef's special-for-four, featuring various platters that we can all share," Guy said hopefully. "What say we go for it, eh?"

It was clear that he intended to pay, and now, as he generously contemplated the wine list, I saw that he had absolutely no airs about him. He liked to tell silly jokes, which he himself enjoyed immensely. He even, at one point, slapped Jeremy on the back; and when Aunt Sheila broached the subject of our upcoming wedding, he insisted on ordering a bottle of champagne "for good luck", he said. There was something endearingly genuine when he raised his glass in a toast to Jeremy and me, saying, "I want to wish you both the greatest happiness together, long life and good health", as if he meant every word.

We clinked glasses, and for a moment I thought all was well, until Guy fecklessly and broadly hinted, "Who knows? Someday soon there may be other wedding bells ringing for some other lucky bloke."

And that, I think, was when Jeremy began to despise him.

He didn't really show it. Jeremy was perfectly polite, but I knew he was struggling; and again, I felt that Aunt Sheila had been a bit unfair to him. Of course, it would be a vast understatement to say that she was a secretive woman when it came to her love affairs. Before marrying my Uncle Peter, she had been desperately in love with Jeremy's dad, an Italian-American musician who'd arrived in London's swinging '60s, but died shortly after serving in Vietnam, when Jeremy was a baby. And the thing is, she never told Jeremy about his real father, not until quite recently, when the truth came out during an inheritance kerfuffle over Great-Aunt Penelope's will. So I could see why Jeremy didn't need another shockeroo like this.

"Guy is an horologist, Penny," Aunt Sheila said. "I imagine you and he must have a lot in common, you know, with your history-research background."

"Ah, yes, Sheila told me about your career!" Guy said, and we plunged into a conversation about his business of antique clocks, which fascinated me. While I was listening to Guy's anecdotes, Aunt Sheila, sensing Jeremy's confusion, began to speak in low, soothing tones to him; so I suspected she'd deliberately gotten the conversation to break off into two, giving her some time to talk with her son.

When dessert came, accompanied by an after-dinner liqueur of fennel and other delightful herbs, Aunt Sheila said, with a falsely casual tone, "Jeremy darling, your grandmother telephoned to say she'd like you to bring Penny to meet her, at a little party she's throwing in your honor. Soon. Very soon."

To be honest, I'd completely forgotten about Jeremy's English grandmother on his mum's side. Possibly because, even after all these years, Aunt Sheila has barely been on speaking terms with her own family. Jeremy always acts as if he wants nothing to do with them, but he'd told me that, as a kid, he periodically had to put in an appearance whenever his wealthy grandmother summoned him, usually on landmark occasions, such as his graduation from Oxford. And, his previous wedding. And his divorce, which she tried to talk him out of, for appearances' sake. Now, it seemed, his grandmum wanted to look over his new bride. (That would be me.) Here in London. In a fortnight. I gulped.

At this point we were standing in the front of the restaurant, waiting for our coats, and Aunt Sheila's came first, so Guy was helping her into it, as they murmured companionably together. Jeremy and I exchanged covert, dismayed whispers.

"I do hate to bring you to my dragon of a grandmother," Jeremy said apologetically, "but if we refuse, we'll never hear the end of it."

So here I said one of those things that women in love tend to spontaneously say, but really shouldn't. "Oh, it's okay," I said philosophically, "after all, she *is* your grandmother."

"Thanks," he said gratefully. "I'll tell Mum to let her know we'll come."

"You okay about Guy?" I asked him in a low voice.

"Do I have a choice?" he inquired. Guy and his mum turned to us now, smiling.

"It's such a lovely night," Aunt Sheila said to us as we stepped out onto the street. "Let's all go for a walk together."

I was, by now, highly amused at her attitude, for she was still up to something. We soon found out what. As we turned a corner, she and Guy came to an abrupt stop in front of a locked clock shop with these words lettered in a fan-shaped curve: *The Village Horologist. Clocks Bought, Sold and Repaired.* I thought it was touching that she wanted us to see Guy's business, perhaps to convince Jeremy that Guy was a solid, reliable character.

Guy pulled out a jingling key-ring from his pocket, inserted the key in the lock, and pushed open the door. "Come in, come in!" he cried. "Look around, look around!"

The shop was home to an amazing family of clocks, each with

its own personality. Grandfather clocks, carriage clocks, pocket watches, table clocks . . . some with their movements encased in glass so you could see their elaborate mechanisms at work. Each were ticking precisely like the busy timekeepers they were, and every now and then one would suddenly start chiming from its corner, startling us with its tinkling or tolling, for they were set to various time zones around the world.

"Penny, have a look at this one, and tell me what you think," Guy said, taking my hand and drawing me toward a table where a remarkable fireplace mantel clock stood.

Its case was made of partly gilded silver, with a clockface of champlevé silver and black Roman numerals above a base of rosewood and tortoiseshell, with a movement of brass and steel. The top of the case had thin, flat, overlapping circular discs, looking like silver DVDs, that stacked upon one another like a wedding cake. Seen from overhead, the largest, bottom disc represented the seasons, topped by a smaller disc for the months of the year, which in turn was topped by an even smaller one representing the days of the week, until finally, the littlest one of all, for the hours.

Atop this stack of discs was a small but stunning sculpted silver figure of Apollo in his chariot, holding the reins of his winged horse. They seemed captured in midflight at their daily task of hauling the rising sun across the sky and plunging it into the sea to bring the day to a close. When the clock struck the hour, as it was doing now, the figure of the sun god and his horse rotated, to point to the hour, day, month, and season, displayed on the outer rims of the stacked discs, which simultaneously, incrementally moved into place beneath the figures; and the clock's chime gave out a mellow, golden sound. There was something very appealing and dear about the way the Apollo figure moved, as if it were trying to engage us, to tell us that our time, and so our lives, were as fleet as a winged horse.

"Beautiful," I breathed. Guy waited expectantly for my professional assessment. "I'd say it's early to mid-1700s, maybe French?" I asked. "Although there seems a German influence, too . . ."

"Augsburg," Guy nodded. "But, made by a French clock maker and his astronomer wife."

I was captivated by its traditional images and mysterious mechanisms, and Guy was delighted to answer all my questions. "And what does it say here?" I asked, peering at an engraving in Latin. "*Tempus est circulus grandis sine finibus,*" I read aloud.

"It says 'Time is a great circle without end'," Guy translated. "The Latin proverb also gives you the exact year the clock was made—" He broke off when Jeremy accidentally knocked into a table clock; but as it wobbled, Jeremy moved swiftly to catch it, just in time.

Aunt Sheila said playfully, "Well, come on, Guy, *tell* them!"

"Anyway," Guy said with a bit of a flourish, "I am pleased to say that this is the very clock which Sheila and I have chosen as our wedding gift for you two." I saw Jeremy's jaw muscle twitch.

"Oh, no, that's too much," I protested. "I didn't realize what you were up to!"

Aunt Sheila said firmly, "It is *our* gift to you both. So, you cannot refuse. We hope it keeps track of many good times, and many years of happiness for you both."

Jeremy bore up manfully, overriding his misgivings about Guy, and thanking them with true appreciation. Guy beamed, and said he'd deliver it to us as soon as he cleaned and polished it up. We went back out onto the street, where Guy had a parked car waiting. "Give you a lift?" he inquired.

"No, thanks," Jeremy said decisively. "It's a nice night, and a walk will do us good."

"Right, then. Have a great time in Moo-gans!" Guy called out, as he and Aunt Sheila drove off.

Jeremy stood watching their car disappear, a look of disbelief on his face. "Bloody hell," he said. "Everyone's gone barmy. Can you believe that jerk?"

"I think Guy is really sweet and genuine, under all his bluster," I offered. "And he clearly adores your mom."

Jeremy glanced at me, slightly accusingly. "Do you really like that Trojan Horse of his?" he said.

"I do," I replied. But I knew he meant that I was helping this stranger muscle into the family. "Look," I said, "I realize the last thing you need right now is even the suggestion of another stepdad. But think of it—you're getting married, and no matter how close we are to your mom, it's as if she's losing the only man she cares about—you. So, don't you think she's entitled to good companionship?"

"I don't deny it," Jeremy said stiffly. "I merely suggest she could have done better."

"On the other hand, she could have done a lot worse," I warned.

Jeremy shook his head, then gazed upward and broke into a sudden smile, saying, "Look."

We'd reached an old, curving, narrow street of cobblestone, lined with fascinating hobby and antiques shops. Heirloom furniture, rare books, coin and stamp collectors—but he was pointing to a jewelry store. Beneath the main sign it said, *Classic Wedding Bands for Timeless Young Lovers.* We drew closer. The place specialized in wedding rings designed in various retro styles like Deco and Art Nouveau. The shops on this street were open late tonight, so Jeremy took my hand and said, "Let's go in."

We had agreed to keep our wedding bands simple, yet for weeks we'd searched in vain, because somehow everything we saw seemed overblown, and had left us unenthused. But tonight must have been one of those occasions when the tide of fate turns, and things that were once difficult suddenly become effortless. For here in this little shop, we immediately spotted displays of appealing, original designs, quite unique from one another, without the usual look of modern, mass-produced bling.

As we peered into the glass cases, the smiling, bald-headed proprietor pulled out a particular set of rings that we pointed to: elegantly understated, modestly priced matching bands of antique gold with a nicely engraved Deco swirl. We tried them on, examining them in the light.

"That's it," Jeremy said positively, "this is the one I like." I nodded in happy agreement. The jeweler measured us and said he would size them, and have them engraved on the inside in the script we selected, to say *Penny and Jeremy* and the year.

"There's an excellent engraver on this street who does all our work," the jeweler assured us. He took down our names and address. Jeremy paid for them, and, feeling his mission accomplished, drifted to the front of the store, as men do when they're waiting for a woman who's still browsing.

"This wedding band will make a perfect complement to your engagement ring," the jeweler told me, pointing to the ring on my finger. It was of a similar antique gold, which Jeremy had had specially made with a ruby that his mom handed down to him, who in turn had gotten it from her mother. I trembled slightly at the thought of soon meeting Jeremy's ruby-bequeathing grandmother in person.

"I'd like to get my fiancé a groom's gift," I confided in a low voice to the jeweler, nodding surreptitiously toward an interesting case of men's cuff-links, tie-clips and rings, all with unusual designs. But before I could examine them further, Jeremy chose that moment to come drifting closer, eager to move on. The jeweler smiled at me without betraying our secret conversation, for he knew I'd be back.

On the way home, the night air had a velvety freshness to it, with the scent of budding blossoms and leaves on the trees, so welcoming after the cold, nearly scentless winter. We passed other people who were also lingering in the longer daylight hours, meandering by with a pleasant nod to fellow strollers, instead of the usual hurried indifference.

"Boy, everyone's in a good mood tonight," I commented. Jeremy gave me a smile.

"Are they?" he asked, his hand tightening in mine. He drew me closer into his arms, and gave me a long, lingering kiss that made me feel as if we were on a little planet of our own, suspended in time and space, spinning sweetly, with only the support of sheer air and light, yet as secure as any star in the nightly firmament. It felt deliciously dangerous to be this much in love.

Chapter Four

When we arrived home, the whole first floor of the townhouse was bright with lights.

"Bet she's invited all her friends to your sleepover jamboree," Jeremy commented, putting his key in the lock.

We stepped into the vestibule, and peered into the reception room, where Honorine was quietly and happily ensconced at the little walnut desk with a computer on it. She didn't even hear us come in, because she had earphones on her head, and suddenly began singing to herself in French to the jazzy tune she was listening to, loud, in the way people do when they can't hear their own volume.

I surveyed the room in amazement. The cluttered, old-fashioned reception parlor, previously overwhelmed with mail, files and news clippings waiting to be sorted, had quickly yet brilliantly been transformed into a neat, orderly front office.

On closer inspection I saw that the unopened mail was now carefully arranged into desk trays, labelled according to the week of the postmark. Honorine was still clacking away at the computer, but she must have felt my gaze now, so she looked up, blushed a little, and smiled. "Oh, it's you!" she cried, pulling off her earphones.

"What's going on with the computer?" Jeremy asked.

"Hope you don't mind!" she answered, beaming. "But I got so bored watching TV. I was dying to go on the Internet." She slid her chair aside so Jeremy could see the screen, and she demonstrated how she'd got it working again. "It's just that the older software was fighting with the new. Mostly, it needed an upgrade, and a couple of other changes, to tell it which voice to listen to. You see?"

Jeremy, suitably impressed, said, "Are you a programmer?"

"No, not at all. Really it's not that complicated," she said modestly, "once you figure out how to get in and talk to it . . . See . . ." Honorine clacked away some more, whizzing through a demonstration of the new system, brisk and efficient. "Now it should be much faster for you."

I could see how hard she'd worked to impress us. "Honorine," I said. "You're incredible."

I gave Jeremy a meaningful look. "Well?" I said. "Who says a philosophy student isn't marketable?"

Excited, Honorine reached into her backpack lying beside her on the floor, and she pulled out a wad of papers and handed them to Jeremy. I peered over his shoulder. Page after page, in French and English, were recommendations from her teachers, saying that Honorine was scrupulous, hardworking, highly intelligent, as honorable as her name implied; and one teacher in particular made a point of saying that Honorine possessed an exceptional mind that was *très subtil*.

Subtlety, evidently, is highly prized in a philosophy major. So is argument and persuasion. I read on. Honorine was versed in five languages, including Chinese. Jeremy, who'd initially taken her for a slacker, was profoundly impressed by both her accomplishments and sincerity.

"You know," Honorine suggested shyly, blushing a little, "perhaps . . . you think . . . I might be a suitable personal secretary here in London. Do you know of anyone who needs an assistant?" She turned beseechingly to me, obviously asking-without-asking for a job.

"Well," I admitted, "it's true we need someone, but honestly we really don't know how it will work or where things will lead . . ."

Her face lit up with pleasure. "*Parfait!*" she cried.

"Now, hold on," Jeremy cautioned. "For one thing, you are vastly overqualified."

"It could just be temporary," she assured him quickly, "only until I can find my true vocation." If anybody else had put it that way, they might have sounded affected. But in Honorine's voice, it seemed totally natural. "A little experience for me, without a long-term commitment for you."

I saw that it wasn't really fair of me to leave Jeremy the role of "the heavy" in all this, what with Honorine's face all alight with hope. So I added more cautiously, "I think we should see what your mother has to say. Why don't we ask her when we go to visit this weekend? All three of us?"

Honorine understood the bargain, and now she had a look of confident determination. "Yes, I will come with you. I know we can lay out a convincing case," she declared. "*Bonne nuit!*" she said brightly, and scampered up to the guest bedroom.

Jeremy waited until she was completely out of earshot; then he said, "Look, she's a nice kid, and you handled her fine—you got her to agree to go back home. And I wouldn't want to hurt her for all the world. But you really don't want to get mixed up with a runaway; if anything happens to her, your entire family will blame us."

"But we need a good assistant. Someone special, not just a secretary. Doesn't it seem as if fate has already taken a hand?" I argued enthusiastically. "Like there's a *reason* she appeared on our doorstep at this point in our lives."

"Maybe so," Jeremy said affectionately, "but all I'm saying is, tread carefully."

I had been rummaging through a drawer where I kept all my maps. "Look, the odds are that Honorine's mother won't let her stay with us in London anyway," I said. "Let's see where we're going this weekend. Hmmm . . . Mougins . . . must be away from the coast, so that would be the opposite direction from Great-Aunt Penelope's villa in Antibes. . . ." It was our villa now, but we still referred to it as Great-Aunt Penelope's. "There it is. Mougins is an old town up in the hillside. Not terribly far from Cannes, as the crow flies . . ."

Jeremy groaned. "Somehow, the minute that kid showed up," he said, "I knew, in my heart of hearts, that our goose was already cooked."

"Don't be silly," I replied. "It's only a weekend in the country. Good food, nice company. What's not to like?"

Part Two

Chapter Five

So Jeremy, Honorine and I went winging our way to visit what I had begun to think of as *ma famille française*. I was pretty excited. Deep down, I'd secretly hoped that I harbored the potential to be a devastating French female . . . I merely needed a little exposure to that side of my lineage. Perhaps I could learn by some sort of osmosis. Take Honorine, for instance. She just had that natural sleek, radiant quality that is somehow the heritage of French girls, mysteriously acquired amid all those school days of wearing navy blue cardigans and white Peter Pan blouses and good wool pleated skirts and serious shoes, and being fed *pain au chocolat* after school without guilt. Yep. A weekend in a little French country house would be a great crash course for me.

When we landed at the airport in Nice, I immediately felt the soft sunlight streaming in the windows, indicating that the Riviera had already gotten a head start on the warm weather. Since we were in town just for the weekend, we'd rented a car at the airport.

"We could stop by the villa to check it out," Jeremy said, tempted by the relaxed atmosphere.

"Detour to Antibes now?" I said, glancing at my watch. "That would make us quite late. Besides, Celeste would be highly insulted if we showed up without warning. She'd think we didn't trust her to look after the place." Celeste had worked for Great-Aunt Penelope, and was now our housekeeper. She had a naturally proprietary air, and she liked things to be properly scheduled, *comme il faut*.

"How do you know she's not down in the wine cellar, drinking up the sherry?" Jeremy teased.

"You don't have sherry," I retorted, thinking of his recently stocked collection. "You have port."

From the back seat of the car, Honorine was watching us in amusement. Jeremy steered the car out of the airport labyrinth, and we were climbing up to the *Moyenne Corniche* road, which wove its breathtaking way along the cliffs above the splendid coastline of the Mediterranean Sea. We were immediately enveloped by the cheerful Matisse colors of blue-white-and-yellow for sky, clouds and sun, brilliant in the Côte d'Azur's inimitable combination of brightness and softness. The air was redolent of flowers, fruit and that salty sea, that sparkled and shimmered as if the fish were dancing just beneath its surface. Every harbor we passed was dotted with fishing boats and yachts. I inhaled contentedly, leaning my head back, letting the Riviera once again soothe me and smooth me. But, since I wasn't exactly born into this lifestyle, I didn't dare close my eyes, for I still can't quite believe my little Cinderella luck.

We headed north from Cannes, away from the coast, climbing up, up into the hills, where the winding local roads lead eccentrically to one rotary after another, so it was like circling halfway around a clock and then darting away onto an even smaller road with yet another rotary to circle. I'd never seen this part of the South of France before, so very high up, and miles away from the coast. The air was a bit more humid, and the vegetation more lush.

As we reached the medieval town of Mougins, the steep roads narrowed even more, with ancient walls rising high on both sides, at times to the point of absurdity. There was a fairly dicey moment when Jeremy had to slow the car to a near stop in order to get through a terrifyingly narrow passageway under an old stone bridge.

"Another coat of paint on this car and we wouldn't make it," I observed, as we squeezed through the tight pass, with the stone walls pressing in on either side of us. But after all, I told myself, these villages had been built not for cars, but for horses, donkeys and mules, long before today's fancy restaurants and spas began attracting modern traffic.

Higher and higher we climbed, with a brief, stunning glimpse of fertile farmland spread out in valleys far below, impeccably sculpted into neat lines of contrasting shades of green—endless rows of vegetables, herbs, silvery-branched olive trees, and gnarly fruit trees openly basking in the abundant sunshine. Beyond this, off in the horizon, were other villages, with plumes of smoke rising from the tiny chimneys of faraway stone farmhouses, and villas with terracotta-colored tiled roofs.

Returning to her roots had a slightly dampening effect on Honorine's high spirits. She was slumped in the backseat, closing her eyes to the magnificent views, with her earphones on again. But when we drew nearer our destination, she seemed to sense it, for she opened her eyes just long enough to tell us which turns to make. Then she went right back to her private earphone world of canned music.

Jeremy glanced at her in the rearview mirror, and whispered to me, "Geez, I feel like we've inherited a grumpy adolescent kid that we're forcibly taking on vacation."

"She certainly is drooping like the last rose of summer," I

agreed. We drove a short way in silence; then, glancing at the map, I confirmed, "Right turn here."

Now Honorine sat up alertly, yanked off her earphones and directed us down a private driveway, which turned out to be a long, elegant avenue slicing through a private park of tall, beautiful old pine trees, and big leafy chestnut trees that demonstrated how gloriously a tree can grow when given ample space. Seated grandly at the far end of the drive, behind several squares of lawn rimmed with formal flowerbeds and potted topiary, was a fine old château, its multitude of rooms laid out with intellectual precision, its long windows and French doors like regal proud eyes, watchful of our approach.

I gasped. Was this the "country cottage" that Tante Leonora invited us to? Phew! Even Jeremy, with all his bigwig, world-wide connections, was impressed.

"Blimey," he said drolly, slowing the car as we pulled up to the entrance.

Honorine reached for her backpack on the floor. "You can turn left and go halfway down the drive to the garage. Park anywhere you like. It's fine. Leave the suitcases in the car," she instructed. "And the keys." She didn't elaborate, so I assumed a servant would take care of it. We left the car, and followed her to the front path.

The château was a pale, yellowy-cream-colored building, with dark green shutters and a dark green roof. It stood three stories high, and was laid out very widely, with window after window in perfect symmetry; and on the left, there was a square four-story tower with a matching roof of its own. Honorine now scampered up the five steps to the big front door, and she offhandedly led us inside with the natural ease of a well-bred girl who is so accustomed to her elegant surroundings that she barely notices them. She put her key in the lock of the front door, and pushed it open.

The dark wall panelling of the great, high-ceilinged entrance hall made the interior feel cool and somewhat somber. We crossed the polished cherrywood floor to a wide staircase with two curving, coffee-colored banisters. Just before we went up, Honorine pointed out a doorway to the left, and told us that it led to the salon, so that we could find it when we came back downstairs.

Our footsteps echoed on the staircase. When we reached the second level, Honorine went bounding down the hallway ahead of us, like an enthusiastic puppy who wants to show you the way. She stopped at the very last room at the end of the corridor, whereupon she pushed open a big, heavy door. We entered an enormous bedroom that overlooked the front park, designed to make its occupant feel very grand and important, just gazing out at the view.

"You can sleep or relax awhile," she said, smiling. "Come down when you hear the bell for champagne before dinner, in the salon." She stepped out and closed the door softly behind her.

The room had that nice scent of polished wood furniture and floors. I glanced at the finely embroidered, upholstered chairs, the antique commode, the hand-crocheted bedspread, the Savonnerie carpeting, the brocade draperies, the gorgeous framed mirror, the gilded chandelier, and the large round crystal vase of pink and white flowers that added their springtime fragrance.

Passing the huge canopied bed heaped with pillows, I walked over to the adjacent bathroom, which had a lovely antique tub, and a deep sink with very old but fancy brass taps. A white antique cabinet was piled with fluffy white towels monogrammed in dark green. Another white cupboard was stacked with plenty of fine Provençal soaps, sachets, shampoo, bath salts and scented lotion from nearby Grasse, the capital of the French perfume industry. On the windowsill was a pale yellow vase with fresh violets.

While looking out this bathroom window, I saw a Vespa come

puttering around the side of the château, its helmeted rider steering it in the direction of the garage in the back.

"This soap smells really good," Jeremy commented. As we were freshening up, we heard a thump in the hallway outside. Jeremy opened the door, and found that our suitcases stood politely in the hall. "You didn't tell me you came from the landed French aristocracy," he joked as we unpacked. "Had I but known, I'd have asked your father for a dowry."

"It would have done you no good, you cad," I said. "We're the poor relations, remember?" I peered into my suitcase. "What do you suppose we should wear to dinner?" I asked, anxiously scanning my overnight bag, suddenly comprehending a cryptic e-mail my mother had sent me just before I left, almost as an afterthought: *Darling, you should bring a nice cocktail dress, elegant shoes, a good pantsuit and a silk blouse. Also, this is as good a time as any for your best jewelry. Love, Mum.* I glanced up and saw that Jeremy was unpacking a nice weekend suit that seemed perfect for the occasion.

"How did you know how to dress for this 'country' shindig?" I asked suspiciously.

"Darling, I'm English," he said maddeningly. I almost threw a small pillow at him, but when I noticed the fine old eyelet trim on it, I put the pillow back down again. "After all, I'm going to meet my little French fiancée's family," Jeremy said. "Did you think I'd show up in sweats?"

"Hook this chain for me, will you?" I said, holding up my graduation-day diamond pendant, adding jokingly, "I'm scared."

At that moment, we heard a soft, low bell that resonated through the house. "Show time," Jeremy said, kissing the back of my neck after he'd hooked the necklace.

"I hate to tell you this," I said, "but my French is not nearly good enough for a dinner party."

"A fine time to say so!" he responded in mock dismay. "We're ruined."

"Honorine can surely translate for us if necessary," I said hopefully.

But when we entered the salon, Honorine was nowhere to be found. A group of total strangers were milling about, cocktail glasses in hand, speaking French in low, melodious voices. As we arrived, they switched seamlessly to English, which I thought was considerate, yet typically French.

The first thing that struck me about this room was the way it was softly scented with lemon blossoms, from little plants with their shiny green leaves, installed in pale peach china pots that nicely contrasted with the dark panelled walls. A large fireplace—flanked by iron tongs and pokers with handles shaped like angels and ogres, and a fire screen with embroidered dragons, knights and other medieval images—was occupied by an urn-shaped basket filled with sprays of long-stemmed fresh flowers. The multiple windows looked out on the same view of the lawn and avenue in front, but heavy velvet curtains were partly drawn, a signal of the evening hour.

A fine, upright-looking man who appeared to be in his early thirties stepped forward and said, in perfect English with a polite French accent, "You must be Penny and Jeremy. I am David."

This was Honorine's older brother, whom she'd described as colluding against her with her mother. He was slender, dark-haired, pale-skinned and dark-eyed, just like Honorine. He had a graceful way of moving, as if his gestures were timed to music; but he also had an animated, slightly high-strung quality. As he handed each of us a glass of champagne, he introduced us to the other dinner guests.

There was a stout mayor and his wife; a muscular-looking retired general and his petite wife; a couple in their thirties who both taught at university and had grown up with David; and an elderly doctor and his white-haired wife. There was also a slim, pampered-looking, curly-haired man in his early twenties, conspicuous for being the youngest person in the party. This was Charles, a law graduate, and he was accompanied by his doting mother and his tall, broad-shouldered father. As soon as I heard the name Charles, I realized that this must be the fellow that Honorine was supposed to marry. Someone mentioned the Vespa he'd received as a graduation gift, so he was the rider I'd noticed earlier.

David's wife was the very proper Auguste, a woman with mildly blonde hair pulled into a chignon at the back of her head, and she was dressed in varying shades of beige. They had three children who'd been romping about on the side lawn, until they were summoned to come inside and bow and curtsy to us, before being sent to have their dinner in the first-floor tower room, which was the children's dining salon. The adults serenely continued chatting, and I learned that David was in charge of the family perfume business. I could tell, from the way that everyone listened attentively to him, that he was highly respected among their friends and neighbors.

The guests had now seated themselves on various upholstered chairs, which left the swooping grey silk sofa available for Jeremy and me to sit on. David remained standing by the enormous fireplace. I stole a look at the women, who wore finely cut dresses of silk or linen, in soft, pale colors of the season, and delicate jewelry remarkable for its subtlety. The men wore dark suits that draped very naturally and made everyone looked polished yet relaxed. Only the older gentlemen wore ties.

Gradually the guests began to ask us polite, tentative questions, whose answers they received with sincere and gentle interest. How did we like life on the Côte d'Azur? Did we prefer winter in London? How did my parents feel about me living abroad, so far away from them? It soon became clear that they were all assembled here in our honor, and, like Honorine, they were curious about the "American heiress and her Englishman" whom they'd heard so much about. The funny thing is that they were just as exotic to me as I was to them; and, as far as I was concerned, the real celebrity of the evening was the matriarch of this attractive family—my dad's cousin, the ambitious Tante Leonora, who now made a grand entrance as hostess, accompanied by her very dignified husband, Philippe.

"Welcome, *chère* Penn-ee!" she cried in delight, in a high, rather theatrical, feminine voice. "And this must be Zheremy." I very nearly giggled, for she pronounced our names exactly as my father did.

Tante Leonora was a tall, impeccable, dark-haired woman in her mid-fifties. She appeared as alert as a hawk; and in fact, she had a way of sweeping about in her black taffeta dress that was very much like a great-winged bird. She wore a necklace and earrings of gold and onyx. With her pale, flawless skin and oval face, dark eyes, high forehead and high cheekbones, she was attractive in a "handsome" way, like a particularly formidable goddess.

Leonora kissed me on both cheeks, then moved in a gust of soft scent to do the same with Jeremy. She seemed delighted that we'd cared enough to come and grace her home, and I found myself wanting to do my part to make the evening a great success. She immediately inquired about my parents, asking of their health, saying how proud they must be of me.

"What happy summers your father and I had as children!" Leonora proclaimed warmly, with a fond smile. For the first time I felt that we truly could be related, and I experienced an unexpected pang of regret that I had not grown up with the kind of old-fashioned, traditional exposure to an aunt like this, who'd give you sweets at Easter, and whom you must respectfully visit at Christmastime.

The conversation continued along pleasant topics of travel and weather, yet Tante Leonora was such a compelling presence that I couldn't take my eyes off her. Certain people have a way of glimmering with energy and sparkle from the moment they enter a room, so that the very vibe of the assembled group changes in an exciting manner, as if we were all satellites that rotated around her strong, magnetic pull. She seated herself like a great diva, regal and in perfect control, her expression serene and confident of an enjoyable occasion.

Her husband, Philippe, who appeared at least ten years older than she, was silver-haired and straight-backed, spry and spiffy in his velvet olive-green jacket. Secure in his own exalted position, he was content to let his wife shimmer in the spotlight while he watched with appreciation of her gifts.

Only once did I catch a little crease of displeasure in Leonora's brow, and that was when she glanced around the room, and saw that her daughter was still AWOL. Then she turned to David and asked, quite sharply, *"Où est Honorine?"*

At the mention of his sister, David shook his head and said resignedly, *"Qui sait?"*

Very soon, a serving woman in a black dress, black stockings and white apron entered and murmured to Tante Leonora that dinner was served. Tante Leonora rose, and instructed us to adjourn to the dining salon. Oncle Philippe graciously offered me his arm to lead me to table, and something in his gesture made me feel especially honored as I followed him. Tante Leonora selected Jeremy to escort her, and, two by two, we all went to dinner, by way of a long corridor that led to the back of the estate. We passed several tall pedestals bearing sculpted busts of France's great kings and thinkers . . . and I had the oddest feeling that they, too, were watching us expectantly.

Chapter Six

"*Alors,*" said Oncle Philippe as we entered the formal dining salon, which was a long room with dusky plum and silver baize papering on the walls, very old-fashioned, and two beautiful chandeliers above a long, candlelit table laid with snowy cloth, shining silverware and crystal. But it was the exhilarating scent of the fresh pink and blue flower arrangements that gave the room a heightened atmosphere of celebration.

Oncle Philippe and Tante Leonora sat across from each other, but not at the far ends of the table. Instead, they were seated right in the center, facing each other. My father used to argue with my mother about this, telling her it was the only civilized way for a host and hostess to preside over dinner. My mother, of course, subscribed to the Anglo-American habit of placing the hosts at hollering distance, on opposite far ends.

I was seated to Oncle Philippe's right, and Jeremy was seated to Leonora's right, so that Jeremy and I were not directly across from each other. Still, this put us much closer than the other couples were to their mates. Leonora must have read my thoughts, for she said laughingly, "You see, you and Jeremy have been spared—you sit closer, because you are not yet married, and are still in the lovebirds stage."

"Enjoy it while it lasts!" cried the retired general, who had a very stiff-necked, military way of holding his head. "While you still adore the sound of each other's voice." He patted Jeremy on the shoulder as he passed his chair, en route to his own seat.

"And you?" said the stout mayor to the general. "Is your wife's voice not music to your ears?"

"But of course!" replied the general, clapping his hands over both ears as if to shut out the sound. "All the more so, as I grow older and harder of hearing!" This was all done in a jocular way, but the general's petite wife shook her head in resigned tolerance of these dumb I-love-my-wife-but jokes.

The mayor's wife, who was thin and soft-voiced, retorted, "Yes, a deaf husband is a blessing, but a blind one is even better, so he cannot see the young girls and embarrass them with his flirting!" She nodded toward me, as if to reprimand the general for teasing a woman young enough to be his daughter.

It was good-natured banter, but I suddenly experienced one of those strange involuntary "irks" I'd been having lately, whenever somebody disparaged marriage. In the past, such jokes struck me as silly, but I had supposed it was just a way of letting off steam, although I never found them particularly funny, and I noticed that most wives didn't, either. Now, however, with these remarks deliberately made for my benefit as a bride, or, even worse, as a warning to Jeremy, the groom, I found myself less inclined to laugh them off. It provoked an image in my mind, of Jeremy and me, years from now, behaving just like these couples, exchanging jokey insults, and feigning a desire to escape each other's company. Yuck-yuck, hoo-hoo. I didn't think it was so damned funny.

While I silently pondered this, Jeremy deliberately caught my eye and gave me such a smile of comprehension and reassurance that I instantly felt better. Plus, the arrival of the food also helped alter my mood—starting with the appearance of an appetizer of the tiniest, most tender artichokes of the season in a light butter sauce, sprinkled with delicate fresh goat cheese in herbs, accompanied by a lovely white wine the color of pale gold. Glancing around the table, I admired the way everything in the room—flowers, bowls of fruits on the sideboard, plates of perfectly proportioned good food, and the ladies' dresses—all served to remind us to rejoice in the return of the sun.

Oncle Philippe conversed with me in a quiet, charming voice, like an aristocratic country squire who was perfectly content to while away his retirement in the country; but I soon learned that he was the hardworking steward of a family business that originated centuries ago with *gantiers parfumeurs*.

"What's that?" I asked, fascinated.

"Glove-makers," Oncle Philippe said, raising his hands to mime putting on a pair.

"But I thought your business was perfume," I said.

"Ah, well, let me explain. You see, in the Middle Ages, the town of Grasse was a center for tanning sheepskins from herds in the mountains of Provence," he told me. "They used herbs to treat the leather. So, later, when Catherine de' Medici arrived from Italy to become France's queen, she asked the tanners of Grasse to make fine perfumed gloves, which were all the fashion. So the tanners became *gantiers parfumeurs*. In the process, they also became highly skilled makers of scent, using the especially fine flowers and herbs from this region."

"And so, perfumed gloves from Grasse became a status symbol for the whole world's royalty, nobility and wealthy merchants," Tante Leonora interjected proudly.

The other guests appeared familiar with this story, and now the elderly doctor chimed in, offering, "They say it was also Catherine de' Medici who first taught the French to eat with a knife and fork." He held up his fork to make the point. Glancing over at Jeremy, his eyes twinkled as he added, "Of course the English took a bit longer to learn. One still hears that they haven't quite got it right, what with scooping up their peas on the knife."

He beamed at their resident Englishman; and Jeremy took the joke with good grace. The doctor's white-haired wife reached out and patted Jeremy's hand soothingly, as if to assure him that the insult wasn't serious, and she did so in a highly feminine way, indicating that she enjoyed the excuse to touch a handsome younger man. There was something fascinating about an elderly woman still being sexy, and we all enjoyed it, for it was inoffensive even to me, Jeremy's partner.

"After the French Revolution, when symbols of royalty, like powdered wigs and perfumed gloves, went out of style, the *gantiers parfumeurs* focused simply on being *parfumeurs*," Oncle Philippe said. "*En fin*, they created the famous perfumeries of Grasse."

He proudly added that his company still retained their own flower fields in Grasse. This, I realized, explained the wonderful preponderance of blossoms in the château, and the sophisticated toiletries in our room.

When the conversation had begun, I'd noticed that there was an empty seat beside me. Now, as Oncle Philippe was finishing the story of Grasse, Honorine slipped into this seat, almost unnoticed, as if the family was so horrified by her breach of etiquette that they simply chose to ignore it. She kept her eyes focused on her plate, clearly trying to avoid the gaze of Charles, who sat directly across the table from her. Charles appeared to be an intelligent, genial kid, but one who was indulged and petted by his parents; particularly his mother, a tall, attractive woman with light brown hair, who seemed aware of his every move. The broad-shouldered father seldom spoke, but he and his wife listened with watchful expressions; and more than once I saw them exchange glances whose meaning was clear only to them. The fact that they, too, ignored Honorine's entrance made it all the more significant.

Evidently Honorine had been dodging Charles as long as she could, which accounted for her absence during cocktails. She'd missed the appetizer, but now, as the plates were cleared, and a chicken consommé topped with tiny, precisely cut vegetables was served, she turned to me and, under cover of the distraction of food, whispered that her mom had roundly scolded her for intruding on us in London.

"I hope you can find a moment to speak to my parents on my behalf," Honorine whispered. "Could you perhaps tell them that it wasn't so horrible to put me up for a few nights?"

"Sure," I said. "I'll tell them we made you wash the dishes." Honorine giggled conspiratorially, but we both caught the flicker of disapproval in Tante Leonora's face, and this caused Honorine to flush angrily, and jut her chin out a bit defiantly.

Uh-oh, I thought to myself, wondering what dreadful mother-daughter tangle I might have inadvertently allowed myself to become ensnared in. Charles' mother was watching, too, I noted.

"Penny, I do see a great deal of your father in you!" Leonora said, now gazing at me intently. "Perhaps not only in looks, but in temperament, too?"

She turned to the others and said, "My cousin Georges was a restless man, *très indépendant*, who simply had to go away and see the world. New York captivated him, and would not give him back. Then, he moved again, to Connecticut!" Her tone was bewildered, and ever so slightly resentful. "Now, his daughter also feels compelled to leave home, but her travels have brought her *back* to France, to make up for our loss of Georges."

Geez, I thought, she's making it sound as if my dad was dead—perish the thought—or, that he was one of those ancient explorers who ignored all warnings, sailed away to the edge of the map and fell off. I recalled my father saying that his relatives were so averse to change that "you cannot move a stick of furniture in a room without coming to grief".

"Americans are always moving from one house to another!" observed the professor. There was a murmur of amazement, as if they were all baffled by the size and scale of America, and of the prospect of voluntarily uprooting oneself from one state to the other. In their milieu, I realized, one relied on the family home for centuries.

But this little ripple on the calm surface of the conversation was soon smoothed away by the arrival of the next course—Alpine lamb accompanied by Provençal red wine. The excellent repast soon created a more relaxed, convivial mood where the talk became even more spirited, increasing a bit in volume. It was as if the food, wine, and conversation was lifting us all together, and we'd embarked on an old-fashioned balloon ride, with everyone doing their part to keep the balloon afloat. Even when discussing potentially prickly topics like art and politics and science, I noticed that Tante Leonora was particularly skilled at keeping the talk artfully lighthearted, yet never lightweight.

After a dessert of a small, wonderful airy chocolate soufflé, we took our coffee and liqueurs in the salon. Then, Tante Leonora announced, "And now, we go to the gallery, where we have a little surprise for Penny and Jeremy."

Mystified, we followed her out to the entrance hall, quietly, in a very solemn procession. Leonora pointed upward, to something I hadn't really noticed earlier in this high-ceilinged hall: opposite the main stairs and the second-level landing, right above the front door, was a graceful walkway, like a narrow balcony with a wrought-iron railing, that spanned the entire width of the hall. Two long, splendid windows were centered here, above the door and walkway.

While we stood there, Tante Leonora touched a light switch, which illuminated the area between the windows. Now I saw that a baroque tapestry was hanging as an *entrefenêtre* in the considerable space there. I gazed upward at the tapestry, which looked to be about nine feet high, and five feet wide. It seemed to bear the image of a man and woman asleep in bed, surrounded by other fanciful designs.

With great ceremony, Tante Leonora proclaimed, "As we have two betrothed young people among us, it would give us much pleasure to make a loan of our bridal tapestry to Penny and Jeremy for their wedding day."

There was a collective gasp of excitement and approval, and the little group even broke out in applause. I was stunned. Leonora brought us to a small, spiral staircase in the far right corner of the hall, which led up to the walkway. Everyone ascended, single file, to admire the tapestry more closely. Along the way, I noticed other, smaller artwork hanging on the walls, beyond the windows. But now the guests were considerately arranging themselves so that I could move directly in front of the tapestry, to get a really good look. I drew nearer, fascinated.

I knew a little about tapestries because of all my movie research, scouring artwork and furnishings for the sets of historical dramas. To me, tapestries usually fall into one of three camps: the purely decorative, like a carpet or quilt; the political, which are loaded with either flattery for the patron, or propaganda about a country's wars and conquests; or, the truly artistic, mystical ones, which can be downright spooky, in the way that they seem to beckon you to come closer—as if they want to whisper the secret to a complex riddle of life. The tapestry I was now gazing at was definitely in this intriguing category. In fact, it made me feel as if I had just stepped into another world, where some drama was already in progress, for it was composed of such an elaborate series of pictures that it was impossible to take in all at once, nor even to know where to begin.

It was made of wool and silk and gilt-metal-wrapped thread, which meant that strands of real gold and silver were woven into the fabric, giving it a shimmering quality that was changeable—at times like undulating sunlight reflected on the sea, at other moments like flickering candlelight—and these precious threads were so intricately entwined that, up close, the weave almost resembled fish-scales.

The overall pattern in the main body of the tapestry was deceptively simple: it seemed to be a bedroom, with a husband and wife asleep in bed; he in a peaked cap, and she in a bonnet. The interior of their bedroom—window, walls and floor—were also visible, but it was their flowered bedspread that made up most of the tapestry. Peering closer, I saw that the bedspread pattern was a field full of flowers, with horizontal paths in between. And upon these paths, little scenarios were played out, with groups of small figures walking in formal processions. At the very top of the bedspread, above all the processions, were two rows of oval insets with their own individual "snapshots" of drama, mainly of couples performing various seasonal tasks such as gathering the harvest. And so, the bedspread appeared to be a field of dreams that the sweet married couple were dreaming together.

Above the sleeping couple's heads was a big, fan-shaped window, divided into three pie-shaped sections: one in the middle, with a view of faraway hills, sky and sea; one on the left, where a half-moon shone with an elegant, aristocratic expression on its profile; and one on the right, with a regal sun-face whose fiery rays emanated outward. Meanwhile, in the background of the couple's bedroom, the carpeted floor and wall-draperies were covered with still more images, but these were godly, allegorical figures and faces, personifying the four elements and the four seasons. The entire main body of the tapestry was rimmed on all four sides by a decorative border, which served as a sort of "picture frame" scattered with Latin proverbs, flowers, birds and otherworldly creatures and symbols.

"Oh, she is bewitched by it!" I heard someone say behind me. I realized I'd gone into a private trance of delight, forgetting everybody and everything, as if nothing else existed except me and the tapestry—a sure sign of enchantment.

"But just *look* at it!" I cried, pointing out the fine work. It was an expensive creation, undoubtedly made for someone quite important. The professor sidled up nearer, peering through his spectacles at the cloth.

"Exquisite," he murmured.

"Who made this beautiful work of art?" I breathed, turning to Philippe and Leonora. They seemed touchingly pleased and proud that I was impressed.

"One of Philippe's ancestors," Tante Leonora answered.

"Then, it's been in the family for many years?" I asked.

Oncle Philippe shook his head. "*Ah non*, it did not come into my family's possession until the 1930s, when my aunt bought it at auction. Since she had no children, she gave it as a wedding present to me. In fact, Leonora and I were married before it, just like a king and a queen!"

And so it had come into the eager hands of Leonora, I observed, for she was very proud of it, pointing out this or that particular feature. "*Eh bien*," she concluded meaningfully, nodding toward Honorine, "perhaps one day our own daughter will be married before this tapestry, if she is lucky enough to be asked by a good man!"

The guests laughed indulgently, and someone slapped Charles on the back. I stole a quick glance at Honorine, who blushed furiously. Behind her, Jeremy raised his eyebrows to warn me, *MYOB*.

"But in the meantime," Leonora said calmly, "we have this lovely bride in our midst." Everyone began chattering all at once, peppering me with happy questions, as we descended the stairs.

"Have you set the date yet?"

"Will it be a very large wedding?"

"Will you be getting married here in Mougins, or in Antibes?"

Leonora quickly offered her house for the wedding, basically saying that her château was our château. I was stunned by their warmth and generosity, yet unable to answer their questions about my barely existent wedding details.

"Actually," Jeremy explained, deftly rescuing me, "we are only now just contemplating our plans." And he somehow managed to keep the focus on how we were honored by this too-generous offer by Philippe and Leonora.

Then Honorine helped out, whether she intended to or not. She let out a big cat yawn that echoed in the great hall. "Oh, *Maman*, we are so tired from the airplane, it's time for bed!" she cried with the charming manner of a little girl. Everyone responded warmly, and, realizing that Jeremy and I, too, must be weary from our travels, they bid us good-night.

Chapter Seven

"So, how's this work?" Jeremy asked teasingly. "We get married under the thing, and then take it home and use it for a bedspread, just like that funny-looking couple tucked up in bed with their little night caps, surrounded by all those weird symbols?"

"Some of those images do look like the 'bad news' cards in a tarot deck," I admitted.

"It might give us nightmares," he suggested. "Besides, who knows who else slept under it? What if they had bedbugs? Or plague or smallpox? All things considered, I'd rather have a soup tureen, a most useful item."

"You idiot," I said, playing along. "We are certainly not going to sleep under this treasure, because you can't be trusted not to spill your morning coffee and croissant crumbs all over it. But if we lived in olden times, before central heating was invented, believe me, you'd have been eternally grateful for a bedroom tapestry hanging on the wall to keep out the cold drafts. In fact, you'd also be glad to have it there for entertainment, in the days before television!"

"What, people sat around watching tapestries for fun?" Jeremy said in amusement.

"Sure! Louis XIV had his favorite Aesop's fables all over the draperies in one of his bedrooms. He could lie there and look at them, like watching a cartoon movie," I said as I climbed into the big bed, which required ascending a small, elaborately embroidered step-stool. "And they put tapestries in waiting rooms, so you could stare at them while waiting to curry favor with some big mucky-muck."

"I suppose it beats sitting around leafing through old magazines in a doctor's office," Jeremy commented. Then, indicating that he understood the significance of Leonora's offer, he said affectionately, "I like your French folks. They're beautiful and smart and elegant . . . just like you. And, I'd say they're totally enchanted with Miss Penny Nichols, too. Very nice of them to offer the tapestry for the wedding. However, I can't help noticing that everyone is assuming we'll be married in France."

"Can you blame them?" I said. "If that were your tapestry, would you ever let it be taken out of the country? They probably want to make sure it's handled and displayed correctly."

Jeremy grinned. "Better watch out, though. A woman like Leonora will take over the whole wedding if you let her."

"Shh! They'll hear you!" I cried, "with your big booming voice and these big booming rooms."

Jeremy obligingly lowered his tone to a stage whisper. "Do you want to get married here?"

I hesitated. "You're right about Leonora. She'd expect to be in charge. My dad says his relatives used to drive him crazy, always wanting things done exactly the way they expected them to be, according to tradition. Philippe's family goes back a long way. They must have been very honored and quite wealthy."

"Maybe so," Jeremy said gently, "but it looks as though they're struggling now."

"What are you talking about?" I demanded. "Did you not see how incredibly big the estate is?"

"Haven't you noticed all the shabby edges around the old château?" he asked.

"Nonsense," I scoffed. "Frayed carpeting and dusty old drapes and scuffed furniture are sure signs of old money. Aristocrats don't spend their fortune on ostentatious new purchases. Everything is *supposed* to be musty and moth-eaten, to prove it was handed down through the centuries."

"True enough," Jeremy allowed, "but these people have no valet and very few servants. I'm not sure who carried our bags up. Looks to me like a case of land-rich, cash-poor."

I pondered this. "Then their offer is all the more generous," I said. But I felt a trifle uneasy. It occurred to me that Tante Leonora, having achieved her social position through marriage, now saw herself as protector of the family, watching over her children to ensure that, like actors, they played their assigned roles, so that the fabric of her family didn't fray at the ends and come unravelled. She clearly saw my free-spirited father as a threatening loose end.

Being an only child, I harbored romantic ideas about big families, but I could see why my father wasn't in such a hurry to return to the provinces of his youth, despite his deep and abiding love for France. He'd said he felt hamstrung by the watchfulness of small-town life, even in Paris, with its highly structured society of age-old privilege and connections. America had offered him the anonymity of a new place, where no one could admonish him for not playing his part exactly as they wanted. It made me wonder what role my French relatives now expected me to play.

So that night, as the entire household settled into sleep, I lay there listening to the creaking floors, the groaning pipes, the wind making trees scratch against the windows like cats. The château was undeniably beautiful, and it stood as a bulwark against time and all the uncertainties of life—wars, plague, storms, persecutions. It had the quality of a museum or a church; a place that reminded one of death as well as life. For the first time, I felt I understood Honorine's flight. With all these medieval, cryptic images surrounding us in every carving, painting and artifact—those angels and ogres, knights and kings, youth and age—I fell asleep dreaming of galloping off on a white horse, beyond the avenue of trees, beyond the woods, all the way down to the coast . . . and the wide-open, liberating sea.

Chapter Eight

The next morning, at the breakfast buffet—laid out in a smaller dining salon overlooking the garden and woods at the back of the house—our hosts surprised us by casually announcing that they had arranged "a shooting party" in Jeremy's honor. After David delivered this invitation, Jeremy marched upstairs to change clothes. I followed him.

"Shooting!" I cried, appalled. "Are you going to go off and kill some poor little deer or duck?"

"No, mercifully," Jeremy told me as he rooted around in his suitcase. "They gave me a choice, of either slaughtering animals or shooting trap. They are operating on the huge assumption that, just because I'm English, I fancy a hunt."

"Do you shoot?" I asked in amusement.

"I can if I must."

"I mean, do you like it?" I persisted, wanting to know if my future husband had hobbies I'd been entirely unaware of.

"I loathe it. Therefore I opted for trap. One can only guess at what inferences they will draw from my choice," he said. "I wonder, do you suppose this will scotch our chances for being married under the tapestry?"

"It's 'before' the tapestry, as in, 'in front of'," I corrected. "Not 'under', which implies they're going to toss it over our heads."

"Well, either way, it's curtains for us now," he joked.

"If you loathe shooting, why are you going?" I asked.

"For love of a Penny," he said, kissing me and then hurrying off.

I went downstairs shortly after Jeremy left, wondering uncertainly what I would do with the day while he was out. I needn't have worried. Oncle Philippe emerged from the little dining salon, having lingered over his coffee, fresh brioche and newspaper; and he now said, with a twinkle in his eye, "You seemed interested in the history of my family's perfume business. Would you like to come to my workshop in Grasse for a private tour of the best perfume in France? It's all been arranged, if you'd like."

"Oh, yes!" I cried. I loved his rich French accent, which made "arranged" sound more like "orange-ed." He wore a fine, formal straw hat and a linen suit, white shirt and pale blue tie.

Nobody else in the household seemed to be around; it was just Oncle Philippe and me. He escorted me out the front door and down the pretty stone steps. The sun was already bathing the air with its warmth and the promise of a beautiful day. A long black car awaited us, and a driver opened the door so that we could slip into the cool interior. Then he steered the car down the driveway past the allée of trees, and whisked us off to Grasse.

We took the "Route Napoleon", where the irrepressible emperor had escaped his island exile and marched back to Paris. Despite the roar of traffic on this now-modern highway, the South of France—with its prehistoric caves, sheltering Alps in the distance, and *villages perchés* clinging to ledges and cliffs—still seemed like something from a fairy tale.

"Where is Honorine today?" I couldn't resist asking.

"Her mother has taken her to call on a few friends of the family," he replied, and I wondered if this had to do with Charles' family. He smiled and said, "I am sure that she would much prefer to come with us today." It seemed like an opening to ask him how on earth he could want a bright young daughter to sacrifice her future happiness for their present business interests, until he added rather presciently, "But I do not interfere where the ladies are concerned."

"Honorine is very, very bright," I ventured. "She's already been so helpful to us at our office. And her school record is amazing! She's really quite special."

"*Oui*, Honorine has always been bright and high-spirited," Philippe said, "and with that comes a certain independence of mind." He was careful, in that French way, not to make this sound like either boasting or complaining, but I could tell that Honorine both delighted and vexed him.

We'd reached the town of Grasse, whose name, Oncle Philippe said, came from the word for "grace". Once upon a time it had been an independent Italian city, before falling under French rule.

At the flat top of a high hill was a modern, bustling tourist area with lots of shops and traffic, and a pedestrian plaza, rimmed with stone balustrades, reigned over by an imposing war memorial. From here, one had a view of the old city, which lay below us, at the foot of a wide, steep, stone staircase. Nestled in those narrow, medieval streets were tall stucco and stone houses in pale washed colors of desert sand, faded terracotta and violet-grey.

I would have been delighted to stop, get out and explore the old streets on foot, but the driver was steering the car away from the shops, museums and churches, making several turns down side streets, so that he could approach a parking lot at the rear of the old factory that belonged to Oncle Philippe. The car stopped at the back door, and I slid out first, followed by Oncle Philippe.

A brisk, alert-eyed woman in a white coat, carrying a clipboard, greeted us, ready to guide our private tour. Oncle Philippe introduced her as Lisette, one of the managers. Although the factory was technically closed today, some of the workers had come just to help in this tour, presided over by Oncle Philippe himself, which made it a very special day indeed. From the moment we entered the factory, his employees snapped to attention and greeted him with genuine warmth and excitement.

"I am what you might call 'semi-retired'," he explained with a smile, aware of his celebrity status.

"Theeze way," Lisette said politely as she led us past the foyer. The factory was a series of cavernous, echoing, high-ceilinged rooms with no windows, and various big machines, each operated by an employee who neither glanced up nor spoke to us unless Lisette addressed him. "First, we have to get the flowers and herbs, many of which we still grow and pick from our own fields," she said as she began a narrative of the process of perfume-making. "Only about thirty years ago, there were still thousands of flower growers in this area, but now it's down to less than a hundred fifty growers."

"So we are a vanishing species," Oncle Philippe said, shaking his head. "We go the way of the dodo."

"We grow many flowers, particularly roses and jasmine," Lisette continued. "These require experts to pick them, and we like to get them super-fresh, within an hour. They are here." She pointed to big burlap sacks on the floor, which had flower petals and herbs that were in various stages of drying or storage. "Our task is to extract the fragrance from the flower petals," Lisette explained. "The oldest method is 'expression' or cold-pressing, but nowadays we only use this method for oranges and lemons, because they have so much oil in their peels." Oncle Philippe pressed the palms of his hands together.

"Like olives for olive oil?" I said.

He beamed at me. *"Précisément."*

We moved through another room, full of big copper and stainless steel vats with long, old-fashioned curling pipes and funnels protruding from them. Lisette explained that this was the method of distillation, or steaming out the fragrance. Then, in the next room, we paused in front of stacks of mysterious wooden trays that seemed to go up to the ceiling.

Lisette said with a flourish, "But now, you see the method that was developed here in Grasse. It is called *enfleurage*. Here, fresh flower petals are put into odorless animal fats, which absorb the fragrance from the flowers."

She pulled out a tray made of glass and wood, containing a smooth, thick layer of fat, topped with orderly rows of whole flowers looking like delicate butterflies who'd gotten their spread wings trapped in the waxy substance. "Fats that have fully absorbed the fragrance are known as *pommade*, which is then soaked in alcohol to extract the scent from the fat."

As we left the room Oncle Philippe said with a smile, "But, afterwards, the remaining fats still have some fragrance left in them, so what do we do with that?"

"Soap?" I guessed delightedly. He nodded, and we entered another room, where a very big, elaborate machine cranked out wide tubes of soap, as if it were a giant toothpaste tube. A conveyor belt circled it, loaded with egg-shaped soaps in Easter colors, packed in neat little rows in cartons.

"*Enfleurage* is time-consuming," Lisette concluded. "It takes months. That's why so many of today's perfumers use chemical solvents instead, which requires only a few days."

"We work with all methods," Oncle Philippe explained, "but

for our most special lines of fragrance we still use the old ways, because it results in a more natural perfume."

I kept sniffing rapturously at everything he offered me, and I felt totally seduced by the heady atmosphere of secret formulas and glamorous scent. The mysterious, complicated process of coaxing fresh flowers to relinquish their perfume was fascinating, as if I'd come upon ancient alchemists cooking up magical love potions. I could see how easily this world might become a lost art if it were not passed down through the generations, by sophisticated elders like Oncle Philippe, who would share their secrets only with people they trusted. It occurred to me now that, despite his casual comment about taking me here because I'd seemed interested in our dinner conversation last night, clearly this tour meant a great deal to him.

We had now entered what looked like an artist's studio, with multiple easels. On closer inspection I saw that these "easels" were really wood boards with squares of varnished color photographs of various perfume sources: vanilla pods, gardenia flowers, mint leaves, honeysuckle blossoms, even apple and cocoa. Each square had a circular hole drilled through it. On a nearby table were jars of waxen fragrance, about fifteen in all, with no names on them, only numbers.

"Now it's time for you to test your nose," Oncle Philippe said, enjoying this as if it were a children's game. "See if you can match each jar of fragrance to its source, by smelling them and then placing them in the correct slots."

Lisette unscrewed all the jars, then took out a stopwatch to time me. "Go!" she cried.

I was confident I'd "ace" the test. I picked up each jar and sniffed its waxy scented contents, identifying the scent, and then quickly putting the jar into the slot with a picture of its source. It was a delightful, sensual experience, but I soon found myself hesitating. Apple or pear? Orange or lemon or lime? Rose or jasmine or gardenia? Chocolate or coffee? It wasn't as obvious as you'd think. As the seconds ticked by, I became less certain.

"Time!" called Lisette. I still had two to go. Quickly I placed them into slots. Lisette inspected my work at the easel; then she pulled out four jars that I'd got wrong—including the last two—and she relocated them to where they belonged.

"Did I flunk the test?" I cried, and they both laughed.

"No, no, you did rather well," Oncle Philippe assured me. "Very few visitors recognize more. But some people are born with the natural ability to differentiate hundreds of fragrances!"

"How is that possible?" I asked. Oncle Philippe wagged his finger.

"It's a gift," he said. "But even they must pass a test to qualify for admission to perfume school, where they learn to identify *thousands* of the flowers, herbs, spices and other sources of scent."

"Wow," I said, trying to imagine that level of subtlety.

"But the *crème de la crème* of scent-finders," Oncle Philippe proclaimed, "is the *nez.*"

"*Nez?*" I repeated.

"Ah . . . the Nose," he explained. "Those who are born to sniff, like a wine specialist."

"There are only about fifty of these 'Noses' in the whole world," Lisette told me. "They are in great demand."

We passed through the bottling room, where rows of little stoppered bottles, with their medicinal-looking rubber droppers, trundled by in trays on assembly-line conveyor belts; and then we reached the final destination, a guest shop, filled with crowded tables laden with boxes of every imaginable perfume gift, including fountain pens with scented ink, and plump little pillows of dried sachet tied with bright ribbon.

We stopped walking, and Oncle Philippe nodded to Lisette, who vanished mysteriously, but soon reappeared with two pretty antique bottles of dark glass: a rose-colored one for me, and a blue one for Jeremy. I discovered that, each step of the way, Lisette had been carefully noting every scent that I had particularly liked, which explained those moments when she and Oncle Philippe had conferred in French, guessing at what would make a winning combination for a custom-made perfume *pour la dame* (that would be me) and an aftershave *pour l'homme*, for Jeremy.

"We will keep your secret formulas on file, and you call us any time you need more," Oncle Philippe declared. He and Lisette looked at me with eager, expectant expressions, as if they dearly hoped I'd approve. How could they even doubt it? I found their generosity of spirit deeply touching.

"Oh, Oncle Philippe!" I said, feeling tears spring into my eyes. "How wonderful!"

"*Zut!* No time for tears, not until the wedding, and even so, a bride should never cry. The other ladies at the wedding will do the crying for you," Oncle Philippe declared. The bottles were placed in fine inlaid gift boxes, wrapped in colored tissue and ribbon, and handed to the driver to put into the car for us. Lisette smiled at me indulgently as we waved goodbye.

On the way home, Oncle Philippe asked, "Would you like to see the flower fields that produce our perfumes?"

"Absolutely!" I cried.

The sun had now climbed high overhead, and the sky was a stunning bright blue. A soft breeze stirred the green fields, rustling through the herbs and grasses, and making the trees and flowers toss their heads. The car turned onto a dusty unpaved dirt track with the occasional jolting hole or rock that made us bounce along. As the car slowed, Oncle Philippe rolled down the windows, gesturing out at flower-covered land as far as the eye could see. The first scent was of the warm baked earth, from the turned fields.

"These," he said proudly, "are the very flower fields you saw on the bedspread in the tapestry."

We drove around the corner, into a wide, short driveway protected by a wrought-iron gate that arched overhead. The driver punched in a code, the gates opened, and we entered and parked. Then we set out on foot.

The fields were neatly comprised of long rows of plantings that stretched out ahead, basking in the warmth of the day. We walked down well-worn paths between the tall rows of flowering climbers and shrubs, where bees buzzed contentedly, and butterflies flitted around us. I followed Oncle Philippe, who trotted along with a surprisingly strong, steady gait, like a man who deliberately walks every day to actually get somewhere, not just for exercise. He pointed out the various herbs and flowers en route.

"Come, let me introduce you to my ladies," he said. Fascinated, I followed him through multiple rows of tall climbing roses. He paused at a section of bright yellow ones with cabbage-style blooms, that had a sweet, powdery scent. He touched the green leaves almost as if he were shaking hands with the plant, like an old and dear friend.

"Here you see the Marie Rose," he said, "named for my grandmother, who was born the year that this variety was first created." He moved on to the next row: white roses with a spicy odor, which he called, "Petite Julie", planted for his mother. Next were roses in such a dark shade of purple that they were almost black, and they had a musky violet scent. "These are the Venetia Rose," he told me with a smile, "named for my Tante Venetia." As we approached a row of cherry-red roses with a strawberry fragrance, he said, "The Rose Leonora, planted the year we were married." We came upon a row of little pink honey-scented ones, whose petals were unusual, not wrapped tightly around one another like most roses, but distinctly apart, almost like daisies. "*En fin* . . . as you may guess . . ."

"Rose Honorine!" I cried. He nodded. I gazed in astonishment at the continuing, seemingly endless rows of other heirloom roses beyond us, their heads bobbing and nodding in the breeze, as if they were living, breathing ladies who enjoyed gossiping with one another, down through the centuries. Following my gaze, he said, "You see how far back my family goes!"

We had reached the end of the fields, and just ahead of us was an octagonal-shaped gazebo, whose interior was entirely rimmed in wooden benches. As we sat down gratefully in its welcoming shade, Oncle Philippe said, "Once, the home of my ancestors stood on this spot."

He explained that one of the glove-makers in his family built a house here for his son in the 1600s, but it was eventually torn down in the 1700s, when the family moved into the elegant château in Mougins, where Philippe and his family now lived. This gazebo was then erected here to mark the spot.

Earlier, when we'd left the car, I vaguely noticed that the driver had gone around to the trunk and opened it. Now I saw that he was following us, and he arrived slightly breathless from carrying a big wicker hamper that contained a picnic lunch. He quickly unpacked it, and began setting up china plates and linen napkins, and he opened a bottle of very light, delicate sparkling white wine. Then he took his own sandwich and returned to the car, to give us privacy.

Oncle Philippe and I ate in companionable silence, feasting on pâté, cheese and a long narrow loaf of bread. The gazebo was pleasantly cool in the midday heat, and as the breeze shifted, gently rustling through the fields, I inhaled not only the mingled scent of flowers, earth, grass, trees, but even, perhaps, a whiff of the far-off sea. Oncle Philippe, his eyes slightly closed, raised his head to it.

"You must be so proud of all this," I said, gesturing toward the flower fields, after we had rested a bit, and I spotted the driver making his way toward us, to collect the picnic basket.

A shadow seemed to cross Oncle Philippe's expression as he gazed at his roses, saying, "They are costly to keep, as all fine ladies are. The world wants everything fast and cheap," he exclaimed, shaking his head in disapproval. "If they are not careful, there will be nothing left but artificial scent that comes from nothing of this earth." He wrinkled up his nose as if he'd smelled something bad. "Junk!"

I'd seen this very expression of scorn on Honorine's face when she spoke of things that annoyed her. I tried not to smile at the resemblance. I wondered how she was doing; I imagined that she'd been shanghaied into having lunch with Charles' mother.

When we returned to the château, Oncle Philippe allowed me to kiss his cheek before he toddled off to have a nap in his own room. "I go to take the afternoon sleep of babies and old men," he said self-mockingly. This was the first indication that our outing had tired him. "Leonora has planned a little early dinner for you with the ladies in the conservatory." He waved his arm to give me directions to where I'd find it. "You will hear the dinner bell. And so, *au revoir*."

Chapter Nine

I began to get an inkling of the family conflict when I attended the ladies' supper. The conservatory was a large room at the far end of the house, with glass walls and skylights, filled with big potted citrus trees and hothouse flowers. It was just Leonora, David's wife Auguste, and me, seated at a round table laid with a blue and yellow cloth. Still no sign of Honorine, and no place set for her, either. I asked as casually as I could about her.

"She dines out with Charles tonight," Leonora said calmly, without a hint of duress. Yet something in her tone warned me off further questions about her daughter. I didn't want to cause Honorine any trouble; history was full of such families who might just bundle their daughter off to a nunnery if she got too rebellious.

So I talked about my day at the perfume factory, but was surprised when Leonora said, a trifle impatiently, "Yes, yes, in the old days, when Honorine and David were children, Philippe loved taking them there, but how he spoiled them! Why, even now, he'd just as soon have Honorine remain a little girl forever, hanging about the perfumery, chatting with the workers for gifts of soap!"

"My children know better," Auguste said. "David took them there one Christmas, but he made them sit on a bench and watch from morning till night, until they were so dusty and tired that they fell asleep. *They* know it's not magic made by elves! You won't see them asking to go back to the workshop. David himself can hardly bear to set foot inside the factory now."

It didn't take a genius to catch that whiff of snobbery from Auguste, and it was clear that both ladies looked upon the perfumery and flower fields as a grubby business, merely a means of financial security. They took pride only in David's wheeling and dealing, although they didn't go into the details. They also seemed to expect that I wholeheartedly agreed with them on the need for modernization, not preservation; but since they didn't actually ask my opinion, I didn't offer it.

"Times change, and the business must change with them," Auguste said primly, in the attitude of a woman who was quoting her husband as if it were gospel. I got a slight stab of terror, envisioning myself as a wife who went about announcing, "*My* husband thinks this" as if it were a competitive sport.

But frankly, I was starting to miss Jeremy very much, and I was relieved when everyone rose from the table, and Auguste murmured about going to look in on the children. That left me alone with Leonora as we returned to the entrance hall. When she saw me glancing up again at the tapestry, she said encouragingly, "Go ahead, have another look." She watched from below as I ascended to the balcony.

This time I noticed the other artwork that hung there. There were two good landscape paintings, one of old Mougins, one of turn-of-the-twentieth-century Cannes fishermen hauling a day's catch in beautiful light. Also, there were two medieval portraits, done in those deep, rich, chocolate-y colors, one of a monk, another of a lady wearing a spiky crown and her hair in a long braid.

On closer inspection, I saw that the pictures seemed to be

spaced apart in an odd way, as if to cover up for the fact that, originally, much more artwork had hung here, but was recently removed, leaving some telltale dark square "shadows" on the walls. Leonora, who'd come up the stairs and now appeared at my elbow, said, lightly, that over the years they had indeed sold off some of their art.

"Eventually, one tires of looking at the same old pictures," she explained airily, but rather unconvincingly. "This house has had many visitors who speak of our collection, and the next thing you know, some museum makes you an offer, and they can be very persuasive." She paused. "We recently had an offer for the tapestry, but I, myself, am convinced it was far beneath what the tapestry is worth. Perhaps you, my dear Penny, would like to look into it and render your professional opinion?"

I now realized that there were many reasons for this weekend invitation. But the intriguing tapestry was simply irresistible, and I had an automatic urge to photograph it with the camera I always travel with, out of habit from my research work. When I asked her permission, she agreed, so I went to my room to fetch it from my suitcase; then returned.

At first I just stood there gazing, wondering where to begin. It was too big to fit the whole thing into the frame of one photo, and still see any details. I began snapping sections of it here and there. Finally I paused to ask, "Can I get a shot of you near it?"

Leonora looked surprised, then flattered, and obligingly stood alongside it. Our voices must have carried up the hallway to the other wing where the family bedrooms were, because Philippe emerged and came wandering out. He was wearing a red and gold smoking jacket, and carrying a pipe. He posed naturally beside the tapestry when I asked him to, with that friendly ease that continental men often have, obliging and relaxed. Then he went right back into his room, silently, like a horse returning to its stable, and Leonora wished me *bonne nuit* and followed him.

A few hours later, the other men returned, and Jeremy bounded upstairs where I was waiting in our room. He grinned and kissed me, then headed straight for the shower. When he peeled off his shirt I saw a large, black-and-blue bruise on his chest and shoulder.

"Holy cow, what is *that*?" I cried.

Jeremy looked embarrassed. "Just a little knocking about," he said.

"Did you get into fisticuffs with David?" I joked.

"Ho, ho. No, it's from the 'return' of the shotgun. Been awhile since I've gone shooting."

"It looks awful! Does it hurt?" I asked.

"What do you think?"

"Want me to ask for some ice?"

"Lord no, don't rat me out," he said. "I could kill for a cup of espresso, but they assumed that I, being English, preferred tea, so they went to a great deal of trouble to produce a fine afternoon tea, in a tent, no less, right after the shooting. Later, we went to the local pub for a beer and supper."

I told him about my day with Oncle Philippe. "Look at what they gave us," I said, and I showed him the beautiful antique perfume bottles and personalized scents. "Perfume for me, and aftershave for you. Did you know that perfume is made only for women? Men get cologne, or aftershave."

"That's nice," he replied.

"*Nice*?" I said incredulously. "Is that all you can say for this incredibly rare gift they made especially for us? By hand, from local flowers and ancient methods? Do you know what this would cost if you had to pay for it? No other man in the world will have an after-shave like this, you dope."

"Oh. Can I open mine?" Jeremy asked.

"Why not?" I said. Once he handled the bottle, I think he understood its value. He opened it reverently, as if fearing it might break. Then, he sniffed appreciatively.

"Hey, you're right. This is pretty good stuff," he said. "Subtle, yet potent. I'm going to douse myself in it after I shower," he exaggerated.

"Listen," I said, "I found out something about why they're being so nice to us. Tante Leonora wants me to research the tapestry so she can sell it for a high price. I suppose it's a harmless enough request, but maybe you were right about the family being a bit cash-strapped."

"Yes, well, there's a little more on the agenda than that," Jeremy told me. "This whole hunting party took place at the lodge of Charles' father. Afterwards, David hinted that we might want to invest in Philippe's perfume company. Never said the words outright, no pressure, but I got the drift. So your little perfume tour and picnic out in the flower fields could have been a subtle part of the overall pitch."

"Really?" I asked, intrigued. Going over the day's events in this new light, I supposed it was possible that Oncle Philippe had been assigned to do his part to entice our interest; yet, there was something slightly subversive about him, or at least, ambivalent about the future course of his company.

"I can also shed some light on why they're so keen for Honorine to marry Charles," Jeremy added. "Her family's perfume company is merging with Charles' family's business of pharmaceuticals."

"Oh," I said. I paused. "So, what kind of a guy is Charles?"

"He's a nice enough kid," Jeremy said. "Intelligent, but rather cautious and reticent."

I recalled what Honorine had said about how Charles did whatever his parents told him to do. Something in her tone had convinced me that he just wasn't the ideal match for the spirited Honorine.

"By resisting Charles," Jeremy warned, "Honorine is gumming up the works."

"Why . . . that's positively medieval," I spluttered indignantly.

"Nevertheless," Jeremy said, "David really wants this deal. He's been trying to drag his company into the twenty-first century, modernizing the equipment, the chemistry, et cetera. That takes capital. With such a labor-intensive company and expensive materials, the debts can be big. Very big. So," Jeremy concluded, "I lovingly suggest that you butt out of this Honorine debacle."

"But we promised her a job," I objected.

"If she asks, and *only* if she asks, we can say the offer stands," Jeremy said firmly, "but don't be surprised when Leonora mows down the idea. If so, then leave it be."

The next morning, I arose with some trepidation. As we packed our bags and prepared to depart, I just knew things would have to come to a head with Honorine; and, sure enough, right after breakfast, when Jeremy and I were at the foot of the staircase, thanking everybody, ready to skedaddle back to London, Honorine appeared, dressed to travel, and carrying two little suitcases. Just like that, as if it had all been agreed upon. All weekend she'd acted dutiful and obedient, but only, as it turned out, to lull her mother into a false sense of security. She'd waited until now to spring it on her *maman* that she intended to return to London as a personal assistant to me and Jeremy, because we needed her help.

"It's all set," she informed them grandly. All "orange-ed".

Tante Leonora's smile immediately vanished, but Oncle Philippe stepped into the breach and declared this an excellent idea. "Let her go with Penn-ee. Much better than backpacking around with her scruffy *artistes* and bohemian friends, sleeping God knows where," he said, and, with typical French rationality, he declared that staying with Jeremy and me would surely be a more *profonde* influence.

"After all," he said, "Penn-ee is a successful career woman, and she will be a beautiful bride and a gracious mentor for Honorine. I would hope our daughter will make herself indispensible, not only in their office, but for the wedding plans, too." I saw that he'd been listening to me much more closely than I realized, when I had been singing Honorine's praises about how useful she was to us in London.

To my surprise, this worked like a charm with Leonora, giving her pause, just as she was on the verge of throwing a fit of pique with her impossible daughter.

"Yes, it's true," Leonora murmured thoughtfully. "Think of all the wedding tasks to be done! The flowers, the menu, the music . . . Honorine can surely help."

Despite the instant alarm I always feel whenever someone mentions my "wedding tasks", I was deeply impressed with Philippe as a man who knew exactly how to get around his wife for her own good. Right before my eyes I'd seen Leonora do a complete *volte-face* and visibly warm to the idea. It was the only time she lost some of her artful subtlety, for I could practically see her thoughts moving across her face in plain view, as she rapidly sized up the situation, weighing how she might come out ahead. I imagined her sly musings along the lines of: *Well, Penny has clearly made a good match and succeeded in life, she is a sensible woman. If Penny will immerse Honorine in bridal plans, she might lead Honorine to discover that being a bride isn't such a terrible thing; meanwhile, Honorine can influence Penny to have her wedding in France. Parfait!*

But all Leonora actually said was, "Ah! I can see it is a waste of time to argue. This decision has been made without me, but who am I? Just a weary mother, that's all."

And while continuing to pretend to throw up her hands, having been outnumbered and overruled, she then, quite casually, told me that she would send Honorine a list of family members we might wish to invite to the wedding. I could mentally see my guest list expanding by leaps and bounds, and I couldn't wait to get home and telephone my mother to inform her that she was utterly wrong about the French side of the family. They were definitely planning on attending the wedding—in France!

Part Three

Chapter Ten

When Honorine, Jeremy and I arrived back in London, we found that an enormous amount of work had piled up in our absence. In particular, there was an environmental charity that I'd become involved with, called Women4Water, which supported studies to protect the world's oceans, lakes, streams, and aquatic life. (Our motto was, *Let's make waves.*) This year we were trying to raise money to provide good drinking water for children in poor countries.

Jodi, the director, informed me that they simply must come up with something special, some new way to lure more donors, but, as she told me, "Times are tough for charities, and the competition is fierce. Rich people have seen and heard everything. Celebrities help, but one must captivate them with something new."

Meanwhile, I was now getting impatient phone calls and e-mail messages from my friends and relatives who all wanted to know where my bridal registry was, even though I'd plainly told them that I didn't need fancy gifts, and would prefer instead that they make donations to this charity.

"But darling," Erik patiently explained to me on the telephone, "of course we'll make donations to help you save the world, but meanwhile, people want to do things that are *fun* when their little sweet friend is getting hitched. You're only going to get married once in this lifetime—I *hope*—and this is a big deal for you, you funny little thing. So put your wedding day at the top of your to-do list, sweetheart, or it is just *not* going to happen the way you want, and you're going to lose control of it to your mother or somebody."

His affectionate words of advice rang true. Erik and I have worked together for years on more film sets than I care to count, and he knew me better than most. But I couldn't even explain to him that the truth was, frankly, every time I sat down with my lists and my planner, I experienced a very strange mood, which I found profoundly baffling. It was as if my brain went into a dead zone, and I sat there at my desk utterly stymied, not knowing what to do first. I put this down to total overwhelm, like when you have to cram for an exam on a subject that you really don't seem to have any affinity for. I couldn't figure it out. Every girl I knew harbored a fantasy of how her wedding day would look, right down to the dress, the music, the flowers . . . and so had I.

But, now that it was for real, there was just something about actually orchestrating my wedding that unnerved me in a most surprising, peculiar way. Worse, I found myself clamming up. I couldn't even raise the subject with my mother or my friends. Something inside me felt secretive, as if a wedding ought to be a private affair and was simply nobody else's business. Would anyone understand this? I doubted it. There was, perhaps, only one person that I felt I might actually confide this to.

Jeremy. He came into my office one day to tell me about various conversations he'd had with potential clients, and he was regaling me with what he thought was a particularly funny anecdote about a guy who wanted us to handle his estate—to ensure that, upon the man's death, he would be buried with his favorite Picassos and Monets. I must have been staring blankly at Jeremy with glazed eyes, nodding automatically, because he broke off in the middle of a sentence and said in amusement, "Pardon me, am I boring you into total catatonia, or what?"

I blinked. "Sorry."

Jeremy flung himself into the chair at the opposite side of my desk. "What's the matter, Penny?"

I didn't really want to admit to failure as a bride this early in the game, so I attempted a casual tone, but to my surprise my voice sounded woeful as I said, "Oh, it's just the wedding plans. The dress is no problem; I finalized that awhile ago. But I really can't seem to pull the rest of it together, and I'm running out of time." When I reached the end of that sentence, I sounded as if I was on the verge of tears, which horrified me.

Jeremy absorbed this in that intelligent way of his, then said, "Hell, why don't you just hire somebody to deal with all the details? Aren't there professionals who do this stuff?"

"Wedding planners," I said in a small voice. "Jodi recommended one, right here in London."

"So? Why not?"

"It just seems impersonal, and I feel like I ought to be able to do this myself," I said.

"Can I help?" Jeremy asked.

"We could pick out the music," I said, shuffling through my notes. "And the caterer, although all the good ones must surely be booked up by now." There it was again, that panicky edge in my tone. I was deeply embarrassed. What an idiot. Besides, there were things on my list that I didn't want to consult Jeremy on. The groom's gift, for one thing. I wanted to find him something truly special.

My intercom buzzed. Honorine had an important call for Jeremy. When I gave him the name of the person, he said apologetically, "I have to take this call. Don't worry, we'll get the wedding sorted."

After he had gone, I looked out the window of my office, which had a view of a pretty little garden in the back, with a cherry tree and a bird hopping about, singing. Jeremy, the sweet guy, had let me have dibs on this room, with its lovely sunlight. His office—on the opposite side of the townhouse, overlooking the tree-lined square and street—was big, dark, clubby-looking, and private in the way of a man who prefers to work like an undisturbed bear in a cave. The day that we'd fixed up our dream offices, I'd vowed to become the productive best that I could be.

Remembering this, I said aloud, "Pull yourself together, ducky. Take Jeremy's advice, and let the professionals get you started." Then I picked up the telephone and called the wedding planner. She told me to come right over.

Chapter Eleven

The wedding planner's office was smack-dab in a posh section of town that was known as a shopping haven for the wealthy daughters of the world's moneyed families. Old townhouses had been combined and converted into exclusive, discreet salons for exercise, hair, diet, couture, and surgery. Many of these places were by-appointment-only, their front doors locked to discourage drop-in browsers. The wedding planner, however, was supposedly not just another caterer to the idle classes; she was the businesswoman's businesswoman who could "get things done right the first time". Everyone I'd talked to in London said that this was the wedding guru who couldn't be topped. She had "done" most of the "important" weddings in the world, specializing in exciting ceremonies for brides determined to make a splash; yet she could also engineer discretion and privacy for shyer celebrity clients. Her banner, *Roberta's Rapturous Weddings*, hung in one of three enormous windows in her second-floor office.

So, up I went, in a glass-and-chrome elevator run by a sphinx-like little gnome of a man in cap-and-uniform. The door opened onto a surprisingly large lobby, blindingly decorated in every conceivable shade of white, with white feathers pluming out of flower-pots; white chiffon curtains in the hall doorway; and a circular white reception desk presided over by a bevy of sharp young women in white suits, which gave them the antiseptic, no-nonsense look of nurses running a mental asylum for particularly difficult patients. I could not help thinking of that old joke about a blank white sheet of paper supposedly being a painting of a "polar-bear-in-a-snowstorm-eating-a-marshmallow".

The white-suited females all smiled when I came in, and they immediately began to bustle solicitously around me, with offers of spiked passion-fruit cocktails and all manner of cookies and pastel-colored candies. Despite the enormous size of the waiting room, nobody else was sitting there; this hour was to be exclusively mine. Apart from receptionists speaking in short staccato sentences into their multiple phones, the room was quiet, with low, dreamily romantic music that made me want to doze off. I was handed a clipboard with a five-page questionnaire.

"Fill out everything," one girl ordered with a smile. "Don't leave any blanks." She gave me one of their fat white pens that were like big cigars.

The multiple-choice questions were the kind that you wished had one more choice for each question, because you can't connect to any of the options they're offering. I studied each with mounting panic, such as: If you had to decorate a one-room shack on a desert island, what color would you choose? (*Red. Pale grey. Yellow.*) What's your idea of a great evening? (*Alone on a mountain-top. A rock concert. An exclusive nightclub.*) A great vacation? (*Extreme hiking. Snapshot safari. Arctic rafting.*) How would you like to express your gratitude to your guests? (*Edible favors. Jewelry. Handmade scrapbooks.*) Then there were photographs of three brides displaying their wedding "styles", with a "unique" dress, shoes, jewelry, and table setting. Which is your wedding style? (*Romantic.*

Nature-lover. Modern.) Trouble was, I could see very little difference in the accoutrements of each. Finally, there were what I considered some very nosey-parker questions about the health of the bride and groom, their diet and body structure.

Just as I was beginning to consider sneaking out and consulting a fortune-teller instead, I was summoned, and the white gauze curtains were parted for me. I was led down a long white corridor whose walls were covered with gigantic framed photos of bridal couples. Every size, every age, every pairing imaginable. By the time I reached the end of the corridor, I was already sick of the idea of coupledom. There is nothing less inspiring to the course of true love than visions of self-conscious strangers enamored with the limelight, and putting on amateur expressions of being inspired by love. The thought of hoisting Jeremy and me into this rogue's gallery made me actually feel faint.

But I'd apparently succeeded in running the gauntlet, because now I was in a sunny office, the very room with the big windows and the banner that fronted onto the street. Here I would have my free initial consultation with the queen bee of this hive—Roberta of the Rapturous Weddings.

She sat at a rectangular glass table with a computer, a pen and a telephone on it. There were two chairs in this minimalist room, both black; one for Roberta and one for me. When she rose to greet me, I discovered that she was the only woman in this entire establishment dressed in black. Her tight suit had a frighteningly tiny, nipped-in wasp waist. Her ash-blonde hair was spiky and short. She had startlingly pale skin, in sharp contrast to her fearless blue eye shadow, and lipstick of dark vampire red. But she had a disarmingly friendly smile, and a cheerful bluntness.

"Hullo!" she said in a melodious, whispery voice that gave her a deliberately otherworldly aura. "You're here not a moment too soon, you look *so* scared," she informed me; then, speed-reading my questionnaire, murmured, "Mmm, mm-hmm. Mmm. You are *definitely* the No-Fuss No-Muss Bride."

Glancing up with a confident smile, she proclaimed, "You hate details and like to delegate. You want to simply show up and get it done. You'd love it if someone just handed you the dress, the cake, the church, the vows, the reception, and the limo. You want everything stark, simple, modern, clean, and easy. You don't like a lot of fusty, musty traditional clutter. You're not sentimental, you'd rather eat out than cook, and go to parties rather than read a book. Your taste is trendy, modern, edgy. Am I right?"

She was so entirely off-base that I actually felt embarrassed for her. Yet with all her aggressive blissyness, I noticed that she never once looked me directly in the eye. As for myself, I struggled mightily to repress a weird giggle that was filling up my nostrils and threatening to become a snort.

"Actually," I managed to gasp out, "I just want to get organized with a few things." But I didn't dare take out my overstuffed organizer, with all its slips of paper and sticky notes. I just couldn't. Where would I put it? Not on that pristine table.

"Oh, sure," she said. "That's what we *do*. Wait till you see how *easy* it can be. We could make it all happen for you. The cake. The invitations. The favors for the guests. The attendant's dresses. The rehearsal dinner. The groomsmen's gifts. The venue. The gift registry. The music. The testimonials. Are you journaling? You really should. It will help you write your vows, and your Bride's Speech with your 'best memories', so you can tell each and every special person in your life how much you appreciate their support and love. We can even do the Best Man's toast. Or, you might consider a little bride/groom duet on video; for shy people like yourself, the prerecorded testimonial is the best way. You can always run it with a modified laser light show to make it feel 'live'."

You may wonder why I sat silently through this list. Actually, I was, the entire time, struggling to speak. But it was like a bad dream when you are being chased by an axe murderer, and if you try to scream for help, your words just get caught in your throat and lodge there, until finally you wake up.

Well, it was the word "laser" that did it. My voice started out as a little mouse-squeak, then developed into a full-blown roar. "NnnnoooOOOOO!"

At least she put down her cigar-shaped pen. I quickly explained, "We're not doing a rehearsal dinner. Or favors. Or attendants and best men. Or speeches to our parents, or a bridal registry." I suddenly realized that this meeting had been productive, after all. I'd discovered that all I really had to do was pick the date, the time, the place, the music, and the food. Compared to all this other hoopla, they suddenly seemed like the modest tasks they really were.

A tiny crease of displeasure appeared on her face, between her perfect brows. I realized I'd just accidentally discounted her most expensive packages. But then wispy-voiced Roberta said something truly unkind. "Sweetie," she responded. "It sounds to me like you just don't want a wedding. Are you sure you even want to get married?" She laughed a little, as if to imply that it was a joke. But it wasn't funny. For a second we just sat there, until the silence forced Roberta to finally look me in the eye.

"Is that what you really meant to say?" I asked her quietly.

"Okay," she said briskly, "in these economic times, I understand perfectly. If you don't want the Full Fabulous Wedding, then I would say you're a perfect candidate for the 4-Day Consultation, which means that we put it together for you in four half-hour sessions. You might also want to do our BrideBody Boot Camp"—here she glanced at my figure—"because let's face it, we can *all* use a little resculpting. Brides are into being sexy now, and you're the star, so *yours* will be on view, you know. It's five sessions; the last visit includes one Couples Yoga Massage, to help you and your man de-stress, detox and unwind."

I could just see Jeremy showing up here and being told by Vampira to strip down and detox. Roberta ignored my disconcerted look and said, as if speaking to a child, "Even if you are on a tight budget, I *do* think you and your fiancé are perfect candidates for video testimonials. You can express your love for each other and your parents, and you might even want to write a song together."

She rose, went to a closet and retrieved a black folio containing what appeared to be a twenty-page contract. She returned, clicking that enormous cigar-pen. "So," she said briskly, "let's make Your Big Day a reality."

At this point, the sound that came out of my mouth was something between a hiccup and a hoot. "Shhrwy," I said apologetically, rising. "Terly Thhks. Bleebye."

The rest was a blur. My mind froze, but somehow my feet took over, and propelled me past the hall of grinning couples . . . I believe at that point some of the girls-in-white began to chase me, so I must have sped up . . . then I sprinted across the waiting room, past the reception desk where someone called out to my deafened ears as I went bursting out the doorway . . . into the pixie-man's elevator . . .

. . . and baby, I didn't look back.

Chapter Twelve

I ended up in some tea shop, sitting at a table in the window area, in utter defeat, watching the world go by. Obviously, I told myself as I sipped tea from a big china cup, it was not simply the wedding and all its details that were overwhelming me. Much more important to me was the prospect of marriage itself.

So, in my usual earnest-but-dopey way, I'd been trying to "research" the secrets of a happy one, and I was therefore seeking more substantive guidance. But you can't get that from a wedding planner or a florist. Nor even from the spate of relationship self-help books, which all seemed to begin with the premise that men are Neanderthals having absolutely nothing in common with women, who nonetheless desperately want to hook them, God knows why. As usual, I was finding the modern world somehow bereft of the magic and sweetness that I wanted as a guiding light for my married life.

Sheesh. Sitting there surrounded by carts of tea sandwiches and iced cakes being trundled back and forth, I pulled out some of the close-up photographs I'd taken of the tapestry's details, which I'd tucked in my purse on my way out today. I'd never even come close to wanting to share these with the wedding planner. But now I considered that I might want to coordinate the wedding decor with the tapestry's lovely colors of deep burgundy-red, gilt-edged cobalt blue, and velvety green.

When we'd returned from Mougins, I'd tacked up all my tapestry photographs, and they completely covered the bulletin board in my office. So, every morning I found myself gazing at haunting images that were beginning to speak to me. Scrutinizing some of these photos now, I wasn't entirely sure that I liked or understood the tapestry's message. And here was yet another decision to make. Did I really want to get married in front of this thing? I couldn't commit to such a grand gesture unless I understood the tapestry's take on marriage. I stared and stared at the obscure symbols.

On the one hand, there were those oval insets with lovely, happy, rural images of couples engaged in sowing the spring planting, and gathering fruit in the summer ripening season, and collecting the autumnal harvesting, and making grapes into wine. On the other hand, some of the pictures were a bit disturbing and cryptic, to say the least. There was a man brandishing a scythe, reaping the wheat fields—was that a life or death image? There were soldiers leading a man away in chains, obviously a prisoner. Was this a comment on the burdens of married life? Like those jokes around the dinner table?

Plus, there was an actual bridal procession, with groomsmen carrying the bride's dowry cask, but with black dogs nipping menacingly at their heels. The groom himself seemed to be walking far ahead of the bride, instead of alongside her. Was he Orpheus, who'd been warned not to look back over his shoulder at the girl he was rescuing from the kingdom of the shades; but he couldn't help peeking, and he lost her forever? Or was it about the subjugation of women, like the notion of traditional Chinese wives walking ten steps behind their husbands? I knew that tapestries, especially those designed for women, were meant to serve as a guide to married life, but that usually meant exhorting brides to be virtuous, faithful and obedient. Humph. What about the guys? What were they supposed to do?

However, there was one simple image I particularly liked: a circular inset of two medieval figures, woven in red and gold thread—a French knight astride a horse, with his lady seated in front of him, her hair flowing in long romantic waves. This pair looked like young lovers fleeing the world, leaving its noisy strife behind, riding off to a triumphant—and private—destiny. Something about the way these archetypal figures were rendered, so lovingly, was appealingly elegant and vital.

Not far from this, inset in another circle, was a coat of arms with the ornate gold initials of "J.L." These just happened to be Jeremy's initials. Behind the letters was a half-moon. These were not the initials of the tapestry-maker, for his mark was clearly in the lower right corner. Idly at first, I began sketching what I saw, copying both circlets as they were; and then, suddenly inspired, I made my own composite, coming up with several variations.

For awhile I sat there, totally absorbed, until I landed on one version I really liked. Excited, I signalled to the waitress for my check; then I rose, packed up my sketches, picked up my handbag, and headed for that little cobbled street where Jeremy and I had found the jewelry store. After weeks of paralyzing uncertainty and inactivity, I felt suddenly energized, and it seemed important to take an action, any action. Jeremy's gift was a big one.

The sky had that lowering, threatening attitude of rain, but it didn't look as if it would erupt into a full-blown storm. When I entered the shop, the jeweler glanced up long enough to smile encouragingly at me while he was wrapping up a package for a customer at the counter. The customer, upon seeing that he was keeping someone waiting, deliberately squared his shoulders as if to block me from getting the jeweler's attention, and pretended that he was considering making another purchase; acting rather like a driver who sees that you want the parking space he plans to vacate but is now suddenly loathe to give up.

I didn't care. It gave me a chance to prowl among the jewel cases without the pressure of the shopkeeper watching me. I looked everything over, to be certain I hadn't missed anything new, but I knew what I wanted to see, from the moment I'd spied it on my first visit here.

It was a case of men's signet rings. These were bands of gold or silver or pewter, each with a flat round disc on the top, some of which looked like authentic antique coins, while others seemed to be newly minted medallions engraved with family crests. Upon closer inspection, I saw that a few were actually engraved backwards, so that they could be used to imprint one's mark on the sealing wax of letters, envelopes and documents. Others bore images of titans of history: Julius Caesar, Napoleon, Beethoven, Mozart, Shakespeare. And some were simply replicas of old money, specially designed to look like worn, beaten metal.

I was so absorbed that I didn't notice when the previous customer had left, until the jeweler moved over to my counter. "You must be prescient," he said now. "Your wedding bands just arrived from the engraver. Do you want to take them with you? You can try them on at home, and if they need any adjusting at all, just let me know."

He went to the back room and returned with one blue velvet box. He opened it to show me where our two rings, gleaming gold, were nestled, side by side. The sight of them had a sudden, unexpected effect on me. They looked so sweetly companionable—with mine smaller but matching Jeremy's—reminding me of the two of us, and all our little hopes and plans for the future. I felt a sudden kinship to all hopeful couples; for nobody really knows how much time we'll actually have together with the ones we love. Life seemed suddenly brief and fragile, and I felt a little catch in my throat.

This unpredictable wave of emotion was so unlike me that I hardly knew what to do or say, so I just stood there for a moment, not daring to even try to speak. Then I recovered, somewhat, and blinked, and looked up to thank the jeweler. He was smiling as if he understood.

"I'll get you a nice bag to carry it in," he said. He gestured down at the counter. "Something else you'd like to see?"

"That's not a real Roman coin, is it?" I asked, pointing at the men's ring.

"No, it's a copy. The engraver has a brother who's a coin dealer. They work together on these; their shop is just around the corner. Sometimes they use real antique coins when they can get them, but the old ones are costly, so the brothers often make their own designs. These rings are wedding gifts, like the men's version of an engagement ring."

"They're very good," I said. They were reasonably priced, too. "Could your dealer make one on commission?" I asked tentatively. "If I had my own design that I wanted done?"

"Sure," the jeweler said. "That's what he did here. This is a family crest someone gave him."

Thrilled, I pulled out my sketches. "Could he do this? I'd like to copy the initials from here," I said, showing him the "J.L." with the half-moon behind it. "But see, I want to take out the moon, and put these figures behind it instead," I said, pointing to the knight-and-lady on horseback, "and have the letters be sort of entwined, like vines," and I showed him a third sketch, the best composite I'd drawn.

"Ah! Lovely," the jeweler said approvingly. He made a few practical alterations, sketching, and said he believed it would be possible to engrave my design into one of the flat discs, to make a special "crest" for Jeremy.

"This style would work very nicely," said the jeweler, showing me some sample blank gold discs. "Your design is French medieval?"

"Yes," I agreed, "although I believe it was actually made around the mid-1600s."

"Where did it come from? Do you have the original art for me to look at it?" he asked curiously.

I shook my head. "It's not mine. It's from a family heirloom."

"Your sketch is pretty good," he mused. "I'll ask the boys to have a look. Then I'll get an estimate for you."

I went back home feeling triumphant. Within days, the jeweler gave me a very agreeable estimate, which I approved. I smiled to myself, feeling I'd finally accomplished something. Jeremy would love this gift, and it was unique and heartfelt. So, maybe now my wedding could start to feel like my own, and not something that someone else had dreamed up. Perhaps I'd soon tackle all the other things on the list, too. One little victory, I told myself, begets another.

Chapter Thirteen

One thing I'd completely forgotten about, in my new freaked-out-bride mode, was that Jeremy and I had been summoned by his Grandmother Margery, for a cocktail party to introduce her friends to Jeremy's "new" bride . . . as opposed, I supposed, to his "old" bride. I already didn't like the sound of it, guessing that Margery had thrown a similar bash for Jeremy's first wife prior to their brief marriage.

Jeremy admitted as much. "But don't worry," he said. "Nobody in that crowd remembers anything from last season, much less a wedding from a million years ago."

"Are you kidding?" I asked incredulously. "This kind of gossip has a shelf life of forever."

I wasn't fooled, and I knew there would be inevitable comparisons, but I'd already dealt with the ex-wife, and I wasn't about to backtrack now.

Jeremy gamely switched tactics. "They will adore you," he promised.

And so, on the appointed evening, we dutifully climbed into his green Dragonetta and drove out. It was one of those foggy, soggy evenings that London is famous for, where it isn't actually raining, but "misting". This means that the rain just hangs in the air, not bothering to land, yet constantly giving you the sensation that it's falling . . . mostly on your hair and skin.

We'd had weeks of constant "misting", as if we were all a bunch of potted plants; but the poor English weathermen kept trying to make it sound different each morning, employing nearly seventy-two synonyms for "wet", and reporting every lull, no matter how brief ("evening showers, followed by morning dry spell, with afternoon rain, and light drizzle in the evening, with storms developing at daybreak") all in the Herculean attempt to vary the forecast, so that the good citizens of Great Britain wouldn't shoot themselves in despair, but instead feel that we were all slogging our way toward a sunnier tomorrow.

"You look nice," Jeremy commented appreciatively as we drove off. "Like a self-assured woman of the world, except for that expression you're wearing, which is of someone being carted off to the Tower of London."

"Actually, I feel like I'm about to meet the Queen in *Alice in Wonderland*, the one who kept saying 'Off with her head!'" I admitted.

Jeremy said reflectively, "Yeah, that's about right."

"Thank you," I replied. "That's mightily reassuring." I had good reason to feel apprehensive. After all, this was the woman who'd kicked her own daughter—Jeremy's mother—out of the house when she got pregnant without the benefit of marriage. Margery's husband had been alive then, but the pair of them wouldn't give Aunt Sheila any financial support, despite all the money they had to burn. So she was left to fend for herself and her baby Jeremy, all alone.

Eventually, however, Aunt Sheila did get married, to a relative of mine, no less. My Uncle Peter, mom's brother. He adopted Jeremy and raised him to be such a good, posh Englishman that, one day, round about Jeremy's tenth birthday, Margery finally woke up to the fact that she had an intelligent grandson on track to go to Oxford. She began taking an interest then, which was a mixed blessing for Jeremy. Suddenly, the grandmother who'd wished he'd never been born, and who was still quite chilly toward his mother, was now summoning him to visit her on birthdays (hers), graduations (his), and Christmases (very tense, with his mother being treated as a black sheep).

"I always felt it was my job to please Margery. I thought if only I could, then she'd love Mum more," Jeremy once confessed to me. "It never worked, so I thought I must do better on the next visit."

Remembering this, I gazed at him tenderly, thinking of what a stoic kid he'd been. Plus, he'd acted so gallantly with my French relatives, gamely going out and shooting and doing whatever it took to ensure that a friendly bond was created with them. So, I was determined not to make this any more difficult for him with Grandmother Margery.

He caught my glance, smiled and said, "Just be yourself, darling. I know that you will triumph over all my sorry relations. The trick I've learned with my grandmother is, just don't tell her anything you really care about, and you'll be fine."

"Marvellous," I replied. "Be yourself, but then again, don't."

By now Jeremy was busy negotiating with London traffic. "Bloody hell," he muttered, glancing into the rearview mirror. "That wanker's been tailgating me the whole way. Look round for a parking space, will you? That's the house, on the corner, and I don't want this idiot to beat me to a spot if it becomes available. Which it never will, at this hour."

"Just hover until somebody goes out of one," I advised. Jeremy pulled aside, forcing the tailgater to go on without him. Miraculously, within minutes, a man came down the steps of a nearby building, flashed his keys, climbed into a car and drove off. "That was lucky," I said. "But then again, maybe not. Now we really do have to go in, and face-the-music-and-dance."

Jeremy swooped the car into the space expertly, turned off the ignition, leaned over and kissed me, then said, "Okay, Alice in Wonderland. Let's go."

Grandmother Margery's house was one of a series of white-pillared beauties that were set back from the sidewalk, and framed by a low, stone wall topped with a wrought-iron fence that went all the way around the corner. Her house had particularly lovely windows, especially the ones on the main level, which was reached by a short flight of steps.

From across the street, I could see that the party was already in progress, unfolding like a movie, as glamorous figures moved to and fro in the window, illuminated by a cozy yellow light. It was the kind of view that normally would have made me wistful, wishing that I could be invited to such parties. However, in all my fantasies, I never imagined myself as the conspicuous interloper in a group of people who'd known one another for a million years and who were not, by nature, particularly welcoming of newcomers. But Jeremy, keeping his hand lightly and reassuringly at my elbow, now ushered me across the street and up the steps.

We entered, stepping into a small hallway where a butler took our coats and put them into a closet. We peered into the room on the left, which was the scene I'd glimpsed from the street, where some of the guests were milling around with their drinks in hand, their laughter buoyant from the cocktails. These folks were young and snappy and urbane in their dark suits and fine shirts. I saw that, in contrast to the French party, this one was much less formal. Guests were constantly arriving or departing, speaking in brief loud bursts of conversation in passing bites, like the delicate finger-food they nibbled on that was carried about on gold trays by the uniformed servers.

Jeremy waved to the guests and we exchanged a few greetings, but he led me farther down the entry hall, pausing to say brief hellos to the people we passed along the way. I actually wished we'd lingered longer in that front room with the younger members of this set, for I could see, as we progressed farther back, that we were heading toward an older crowd.

And I knew what that meant. We were getting nearer the inner sanctum, a drawing room at the rear of the house, where Jeremy's grandmother was holding court. With more hellos and speculative glances from the guests, Jeremy's mere presence parted the crowd, who were watching for Margery's reaction as I approached her.

"Grandmother," Jeremy said, "this is Penelope Nichols. Penny, this is Margery."

She was not an apple-cheeked and cozy granny-ish widow, not nearly. Something about her did not even seem very elderly, as if she would not deign to grow old. Margery was very thin, straight-backed, with pale powdered skin. She was expensively but conservatively dressed in cream-colored cashmere, with low-key gleams of gold and diamonds on her fingers, a long pearl necklace and pearl earrings. She held a cigarette-in-a-holder in one hand, and a glass of scotch in the other, which, despite her stiff correctness, gave her an unexpectedly defiant air.

"Y-e-e-es, how nice of you to stop by," Margery said with a faint, distant smile, as if I'd just taken it into my head to pop over here, instead of having been summoned by her. Aware of her watchful friends, she extended a thin welcoming hand and clasped mine briefly, then asked a few polite, inconsequential questions about how I liked London.

"And your parents?" she inquired. "They are living in America?" She said this as if the United States was still one of those far-flung colonies of the empire, where the lesser folk who couldn't cut it in England were sent to make something of themselves. She inquired about my "line of work" and smiled tolerantly, less in the manner of the Alice-in-Wonderland queen, actually, and more like the real Queen of England, in that Margery behaved as if she were accustomed to patiently receiving visitors who could only be her inferiors. She observed me through slightly slitted eyes, making a quick assessment of me, which I sensed would stick forever.

Not to be daunted, I studied her back, noting that, yes, because she was blonde and green-eyed, she did bear some resemblance to Aunt Sheila . . . minus the warmth.

Once she'd dispensed with a reasonable greeting to me, she turned her full attention to Jeremy.

"What a charming girl," she told him, looking inscrutable.

I watched for Jeremy's reaction, but he appeared just as inscrutable, although he received the compliment by smiling at me, and then saying to Margery, "Yes, I'd like to introduce Penny to your guests, shall I?" while putting his arm around my waist. The warmth of his touch was bolstering, as if he were ready to leap to my defense if necessary. But why should that be necessary?

"By all means," said Margery, and Jeremy quickly steered me back through the crowd. As an older gentleman came over to shake Jeremy's hand, Margery floated off to resume her hostess role.

Wow, I thought. That was fairly painless. Since we'd gotten through the introduction to Margery well enough, and we were now navigating more friendly encounters with a few other guests, I figured we were doing okay . . . until I overheard one of the older female guests say, with ill-concealed glee, "Of course, Margery's being very big about it. You know she adored Jeremy's first wife."

Jeremy heard it, too; I guess he was meant to, since these old darlings were chatting in troublemaking stage whispers. But his neutral expression revealed nothing, and I didn't think anyone guessed that he'd heard. There was a time when I might have been fooled by that impassive look, too. But now I simply copied it as best I could, pretending to be raptly attentive to a jovial male member of Parliament with a booming, nonstop voice and the chubby cheeks and moustache of a walrus. He was what the French call *un vieux beau*, the kind of older guy who likes to stand really, really close to younger women.

Jeremy steered me away from the walrus, and, knowing that I'd overheard the old biddies, he murmured, "For the record, Margery detested Lydia, and only started saying nice things about her when it was absolutely certain that we were getting divorced, just so I could feel like a loser."

"Why would she want to make her own grandson feel crummy, when getting divorced is bad enough?" I asked in a low voice.

"Sport," Jeremy muttered. "Habit. And opportunity, not to be missed. The trick is to keep moving here, don't stay in one spot too long. Stick with me and we'll get through it."

As he guided me through the labyrinth, I saw that this was actually a fairly swish and sophisticated affair, with loads of impressive guests, young and old, who all felt obliged to show up at Margery's cocktail party or else face dire consequences: an earl here, an ambassador there, a music conductor there . . . but Aunt Sheila was not here. Her younger brother Giles was, however.

"Uncle Giles, this is Penny Nichols," Jeremy said in the tone of a man determined to run the gauntlet and be done with it.

When Uncle Giles turned round to see me, I tried not to grin, for he actually looked a bit like Jeremy. True, there were significant differences: Uncle Giles was older, heftier, with green eyes like

Aunt Sheila. He had a silvery-blond receding hairline, and the tightly wound body of a man who worked out religiously at his private gym. This was very different from Jeremy's natural slenderness, and deep blue eyes and dark hair, which he'd inherited from his Italian-American father. Nevertheless, Uncle Giles made certain expressions involving the eyebrows, nose, mouth and jaw exactly as Jeremy did; and the bone structure and shape of the face was undeniably similar, so there was definitely a family resemblance here, which I had not seen with Grandmother Margery. Perhaps it came from the English grandfather, who was no longer alive.

"Ah, so this is 'the one'," Uncle Giles said. "Penny Nichols! Whoa, you won't be saddled with that name much longer, eh?"

"Actually, we rather like it," Jeremy replied, nipping that old joke in the bud.

I'd been intending to call myself Penny Nichols Laidley once we were married, but I said nothing, mindful of Jeremy's warning not to volunteer information about my own thoughts. I figured that this caveat extended to uncles as well. Still, how could a man of this century automatically assume that I'd dump my maiden name? Didn't he know any career women at the office, for Pete's sake?

"My wife, Amelia," Giles was saying. "She ran a sewing magazine, years ago. Before she married me and had the kids, of course." Ah. That would be that, then.

Amelia had the carefully straightened, blonded hair identical to so many of the other women her age in the room. She studied me with a friendly but wary look that she probably used with all new females. "Welcome to the family," she murmured.

"And what have you two been up to lately?" Jeremy asked quickly. To my surprise, this caused Giles and Amelia to launch into a recitation of what schools their kids had gotten into, where they'd spent their last vacations, the styles of their new cars (his and hers), the endless remodeling of their house in the suburbs, and what lovely misfortunes had befallen their mutual acquaintances.

I grinned at Jeremy, who carefully avoided smiling back. It was as if he'd just pressed a button, and the conversation went into automatic pilot. It was restful, in a way, since the spotlight had moved off us. But then Jeremy's mobile phone rang, so he vanished into a nearby study to take the call.

By now I was approaching this party with the interest of a bridal anthropologist doing research on a foreign tribe she'd just stumbled across on some remote island. Marriage was very big in this neck of the woods, I could see that. But what did it mean to them? The joint recitation of Giles and his wife seemed designed to prove what sterling trophies they were for each other in a "perfect" marriage: he as a big moneymaker, and she as a well-placed society girl with a father retired from the diplomatic service. They were hugely pleased that they'd outlasted all their friends without the taint of divorce; yet whenever one of them spoke of a hobby (her tennis club or his favorite cricket team) the other wore a look of resigned patience, as if they each knew the other's best anecdotes and could perhaps recite them verbatim. Particularly Amelia, calmly but absently listening as Giles nattered on about his investments.

When Jeremy rejoined us and spoke to Giles about businessmen they both knew, Amelia turned away from the guys and said to me, "How nice that you and Jeremy are getting married. I envy you!"

"Why?" I asked.

"You're just starting out," she said. "You're free and unfettered. Enjoy it. It won't last." She took a deep sip of her white wine. "Well, you'll find out what I'm talking about, soon enough," she said, in the manner of a fortune-teller predicting cards of doom that could not be avoided.

"How did you two meet?" I asked, trying Jeremy's trick of keeping the focus off myself.

"Oh, school and chums," Amelia replied, as if an unimaginative god of destiny had arranged the whole thing. "Practically everybody here grew up with everybody else."

I wondered if Giles and Amelia had ever been giddy-in-love. Surely they had, for there was definitely a partnership here. And, despite her stoic attitude that the glow of excitement invariably wears off after the knot of marriage is tied, I saw a flicker of spirit in her eyes, as if she possessed a lingering romantic hopefulness. This made me like her, and I suddenly had one of those inconvenient moments when I feel sorry for the whole wistful world.

"You and Jeremy seem to enjoy each other," she noted. "But, you have to work at it," she added in a lowered voice, eyeing the guys. "You have to be *really* organized with husbands, and tell them exactly what you want. They don't *actually* like to discuss things endlessly."

We both fell silent, staring at our menfolk. And, as I said, they did look a bit like each other. Could Giles be what Jeremy would become, a decade or two hence? And would I end up pouncing on "new" brides and wishing on them the same slightly disillusioned life I had? As we all stood there nibbling canapés, I experienced a small, clammy sensation of dread. I began to feel trapped, restless. We'd "done" the entire group now, and some of the guests were already departing for the theatre or other engagements. Surely we might escape as well.

Jeremy apparently thought so, too, because he managed to steer us away from Giles and Amelia; and I was sure we'd be able to slip out gracefully in all this flux, but no such luck, for Margery was moving purposefully toward us, this very minute.

"Jeremy, stay," she said firmly as she spied us edging toward the door. "I want a word. Let's go into the study." I wondered if this was as ominous as it sounded. Jeremy remained impassive as we marched into a small room beside the stairs, but he instinctively closed the door behind us.

Margery sank onto a wheat-colored sofa, and said directly to him, "I want you to talk some sense to your mother." She grimaced with displeasure in a way that pulled down the corners of her mouth, making her look momentarily like a grim fish. "Sheila simply cannot bring that ridiculous man to the wedding and make a fool of herself to all of London, when, as it is . . ."

She didn't bother finishing the sentence, but even I could figure out the ending. As it was, Aunt Sheila had insulted everyone in this crowd by not adhering to their rules, living on her own and enjoying London in its rock-and-roll heyday. But good heavens, were there still people who hadn't gotten over the 1960s? And what did Margery have against poor old Guy, Aunt Sheila's nice little horologist? I tried to picture Guy Ansley at this party. Perhaps he might stick out a bit, but, so what? He'd surely fail to notice, and Aunt Sheila would probably just defiantly turn up that pretty nose of hers to anyone who scorned Guy. So where was the harm? Besides, it wasn't Grandmother Margery's wedding. It was mine.

"Oh, Guy's okay," I said unwisely. This, apparently, wasn't even worthy of a cold stare. Margery just looked momentarily startled, then ignored me and focused on Jeremy.

"It must be done immediately," she said emphatically. "We cannot have that buffoon in all the wedding pictures, because you'll have them forever, long after he's been purged from Sheila's life."

Oddly enough, Jeremy didn't protest. He only said, "Well, Mum is surely aware of your feelings on the subject, but I will convey your thoughts to her." He rose, as if to put an end to it.

"Another thing," Margery said in a resentful tone at his attempt to flee, "I have your railroad all packed up for you to take with you. So please see to it now. It's upstairs."

This totally mystified me. At first, I wondered if they were talking about railroad stocks and bonds. But Jeremy rose, muttered to me, "I'll be right back," and disappeared. Into the attic, I guess, judging by how long it took him to return with a big cardboard box, which he carried straight outside to the car, without a word. Then he came back, methodical as a moving-man, and went right back upstairs, and did the same thing. Over and over. The look on his face was so sober that I felt a strange urge to giggle. But Margery had further business to conduct—with me.

"Sit down, dear," she commanded, gesturing toward the other end of her sofa. There was a low table before us. She picked up a pair of gold-framed reading glasses and perched them on her thin nose.

"Now, Penny," Margery said briskly, uncapping a slender gold pen, and reaching for a white leather planning book from the table before her, "as to the wedding."

I glanced up sharply, watching her open the leather book. "I want you to know," she said as if she were doing me a tremendous favor, "that I've had a long talk with the vicar, and he has managed to juggle his schedule to allow us to have the wedding at our church in the Cotswolds. Jeremy tells me you're thinking of September."

"Yes," was all I could manage.

"Well, of course, that's out of the question. But if we move quickly, we can still book an early November, with a brunch reception at a local inn. I know the owner and he owes me a favor. So, a late-morning wedding would fit the schedule nicely . . ."

I gulped. Aunt Sheila was such a great future mother-in-law, not the least because she couldn't be bothered with conventions and had a full life of her own. So, foolishly, I'd imagined I was home free. I hadn't factored one imperious grandmother into the bargain.

"Um, that's very kind of you, but—" I began, but she didn't even give me a chance to tell her that we might have the wedding in France. In September, damn it.

"Not-tat-tall," Margery said dismissively. "But to get a firm booking, you really must finalize the guest list this week," she said crisply. Clearly, there was to be no shilly-shallying, and she flipped to the back of her book where, tucked in a folder, were several printed pages stapled together. These she handed to me, with no more ceremony than if I were her private secretary.

"Here are the guests from *our* side of the family," she said. "Jeremy may have a few others to add, but these are the important people. The invitations must go out to them in a week, or I can't vouchsafe that they'll come. I'll take a look at a sample of your stationery and then we'll move ahead." She returned to the tablet in her leather book, with her gold pen poised above it. "Now then, where is your bridal registry?"

"Oh, well, actually, Jeremy and I feel very strongly against such wedding gifts," I said, suddenly feeling myself on terra firma here. "We would like our guests to make contributions to any of our favorite charities. I can send you the list tomorrow—"

Margery gave me that distant smile again. "Yes, that's all very trendy, but you may not get very far with it. People like things to be a bit more personal." The idea was so absurd to her that she didn't even bother to get upset about it. She just said, "Amelia can send you a list of the best shops. She has the e-mail capacity," as if it were a vacuum cleaner or other necessary but lowly household appliance that Margery herself would never touch.

Well, it was time for me to abandon Jeremy's advice about not revealing my own thoughts.

"Margery," I said, as respectfully but firmly as possible, "I will have to get back to you on all of this, so I'm afraid we can't quite 'firm' anything just yet. There are other family members to consider. So, you'll really have to leave all this planning to me."

She peered at me in amusement over the tops of her gold-rimmed spectacles. "Why, of course, dear," she said, having managed, anyway, to get her list into my hands. "I'm counting on you to do this correctly, and I'm sure you'll do just fine."

Jeremy was still inexplicably walking back and forth with his boxes. I glanced up at him imploringly, thinking, *May Day, May Day*. He saw the expression on my face, and hurriedly went outside, then returned as if the job was done, kissed his grandmother, and swept me out of there, but not before Margery said meaningfully, "I'll expect to hear from you tomorrow, Penny."

You can expect whatever you want, I thought to myself. "Thank you. Goodbye," I answered.

"Jehoshaphat!" I said indignantly to Jeremy as we got into the car. "How could you leave me alone with her? She's practically got us booked into some church in the Cotswolds. Between your grandmother and Tante Leonora," I said dramatically, "I'd say our families are assembling on the battle lines, with the English on one side, and the French on the other."

"We will surely end up re-igniting the Hundred Years' War," Jeremy agreed. "But don't mind Margery. Guess who that call was from on my mobile tonight? It was a public relations man for a guy called Parker Drake. You should have seen the look on Giles' face when I told him. I couldn't resist."

This gave me pause. Even I had heard of the world-renowned adventurist, philanthropist and multibillionaire banking mogul. Jeremy's old law firm, among many others, had been vying for his business for years without a nibble. Now, apparently, Drake's right-hand man, impressed with what he'd been hearing in the news about our new operation, had asked to arrange a series of "exploratory" meetings to see if Drake might wish to become a client.

"A connection like this," Jeremy said, "could really put our little enterprise on the map."

He looked so happy, and frankly, it was a relief to talk shop after this night among those rarefied orchids in Margery's little hothouse; but I kept twisting around to look at the boxes piled up on the back seat of the car. I knew there had to be more of them in the trunk, too.

"What on earth is inside all these boxes?" I asked incredulously. Jeremy sighed.

"Model trains," he said. "Very old set. Probably valuable as a collector's item; you can assess it. Grandfather never really gave it to me outright," Jeremy explained. "He and Margery used it to jerk me around as a kid. I couldn't play with it unless they invited me here. Grandfather made his millions in railroads, and I think the old duffer just wanted an excuse to set it up in the attic and play with it himself. There was no question of my ever taking it home; they said that Mum's little apartment 'wasn't suitable' for such a treasure. Margery still thinks Chelsea is riddled with beatniks and drug addicts."

I imagined how a little boy would feel, to be told that his own home wasn't safe enough or posh enough for valuable items. "So, how come she's giving it to you now?" I asked.

"She is 'disposing' of the entire set," he corrected. "Therefore I am rescuing it from being thrown out with the trash, which would be stupid. It's vintage. They don't make these models anymore." I saw that the collection was worth a great deal, emotionally at least, yet Margery had been serious about being ready to dump it in the garbage.

"What are those papers I saw her handing you?" Jeremy asked. I pulled them out of my purse.

"Wow," I said, squinting in the light of the street lamps we passed. "There must be at least a hundred people on this guest list. Are these all your friends?"

I read off a few names, but Jeremy stopped me. "Look," he said, "they're mainly *her* friends and people in society who, you know, matter. But I have no desire to get married in that stodgy old parish with a flock of people who don't really know or care about us, yet will expect to get expensively drunk, and probably use the occasion to shag one another's wives . . ."

"So what do we do?" I asked.

"Elope," Jeremy said uselessly. I made a face at him.

"Well, what do *you* want to do?" he asked.

"I don't know. My relatives want us to get married in France. Yours want us in England. My parents say either country is fine with them. America's too far away, and most of my friends in the States are looking forward to having an excuse to come to Europe; and the ones who can't come told me they're okay with just having a party with us the next time we're in New York."

"Well, that's helpful," Jeremy said. "Therefore there's no reason to have the wedding across the pond. So we might as well just piss off only half the family in Europe instead of all of them. The question is, which one?"

I refolded Margery's list. "Speaking of guests, why didn't you stick up for your mother and her new boyfriend Guy? Why shouldn't she bring him to the wedding?"

Jeremy shook his head. "When it comes to Margery, it's best to just pretend to go along with her and hope she forgets about it," he said. But I suspected darker motives.

"You actually agree with Margery about your mom's beau, don't you?" I said.

Jeremy admitted, "The guy's a fool, nobody likes him except you."

"Your mother likes him," I pointed out. "Why isn't that enough for Margery?"

"All she ever cares about are her social rules and a spotless reputation. Forget Margery," Jeremy advised. "Just figure out what you want, and do it."

"What I want," I said, "is to set up your railroad. To play with any old time we feel like it."

"Trying to make up for my misbegotten childhood?" Jeremy asked.

I kissed him. "Absolutely," I said.

"Then, what's mine is yours," he replied, with a warm, contented note in his voice.

When we returned to the townhouse, Honorine was sitting in the kitchen, watching TV and having a cup of tea, looking a little more animated than usual.

"A strange man was hanging around the front door earlier," she announced. "Naturally, I thought it was Jeremy."

"Naturally," Jeremy replied.

"But the minute he saw me look out the window at him, he ran away scared," Honorine said with some pride. I thought in amusement that we'd found our watchdog, after all.

"We do get some kooks now and then," I said rather apologetically. "They're usually harmless."

Honorine, possessing French tact as well as sensitivity, asked, "How was your party?"

"Fine," we both said in short unison.

She smiled knowingly and said, "People are funny about weddings, are they not?"

"Yes," I replied. "They sure are."

I told myself I really had only one task regarding our wedding: to find a genuine way to make it meaningful to us, not mere style over substance. It wasn't an exercise in "event planning" to me, and I didn't give a hoot about impressing people with my showy "creativity". It would be the start of our marriage. I once knew a dancer who told me that the way you begin a movement already determines the way you will end it. Therefore, the wedding was a foundation, which, however imperfect, must at least begin with the love we had, not only for each other and family and friends, but for the sweet joy of life itself. Yes, this was a challenge I absolutely intended to meet.

Chapter Fourteen

Jeremy's favorite "railroad" now occupied a small room just beyond his office, and it immediately fascinated all his male visitors, especially Rupert, the younger associate from his old law firm, who occasionally stopped by for advice on dealing with some of Jeremy's previous clients that he'd gradually been handing over to Rupert. When I entered the "train room" at the end of one particular day, I discovered that Jeremy was allowing Rupert to operate the switches for the inaugural run that sent the trains chugging.

I couldn't believe the elaborate network of tracks now snaking around the room on numerous tables, raised platforms and the floor itself. I loved the wonderful vintage replicas of old-fashioned railroad cars, including Pullmans, Wagon-Lits, other Orient Express trains—all choo-chooing and whoo-whooing with mournful and wistful whistles.

And some cars even had little wooden figures of passengers who were sitting up eating their dinner in the dining car, or lying down in pajamas in sleeping cars. There were uniformed porters in luggage cars with tiny suitcases, and a chef in a big white hat and apron in the cooking car, which blew off real steam. And adorable miniature chairs, tables and lamps.

This was too irresistible to me, and to Honorine, who had followed me into the room after hearing the little whistles. We stood there gazing at all the complicated signals and switches, with flashing green and yellow and red lights, that enabled the "engineer" to make a train switch tracks at the very last minute, just in time to narrowly avoid collision with another train chugging straight at it.

"Great viaduct," Rupert said, admiring the little train-bridge that spanned a model gorge with tiny pine trees around it.

Honorine informed us that she'd set up a coffee tray in Jeremy's office, so we all trooped in there, and she began to pass the cups round. When she handed Rupert his cup, he rose to accept it, but paused to gaze at her in wonder, and then none too subtly spilled his coffee on himself in the process.

"Oh!" was all he could say in embarrassment, blinking. Jeremy just handed him a bunch of paper napkins, and Honorine pretended not to notice, leaving the tray behind as she slipped out of the room.

After Rupert left, I told Jeremy, "Leonora apparently called Honorine today to ask if we plan to use the tapestry for the ceremony. To tell you the truth, I think I should learn a little more about it before deciding if it will be a part of our wedding. So I'm thinking of doing some research on the tapestry, which Leonora wanted me to do, anyway."

Jeremy shrugged, as if it was basically a female hobby, like quilting or something. "Have you settled on getting married in France?" he inquired.

"Not yet," I replied. "I'm looking into venues in both countries."

"Well, then, do you really have time to do tapestry research?" he asked. "Why don't you let Honorine do it for you?"

"Maybe I will," I said, but I had my doubts. I've never delegated serious research, because I often discover some of the most valuable stuff quite by accident. The aisle in the bookstore that you wander down serendipitously; the side gallery that nobody seems to notice in a museum; even the dog-eared clipping or photograph in a forgotten folder in the library. Little buried treasures, just sitting there waiting for a fairly distractible snoop like me. But, I thought, maybe it was time to learn to run a bigger, more efficient operation instead of being a one-man band.

I asked Honorine to join me in my office, where I tentatively broached the subject with her. She had a shy, observant, schoolgirl way of looking up at me as if I were a big sister leading the way to an unconventional, grown-up life. But today I discovered that we differed from each other in one particular, fundamentally surprising way: Honorine was absolutely bored stiff with history. Couldn't stand old things. Couldn't see the point. She rolled her eyes and told me that there was so much of "that ancient stuff" in her "old museum of a house" that she was sick of it.

"We're supposed to devote our lives to taking care of it all, to pass it on to our kids," she said incredulously, "even if we have to starve to do it! And it's like homework, with so many rules about how to do everything!"

"But it's not just about *things*. Looking into your family history is like being a detective," I told her, amused. "You might find out really interesting stuff about your ancestors. Sometimes it's like getting a message from them, across time and space."

"Oh, I have had about all the messages I can stand from my elders, thanks very much!" she cried in mock horror, glancing up at the photos of the tapestry on my bulletin board. It occurred to me that, beyond her aversion to old artifacts, the tapestry perhaps had too much emotional baggage for her, because her mother was literally holding it over her head until she got married.

"Well, if you really want to know all about it, you should talk to

Papa's Aunt Venetia," Honorine said, not wanting to be totally useless. "After all, it was she who discovered it when it was put up for sale, and she bought it for her own wedding, which by all accounts was very, very glamorous. Then she passed it on to Papa and *Maman* for their wedding. She is very old, and lives alone in Paris."

"How old is she?" I asked, intrigued.

"*Zut*, she must be in her nineties now, but she won't tell anybody her exact age. She was a ballerina in the 1930s, and married a very rich newspaper man. Her life was *très romantique,* and she knew everybody-who-was-anybody 'between the wars'. You would adore her scrapbooks, I think. Tante Venetia used to show them to me when I was a little girl and went to visit her."

"A ballerina. She sounds great!" I cried. The name Venetia rang a bell. Then I remembered Oncle Philippe at the flower fields, showing me a deep purple, musky-scented rose he called the "Venetia". Honorine confirmed that this was indeed the woman for whom the rose was named.

"By the way, *Maman* says it would be good of you if you could send Tante Venetia an invitation to your wedding, so she feels included," Honorine said delicately. "But of course she won't come, as she never leaves Paris now, she hardly ever goes out of that apartment, even."

Jeremy appeared in the hall, poking his head in my office. "Hey," he said.

"Hey yourself," I said. Honorine smiled and went out, leaving us to talk.

"I just heard back from Parker Drake's P.R. man," Jeremy said, lounging in the doorway. "Got a clearer picture of what they want."

"That's terrific," I replied, impressed.

I'd already gotten Honorine to trawl the Internet for info on Parker Drake, which she did gladly, since he was a living, breathing contemporary mover-and-shaker, as opposed to a dead ancestor. Within a day, she'd sorted and assembled an impressive bio: Having made gazillions in banking, Parker Drake had a vast art collection and was an expert yachtsman. He was based in Monte Carlo and Switzerland for tax reasons. In addition to their staggering wealth, Drake and his wife were darlings of the media, mostly because they were both so attractive, with that smiling, tanned, well-rested, confident look of powerful people who knew how to make the world spin.

I was particularly interested in his wife, a former model named Tina, who was very generous and active in charities. When she threw a party, she actually managed to raise real money for it, instead of just attracting the attention of the society columns for the party-du-jour. She'd been called a "good influence" on her notoriously penny-pinching husband, having convinced him that rich people should, after all, share the wealth with the less fortunate. Her pet charity was for the world's orphans, and she'd fearlessly gone into diseased areas to care for kids and draw worldwide attention to their plight.

Plus, on a more personal front, she'd managed to have a tasteful wedding, despite the barrage of advance publicity. All in all, I thought this might be a woman from whom I could learn something about how to maintain an authentic, personal life while wisely navigating the treacherous, uncharted waters of conspicuous wealth and media attention.

"He says Drake may want to put us on retainer, to check out artwork for him, to authenticate antiques, attend auctions," Jeremy told me. "If he were a client, the income he'd generate might make it easier for us to pick and choose who else we take on; and I could hand off more of my corporate clients to Rupert, too. Drake's man says they'd also want our input on the charity events he and his wife get involved in, like museum galas and stuff."

"This is perfect," I said with feeling. "My Women4Water gals are desperate for new infusions of cash, and I haven't got a clue how to help them. Nobody's buying my idea of making donations for our wedding gifts. Our guests all seem fixated on giving us punch bowls and table linens. What's the plan?"

"Well, the P.R. guy wants me to fly to Paris and pow-wow in person," Jeremy explained. "He says it's just for 'face time', but I gather it's a preliminary meeting, because he said if all goes well, I—and you—will eventually meet Parker Drake himself at one of those exclusive parties of his."

"Me?" I echoed. "I don't do 'face time' with clients." I had envisioned a quiet talk with Drake's wife, not some public-event spotlight.

"You do now," Jeremy said briskly, "if you want him to fork over for your charity. But don't worry, the party isn't for weeks yet, and I still have to pass muster with the P.R. guy."

"Wait, did you say Paris?" I asked. "Okay, here's the deal. I'll do 'face time' with your mogul when he becomes a client . . . if you'll visit a ballerina with me now, while we're in Paris."

"A what?" Jeremy asked, looking surprised.

"Never mind," I said, picking up the phone to ask Honorine to book our tickets. "I'll explain it all to you on the way there."

"While we're in France, I'd like to go down to Antibes and meet with Claude," Jeremy said. "He's been wanting to talk to me about getting the yacht ready for the summer."

"We may as well alert Celeste to open up the villa for us, then," I suggested. I picked up the phone and relayed all this to Honorine, and when I hung up, I felt a surge of anticipation. The high season on the Riviera would be kicking off soon, and there was always a bustling excitement in the air.

"Off we go, then," said Jeremy, looking pleased himself.

Part Four

Chapter Fifteen

Every time I set foot in Paris, I feel as if I'm receiving a fresh infusion of optimism. It's not simply that it gives me hope for the future; or that it offers a real home to anyone who loves beauty; or that it welcomes lovers; or even that it lives in your heart long after you leave it. Paris is all these things, yet what is most remarkable to me is simply this: Paris is the triumph of making every day a heightened experience of being alive.

I felt this again when I awoke in a pretty blue-and-white hotel suite, and drifted sleepily into a cozy sitting room containing a low marble-topped table, an eggshell-colored sofa, and a wonderful big window with a splendid view. It had been Jeremy's idea to pick this romantic, old-fashioned hotel on the Right Bank, because, as he said, "What the hell, we're getting married. Let's celebrate."

When we parted the curtains to watch Paris awaken, I could almost hear an orchestra of musicians tuning up beneath the hum of shopkeepers briskly sweeping their sidewalks, and office workers rushing out of the Métro, and café owners brewing their coffee, and everyone greeting one another with the first, invigorating *Bonjour!* of the day. From this height, we admired the graceful order of wide boulevards that emanate like spokes of a great wheel, and we could appreciate the wisdom of the city's creators, who'd made strict rules about each building's height and position, so that nothing would disrupt the balance, harmony and light that now gave the morning a particular Parisian bluish-grey-white color.

And clearly, Paris is a city that loves its river, for the Seine was bedecked with a necklace of its best treasures: glorious museums, gardens, cathedrals, palaces and parks; and, most of all, a series of incomparable bridges—some made of stone, some of cast iron, another of wood—linking the left and right riverbanks again and again and again.

The room-service waiter obligingly arranged our breakfast plates on the table by the window so Jeremy and I could continue to observe the panorama below, as we ate French *epice* rolls, which came baked all attached together, like a tree's branches growing out of one long, main "stem" of bread. We ate these with perfect cups of *café au lait*. Our plan this morning was to go our separate ways, then meet up again in the afternoon to call on Venetia together. Jeremy would have his pow-wow with Parker Drake's man, and I was determined to make progress with our wedding plans. Paris, I felt, would make my agenda more of a pleasure, and less of a chore.

We rode down in a gold elevator that barely made a sound. The doorman sprang into action as we left the hotel and stepped out onto the street. "Want a taxi?" Jeremy asked.

"You take it," I said. "I'm not going far from here." He kissed me so tenderly that the doorman, and the taxi driver, and the lady who got out of the taxi, all smiled. I walked on, feeling purposeful and inspired.

The first item on my list was the invitations. Honorine had given me the name of a venerable stationery shop, not far from the Jardin des Tuileries. Here, she told me, was where I could get fine paper for the wedding invitations that would be hand-engraved in the same timeless method they used centuries ago; and she advised me to order matching thank-you notes and old-fashioned calling cards as well.

I loved the idea of future occasions when I'd arrive at someone's door and give the butler my card by way of introduction; or, I'd leave a card behind after calling on a friend who was out. Just exactly when or with whom I would ever do this was beside the point. I knew that if I had the cards, I'd do it someday. It would be a lot more fun than just leaving a voice message or an e-mail.

After the noise and bustle of the street, the inside of the shop was cool and invitingly quiet. So quiet, in fact, that I could hear a snore coming from the sleeping cat who lay in a curl beside the counter. The proprietor was expecting me, and he and two family members stood ready. They made an attractive trio—a very tall man in a black cashmere sweater, a petite woman with spectacles, and a young girl wearing a black velvet headband. I guess they were all curious to see who turned up after Honorine's crisp instructions ahead of my arrival.

The woman picked up a leather-trimmed desk blotter that looked as if it had been made for Madame du Barry (it probably was), and she placed it on a glass-topped counter. Upon this blotter, she laid out, one by one, several sheets of fine paper in pale Easter colors of bluish white, pinkish white, and one the color of melted vanilla ice cream.

"For your consideration, mademoiselle," said the man. Since Honorine and I had already decided on a burgundy monogram, I now chose the cream-colored stationery, which I felt would be perfect. All went smoothly . . . until it came down to the number of guests, and the date, time and location of the wedding. Er, I'd have to get back to them on that. Nevertheless, one item on the checklist was done. The invitations were going to be just lovely.

Having accomplished my first mission, my spirits rose. Perhaps this wedding jazz wasn't so insurmountable, after all. Now, on to the dress. Thanks to Aunt Sheila, I had an "in" at a terrific fashion house, and this process had already been put into motion, months ago. In fact, Monsieur Lombard previously helped me out of a very nerve-wracking social occasion last year, and I trusted his excellent judgment. But I'd been only to his London outpost, and had never seen his Parisian atelier.

It was located at that great big "X" where the Avenue Montaigne meets the Rue François I. The front windows displayed his latest summer creations on mannequins posed on a fake beach, with sand and scattered seashells at their feet, and whimsical pails and shovels. I tried not to be distracted by the pretty sundresses, the nostalgia-inspired ruched bathing suits, and the white trouser ensembles with big straw hats and headscarves that looked like something out of an F. Scott Fitzgerald novel.

I pushed through the revolving door, and walked across the elegant showroom, straight to the reception desk at the back of the shop. As soon as I gave my name to the lady at the big desk, she immediately picked up her telephone.

"Mademoiselle Penn-ee Neekolls," she proclaimed into the phone, and my name echoed in the room as if she'd just announced the arrival of the president's wife. From his office in the back, Monsieur Lombard came forth. He still had the look of a French intellectual, with those black-rimmed eyeglasses and the preoccupied air of a man with many complex thoughts on his mind. But as soon as he saw me, he let out a cry of joy, as if I were a long-lost friend, and he kissed me on both cheeks.

"*Ça va? Eh bien?* You are always adorable, but now you look radiant. Come, I think you will like what we've done," he said in one of his usual modest understatements.

I felt suddenly shy, as I always do whenever people are kind to me. He gave my hand a light, reassuring squeeze, then released it and turned to his staff. He clapped his hands, and his lady attendants swung into action. A cavernous dressing room was immediately placed at my disposal, with enough mirrors to evoke Versailles and to please even the most demanding narcissist. There were several upholstered antique Louis XV fauteuil chairs in red, white and gold. In the corner was a table with a bottle of champagne in an ice bucket, already chilled; and an espresso machine was hissing at the ready, alongside a tray of little sandwiches and pastries waiting for a nervous bride to nibble on.

And there, across the room, hanging on a satin-padded hanger with a gauze dust covering, the sole item on a long antique brass rack . . . was my wedding dress, ghostly white, waiting like a phantom in the corner.

As I approached the dress, the very sight of it made my heart flutter, like a bird who cautiously hops nearer, branch by branch. But these attendants knew their way around jittery brides, and nobody rushed me. Monsieur Lombard had already discreetly left the room, and one attendant brought in accessories and placed them on a low tufted ottoman covered in pale pink satin, while other women appeared with more padded hangers that they added to the rack.

Gently, they helped me out of my street clothes and into the soft, silky stockings and lingerie, which they'd selected for this dress, all in white silk with gold trim. The shoes had a deliberately old-fashioned shape to them, with ever-so-slightly rounded toes, and pretty golden heels.

Now, at last, it was time for the dress. Three attendants lifted the covering reverently. The under-layer was actually one of Great-Aunt Penelope's magnificent 1930s gowns, cut on the bias to sensually caress the hips. Monsieur Lombard had made a new over-layer for this, of fine silk chiffon, decorated with gold and silver thread, and pink and pale blue beading, that his incomparable sewing ladies had stitched on by hand. The effect was of a unified shimmering creation which, depending on how I turned and caught the light, looked now silvery bluish, now golden pinkish, making the dress appear as if it had trapped a whole bunch of sunbeams and moonbeams in its folds.

I was looking down as I stepped into the shoes, while casting a wary eye at the ladies with the pins in their mouths while they made the final fitting. But now, as I lifted my head, I caught sight of my own image in the mirror, which was replicated in all the other mirrors. The room and its surroundings, and the ladies attending me, also appeared in the reflection, and I experienced an eerie feeling, as if I were getting a glimpse of some secret parallel world that my soul inhabited, along with these otherworldly creatures fluttering about, as they do in those magical, dreamy ballets, when seemingly ordinary women turn out to be enchanted swans.

The attendants made me turn this way and that, so they could assess, and show me, the full effect. I obeyed them, speechless, still keeping an eye on that floating, fleeting creature in the mirror, who might just tiptoe on air and ascend all the way up to the clouds and vanish. Monsieur Lombard had quietly re-entered the room and surveyed the dress, without making a single sound, until now.

"And so," he said softly, "the veil."

The chattering ladies fell silent as he reverently carried the veil himself and placed it on my head. It had a lovely round cap of crocheted silk, adorned with little pearls and tiny pale pink delicate flowers. The cap fit nicely on the crown of my head. From this sprung the long veil of billowing tulle, floating out behind me, light as a whisper of smoke.

Monsieur Lombard motioned to one of the gals to give me a drawstring bag made of crocheted silk, with the same beading as the dress. Then I slipped on a pair of Great-Aunt Penelope's white elbow-length gloves that I'd selected from her treasured collection. Monsieur Lombard fussed, gently, with a few seams here, a few beads to lay flat there, brushing away invisible stray threads; until finally he stepped back and appraised the dress carefully from afar. The other ladies held their breath.

"*Ah, bon*," he said finally in approval. Then he looked directly into my eyes, and whatever he read there made him smile gently. "*Très belle,* mademoiselle," he said.

I heard gasps of relief and pleasure from the attendants. I looked gratefully from them to Monsieur Lombard, then to the creature in the mirror again. I had begun to tremble, and now I let out a little tremulous sigh. "Ohhhh!"

That was the first time that I really, truly felt like a bride.

Monsieur Lombard said, "You will be a beautiful long-stemmed white rose. Enjoy it, mademoiselle. Bask in the sunlight of your dreams."

After that, I existed, for a few hours, in a pleasant blur. I vaguely remember stepping carefully out of the dress, into my street clothes again, and being served those nice pretty sandwiches that I now devoured with a sudden robust appetite. I was given a pretty flute of champagne from a bottle that Monsieur Lombard popped open. He drank a glass with me; then he let his main lady take over, with her notes about the final delivery of the dress and accessories. Honorine would handle it from here.

"And you will let us know, as soon as possible, whether the wedding will be in England or France?" the woman inquired without any trace of impatience, but some concern, as the French always do when they want something to be done correctly, with dignity, and not in some dumb half-assed flurry, which they find utterly appalling. "Because we can easily get it to you through our shop in London, if need be," she was saying. "Only let us know, and we will do whatever you require."

"I will," I promised.

"And the suits for your fiancé to choose from, they are ready for him at the shop in London, but he must try them on soon and decide," she warned; then said lightly, "Well, you will let me know."

"Okay," I answered, still half in a dream.

And so, I went back out onto the streets of Paris, walking on clouds, oblivious to the noise and soot and traffic. Back at the hotel, I freshened up, then waited for Jeremy in the guests' lounge, the kind of parlor that has newspapers from all over the world on long wooden poles hanging like flags. A tall, magnificent grandfather clocked ticked companionably in one corner.

Jeremy's arrival caused a number of heads to turn, because he was carrying himself with even more than his usual confidence; and when he spotted me, his face lit up with such pleasure that people curiously glanced at me, to see who he was meeting. *Whew*, I thought, feeling tremulous again. Why didn't someone ever tell me that love could feel this good? But at the same time, I felt as if I might faint, too. Imagine that. In this day and age, a woman swooning at the approach of her guy. It was so crazy, to have my emotions tumbling all around me, threatening to be explosive, like some chemistry experiment, which might prove to be too much, and blow me right out of the lab.

"Hi," Jeremy said as he sat beside me. "Drake's man insisted I eat some lunch with him. Have you eaten?"

"Monsieur Lombard gave me lots of nice lady-food," I said,

adding softly, "the dress is beautiful." Jeremy saw the emotion on my face, and he kissed me.

I asked how his meeting went with Parker Drake's man. "Extremely well," he said. "The guy asked the usual questions, you know, like what other projects we're working on, and about our partnership, and all that other stuff they ask when they're trying to see if I'm a family man, reliable, et cetera." Jeremy smiled, adding, "So, I explained that we've got an upcoming wedding, and we're visiting some of your relatives in France. In the end, he told me we're on the right track, and he will recommend the firm of Nichols & Laidley to Parker Drake."

"Great!" I said, feeling that this, too, was simply a part of the enchantment of being in Paris. "What happens next?"

"If all goes well, we'll be invited to meet Drake himself," Jeremy said. "They'll let us know when." He checked his watch, then said, "Time to head on out to your ballerina's place. We should get there spot-on, if we leave right now."

This woke me up a little. "Holy smokes," I said. "I almost forgot about Venetia. Do we have time to get her some nice flowers? Good. I think she'll like it."

Chapter Sixteen

Venetia was ensconced in a grand turn-of-the-twentieth-century apartment house on the Left Bank, not far from the Boulevard Saint-Germain, the Sorbonne and the Luxembourg Gardens. Her building, decorated with globe lamps and flanked by two catalpa trees, was set back from the street with a pretty gated courtyard in front, made of white and grey flat paving stones. Inside, the building had an old wood-and-glass elevator with a little wooden bench inside, so that an elderly ballerina like her could ride up and down in style and comfort.

When we rang her bell, a plump maid let us inside an apartment with a long, dark corridor. We passed a flock of thin, long-legged, long-necked girls in their late teens who were just leaving, and thus going in the opposite direction; they were strange big-eyed beauties who scampered past us, walking in that telltale way, with their hips and feet turned out.

"Ballet students," I explained to Jeremy. "Honorine told me they still pay homage to Venetia, in the hopes of learning her secrets about how to dance a particular role. Honorine says they're all very gossipy, and Venetia loves having their company to dish about the new dancers."

Venetia was awaiting us in a large, high-ceilinged room that overlooked a quiet side street. There was one big window, through which, presently, we could see the dancers walking and chattering to one another in the street below, as they headed toward a nearby ballet school. Shafts of light from this window fell upon the butterscotch-colored parquet floors. The room at first appeared to be nearly empty, with just a mirrored wall to the right, and a free-standing ballet practice barre.

Then I noticed that the rest of the room's furnishings were all assembled in a sitting area against the left wall: a few chairs with crimson padded seats and backs; a low round table, piled high with dance magazines and large dance books; a tall, fringed lamp and a telephone on a chest of drawers; and an open trunk of costumes. Two floor-to-ceiling bookshelves contained several framed publicity stills of Venetia as a young ballerina, and rows of satin toe shoes on display, in every shade imaginable. Between the shelves was a fancy daybed, whose back and arms had a dramatic swooping shape.

And there sat Venetia, enthroned upon this sofa like an Egyptian queen, with a small bulldog at her feet on a pillow of his own. He opened one eye to size us up.

"Madame?" I said to Venetia. "So pleased to meet you. I'm Penny, and this is Jeremy."

"*Bonjour!*" she purred, in the low, husky voice of a woman who has smoked cigarettes all her life. She had dark, full eyebrows above slanted violet eyes, and a foxy, pointed chin that bore a resemblance to Honorine's. Her expressive mouth moved into a wry smile, and her eyes were shrewd and observant. When Jeremy handed her the flowers, which were beautiful and fragrant, Venetia accepted them with a coquettish smile, as if he were an admirer who'd come backstage after a performance. She buried her nose in the bouquet, saying, "Mmmm," before letting her maid put it into a blue vase.

The maid had returned with a silver tray and silver pot of hot chocolate, which she poured into red-and-white china cups and topped with a little daub of freshly whipped French cream. The chocolate was very good, rich and dark. Venetia sipped hers while holding the cup with both hands, which were adorned with rings of bright, chunky, colorful stones.

She looked at us together now, in that speculative way people do when they are assessing lovers. "So, you two are about to be married, eh?" she said, her gaze going from me to Jeremy, and resting there. "You are both very brave," she drawled. "Ah, but mademoiselle is *très jolie*, and he is a handsome devil, and you seem to move well together. That sort of coordination cannot really be faked or taught. You have money, I hear, so that's a good start, all told."

Jeremy appeared amused by her, and she enjoyed this; she had the soul of a born performer, and I think our receptiveness caused her to become more animated, as if she wanted to hold our attention by continuing to entertain us. So, as soon as possible, I asked her about the tapestry.

Venetia was quite savvy, and said slyly, "Hah, Leonora wants to know what it's worth, and she's thinking again of selling it, eh? Well, I gave it to Philippe, so it's theirs to sell, if they wish. Leonora told me the last price she was offered; it seems fair, but does that make it worth giving it up? I wonder. Is she still hoping to find out that the king himself commissioned it? I told her I already looked into it, quite extensively, because, you know, it was made by one of my ancestors."

"Yes, I heard, but I never got the details," I said eagerly, being on turf that was comfortable for me as a researcher. "What time period?" I asked.

"Oh, the mid to late 1600s, during the reign of Louis XIV," she said.

My father had told me that all French schoolchildren must learn to recite the names and dates of every one of their kings, yet so many are a Louis or a Philippe, that I often lost track. But of course I knew about Louis XIV, the Sun King who had expanded the palace of Versailles and used it as the seat of French global power.

"And your ancestor who made the tapestry?" Jeremy asked. "Can you tell us about him?"

"*Mais, oui!* Shall I tell you a nice, sentimental story I heard about my family, and the very first wedding connected to that tapestry?" she asked with a gleam in her eye, as if offering a bedtime tale to youngsters. When we nodded eagerly, she proceeded.

"You see," she said, settling herself back on her satin cushions, "there were once two boys from Genoa who were great friends. Rinaldo was a glove-making apprentice, and Armand was a tapestry apprentice. They came to seek their fortunes in France, bringing the arts of the Italian Renaissance with them. Rinaldo the glove-maker went to Grasse, and Armand the tapestry-maker went to Paris, where the king wanted the tapestry industry of France to become *le plus ultra* of these high-quality luxury goods.

"The two friends flourished, and each married and had children. The glove-maker's son Edouard became betrothed to Eleanore, the *tapissier*'s daughter. She and her father were very close, as he had educated her, and she often worked with him. Now, I must also tell you that the tapestry-maker had, as a client, a fine Parisian nobleman named Jean Lunaire."

I had to bite my lip to keep from squealing with glee. "Is this the 'J.L.' on the tapestry?" I asked excitedly. Jeremy, of course, had no idea what I was talking about.

Venetia looked at me with renewed respect. "You're the first person in the entire family to even ask," she said. "All anyone ever notices are the flowers, and the couple in bed. The answer is, *oui*, those are the initials and crest of Armand's patron. Yet, the auction house certified that this particular tapestry was not made for Lunaire, nor even for the king, as Leonora would have you believe. No, it was made for Armand's daughter Eleanore, from his prison room."

"Prison!" Jeremy exclaimed.

Venetia smiled, enjoying the effect of her own storytelling. *"Oui!"*

"Whoa," I said involuntarily. "What did he—er, do?"

"Nothing! Really it was all the fault of Armand's patron, Lunaire, who was arrested for trying to poison the king. Poor Armand was dragged into the mess, accused of being dispatched to procure the poison from his, how would you call it, his 'herbalist' friend in Provence." She paused significantly.

"The glove-maker!" I cried, envisioning all those herbs and flowers in Grasse. What a thought. I supposed it was possible to hide a few odd, sinister plants amidst them.

Jeremy smiled at Venetia, and said, "Well, *did* Lunaire try to poison the king?"

She shrugged. "Who can say for sure? Those were troublesome times, where many conspired against the crown. And, when the police investigated the poison suppliers, they discovered more than they bargained for. They found that quite a few of the poisoners' clientele were members of the upper classes, who sneaked off to buy deadly draughts and 'love' potions. So, many people—including nobility, and especially women—were arrested and tortured into confessing. It was like an epidemic."

"Like witch burnings," I said.

"Quite so," Venetia said. "This spread like wildfire, until finally, the investigations went too high, and they accused one of the king's own mistresses of trying to poison the king, although, my personal opinion is that she was merely sneaking aphrodisiacs into his wine to, shall we say, revive his ardor, and keep him out of the clutches of other, younger mistresses. This only gave the king headaches, so they say." Again, that flirty smile.

"But," I said, "what happened to Armand the tapestry-maker?"

"Well, we know from court documents that he was arrested, even though he protested his innocence. Fortunately, he was such a respected tapestry-maker—and, as I said, this being one of the arts that the king wished to encourage French supremacy in—Armand was not executed, but instead, exiled into house arrest outside of Paris, where he was permitted to keep spinning his tapestries."

"That was a lucky break," Jeremy muttered.

"Even so," said Venetia, "he was not allowed any visitors, not even his daughter, who'd been away visiting her fiancé's family in Grasse when Armand was arrested. He begged to be allowed to attend her wedding, but his plea was refused. So he asked permission to finish making his daughter's bridal tapestry, and the request was granted.

"But alas, he died before the wedding, and the tapestry was never delivered to the girl. It vanished into someone's private collection, and did not surface until 1933, when I, Venetia, who grew up hearing about this mythic tapestry, learned about it by chance when it came up for sale at auction, and my husband bought it for me as a wedding gift. That is all I know."

I sat back, having been totally enthralled as she wove this tale, and now feeling so sorry for poor Armand.

"And you were married in front of the tapestry?" Jeremy asked.

"Yes," Venetia said, smiling fondly now at the memory of her own wedding.

"It must have been a beautiful wedding," I commented.

"Oh, of course! My husband adored me. He was quite handsome, and we made a good couple."

I glanced at the photos on the bookshelf, but saw no wedding portrait. "Do you have a picture of your husband?" I asked tentatively. I couldn't help wondering what man would be able to capture such a rare, exotic bird as Venetia. She leaned forward to the nearby table, reached into a black lacquer drawer, and pulled out a framed photo of a very handsome man with dark, pomaded hair, bushy eyebrows, and full sensuous lips. There was undeniable power and vitality in his face.

"Oh, I see," I said with a smile. "How did you meet?" I asked.

"He was a rich boy but a bad boy, cast out of his schools, so his father sent him to Europe. He became a *balletomane;* that is, a connoisseur of *la danse* in general and an admirer of pretty dancers in particular. But he made his real fortune gambling in the casinos! He came backstage one night in Monte Carlo to meet me," Venetia said dreamily, "and *Pfft!* That was that, as you say."

"Were you married in Paris?" I asked, eager to hear about what kind of wedding this glamorous creature would have had.

"My wedding *began* in Paris," she said proudly, "in the little church around the corner, and then we took the *train bleu* to the Côte d'Azur for our honeymoon."

"What's this *train bleu*?" I asked, fascinated.

"Oh, it was a famous train line—quite luxurious—to take kings and millionaires and their ladies in high style and comfort to the Riviera," she said patiently, as if speaking to a poor, uneducated child. "The cars were each fitted out with a unique, beautiful decor. But ours," she said with a theatrical flourish, "was the most beautiful of all! My fiancé bought his own private car on the *train bleu*, and had it specially decorated in my favorite colors, to take us to his villa by the sea. Ah, life was beautiful in those days," she sighed, looking far off, as if remembering every detail. "True luxury, not like now, pah!"

She fell silent. I asked hopefully, "Were you very much in love?"

"*Oui, naturallement!*" she exclaimed, "but passionately, darling! Such jealous spouses we were. I don't mind telling you, in the years to come we both had many affairs, well, that's to be expected, we were young, yet we remained fond of each other to the very end."

Nuts, I thought to myself. Just once I wanted somebody to tell me that their marriage was both passionate *and* loyal. Was that really too much to ask? And parents don't count.

Venetia yawned and stretched out like a cat, groaning. "Arthritis, *mon dieu!* It's what happens to old dancers, but, considering the alternative, I am grateful to be alive."

I knew it was time to go. Jeremy and I rose, and she said, "Well, I wish you both the best on your wedding day. I hope the tapestry brings you luck. Please give my love to *ma petite* Honorine."

"Thank you so much," I said, rising. "We loved your stories."

"*Merci à vous* for your charming company," she said, eyeing Jeremy speculatively as if thinking of what she might do if she were only younger. "*Adieu!*"

Chapter Seventeen

We lingered in the courtyard outside Venetia's apartment before returning to the streets of Paris. Jeremy had stepped aside, talking into his mobile, looking a bit more mysterious than usual.

"What are you up to?" I asked finally.

"Venetia gave me the idea," he said; then he held up his hand for me to wait, as the person on the other end of the phone said something to him. Jeremy said triumphantly, "Perfect!" and hung up.

"Well?" I demanded.

"Come with me," he said briskly. "We are going to dine at Le Train Bleu."

"A train?" I asked, intrigued.

"No, darling. It's a restaurant. Very old, right at the Gare de Lyon train station. They built this restaurant to attract visitors during the 'Universal Exposition of 1900'," he explained to me as we hopped into a taxi. "It was like a World's Fair. One of my professors took me there once. It's perfect for a romantic like you, and you're in good company—Colette, Cocteau, Chanel used to come here to watch people on the platform, coming and going."

When we arrived at Le Train Bleu, I immediately saw that he was right. It was just the kind of romantic place I'd make up, but, apparently, I didn't have to. Actually, it looked as if King Midas had invented it—with gold, gold, gold everywhere, gleaming under the light of spectacular chandeliers. Forty-one beautiful frescoes adorned the salons, and it had those tulip-shaped wall sconces that I adore. The arched doorways had sumptuous portières dividing the rooms, and there were countless rows of leather-and-wood chairs, banquettes and tables, all lined up neatly, with folded-up snowy napkins standing like white miniature Christmas trees on each waiting plate.

Yet as we were led to our table, the most striking impact was not simply of the elaborate decor, nor the speed of the spiffy fast-moving waiters, nor the fabulous food they presented . . . No, above and beyond these sensual delights, I was struck by the great big sound—*Ah-whaaahhh!*—of mingled human voices, like the powerful chanting of Buddhist monks, that drifted upward to the vaulted ceilings, bounced around there, and then reverberated back to my eardrums. It was as if we had walked into a giant golden horn.

We took our seats, and our napkins were snapped open for us by our waiters.

"This restaurant is known for their escargots," Jeremy informed me.

But there I drew the line. "Snails? No way," I said. "I had them once, and my father has never been able to get me to eat them again. Nope. I can't do it. I keep thinking of the little fellow who ate my hollyhocks. Pick something else."

The waiter had approached us now. "Today's special is steak frites, because of a visiting American delegation who requested it," he volunteered.

So, out of deference to my hollyhocks, Jeremy and I ordered the steak frites. Which, I suppose, you could get anywhere in Paris. On the other hand, you never forget a great steak frites. I can remember every single one I've ever eaten, and where I was, and who I was with. And I must say, that I can't ever remember a better steak, a better table, and a better man. Jeremy picked out a nice bordeaux to accompany it, and I pretended that I was a 1920s flapper with a little fur-trimmed coat and a cloche hat and piles of luggage plastered with travel stickers from the four corners of the world.

We would have lingered there, but we had to get back to the hotel and pack. As Jeremy signalled for the check, I went into the ladies' room. There was quite a contingent of women already clustered around its opulent mirror as they fussed with their hair and makeup, so I slipped in and out as quickly as I could negotiate my way around, and then headed back out for the dining room.

I'd barely just emerged from the powder room, when a short, beefy man came barrelling from the opposite direction with the force of a cannonball, and knocked straight into me, sending me sprawling to the gorgeous floor like a billiard ball that had been hit dead-on.

It was such a hard blow that it took me a full moment to catch my breath. I was so stunned that I didn't even realize I'd dropped my handbag, until another man picked it up, brushed it off and handed it back to me. The big bull of a man who'd caused this rude shock had already departed, like a speeding locomotive.

I quickly inspected my handbag to ensure that all its contents were still there. I was surrounded by several concerned faces and a cacophony of excited voices, mostly in French, exclaiming about it. One waiter kept asking me in English if I was sure I was all right. Still a bit dazed, I said I was okay, and finally I made my way back to the table.

Jeremy's back had been to this whole scene, so he didn't know anything was amiss until I slid into my seat. He told me later that I looked pale, and my hair was a bit askew. "What's the matter? What happened?" he asked immediately at the sight of me.

I told him, and he fussed over me, finally saying, "Let's get out of here."

The maitre d' had heard about it by now, and as we reached the door he inquired solicitously. It was all very kindly, but the fact is, when you've just had a rude shock, the last thing you want to do is spend the next fifteen minutes assuring everybody that you're just fine, thanks.

After that, I didn't mind heading out for the soft soothing sun of the Riviera, and a little privacy, peace and quiet.

Chapter Eighteen

When we arrived at our villa in Antibes—which I still can't help thinking of as Great-Aunt Penelope's villa—the fountain in the circular front drive was gurgling invitingly. At the sight of the pale peach walls and blue shutters, and the sound of gravel crunching beneath our feet, and the rarefied scent of jasmine from trumpet-shaped flowers on the vine, I felt summer had started at last. I envisioned long, lazy days by the swimming pool in the yard. But our housekeeper Celeste had some rather strange news.

"You have had a visit from your cousin Rollo Laidley," she informed us.

That stopped us in our tracks. Technically, Rollo is my mother's cousin. He has never had a job in his life, although he adores collecting antiques. Nor has he ever really lacked for money; but his father's legacy is doled out to him in monthly installments by his mum, the formidable Great-Aunt Dorothy. This precaution was meant to prevent Rollo from blowing off all his funds on gambling, substance abuse and generalized carousing; however, his tight leash periodically results in debts to dubious lenders.

Generally speaking, it is not good news when he makes a sudden appearance, but, to be fair, he has been working to convince us that he's good company. Jeremy thinks Rollo's efforts are inspired by a desire to ingratiate himself with anyone who can provide him with free luxury. But I tend to think that Rollo secretly needs to feel he's a member of a real family.

Celeste explained that he had dropped by here looking for us several weeks ago, and, ever since, had been making quite a spectacle of himself, up and down the bars of the Riviera, knocking around one particular dive, in a slightly seedy area of Antibes. All the locals were chattering about it. The Riviera is a big place, but people who make a living here also make it their business to know everybody else's, and Celeste and the gardener felt duty-bound to notify us that good old Rollo's recent shenanigans were threatening to tarnish our family's reputation.

"He has a girlfriend from Tunisia who is a bad lot," she warned. "Every night this week they've been out on the town at a club—the butcher's son tends bar there—and your cousin has been throwing away his money on gambling and drinks. And now, this girl has a very strange brother who has suddenly appeared. He's trouble, all right; he has the face of a brute."

"Rollo has a girlfriend?" I asked in disbelief. I don't know why, but I just couldn't picture it.

"Well, the world is full of girls looking for a man with *l'argent*," Celeste exclaimed, rubbing her fingers together to indicate money. It dawned on me that perhaps Rollo's share of Great-Aunt Penelope's legacy was now presenting him with a new set of temptations.

And indeed, Celeste told us that Rollo had been showing off, acting like a rich man with an endless supply of dosh to buy drinks for any pretty female who'd sit and chat with him. It was not a good idea to fling so much cash around in a bar, night after night, Celeste maintained.

"The glitter of gold will attract the wrong eye," she warned. Her normally serene brow was a bit furrowed. Celeste was probably only in her late twenties, but she'd worked for Great-Aunt Penelope for several years, and still reigned over the villa with the protective air of a wise guardian who knows every nook and cranny of the place. She was tall and wiry, always wearing a spotless white apron over her flowered dress, and her light brown hair was tied back into a smooth braid.

"Yes, well, thank you very much, Celeste," Jeremy said firmly, and she nodded and went home.

"Rollo hasn't been out on a bender in a long time," he told me when she was out of earshot. "I suppose he's overdue."

"Drinking, gambling, or worse?" I asked in dread.

"All three," Jeremy said, sounding weary and all too familiar with this. "Unless we put a stop to it. Sooner than later." Since Jeremy's stepfather was also a cousin to Rollo, Jeremy grew up quite aware of the family stress over Rollo's episodes, and even had to periodically bail him out of jams involving loan sharks, jails and other sordid situations. Resignedly, Jeremy dialed Rollo's mobile phone, and we heard a jaunty recorded message that said, *"Still alive. Speak your piece and get on with it."*

"Rollo. It's Jeremy. I'm in Antibes. Call me the bloody hell back," Jeremy said shortly, then hung up. "What a wally," he added disgustedly. He looked pensive for a moment, then said, "I may have to go out and track him down. Let's get some dinner first. He won't be on the prowl until sundown anyway."

After we'd dined out in a small bistro we liked, Jeremy said he thought he ought to drop me off at home before scouring the streets for Rollo. We were driving in my Dragonetta—the vintage auto that Great-Aunt Penelope whimsically bequeathed to me—since we hadn't yet brought Jeremy's car down from London. I'd let him take the wheel today, because he loves this car.

"That bar where Celeste said Rollo goes is right down this road," I pointed out, after peering at the map. "Let's just take a look."

At first it seemed like a lost cause, because there were so many other nightclubbers milling around on the streets. But when we slowed the car in front of the fairly gaudy-looking club where the butcher's son tended bar, Jeremy said, "Yeah, this looks like his kind of place. I'll go in and get him."

"And leave me in a parked car on the street?" I inquired. "What do you suppose the guys out here will make of that?"

"Well said," Jeremy agreed. "I really should have taken you home, but we're here now, so come on. Rollo listens to you more, anyway. Maybe I won't have to wrestle him to the ground, with you around."

We parked in a nearby lot, then headed for the bar. The odor of stale beer wafted out as we entered. Inside, some ancient disco music pulsed loudly, and the lighting was somehow both dim and glaringly garish, depending on where you stood. Gingerly, we picked our way past the bar's regulars, who regarded us with the same suspicious glance that we probably gave them. There were a few moody male creatures at the bar, staring into their cups. At the far corner of the bar, a gaggle of girls, who'd just arrived ahead of us, were already shrieking at the jokes of younger men seated on the bar stools. The guys would occasionally pull one of the standing women into their laps. Beyond this was a back room, with chairs and low square tables; and nearby, a few pool tables, all in use.

It didn't take us long to find Rollo. There he was, seated at a large, ugly sofa, his pouchy eyes and rumpled suit looking even worse for the wear, and he also had a few days' stubble on his chin. His hair was longer than usual, too, but still smoothed into that Elvis-like pompadour.

As we drew nearer, I saw that he appeared totally soused, swaying slightly even while just sitting there, surrounded by dubious-looking women in cheap dresses. I could see that Celeste had not exaggerated; these gals were clearly trawling for the sort of fellow who, when properly flattered, is ready to spend big sums on free drinks and baubles. The sorry vision of Rollo in this condition depressed me a little, for I'd never actually seen him quite this bad before.

Then, right before my eyes, he stood up, tottering slightly, and selected a pretty brunette from the group to take home with him. This apparently offended a hard-faced blonde with a rose tattoo on her arm, who was perched on a stool at the bar. She'd been venomously watching Rollo and the other women, pretending not to care until it looked as if he was really going home with someone else.

I saw the blonde signal a man at a nearby pool table. He had wiry hair, muscular arms, and a cigarette pack stuck in the rolled-up sleeve of his T-shirt. His sullen, glowering face bore some resemblance to the blonde girl's. He straightened up, set aside his pool cue, and headed right for Rollo, blocking his exit. For a moment they spoke in low, angry growls that quickly escalated in volume, but I still couldn't quite make out the words, because of the pulsing, loud disco music from about a zillion years ago. The brunette with Rollo quickly backed away, returning to her group.

Jeremy, who'd sized all this up and was moving cautiously in Rollo's direction without attracting undue notice, now sped toward him, but couldn't get there fast enough. Rollo had already shrugged and pushed past the pool-table guy, who suddenly swung round, hauled off and *Wham!* He just socked Rollo in the eye, before anyone could stop it.

It happened so fast that poor Rollo didn't even realize what hit him. He staggered back and fell to the ground. The other women at the table, whom he hadn't selected to accompany him home, now shrieked with harsh laughter, and the men at the bar roared. This made me quite indignant. Nobody was going to beat up on a relative of mine, no matter how dumb he was.

Jeremy, well-experienced with Rollo's antics of yore, moved swiftly to stand him up and drag him toward the front door, ignoring Rollo's protestations. The guy from the pool table was watching Jeremy closely now. I held my breath, but Jeremy just gave him one drop-dead glance; and the guy, having figured Jeremy for a formidable opponent, quickly shrugged, turning away as if he no longer cared—a sure sign of a jerk who initially appears brutishly bold, but who only picks on weaker adversaries. He casually sauntered back to his pool game. The blonde, displeased by this turn of events, looked at Jeremy, then noticed me. As we went out with Rollo, she actually gave us the finger. Nice.

"I say, who d'ya think you are?" Rollo demanded to Jeremy, belligerently at first, as if he didn't quite know who was dragging him toward the door—a bouncer, perhaps? Geez. I didn't like Rollo's voice, so angry, growling and low, sounding more as if it came from a bear than a human. He appeared to have learned nothing from being slugged in the eye, because I saw him wink his good eye at the girls he passed, still showing off. Then Rollo finally noticed me, as I was standing there holding the door open so that Jeremy could haul him out of the wretched rum joint.

Rollo came to a dead halt, struggled to focus his wavering gaze on me, and then said, perfectly clearly, in the genial tone he normally uses with me, "Is that Penny? Good gracious, girl, what are you doing in a sinkhole like this? This is no place for you. I ought to inform your mother."

I just gazed at him in disbelief. Rollo looked at Jeremy, and for the first time recognized him.

"Oh," he said. "You came here to stand me a drink, I suppose?" he said dryly.

I was still glancing about apprehensively, dreading that someone would pull out a knife or gun before we managed to hustle him out to the street. Mercifully, we made our getaway without further incident.

"Rollo," Jeremy said loudly, as we reached our car, "what hotel are you staying at?"

Rollo mumbled something I didn't catch, but Jeremy did. "Open the window on his side," Jeremy instructed me, "in case he plans to get sick. Fling him out the window if you must, but don't let him get sick in this car."

I propped Rollo up in the back seat. "Don't worry, Rollo," I said, "we'll put some ice on that eye of yours when we get home."

Rollo, who'd slumped down already, became briefly, suddenly alert. "What's that? You want to pick up some ice? There's a petrol station not far from here . . ."

"No," I said hastily, "never mind, you just take it easy and we'll be home soon."

When we arrived at the surprisingly good hotel where Rollo was staying, the valet and the doorman seemed to know him, and were unflappable about his condition. Jeremy asked the night clerk to telephone us if Rollo tried to go out on the town again. "Please do not, under any circumstances, let him out of the hotel," Jeremy said, passing a couple of bills to the guy, who nodded and pocketed the money easily and quickly.

* * *

The next day, Rollo telephoned my mobile phone—not Jeremy's—to "return Jeremy's call". I told Rollo I really needed to talk to him, and he appeared punctually at the villa. Jeremy had just returned from the harbor where he'd gone to inspect the yacht and talk with the captain. He cast an appraising look at Rollo. For a man who'd been out only hours ago, getting himself seriously sozzled, Rollo didn't look as bad as one might expect, apart from his black eye, which was actually black-purple-red. He was very cheerful, and appeared to be glad to have some company.

"Coffee. How marvellous," he said as I offered him a cup. "Been looking for you two for weeks!" he beamed. "Thought you'd be down here any day to put the boat back to sea."

"We've been a tad busy," I said.

"Ah! That's right, the wedding bells!" he said, grinning. "Still chiming in perfect harmony?"

"Rollo," I said, "you've really got to straighten up and fly right for my wedding. I don't want to have to send somebody to dig you out of a dive on the wedding day. That would bring us all bad luck."

He stared at me. I seem to be the only one who gets away with talking to him as if he's a bad schoolboy. "I'd hate to pick up *Nice Matin* one day and find out that you've been murdered by that guy at the pool table," I continued. "You mustn't go there anymore. At least, not before the wedding. Promise me?"

Rollo looked at Jeremy. "She's a bit of a scold, you know," he said. "Is she like that with you?"

"I don't give her cause," Jeremy shot back. When his mobile phone rang, he stepped into the drawing room to take the call.

"Ah. Well, Penny dear, you wouldn't want me to disappoint all the ladies of the Côte d'Azur, would you? They think I'm frightfully chic, you know," Rollo told me. I stared at him, trying to figure out if he could possibly be flattering himself that such women were attracted to him for his personal appeal, and not the money he kept waving under their noses.

"Do I have to threaten to tell your mum on you?" I demanded, feeling a little cranky myself now.

And that, apparently was the key, because at the mere mention of Great-Aunt Dorothy, Rollo launched into a whole spiel about how his mother was ailing, back in London, but impossible to live with nowadays because she kept "threatening to die" as he put it.

"Bloody depressing," he whined. "She can't stand having me hang about her, she says she's got her maid and her doctor. She says I must start thinking of what I'll do with myself when she's gone."

All of a sudden, his antics made sense. The more he talked, the more convinced I became. Rollo was in some sort of panic mode because, as it turned out, he was afraid of being left alone. But as soon as I appeared sympathetic, he cleared his throat with a great *Harumph!* and said, "Mind if I have a look at your telly? Just want to check the football scores." We had installed a very small white TV in the kitchen, and I allowed this face-saving change of subject.

Jeremy finished his phone call, and rejoined me. "Good news?" I asked hopefully.

"Parker Drake's man," Jeremy said with satisfaction. "He says Drake's wife has heard of *you*, and wants to meet you. So the P.R. guy plans to wangle us an invitation to a party that Tina Drake gives every year. At their place in Switzerland. It's a masked ball, apparently. A charity event."

Jeremy looked puzzled. "He said he'd see if he could get me into Drake's card game there. Apparently cards is the way Parker Drake takes the real measure of a man. I suppose he means poker. I can hold my own in that."

Although Jeremy said this in a low voice, old eagle-eared Rollo looked up from the TV scores, and turned to Jeremy interestedly, saying, "Drake? Did you say Parker Drake invited you to play cards?"

"Yes, why?" Jeremy said warily.

"Why, dear boy, you don't mean to say you may be invited into *that* card game, do you?" Rollo cried. "That's a very exclusive invitation indeed. That fellow Drake conducts his business deals in the summertime over a regular game on his yacht in Monte Carlo. Yes, you may start out playing poker. But if you win and it's down to just the two of you, it's not poker you'll be expected to play. If you want to get on this guy's good side, the name of the game is piquet."

"Piquet?" Jeremy said skeptically. "Isn't that a game old ladies play?"

"Not the way this guy plays it," Rollo said stoutly. "For him it's mano-a-mano."

"I think I've heard of that game," I volunteered. "It's what all the aristocrats played when they were in prison during the French Revolution, waiting to get their heads chopped off."

"Ah," said Jeremy. "I'm thinking in terms of a more current century. Like, this one."

"Got any cards?" Rollo asked in a businesslike tone. I went to the cupboard where we'd stashed all our rainy-day distractions. I managed to scrounge up a box of three unopened decks of cards. Rollo gestured to Jeremy.

"Sit down, m'boy, and I'll deal you in," Rollo commanded, laying out the cards. "For starters, you chuck out all the low-number cards, the ones below seven. The dealer is called 'the Younger' and you, Jeremy, will be 'the Elder'."

We watched closely as Rollo dealt out the cards and explained the game. It had something in common with bezique, whist, bridge, and even gin rummy and poker. You collected cards in suits and three-or-four-of-a-kind, and kept score on a pad. At first I followed the rules pretty well, but when Rollo and Jeremy started trying variations, I got a little lost. I kept watching, but after a half-hour of seeing the two of them slapping the cards down, it occurred to me that now was a perfect time to go back to Leonora's château in Mougins to get another look at the tapestry, now that I knew a bit of its history.

I telephoned Leonora and asked if I could take a few more pictures, and she told me to come over any time I wanted. I ran upstairs to grab my handbag, but when I caught sight of myself in the mirror, I decided to change out of my jeans and into a nice dress. Once I'd done that, though, I had to change shoes. And then, transfer my camera, wallet and keys into a prettier handbag. You can't just march into a château looking like a stowaway.

On my way out, I told Jeremy my plans, and he looked up distractedly, and said, "Okay, great."

He and Rollo were so absorbed with what they were doing that I'm not even sure Jeremy heard me say where I was going. Which was fine with me. I could tell they'd be at it for quite a while. That would give me plenty of time to see what Armand the tapestry-maker had spent the last precious years of his life working on with such heartbreaking devotion.

Chapter Nineteen

I was never much of a driving enthusiast until Great-Aunt Penelope bequeathed me her old 1936 Dragonetta. Cobalt blue and zippy, it was a natural for these curving Riviera roads, and, once I'd gotten it fixed up, it made me a true believer in the joys of jaunting. I felt as if this elegant little auto had its own cheery personality, and was sharing its fearless enthusiasm with me. It took the curves with ease and aplomb, determinedly racing through the roaring traffic in town, skirting around trucks, buses and limousines, and darting through intersections in time to evade gridlock. Then it chugged up those mountain-goat hills to Mougins with spirited determination. Provence was waking up to summer with a riot of hot pink blossoms, and bright blue flowers on long green stalks, and purple fields of lavender that undulated like waves of a violet sea whenever the wind ruffled it with a breath of seaside air.

The château was coming into bloom, too, with its potted miniature trees in full flower now. A gardener and his son were trimming the fancier topiary, making a sleepy *Zzz-zzz* sound with their machines. They nodded cordially to me as I pulled up the front drive. The Dragonetta snuggled into a shady patch of gravel beneath a tree near the garage, looking contented and perfectly at home.

Leonora was happy to see me. She told me with charming candor that she'd almost given up on my doing any research into the tapestry. And although I'd warned her on the telephone that Venetia had sent me the auction house documentation, which convinced me that the offer Leonora had gotten was reasonable, I suppose my appearance here today convinced Leonora that I was "on the case" and would somehow magically find a way to "up" its value.

I couldn't exactly tell her that I was really doing this research for my most important client yet—my marriage. I felt that if an ancestor of Honorine's had gone to all this trouble to make a wedding tapestry for his daughter, then surely this work of art had some wise words of advice for a bride of any century. Something positive. Something for me.

As we moved toward the picture gallery, Leonora commented, "So you've been to see Venetia. She is very *drôle*, is she not?"

"I thought she was wonderful," I said.

Leonora seemed amused and slightly wary of her husband's unconventional aunt. After I declined the need to have anything to eat or drink, she encouraged me to feel free to get right to it, and furthermore, I could come and go as I pleased.

As I unpacked my camera, and began focusing on capturing the details, I commented, "What an amazing story behind this tapestry. Do you know about Oncle Philippe's ancestor Armand, who made the tapestry for his daughter's wedding in the 1600s?"

Leonora shook her head, but before I could launch into more detail, she said hopefully, "That's what all the appraisers say about the time period, but I don't believe it. Auction houses can be mistaken. I think it's from a later period, say, the 1700s, when Louis XIV's grandson got married; the king was very fond of his granddaughter-in-law. See that image of the sun? Surely that alludes to the Sun King."

"Oh," I said, comprehending that she was not the least bit interested in Armand's personal story, and only wanted to hear a royal connection, which might increase its value. "Well, these pictures might help me find out more."

"*Ah bon*," said Leonora approvingly, "I will leave you to it."

It was much better without her hovering over me. As I snapped away, my eye caught more of the details, and I knew that my first task was to figure out how to "read" the tapestry. Some tapestries read from left to right, like a book. Others tell their stories from the bottom—where the images in the foreground are bigger, and represent more recent events—to the top, which represents past events. But this tapestry had all those fascinating horizontal rows of drama, and I wasn't sure where to begin.

The borders acted like a picture frame around the main body of the tapestry. Within this main body was the married couple's bedroom, and here, the top image was the fan-shaped window above the sleeping couple's heads, through which one glimpsed the moon-face on the left, and the sun-face on the right, and, in the center, the far-off horizon of hills and sea.

But the most dramatic images were contained within the "bedspread of flower fields", which the married couple was dreaming under. The top two rows on the bedspread were composed of a series of circular and oval insets. The first row had the "J.L." insignia circlet on the left; and the knight-and-lady-on-horseback in a circlet on the right; and, in between, oval insets of couples of varying ages, doing their rural chores of planting, harvesting, and gathering in fields and vineyards. Beneath this, the second row of oval insets began: on the left, with a young man and woman, carrying a bucket to a water-well, like an elegant Jack and Jill; and on the right were a series of insets of people in seaside scenarios, fishing and hauling baskets of the day's catch.

Beneath those two rows, there were no more oval insets. Instead, the remaining rows on the bedspread all seemed to be part of a great wedding procession that was weaving its way on paths through the flower fields. So, the next row was of the bridegroom and his male entourage. He was at the center-left of his row, walking toward the left. His groomsmen were following him, carrying the bride's very elaborately decorated "hope" chest, which contained her dowry. This was where, oddly enough, the black dogs were snapping at the heels of the groomsmen.

Beneath all that, the next row was the bride and her attendants. She was in the center-right of her row, walking toward the right, and was about to pass under an archway of flowers. So, it looked as if she and her ladies were following the groom's entourage that was "ahead" or above them.

Finally, beneath the bride's line, the bottom row had a stately house situated in the lower right corner of the fields; and, to the left, curiously, was the row of soldiers who were leading a man away in chains. They were walking toward the left, facing away from the house.

As I studied it, I began to realize that the house seemed to be the starting point of the wedding procession. So, the way to "read" this tapestry was as a zigzag, like a maze, beginning at the bottom right corner with the house, travelling to the left with the soldiers; above which was the bride, travelling right; above which was the groom, travelling left again. All of these rows of parading figures added up to the drama of a wedding.

Apart from just a literal interpretation of a marriage ceremony, I knew that bridal processions in art were sometimes about the concept of a "triumph", like the triumph of Love over Death, or Piety over Corruption. Military images in wedding processions could be symbols of the groom's "triumph" of having won his bride and carried off her dowry. That might explain the soldiers. However, I still couldn't find a good spin to put on those black dogs nipping at the heels of the groomsmen. But mythology was full of stories of jealous guests at weddings, disrupting the festivities.

Overall, the tapestry looked to me like a father's tender, loving and bittersweet panorama of the world, with all its joys and sorrows. And now that I knew something about the personal history of the man who made it, these images were infused with new meaning for me. Take the prisoner being led away in chains by the king's soldiers. Could that be Lunaire, his patron? Or Armand himself, bound and unable to keep up with the wedding procession?

Maybe everything here was deliberately cryptic. The tapestry had been made with such painstaking care, right down to the fine detailing of the flowers in the decorative borders. It occurred to me now that these images might actually be homespun marital advice, woven in coded messages from the imprisoned tapestry-maker, so that the prying eyes of the king's guards could not invade the privacy of a father speaking in threads to his daughter.

I was deeply absorbed in all this, when David and Oncle Philippe appeared in the entrance hall below me. They seemed completely unaware of my presence, so engrossed were they in a heated argument in French. I heard something about selling the flower fields; then suddenly the volume of the conversation cranked up a notch.

"You may as well sell them my headstone and my grave, too!" Oncle Philippe said, gesturing dramatically.

David sighed. "Pa-*pa*," he pleaded. "What kind of man would I be if I ignored reality, and put our family and our future generations in peril?"

Oncle Philippe snorted derisively. "Money today, and nothing for tomorrow!"

Something made them look up then, and when they saw me, standing above their heads in the gallery with the tapestry, they both forced a smile and nodded to me. "Ah, Penn-ee," said David, with his correct, graceful manner. "Delighted to see you making your wedding preparations. We knew that you were coming today, but nobody told us you'd arrived. *Ça va?*"

"Fine, it's going well," I said. I imagined that they must have been closeted off in a business conversation too important for even Leonora to interrupt. David looked a bit embarrassed at my having witnessed his exasperation with his father.

But Oncle Philippe was too upset to really care if I'd overheard them. He returned to David, gesturing toward the tapestry. "If we do as you wish, your children—my grandchildren—will inherit only those dead woven flowers, which have no scent!" he exclaimed, and he went outside in a huff.

I wondered if Oncle Philippe understood that his wife was plotting to sell off the tapestry, and therefore, my photos might end up being the only pictures his grandchildren would see of his flower fields. I observed, through the long windows in the gallery, that Oncle Philippe had gone across the lawn to speak to the gardener, who was now clipping the roses and hydrangeas.

I hastily collected my things and went down the staircase. David was still waiting below, apparently defensive after his father's outburst. He glanced up at the tapestry and shook his head.

"My father is stuck in his old ways," he explained. "Like all of France sometimes!" He paused. "You like old things?" he said, nodding toward the tapestry. He sounded, a bit, like Honorine. Perhaps brother and sister had more in common than they realized. Maybe David, too, longed for escape and adventure.

"Yes, I do," I admitted.

"Well, it's very good for a wedding," David allowed, "but as for me, frankly, those classical and medieval images remind me of my schooldays. When I look at that tapestry, I see all the unbreakable rules and traditions that hold France back from the modern world."

"That's just what I like about France," I said. "The traditions that protect the quality of life."

"For tourists, perhaps," David said with a rueful smile, in a charmingly inoffensive way. He went outside, and drove off in his car. I wondered if I should try find a way to say goodbye to Leonora. But I couldn't exactly holler down the hallway for her.

As I stood pondering, I heard Leonora's voice, drifting out from the salon, very distinct, but in French. I couldn't get all of what she was saying, but I was able to make out that she was engaged in a telephone conversation, and I actually heard her telling someone that she wished to insure *le tapisserie* for a higher value, even it meant paying a higher premium.

"Uh-oh," I said to myself. Perhaps this little visit of mine really had been ill-advised. Now she was convinced that her mission would be accomplished. Well, I'd better wrap up my research and report to Honorine about it, and let her deliver the news if it wasn't good. Possibly Leonora would withdraw the offer of the loan of the tapestry for the wedding, but that wouldn't be the end of the world.

There was no reason for me to linger here, waiting for Leonora to figure out that I'd overheard her. So I went outside and thanked Philippe for letting me come, and he looked up from his conversation with the gardener long enough to wave at me as I drove away.

When I returned to the villa, Jeremy and Rollo were still at it, having been sustained by sandwiches and ale that Celeste had given them when she came to do some more cleaning and drop off a few supplies. Neither she nor I had any truly disruptive effect on the card game; the guys just kept at it.

"When it comes to cards, dear boy," Rollo was saying expansively, "there are three things you need: smarts, skill, and luck. Smarts you definitely have, no question about it. With skill, I can surely help. But with luck, well, we're all on our own."

I went on into the drawing room. We had been furnishing the villa a bit at a time, with Celeste showing up to meet delivery men whenever a furniture or antiques shop sent something that one of us had purchased. The drawing room was now mostly Deco design, with two cute striped sofas from the 1930s that look like ribbon candy, and a few tables and lamps, and, in the corner, a roll-top desk and straight-backed chair, with a computer and printer that could be tucked away from view when not in use. I printed out my pictures; then I spread them side by side on a low table.

When Jeremy and Rollo got up to stretch, they wandered in and found me examining the photos. They peered over my shoulder. "I never noticed those soldiers, and the knight on horseback," Jeremy commented. "Reminds me of King Arthur and the games we used to play, pretending our bicycles were horses, and we were knights, jousting with sticks."

"Ouch," said Rollo, imagining it. "Hope you didn't get knocked off too many times." He studied the photos and pointed out the gambling motifs he saw, like diamonds and spades. "Modern playing cards were mainly a French invention, after all," he said. "This looks like a lucky streak to me."

I realized that the tapestry was a bit like an inkblot design that psychiatrists use to determine a patient's state of mind and view of the world. We were all gazing at the same pictures, but we each saw a reflection of our own preoccupations. I wondered about the preoccupations of the man who made it.

"Fancy a real drink?" Rollo asked Jeremy.

"Let's all dine in tonight," I said hastily, sensing that it was absolutely necessary to get Rollo to break his pattern of going out on the town every evening.

"Are you mad, inviting him to dinner?" Jeremy whispered to me when Rollo returned to the kitchen to switch off the TV.

"We need to keep him away from bad company," I said. "I think we should make him come back to London," I added.

"You heard him. He's sick of Great-Aunt Dorothy. Can you blame him?"

"That's not exactly what he said," I corrected. "He's lonesome."

Jeremy sighed. "Then find him a wife," he said. We just looked at each other.

"Okay, I'll cook, and you talk to him," Jeremy conceded.

We returned to the kitchen, where Rollo was neatly packing away the playing cards. I put him to work helping me lay out the table for dinner, which he did with the amused, fascinated look of someone who'd never been asked to do this before. He dutifully followed me out to the dining room.

"Oh, child," Rollo said with some distress when I told him I wanted him to come back to London with us, "really I can't bear London. Too depressing."

"But I need you," I said, suddenly inspired.

The expression on his face changed, and he smiled warily. "What for?"

"You know your way around the best English antiques shops. Could you find me some nice champagne glasses for the wedding reception?" I asked. "I've been reading about how we should have just the right shape for champagne. You know, not too narrow, but not too wide and shallow, either . . ."

"Of course, of course," he said instantly.

"Nothing too ostentatious," I said. "I don't want to spend a fortune on them. Just something nice for a wedding, you know?"

Rollo brightened. "Darling, I know just the thing—Mum has a perfect set, and she never uses it. Lots of them, just laying about in crates. Perhaps I can convince her to give them to you as a wedding present; she may like that, for she won't have to end up spending money on something inferior."

"Really?" I said. I couldn't imagine Great-Aunt Dorothy giving anything away.

Rollo must have read my thoughts, because he added, "Not to worry. I can talk her into it. Or, failing that," he mused, "I can always smuggle them out of the flat."

I could see it was a challenge that appealed to him.

Part Five

Chapter Twenty

So Jeremy, Rollo and I returned to London, with Rollo promising to "touch base" with me within a week. Upon entering the townhouse, I found a pile of messages, neatly categorized, all stacked up. Honorine had also put fresh flowers in vases in each of our offices.

Lowering her voice so Jeremy wouldn't hear, she told me that the jeweler had sent over my groom's gift for Jeremy. She and I examined the signet ring together. I ran my finger over the fine engraving, delighted. "Oh, it's great," I said, locking it away in a small drawer in my desk. "I must remember to thank the jeweler."

"Yes, but, it was delivered by a woman who"—Honorine wrinkled her nose in profound distaste—"wore *very* heavy cologne, *très horrible.*" She rattled off the probable composition of the perfume that so offended her senses. "I had to open all the windows on the entire first floor, for days and days!" she exclaimed indignantly. "And still, I could not get that smell out of my nostrils."

Her little face, all screwed up in outraged sensibility, made me want to laugh affectionately, but aloud I observed that Honorine appeared to be quite a "natural" to follow in her father's footsteps and work in the family perfume business. She knew that I'd been taken on a tour, but now I described it in more detail, which revived her own fond memories of the place.

"At Easter time, we used to take the little soaps and hide them, like eggs," she said dreamily. "I put the lavender ones under my pillow. It helps you sleep, you know."

"Did you ever consider going into the family business?" I asked curiously. She sighed.

"And have my brother and I firing cannons at each other all day long?" she asked. "After all, I *am* a naturalist," she proclaimed, "yes, I am a follower of the philosopher Rousseau, you know, '*Nature never deceives us, it is always we who deceive ourselves.*' Whereas David doesn't really care what he makes in that factory, it could be shoes or can openers," she declared, "so long as it makes profits—but they are never big enough for him. Modernize, modernize, modernize! It's his mantra. But," she added darkly, "when it comes to women, David is not at all *moderne*; he thinks we should all just be obedient wives who stay out of a man's business!"

"And what do *you* think?" I challenged her. Honorine shrugged, pretending to be indifferent.

"What does my famous *cousine* suggest?" she asked tentatively.

"My advice is, follow your heart and do what you love," I said stoutly. "For all you know, you could be a great *nez*!"

Jeremy had come to the doorway of my office just in time to overhear this. Honorine always managed to slip discreetly away at such moments. When she was out of earshot he commented, "I don't suppose it would do me any good to say that *my* advice is, keep your own *nez* out of it."

"Nope," I said, eyeing him, trying to decide when to give him the gift. "It would do you no good whatsoever." I paused. "Was there something you wanted to discuss?"

"Just wondering how things went with the wedding planner," he said, a bit too casually.

"Let's just say we were incompatible," I replied. "They'd have us doing a karaoke rendition of 'our song' or making PowerPoint presentations of our love. There seems to be an assumption that all brides and grooms are secretly dying to get into show business."

"Perhaps I could do card tricks," Jeremy volunteered. "Rollo might teach me."

"Who's asking about our plans?" I inquired, in the same casual tone he'd used.

"I got an e-mail from Uncle Giles. He says Amelia sent you an e-mail you didn't answer," Jeremy admitted, looking a trifle embarrassed.

I turned to my computer and checked. Yes, it had come in yesterday, and was sitting there with all the other unopened messages I'd received. I opened it now, read it quickly, then groaned.

"Oh, God," I said. "She wants to bring the kids to the wedding. How many do they have?"

"Four," Jeremy answered. "The first three were all girls, so they kept at it till they got the son. He arrived rather late in the game."

"Four! If we invite *their* kids, we'll have to invite David's," I said, remembering the shrieking little dears playing on the lawn at the château. I scrolled to the end of the e-mail. "Oh, *no*!" I added in genuine distress. "She says they want to bring the dogs, too, because they are 'members of the family'!"

"Lord, no," Jeremy said firmly. "Draw a line now. No pets, no kids."

"I think we'd better say it the other way round," I said, rapidly reading the rest of the e-mail. "She's not even *asking*. She's *telling* me they're bringing them. She just wants to make sure that we pick a hotel that allows them. It looks like they expect us to pony up for all Margery's guests at the hotel."

"We'd better nip this in the bud. Let me deal with Giles on this," Jeremy said firmly.

"She's also sent me the names of a good stationer, and says Margery wants to see the proofs. But Jeremy, the invitations are already on order in France. The stationer is just waiting for the info—the date, place and a final count of guests." As I said this, I realized how much I still had to do.

"Thank her for the suggestions, that's all. You be the good cop, and I'll be the bad cop," Jeremy said. He paused. "But you know, we really *must* nail down the wedding plans. We can't keep waffling forever."

My telephone line rang just then, and Honorine announced an urgent call from Jodi, the fund-raising woman at my Women4Water group. Jeremy returned to his office, and I took the call.

Jodi came straight to the point. Women4Water was nearly bust. If we didn't raise money this year, it would leave thousands of children in poor countries without safe drinking water. "How do we justify doing nothing about that?" she cried. Since Jodi was normally a very serene Englishwoman, not given to emotional outbursts, I knew it was truly serious, and that money must be raised, and quickly.

But no sooner had I promised to get back to her with concrete suggestions, than my phone rang again. "Your parents wish to speak to you," Honorine said.

They were both on the line. My father coughed in an embarrassed manner. "We heard from Leonora, who was wondering if you found the château unsuitable in some way. She said you visited her recently but never mentioned the wedding at all," he said. "She had planned to show you that they have a little private chapel on site, but said you left before she could do so. Or, you can use the garden if you wish, but either way, the village priest normally does his bookings two years in advance."

I'd thought I'd made the perfect getaway that day, but apparently not. I felt a little ashamed. "Can you just tell them to hang on a few more days and I'll pick the venue?" I said.

"Yes. But you also should decide about bridesmaids and ushers," my mother warned. "They must be outfitted, you know."

"We're not doing those," I said. "Jeremy doesn't like the idea of picking a 'best' man."

I didn't add that his best friend was a fellow named Bertie, who'd just recently married Jeremy's ex-wife. We had politely declined to attend their wedding, and we'd sent a nice gift of a cocktail set, replete with tray, silver-rimmed crystal cocktail glasses, stirrers and shakers, and other fun stuff to play with. Bertie loved it, as Jeremy knew he would, but Lydia was furious that we didn't attend; and, although Bertie said he understood perfectly, he'd sounded wistful. Still, I knew if we went to their wedding, we'd have to invite them to ours, and I emphatically was not going to have that bird of an ex-wife at my wedding. Jeremy agreed, thank heavens.

"I suppose that makes it all simpler," my mother said, perplexed, "but what about the guest list? My advice is, just invite everyone on everybody's list, and be done with it. People harbor grudges for *years*, darling, just years, so why not have a mob and hire a hall?"

"*That's* really romantic, I must say," I responded, feeling wounded.

"Penny is right," my father said unexpectedly. "It is not at all suitable for a thoughtful girl like her to have such a circus for a wedding, and besides, that is no way to spend her money."

"Well, I don't see *you* coming up with a suggestion," my mother said in a testy voice I've seldom ever heard her use with him.

"Hey, guys," I said quickly. "Don't sweat it. I'm going to finalize everything this week. I'll call you back." I hung up, then went to report to Jeremy.

"*Your* parents were quarreling?" he asked, astonished.

I nodded, miserable at having been the cause. "And the worst part is, we left it all unresolved," I said. "They were so cranky, and Mom wasn't any help at paring down the list."

"My mum says it's your day and you should do what you want," Jeremy offered. "But the newspapers think you're a runaway bride."

"You're kidding," I said. He flung it down at me, with the *Lifestyles* section folded open. I glanced at the headline: *American Heiress Gets Cold Feet?* I groaned.

"They think you've lost the 'urge to merge'," Jeremy said with a straight face.

"Oh, God," I said. "They didn't actually *say* that, did they?"

"'Fraid so," he replied.

"Erik and Tim are meeting me for lunch today to hash out some of the wedding plans," I assured him. "I did some film research for them last month, and in return, they're pitching in."

"Good," said Jeremy shortly. He looked at me sympathetically but pleadingly. "The sooner we lock everything down for the wedding, the sooner our relatives will stop badgering us," he said. "I've got lunch with Rupert, to go over some accounts I'm still consulting for. After lunch, I'll be available to do whatever you need me to do."

"Thanks," I said. "I'll get back to you on that."

Chapter Twenty-one

I was determined not to lose the little glow of success I'd felt in Paris. So I lugged my wedding notes with me when I met up with Erik and Tim. They had managed to get a table at a chic new hot-spot for actors and theatre folk in Soho. It was one of those friendly places where the menu is written on a blackboard, and the waiters are all young actors who have definite opinions about the food, so if you ask them about the special of the day they'll either warn you off it, or else say, "Yep, it's great, I tasted that one. Get it while it lasts!"

I immediately spotted my friends in the crowd—Tim is dark-haired, trim and wiry, and Erik is like a big wolfhound, very tall with white-blond hair. His beard was more silvery now, and more neatly trimmed, I noted. They have been working together for ages, specializing in creating film sets for historical costume dramas.

"Penny Nichols!" Erik cried as I approached them. "God, we're famished. How about Dover sole for everybody? It's the special today."

"Yes!" I agreed breathlessly, slipping into my seat. I told them we should discuss the film research project first, before we got bogged down with the wedding plans. They were working on a new version of *The Man in the Iron Mask.*

"Bruce hopes you've got a fresh take on it," Erik said. "His wife's writing the script and she said, 'Ask Penny, she'll find something.' They don't want to just adapt the Dumas novel, saying the prisoner in the iron mask was the king's twin brother. Have you ever seen how *long* those books are? Anyway, Bruce doesn't want to direct another good-king bad-king story. He's done it six times in the soaps."

I said, "Sure, there are plenty of theories about who the guy in the mask was. And, actually, some people think the mask was leather, not iron."

"Oh, dear," Erik said. "'The Man in the *Leather* Mask'? Doesn't quite have the same ring to it."

"Well, anyway," I said, "other theories abound. My favorite is that the prisoner was really a gossipy relative of the king's physician. Apparently, this fellow was spreading the rumor that King Louis XIV was not really the son of the previous king, Louis XIII. But this could all be just baseless gossip."

"Honey," said Tim, "what do you think we're in business *for*? Baseless gossip is our bread and butter!"

"We're going to recreate Versailles—from scratch!" Erik proclaimed.

"Boy, you're brave," I said. "Versailles was a job that took several kings to create—and it killed off a few architects, too. I'd hate to see you guys bite the dust re-inventing it." I handed them my notes, and Erik glanced through the pages with delighted clucks. They were also going to check out the little island off Cannes where the infamous fortress stood that had imprisoned the man in the mask.

"Okay, let's get down to brass tacks," Tim said briskly after we'd eaten. "The wedding. Bruce says he wants to do a three-camera shoot, and he *promises* you'll never notice the cameramen. Says it will all be in good taste."

"Good, that's the least of my worries," I said.

"Tell Papa all your problems and we'll deal with everything, from soup to nuts," Erik said. I opened my planner, with my lists and Post-its stuck in the pages. Erik and Tim are so refreshingly blunt and honest that I actually began to make progress. I showed them a few pictures of the tapestry, and Erik said he'd try to match some of its colors, and would get sample swatches for the table decor.

"But *where* are you getting married? I've got to see the room if you want this set dressed in time!" Erik scolded, not unkindly but exasperated. "This is *so* not like you. Why don't you just make up your *mind*?"

I tried to explain my dilemma of having to choose between what Leonora and what Margery wanted. "Like Romeo and Juliet trying to choose between the Capulets and the Montagues," Tim said.

Knowing that I had Honorine working with me, Erik suggested, "Let the French girl find a place for the reception, and *she* can explain it to the dowagers. Just delegate, delegate, delegate."

"No, she can't let the kid pick the venue," Tim argued. "Personally, I think this is all very psychological. And since there's no time to send Penny off to a shrink, let's cut to the chase. Penny, dear, are you afraid of marriage itself, or simply of having Jeremy for a husband?"

I was shocked, and there was a sudden silence, during which time Erik had to shoo away the waiter, who apparently wished that, while I was searching my soul for hidden conflicts, I'd drink my coffee and finish my dessert, so he could drop the check.

"If I have to pick one of those two things, I'd say it's not Jeremy. It would have to be marriage itself, I think," I said finally.

"Oh dear," said Tim worriedly, "I think that's the bad answer, according to this magazine quiz I read on the plane."

"No, it isn't," Erik said in annoyance, "that's the *good* answer, it means she loves him, but fears commitment. I read that quiz, too."

"You must have read a different quiz," Tim said in a tight voice.

"Yikes!" I said in distress. "Now you guys are quarreling, too. See what I mean?"

"On top of all that, our waiter now *hates* us," Erik commented. "Not to worry, we'll take care of that with a good tip. But honestly, Penny, you have simply got to get in there and hack that guest list to pieces, and tell us all where you want us to show up. Nobody else can do this for you. You, and you alone, must deal with it. Or else, my dear, this marriage is just not going to *happen*."

Chapter Twenty-two

With Erik's warning words ringing in my ears, I went back home, where Jeremy was waiting for me, having decided that we would sit down together and resolve the entire wedding. But as soon as we entered my office, the phone rang. Hoping it might be Erik with a helpful idea, I picked it up.

"Hello, it is me, Auguste," said a familiar, feminine French voice. I mouthed to Jeremy, *It's David's wife*. "I just wanted to ask you to please tell your musical band to play *le fox-trot* at the reception. David and I always dance to it. Okay?" she said, her voice cheerfully shrill. "And we need to know if you are wanting to have the wedding at the château, because of course we must prepare. You must let us know which room you would like us to hang the tapestry in, and there is the priest to consider. Okay?" she trilled, and then rang off.

"Good God, the musical director has just weighed in," I told Jeremy after I hung up. "I haven't even hired a band, because no matter what they call themselves, they all sound like hotel lounge singers to me. 'Tie-ya yel-low rib-bon round the o-old oak tree-e-e . . .'"

Jeremy would normally have grinned at this, but he didn't now.

"I'll ask Mum. She knows a guy at the BBC who can get us audition tapes of musical groups," he said briskly, in that mode of wanting to get everything done as quickly as possible, with little discussion. "What else do we need to do?"

Thinking about Erik's offer to help coordinate the table decor to the tapestry colors, I glanced up at my photos of the tapestry on the bulletin board. "Hey," I said, suddenly noticing something. I'd recently pinned up the new photos alongside the old, but it seemed to me now that some of the old ones were missing. "That's funny. Some of the earlier pictures I took must have fallen off. Like the ones that had Leonora and Philippe posing right next to it."

Jeremy said impatiently, "For God's sake, forget the bloody tapestry! What's next on the list?"

"The ceremony," I said shortly. "We have to decide who to offend—Leonora or Margery. And the guest list. I want to cut it back. They're not going to like that, either."

"Look, just make a decision, stick with it, and tell everyone who's annoying you to bugger off," Jeremy declared. "Stand up to people. If you use the proper tone, then they'll sense you're in charge."

I was already frazzled after seeing Erik and Tim, with that stupid pop quiz. Now, something in me snapped, so what did I do? I wisely escalated it into a full-scale spat.

"Oh, really?" I said testily. "Well, since you're such an expert on getting things done, then what, may I ask, is your role in all this? I mean, it's your wedding, too, and there's a little more to it than just ticking off the boxes on a list. Every now and then *you* look up and realize there's work to be done, so you tell *me* to get on it; and then you expect me to have it all resolved by the next time you ask. You act as if you couldn't care less either way it goes, as if deep down it has nothing to do with you!" I flung out.

He looked utterly stunned, as if I'd just thrown cold water on his face. But he recovered enough to be pissed off, and said in a tense voice, "Fine. Then let me take control of the whole thing."

I was at least observant enough to ask, "Why are you suddenly so concerned today? Did somebody else ask you about the wedding?"

Looking slightly caught out, he said defensively, "As a matter of fact, Margery called, that's all. 'What ails this girl Penny?' she said. 'Why isn't she planning her wedding?'" Jeremy admitted. Ordinarily he might not have told me Margery's exact words, but he was annoyed now.

"Meaning what? That perhaps I'm just not suitable to marry into her esteemed family, right?" I said challengingly, totally unprepared for him to say nothing, with a guilty expression on his face that proved my guess correct. I said, "Well, that's just dandy! Did you tell your mother that she can't bring Guy to our wedding, because he's not 'suitable' either? You want me to stand up to people, all right, let's tell Margery that we want Guy to come to the wedding!"

"Why are you picking a fight with Margery over him? Mum doesn't care whether you invite him or not," Jeremy retorted. "So why are you insisting that he come? Just to spite Grandmother?"

And, to my utter horror, he grimaced with displeasure in the exact same way that I'd seen Margery do it—with the corners of her mouth pulled down like a disagreeable fish. *Oh, God,* I thought. *He got his annoying snob gene from her. If we decide to have kids, will they turn out to be snobby little guppies?*

"Surely you don't really believe that your mum doesn't care if she can't bring Guy!" I exclaimed. "Can't you see that she's just trying to make it easier for us? Which is more than I can say for Margery. I'd rather tell Margery that she and all her snooty friends didn't make the cut."

"Fine!" Jeremy said, raising his voice. "Go ahead, tell Margery that. Just *do* it! Or else let me handle it, I will be more than happy to. And while you're at it, tell your French relatives you hate the damned tapestry. Just please let's just DO *something*!"

Now, I don't know any woman—married or single—who wouldn't get her dander up when a man resorts to that particular *tone*, indicating that he can't understand why you are behaving like a woman, instead of like a guy. That incredulous tone—like he can't believe how addled you are—which borders on jeering. I was hearing just that dulcet tone right now, and I did not care for it. No Sir-ee.

"It is quite unnecessary for you to take an attitude," I said furiously. "We simply do not agree about Guy."

The front bell rang, so somebody was waiting out on our doorstep. Honorine was evidently still out on an errand; I remembered her telling me that she'd tracked down the girlfriend she'd originally been looking for when she first arrived in London. The bell rang again. And Jeremy, blast him, didn't move a muscle, as if males are totally incapable of any form of reception or secretarial work. So I went down the hall to peer out the window.

"It's Guy Ansley," I told Jeremy, who had followed me.

"Right. That's just brilliant," Jeremy said furiously. "You deal with him." He stormed out the back door, rather than face Guy. Therefore, I had to let the poor fellow in.

"Got a little package for a Miss Penny Nichols," he announced, sounding pleased as punch. "It's in the car. Is this a good time?"

"Sure," I said, holding the door open while he retrieved it from his car. He'd come all this way to personally deliver his lovely wedding gift, that beautiful antique clock. I smiled wanly at first, but his vital enthusiasm for his clocks actually cheered me a little. He carried it in as if it were a precious child, and I directed him to the study, where he agreed that the mantel in this room was perfect for it.

"Would you like a cup of tea?" I asked. "I have some in my office I just brewed."

"Lovely, thanks," he said, following me to help me with the tray. As he picked it up, he paused to peer at the nearby photos of the tapestry.

"My, this is all so wonderful!" he said, smiling up at the pictures, and squinting. "Very fine work indeed. French, yes? I should say so. A wedding tapestry, how marvellous. See, the archway of climbing flowers, ahead of the bride? There are many myths about young couples passing under such archways, to test the sincerity of their love. Nice, very nice." He looked up. "Are you thinking of making a purchase?"

"No, it's a loan," I said, enjoying his enthusiasm. He was, in fact, the only person besides me who was really interested in the content of the tapestry. "I keep trying to make sense of all these images," I admitted. "The whole thing's a bit of a riddle to me."

Guy glanced at me now, no doubt sensing that I was talking about more than just the tapestry.

"Life's a riddle, child," he said lightly, "but if you can feel the bumps on the road, it means you're alive and in the game. And that is a good place to be."

We went into the study, and drank our tea and nibbled on butter biscuits while he regaled me with stories of his customers. Then he brushed off his hands, and set about arranging the clock, showing me how it worked. He was genial and jokey, yet quite touchingly serious about his clocks. He showed me how to adjust, if necessary, the revolving, overlapping discs, which automatically rotated to display the hours, days, months, seasons. He was so patient when he explained it all, and I wished that Jeremy had stayed to see what a gentle, generous soul Guy was.

Not until he was leaving did he ask for Jeremy, and when I said he was out, Guy replied in a light, easy way, "Ah, then please give him my best. I hope that Jeremy and I will, in time, become friends. I know that it would make Sheila happy." His face lit up at the mention of Aunt Sheila, as if he was so thrilled to have found her. I could perfectly understand why she treasured him.

After Guy departed, the house was deadly quiet. Normally I find this meditative, but I was unnerved after that dumb spat with Jeremy. I felt apprehensive, because of past boyfriends I've had who were fully capable of sulking in stony silence for days, even weeks on end. I had no idea how Jeremy would deal with this, because we'd never really quarreled in quite this way before. Not over family, which gave it a terrible weight. I couldn't bear to hang around, listening for his footsteps. So I went out for a long walk.

The air was oddly humid tonight. The trees in the little square park on our street were a bit droopy, as if the day had exhausted them, too. I moved on, observing people hurrying home from work, looking stressed but still glad to be released into the summery evening. I saw one woman come to her front door to give her husband a big kiss as he arrived home from the office. He was carrying an attaché case, which he put down on the top step so that he could embrace her. Then they went inside together, stepping under an arched doorway.

Something in this gesture reminded me about what Guy had said, about couples passing under an arch to test the sincerity of their love. I turned and walked steadily home, hoping that Jeremy was there, and yet dreading that he might not be in a particularly forgiving mood. On the other hand, I wasn't going to let our entire little enterprise be defeated by a damned guest list.

When I entered the townhouse, it was totally silent. I went into my office, vowing not to come out until everything on my list was done. But when I sat down, I still felt a little tremulous. I hated being on the "outs" with Jeremy. Feeling foolish, I blinked away a few tears that were hovering in my eyes.

Yet even before I'd picked up my pen, I heard a small whistle. I raised my head alertly. Was it coming from some kid outside? Mystified, still carrying my wedding organizer in hand, I went into the study, where I heard it again, closer now. A moment later, there was an odd clatter of metal; then, out of the corner of my eye I saw something moving along the floor, near the wall. A mouse? Instinctively, I stepped back.

Not a mouse. It was a miniature train that had come chugging in from the corridor, whoo-whooing and choo-chooing its way along tracks which, Jeremy told me later, he had set down while I was out. I stood there, dumbstruck, watching as the train busily rounded the first corner, gently blowing steam, whistling importantly, following its tracks around the perimeter of the room, until suddenly, with a long, shrill whistle, it came to a neat stop, right at my feet.

I stared at it, and saw that it was a mini *train bleu*. Taped to the caboose was a pale blue envelope that said *Penny*. I stooped down to open it. The page inside said:

So sorry, babe. Might I join you for cocktails so we can hash out our future plans? Please fill out the following, return it to the train, and blow the whistle when you're done.

Below this was a choice of two boxes to tick: either, *Yes, you fool*, or *No, get lost forever*. As you may imagine, I opted for the first box. Then, fascinated, I replaced it, and tugged on the tiny cord at the front of the train, and it went, *Whee-ooo!* Jeremy must then have thrown a switch from his office, because a moment later, the train started up again, dutifully chugging back to him, bearing the message.

I waited, silent, holding back my laughter until my chest ached. There was a longer pause; then the little *train bleu* came chugging back; only this time, it was hauling an extra car, a big open-topped one, like the kind that carried coal. Inside this car was a martini shaker, two cocktail glasses, and a dish of green olives. When the train came to its stop, the glasses clinked a little. A second later, Jeremy entered, beaming.

"How do you like the new bar car?" he asked.

I dissolved into laughter. "Pour," I commanded finally.

We sat on the sofa, nibbling on olives and sipping our drinks. After awhile, Jeremy said, very gently, "I think I understand how you feel about that tapestry. Sorry it took me so long."

"*I'm* not even sure of what I feel about it," I commented.

"You want it to really mean something," he observed. "You don't want a single false note in this wedding. Above all, you don't want to be shanghaied into a life that isn't right for you."

"That about covers it," I agreed.

"Your instincts are always right about this sort of thing," he said. He hesitated, then added cautiously, "Darling, you know, we have to face this whole wedding business."

"I know it," I said, sounding stressed in spite of my best efforts, as I began reeling off all the must-do's, but Jeremy stopped me in my—tracks—no pun intended.

"Not that stuff," he said with a dismissive wave of his hand. "We'll get to that. I'm talking about the real deal, that's you and me. This is not about our friends and family and the florist and the caterer. It's nothing to do with them. And I'll marry you any way you want. Frankly, I'd just as soon elope—go off together on our yacht."

"What about your grandmother, and all her posh friends?" I pointed out.

"I don't give a damn what people say, including Margery. Believe it or not, I only humor her for Mum's sake. You'd think I'd know better by now, but I keep falling into that trap of imagining it's my task to bring Margery round, so that she'll be nicer to my mother again. But, she never will. I see that now. And it's nothing to do with our wedding. So, whatever you want is fine with me. Only, Penny, we have to face it, together. Now."

"Face what?" I asked, a trifle confused.

"Well," Jeremy said calmly, with the courage of a true knight, "if it's that you don't want to get married, I want you to know that we don't have to."

I was stunned. Completely taken aback. "Whoa, hold the phone," I said. "Are *you* having second thoughts?" I asked warily. "Ya know, projecting them onto me?"

"Not me, babe," he said firmly. "I love you now and I'll love you forever."

"Oh," I said in a small voice, feeling a lump in my throat.

"But don't let anybody rush you to the altar, even me," he warned. "I can wait, if you're not ready yet . . . or if you don't want to anymore . . . it's okay. Whatever it is, let's deal with it. Just you and me. I'm not going anywhere."

If I thought I loved him before, this just knocked me out. I flung my arms around him and couldn't speak, at first. Then, it was like a dam had burst, and the words just came pouring out of me, accompanied by some tears that dampened his nice shirt, as I was hugging him tightly the whole time.

"I love you so much!" I cried, the fog finally lifting, everything suddenly very obvious to me at last. "It's just that I'm scared that marriage is going to change everything. So, I'm terrified of taking a step in *any* direction, and *that's* why I keep hemming and hawing about each little decision. I don't want us to end up bored or cynical, or taking each other for granted, or snarling at each other, if life doesn't work out as we planned."

"That doesn't sound like us," Jeremy said.

"But everywhere I go, people keep telling me that it'll be no different for us; that, sure, it always starts out good . . . but they all say love can't last."

"Fuck 'em," Jeremy said in a muffled voice, because, as I said, I was holding on tight. "I'm sure your parents never told you that," he said, handing me his handkerchief.

"No," I agreed, "but you know how mysterious they are, they can't explain their secret, either."

Jeremy grinned. "I suspect that's because they're swans," he said.

"What do you mean?" I asked.

"I saw an article in the newspaper, so I did a little research while you were out," he said. "Think you're the only one who can do research? It just so happens that everything you've ever heard about the passion automatically going out of a marriage after the first blush is absolutely wrong. There is, it turns out, a pattern among certain couples that the brain experts call 'swans'. Scientists have actually watched brain scans of these couples who've been married, like, twenty or more years, and who are, apparently, still nuts about each other. No loss of passion. No seven-year itch. Not bored silly with each other. Not unfaithful. They may be rare birds, yet, the researchers say the scientific proof is pretty indisputable, and it blows conventional thought right out of the water. The scientists call these lucky couples 'swans' because swans mate for life."

"You're sure you're not making this up?" I teased.

"I printed it out for you. You can read it later," he said offhandedly, looking a little embarrassed now. "But the point is, Penny, I think your parents are a couple of swans. Maybe that means we have 'swan potential'. I'm no expert," he said, taking my hand in his, "but it seems to me their secret is that they really like each other, and with all that love and compatibility, they have the guts to make their marriage the most important thing in their lives. I absolutely believe that you and I can do that, too. And who is anyone to tell us we shouldn't even try? Nobody's saying we'll have a perfect marriage or even a perfect wedding, whatever that is. But if we stand by how we really feel, then at least it will be *ours*."

I felt as if a giant boulder had been lifted off my shoulders, and I was ready to deal with anything. I told him so.

"You're sure?" he asked tenderly. I kissed him.

"Oh, *yeah*," I said positively.

Jeremy suddenly exhaled aloud in relief, and I now saw how much this meant to him. I mean, there he was, bracing himself in case I had said I couldn't go through with it.

"What were you going to do if I said 'no'?" I asked curiously, the danger so far behind us now that I could kid him about it.

"Oh, pack a few things in a sack at the end of a stick, go off and be a hobo," he said lightly. "Come back the next day and fight for you all over again."

"You really are my knight in shining armor," I said, touching his cheek. Then I remembered something, and I said, wide-eyed, "Hey, this is the perfect moment if ever there was one!"

"Shall I call the minister?" he teased.

"Stay right where you are," I cried, and bounded into my office, unlocking the little drawer in my desk and taking out his gift. When I returned to the study, I was breathless.

"Here," I said, depositing it in his lap. "It's your groom's gift."

"My what?" he asked.

"I was waiting for the perfect moment," I explained.

"Had I but known," Jeremy said, "I'd have waited till you gave it to me, before offering you an 'out' from our marriage."

"Shut up and unwrap it," I commanded.

He pulled off the dark blue wrapping, and opened the nice box the jeweler had given me.

"See?" I said, bouncing on the sofa like a kid, "I took those images from the tapestry, but it's really my own design. That's us, riding away on the horse. And the gold matches this . . ." I put my hand near his, so we could see my engagement ring alongside his gift.

"I love it," he said softly.

We were very quiet again. He pulled me into his arms, which was such a warm and wonderful place to be, and I wasn't afraid of us "changing" anymore. In fact, I felt like a boat relinquishing its moorings, ready to leave everything behind, departing from the land for the sea, to seek out something entirely new. It didn't matter if we weren't a hundred per cent sure of where we were going, just as long as we were going there together... and he kept kissing me this way . . .

Afterwards, we drifted into a deep, wonderful sleep, the kind that, when you wake, makes you feel as if there could not possibly be any troubles on the horizon. I think we must have awakened at the same time; and when Jeremy turned his head to look in my eyes, he smiled. Now, a gal could live on *that* kind of smile for a long, long time.

But what I said was, "Mmmm. I'm hungry. Want something to eat?"

"Let's order out a take-away dinner," he said lazily. While he went to sort through some menus in the kitchen drawer, I noticed that my wedding organizer was still lying on the table where I'd left it, and I began to clear it off so we could eat. Jeremy was watching. "Want to plot the whole wedding out right here, while we're waiting for dinner to be delivered?" he asked. "Let's see that list of yours."

"Oh, God, let's not spoil a good moment," I said.

"Stuff and nonsense," he said. "Come on, be brave." And it was amazing, but suddenly everything seemed very clear and do-able. We talked and plotted, and when the food arrived, we ate and drank and talked some more, sitting on cushions on the floor with my notes spread out all around us.

"We could elope," Jeremy began.

"Don't start that again," I said. "This is no time for jokes."

"I think we should consider all options, no matter how idiotic," he said.

And, for a time, we actually did contemplate eloping—just take off on the yacht, and come back married. But, as we began to picture it, we started thinking of the few people we'd really, truly like to have with us. This turned out to be a good way to begin, rather than working backwards by paring down other people's lists. But when I laid out Leonora's and Margery's lists, it looked pretty daunting, still.

"It's way too big. I'm not Princess Grace of Monaco, for God's sake," I grumbled. "I always pictured our wedding as small, intimate and cozy."

"Fine," Jeremy said. "We'll set a limit, and tell Margery and Leonora that they can pick four guests."

I giggled. "You'd better give them a little more leeway than that. Let's see, if we cap it at seventy-five guests . . . including Leonora and Margery and your mom and mine . . . I guess we could divide seventy-five by four . . ."

"Divide by five," Jeremy said. "You're forgetting us!"

"Oh. Right. Well, that makes it easier. Divide seventy-five by five and you get fifteen. Hmm, that's an odd number, when most people come in pairs . . ."

"Well, this isn't Noah's Ark," Jeremy said. "Look, let's just tell the four of them that they can invite ten people each. The rest are ours."

"Okay," I said. "They can like it or lump it. Or, they can bargain and trade with one another."

"Good. What's next?" Jeremy asked.

"Monsieur Lombard's gals want you to pop into their shop in London, so they can make alterations in time," I said.

"Okay," Jeremy said, as if he expected it to be perfectly easy, a simple matter of showing up and wearing clothes. And I suppose it is, for men. Honestly.

I deposited some sketches from Monsieur Lombard into his lap. "What's this?" he asked.

"Your morning coat," I said, without looking up.

"My *what*?"

"Your groom's outfit," I said briskly. "I believe you'll find all the other necessary accessories, including shoes, socks, tie, and a lovely burgundy silk handkerchief that matches my bouquet of burgundy roses, in honor of my ancestors from Burgundy."

"Good Lord," Jeremy said incredulously, parting the tissue-paper overlays on the sketches for color options. "What, no underdrawers?"

"Keep looking," I said.

"Penny," Jeremy said sternly, "I will keep all this under advisement, but you'll have to let me take it from here. I'll pick out what I'm comfortable with, and you can have final approval to make sure we don't clash, but I won't dress up like some poppet."

"Okay, since I don't even know what a poppet is," I said meekly.

"Let's please move on. What next?" he asked, shuffling through my papers.

"You already said you could get your mum to help with musicians. Can you handle the music?" I asked. "I'd like classical for the ceremony, and anything you want for the reception."

"Sure," he said. "What else?"

"The venue should be next, because that could affect the total number of guests," I said. "We have to decide which country to have the wedding in. Frankly, I know this is ungrateful of me, but I don't really want to be married in that château. It doesn't feel like you and me. Neither does some brunch at an English country inn that means nothing to us. But it will be hard to get a booking anywhere now. Every place I talk to keeps insisting they can't even do this year, let alone September."

"Pick the country first," Jeremy suggested.

"I could do either England or France, I love them both. Just so long as the place where we say, 'I do' feels like a place where we both belong," I explained.

Jeremy stood up and reached in his pocket for a coin. "Okay," he said briskly. "Heads, we have the wedding in France. Tails, England." He pitched the coin into the air. It went straight up, then came down with a purposeful landing, *Ping!* Right on one of the cars of the toy *train bleu*.

"There you have it!" Jeremy declared. "It's heads for France."

And then, as I gazed down at the little toy train, I had a perfect *Eureka!* moment. I jumped up and started waltzing Jeremy around the room.

"What gives?" he demanded.

"Thanks to you," I cried, "I have just solved everything!"

Chapter Twenty-three

My brilliant idea was this: Since we had to deal with the press' interest in our wedding anyway, why not make the "public" part of the day be a benefit occasion for my charity group? Inspired by Venetia's 1930s wedding, I thought we might charter a couple of private railroad cars, decorate them like elegant vintage ones, and give our English and American guests a luxurious reward for coming to France for the wedding. Hopefully this would offset the inconvenience of travel.

"The press and the English guests can start out at St. Pancras station in London," I explained to Jeremy. "They'll switch in Paris, to board our spiffed-up wedding cars, along with our French and American guests; then everybody takes off, down the *train bleu* path to the Riviera, where they pick up Honorine's family at the Cannes station. Our guests will be wined and dined all the way, maybe with some vintage music from that time period; and we'd better throw in some Beatles for our parents.

"Anyway, the final destination will be the villa in Antibes, where we can be married in a more private ceremony, before the tapestry. The villa feels just right for the exchange of vows and the reception; it's like Great-Aunt Penelope will watch over us there. Then, we go off on the yacht for a secluded honeymoon. The guests go back home by train, and *voilà*! It's done."

I brandished my pen. Jeremy grinned. "You are sounding more French by the minute," he said approvingly. "Could it be that you're turning into one of those chic Gallic females?"

"Ooh, I like the sound of that!" I said, beaming.

Jeremy raised a few practical concerns, but overall he liked the idea. "But," he questioned, "how does that help your charity?"

"Well," I said, bursting with enthusiasm, "instead of buying us presents, the guests can simply fill out a box on the invitation's RSVP card, to either make a donation to the charity—which will get them a 'train ticket' to the wedding—or, for those guests who still prefer to buy 'things' instead of making a donation, I'll provide a registry of decorative items we'll want for furnishing the railcars: old-fashioned lamps, and dining-car dishware, cutlery, monogrammed napkins, stuff like that. In place of a bridal registry, see? After the wedding, the entire collection of these 'gifts' can be donated to my Women4Water charity, so that they can use it again for future fund-raising parties, dinners and galas; or they could even auction 'em off if they want.

"And since the press wants to cover the wedding anyway, at least all the publicity will benefit the charity. It will be one big celebration, and at the end of it, you and I will sail away on *Penelope's Dream* and leave the world behind."

Jeremy grinned, "You know," he said, "I think this idea is just crazy enough to be worth a shot."

"Let's go try it out on Honorine," I said, hearing her footsteps as she came in. "If it flies with her, we might have a chance at getting it past Leonora."

We trotted over to Honorine's reception room, and told her the whole story. She had been out shopping with her friend, but now she put down her packages and listened raptly, with a very serious and proper attitude, her face never betraying her thoughts until we reached the end.

Then she announced philosophically, "*C'est idéal.* It will be fun, and how many weddings can you say that about?"

"Hooray!" I cried. "This wedding finally has an engine!"

In the next couple of days, the plan really picked up steam. Honorine eagerly announced that, through family connections, she was able to get in touch with a bigwig at the French rail company, who enthusiastically saw an opportunity to publicize the advantages of rail travel over air travel. My charity gals were ecstatic, and offered to help coordinate the "gift" registry for me.

So I telephoned Venetia for the details of the luxury items of those old railroad cars. She was flattered to be one of my consultants, and she gave Honorine lots of instructions to pass on to Erik and Tim, who were delighted with the concept. You might say that everyone got "on board" . . . except Grandmother Margery. Her comments brought it all to a screeching halt.

"Surely you are joking," she said, not really comprehending the idea, and not particularly wanting to. "Ask *my* friends to take a train journey to France? Why on earth should they do that?"

"You have to understand," Jeremy told me after that deflating phone conversation, "she's accustomed to having her orders obeyed by one and all. It's what she lives for."

But even this couldn't dampen my enthusiasm. Figuring that finesse and psychology were called for here, I said cunningly, "Why not invite her to visit us at the villa in Antibes, to see for herself that it's a totally appropriate venue for her guests? We'll tell her we won't make a move without her input. That way she can still feel like she has the final word."

"And if she says no?" Jeremy inquired. "What's our Plan B?"

"We tie her up and gag her, chuck her in the luggage compartment, and force her to come," I said.

"Ah," Jeremy replied. "I knew you'd think of everything."

"We'll cross that viaduct when we get there," I said stoically.

He returned to the phone, called her back and relayed this new suggestion. At first I couldn't tell what she was saying on her end of the conversation, because Jeremy did some long listening. But finally he said, "Right. I'll call you back." He hung up, then announced, "She bought it."

Apparently the idea of being fussed over and allowed to conduct an "inspection" was just too appealing to Grandmother Margery to refuse. So, for once I had played my cards right. Honorine, who knew a thing or two about protocol, suggested that we prepare the villa for this inspection by sprucing up the place, including the garden, which we'd have to do for the wedding anyway.

"Let's get it done now," Honorine said pragmatically. "We could even hang the tapestry in the villa for her to see. I'll tell my mother it's like a dress rehearsal."

Leonora was actually very happy to receive this news, because when she hadn't heard back from me, she'd assumed that we'd decided to forsake France for an English wedding. She said that she and Philippe and David would be happy to be on hand at the villa, to help us greet and smooth the way for Margery, and they could supervise the proper hanging of the tapestry. Aunt Sheila's beau arranged to transport the lovely clock he'd given us to the villa, so it could be set up in the drawing room to chime like wedding bells after we took our vows.

But of all the hurdles we'd jumped, I counted this one the biggest: even Great-Aunt Dorothy complied, agreeing to let Rollo use her antique champagne glasses for the reception. "I told her that if she didn't contribute, *we* would look the fools, and the press would say our side of the family were the poor relations," Rollo explained. "Blackmail, plain and simple, my dear girl."

So all systems were go. "Okay, troops!" Erik said. "Let's hightail it to the villa, and dress this set!"

And a major production it was. Celeste, the housekeeper, likened it to an invasion of an army. But Erik and Tim soon made fast friends with her, and she pulled in some of her relatives to do garden work, more cleaning, minor carpentry, even sewing. We all swarmed around like busy bees, and soon there was a rather festive atmosphere, since, no matter how much work there was to do, we could always plunk ourselves in the pool at the end of a dusty workday.

Summer on the Riviera was in full swing now, and the famed flower markets and food stalls in Antibes and Nice were in their glory, just bursting with incredibly wonderful earthly delights for our suppers—plump juicy tomatoes, purple and white eggplant, green and yellow zucchini, and fruit so succulent and flavorful that they perfumed the entire house—white peaches, red cherries, giant red and green grapes, sweet yellow pears, and bunches of tiny delicate purple champagne grapes that were so perfect with a plate of cheese.

And flowers, flowers everywhere, in each room, filling the house with fragrance. We planted a few more blossoming shrubs, and Leonora's gardener gave us some potted citrus trees from their greenhouse, to place on the patio. Celeste threw herself into sprucing up the kitchen garden at the side of the house, and now it was fragrant with basil, oregano, thyme, marjoram, parsley, and bay. Even the bees were giddy with delight. The sun shone hot and bright, the air was alive with birdsong, and the night breezes were a sigh of satisfaction, punctuated by the occasional hoot of an owl.

There was never a moment when I didn't silently bless Great-Aunt Penelope for bestowing this lovely villa on us. Moving from room to room, I once again felt her presence, as if she couldn't resist just another good party. One day in particular, after Erik had a piano delivered, he sat down to test it out, and played a couple of 1930s tunes he knew; and when I heard the ghostly music wafting through the house, out the windows, past fluttering curtains, I was certain that we had Aunt Pen's blessings. I could almost hear her say, "Well done, ducky!"

So, I could be forgiven for feeling optimistic, and, as inspection day dawned, I was buoyed up with enough confidence to face down anybody, even Grandmother Margery. Honorine, however, was as pale and nervous as if she'd been cramming for a final exam. Tim moaned that his jitters were far, far worse than an opening night when he'd "trod the boards" in his early and ill-fated attempts to be an actor.

I even caught Aunt Sheila standing outside in the driveway, covertly smoking a cigarette; and the gardener's dog hiding in the wine cellar, where I found him peering out anxiously from under a rack of bottles. Rollo helped move chairs, and he fussed with the glasses on the buffet table, mopping his brow every now and then, as if this were the most physical labor he'd done in his entire life.

By noon, David, Oncle Philippe, Tante Leonora and Honorine finished the last details of hanging the tapestry in the drawing room. Now they stepped outside on the patio, to catch their breath. That left me alone with the tapestry in the cool shady room. Occasionally, the wind would stir the trees outside, and the changing light caused some of the silver and gold threads to glint and gleam. Today, the images in the tapestry seemed benign, calm and balanced; and the slumbering couple's dreams were just that—life's illusions, a set of passing vignettes that came and went like the wind's sighs across the flower fields. There was something sweet and consoling and yet exhilarating about it, as if the tapestry was telling me to move ahead fearlessly into this new realm.

Erik and Guy came out of the dining room now, and lingered on the threshold of the drawing room as Guy held out his pocket watch, waiting for the mantel clock to strike the half-hour. *Ting-tong-tong-Ting, Tong-ting-ting-Tong!*

"Beautiful," Erik said approvingly, smiling at me. "When was it made?"

"Oh, I can tell you the exact year," Guy replied. "See, right here in the chronogram? It says it was made in 1725."

I heard a car coming up the gravel driveway. Everyone else heard it, too, and there was a sudden rush as people assembled expectantly in the circular foyer. I went outside, pausing on the front stoop, feeling the heady sunshine of the day. The fountain sparkled invitingly.

Uncle Giles was driving a rented Bentley, but when it stopped, another man got out of the back seat and hurried around the car to open the front passenger door for Grandmother Margery. She emerged, in a pink and white chiffon frock, with a long pink silk scarf around her neck, resplendent and queenly, as her little narrow ankles and feet in their pink high-heeled sandals touched down delicately and tentatively, like a flamingo.

"Lovely place!" Giles called out to us, glancing appreciatively at the villa. He looked like one of those pale Englishmen who spends so much time in offices that they emerge into sunny climes blinking, like groundhogs. He ambled toward us now, and introduced the other man in their entourage as Hilary, Margery's personal decorator—and definitely someone she hadn't told us about.

Hilary wore pale green linen trousers, a green-and-white striped shirt, and bone-colored loafers with no socks. He had longish blond hair, parted in the center and pulled into a short ponytail, and wire-rimmed spectacles.

"Hmmm," Hilary murmured noncommittally, gazing about appraisingly.

I saw Margery glance alertly at him, and she, too, said, "Hmmm," and in that moment it was clear that, although nothing had been decided yet, Hilary would hold more sway over her opinion than anyone else. The group came inside, chattering excitedly and animatedly, but I had a moment of panic as Jeremy introduced Hilary to Erik. I feared they were bound to clash, since Erik and Tim had worked like dogs to do a spectacular job of decorating the villa. And indeed, Hilary and Erik now warily circled each other, like two extremely opinionated tigers.

Meanwhile, Tante Leonora and Oncle Philippe had been standing calmly in the foyer, waiting to greet our English guests. I watched Leonora quickly size up Margery; I guess I knew my French relative well enough by now to see that she diplomatically decided, in that instant, not to immediately go head-to-head with Jeremy's grandmother. Margery wore her queen-on-the-reception-line smile. It was as if both matriarchs were determined not to be the first one who lost her cool. This, at least, was hopeful.

Aunt Sheila and Guy had been loyally on hand all day, but at the first sight of Margery's arrival, they tactfully retreated to the kitchen to oversee Celeste, who was arranging refreshments on platters; thereby ensuring that Guy's presence would not immediately irritate Margery.

Now I went boldly up to Jeremy's grandmother, and said with my best smile, "Margery, please come with me, we'd love to show you around."

"Attagirl," I heard Erik mutter under his breath.

I let Honorine conduct the tour, and she was well-prepared, giving Margery a brief history of the place, explaining that it was built in the 1920s. We began by inviting everyone into the dining room, where Rollo's champagne glasses were all laid out, along with Aunt Sheila's good china and silverware, and my mother's antique linen tablecloth and napkins, which she'd shipped over to me, and some fantastic gold candlesticks courtesy of Erik. Since Jeremy and I had only just begun to carefully furnish the villa with a few choice pieces of furniture, Erik had borrowed whatever antiques he could from his European friends who "owed" him. They harmonized very well, providing extra seating for our wedding guests.

Honorine explained that, after the wedding ceremony, the food would be laid out in a buffet in the dining salon, and tables would be set up, both inside here, and out on the lawn in tents. Margery followed silently, revealing nothing. Hilary had opened a little note-pad on which to jot his thoughts as we moved across the room, compiling suggestions, which actually weren't bad.

"I know of a marvellous gilt-framed mirror that would work in here quite nicely," he said, glancing at Margery as if they'd discussed this previously. "Possibly a wedding gift?"

"Yes," she murmured, "we talked about that, and I can see that it will help here."

So. She had spoken, at last. Was this a good sign? Or, was her comment Insult #1? At least they were discussing practical matters, which would seem to indicate that they were seriously considering going along with it. Jeremy squeezed my hand encouragingly. But when a severe, queenly look returned to Margery's face, I began to imagine the possibility of her going through all Hilary's pleasant suggestions, only to turn round and say, in the end, "Alas, no."

Honorine was now leading them upstairs, to show them the guest rooms where they would sleep tonight. "It's smaller than I expected," Margery said to Giles, glancing around the bedrooms as we moved through them. (Insult #2.) "What if our guests want to stay in France overnight?" she asked.

But Jeremy was ready for this issue. "We've made an arrangement with a terrific boutique hotel nearby, for any guests who want to stay. The hotel's chefs and kitchen are preparing the wedding feast, which Penny's father will supervise. He is a superb, professional chef."

Margery pursed her lips and looked at Hilary, who made a few more notes. *Just go ahead, I dare you,* I found myself thinking, feeling suddenly pugnacious.

"As we have arranged for transportation from the train station, parking should not be a problem," Honorine volunteered as we all went back downstairs.

It was time to inspect the garden in the back, with its patio, pool, and potted plants; and borders of beautiful hydrangea, rhododendron and climbing jasmine, culminating at the far end of the lawn, with a view of the sparkling Mediterranean Sea. A few obliging yachts and sailboats drifted dreamily by, thereby perfecting the picture. The sun, it seemed, had specially draped the water with a golden veil, and the blue sky had only a few puffy white clouds that floated like heavenly boats.

"Ahhhh," Uncle Giles could not resist saying appreciatively.

Honorine explained that music and dancing could take place on the patio. Margery and Hilary said nothing, walking back and forth, up and down the patio, and across the lawn again . . .

I mean, honestly. Who could go into Great-Aunt Penelope's beautiful garden, right up to the hedges, as Margery was doing now, and peer over at that spectacular view of the sea and the rising cliffs on the other side of the coast, only to squint as if finding it difficult to make up her mind?

Tim whispered to me, "Oh my God, she's going to nix it, and I'll just scream the place down if she does."

"Don't scream," Erik advised. "We'll just toss her over the cliffs."

I looked back at the villa and saw, through the long dining room windows, which had been flung open now, that Guy and Aunt Sheila were quietly helping Celeste lay out the luncheon in the dining room. Guy was carrying buckets of ice for the good chablis we'd brought up from the cellar. Aunt Sheila, glancing briefly out the window before vanishing from sight, had a wary look on her face, as if she, more than anyone else, knew just how difficult her mother could be.

When I saw Margery turn to look back appraisingly at the villa, my heart sank, and I did what no hostess should ever do once the party has started: I suddenly saw my nice sweet home through the eyes of an unimpressed stranger. I began to wonder, very humbly, how this must compare to the sorts of weddings that Margery and her friends attended—at the great rooms in stately homes, in dining halls of Scottish castles, and the gardens of palatial estates. Perhaps I should have accepted Leonora's offer of the château, which would have been beyond the reproach of someone like Hilary.

Honorine, still taking her role as tour guide very seriously, announced, "The wedding ceremony itself will take place in the drawing room. Please follow me now."

We had reached the final leg of the tour: the presentation of the *pièce de résistance*, the tapestry. The drawing room shone, with its polished floor and sparkling windows. Honorine had gotten Venetia to go through her scrapbook for more photos and clippings of herself as a ballerina, and we'd put them into vintage frames in the drawing room, next to framed pictures of Great-Aunt Penelope and her cabaret partner performing in this very room. Hilary studied these closely.

David stepped forward now, explaining about the origin of the tapestry, and how it had been found by Venetia. Margery glided right up to it, and she adjusted her spectacles to take a closer look. What was she doing, counting up how many gold and silver threads it had?

I stole a glance at my French relatives, who looked so eager, so expectant, so proud. I made a fervent wish that, if Margery was going to submarine the whole project, she wouldn't come right out and say it wasn't good enough for her guests, and publicly hurt the pride of these lovely people. She could at least wait to tell me later, and spare the others. That would only be polite. Margery's lips parted, as if she were on the verge of speaking. But then, someone else spoke first.

"Splendid!" Hilary pronounced, unable to contain himself another minute. "This is a most excellent, unique tapestry!" He turned to Leonora, looking newly respectful. "*C'est magnifique!*" he proclaimed, not giving a hoot what Margery thought. "And I *love* the ballerina and the Auntie photographs. I suggest we put them in the dining room, they lend a fantastic aura to the whole place, so dramatic and stylish. This will be a delightful wedding, what with the great party on the train, and then this incredible tapestry. People who've attended it will speak about it for years to come, and won't everyone be jealous who *wasn't* there!"

Erik gasped with delight. I couldn't even look at Jeremy, for fear I'd burst into uncontrollable giggles. Under the circumstances, Margery played the only card she could.

"Excellent!" she agreed. "I applaud your good taste, Leonora."

Not me and my good taste, of course. Oh, well.

Margery politely insisted on a few face-saving additions that she would provide—some china serving dishes, for instance, and the mirror Hilary had mentioned. Then, right before my eyes, the two formidable *grandes dames* joined forces, as Leonora, ever one to take advantage of an opportunity, clasped Margery's hand briefly, with an utterly charming smile, and spoke to her in lilting, encouraging tones. Margery's face was wreathed in enchanting smiles, too, as if she'd been challenged to rise to full wattage, and was now determinedly on board to make the event a great success to all her friends. I could see that both ladies were extremely skilled at being dazzling hostesses . . . when they wanted to be.

Hilary and Erik and Tim now behaved like relieved students who've just been released to summer vacation. They went off into the corner chattering, excited by each other's suggestions, and they began swapping anecdotes and opinions about various period furniture.

"May I suggest we arrange the chairs in a semicircle, so everyone can view the exchange of vows and that enchanting tapestry?" Hilary asked. "We can still have one big central aisle through it, for the wedding procession. Also, I see we'll need more chairs, so I'm thinking Louis XIV, I mean, everyone *thinks* Versailles when you say Sun King, but the fact is that his chairs are plainer and saner and downright *austere* compared to those curlicues and whirligigs that came after him!"

"I totally agree," Erik replied diplomatically, giving me a big wink the minute that Hilary's back was turned. Hilary sighed rapturously. And I watched, totally amazed, as Honorine joyfully guided everyone into the dining room for lunch.

I was getting that tremulous feeling again, especially when Jeremy popped open a bottle of chablis and everyone clinked glasses. It really felt like the wedding was definitely going to happen, right here. And I must say that, once Margery realized the inevitability of this, she plunged right in. Giles was given the assignment of telling me so.

"Penny, my mum has an idea," he said. "She wants to receive and sort out whatever gifts your guests send to decorate the train cars, and she and Amelia could work directly with your charity person. I hope you agree. Amelia is a very good organizer," he added nervously, citing Margery's credentials as an expert on railroads, because her husband had been "a railroad man".

I grinned. "That's an excellent idea!" I said, for it would surely keep Margery extremely and usefully busy. "It will be such a relief to know that Margery and Amelia are taking charge there. Please tell Amelia I'm ever so grateful to have her handling this!" I said. And the funny thing was, I meant it.

I went into the kitchen and found Aunt Sheila, who told me that Guy had tactfully vanished, going off to Nice, where the two of them were visiting for a few days. Aunt Sheila said, "Darling, Jeremy tells me that Mum and Hilary and Giles are staying here at the villa overnight. Here's my hotel number, so call us if you need anything whatsoever. Otherwise we'll just stop by in the morning to touch base."

"Fine," I said, and I hugged her for volunteering to be "on call" to stomp out any fires if Margery should suddenly feel feisty and ready to cause trouble again.

So, that night, after our houseguests settled down to sleep, and it was so quiet that it seemed as if even the owls and cicadas outside had gone to bed contentedly, I allowed myself to breathe a sigh of relief. My wedding was really going to happen, after all. Right here in Great-Aunt Penelope's villa. Everything finally felt right, at last.

Part Six

Chapter Twenty-four

The next morning, I rose early, showered and crept quietly downstairs, feeling like a little kid on Christmas day. The house was very quiet. Celeste had come early, and was in the dining room, preparing a breakfast buffet for our guests. She'd already made a fruit salad of melon, berries, and grapes. I nibbled on some, then took a cup of coffee from her, and I wandered out to the garden patio, settling onto a lounge chair with my organizer, to dreamily indulge in pleasurable musings about my wedding day.

Aunt Sheila had offered to coordinate the RSVPs with my mother, and she would interface with Honorine, who was now the efficient command center, managing all the other details of the wedding. Everything was beginning to come together with a speed and energy of its own, in that pleasurable way when people instinctively start to pull together and inspire one another.

I hummed to myself, going over my notes of the sample CDs that Aunt Sheila, through her old contacts at the record companies and the BBC, had scoured up from various available musicians. Jeremy and I had played them on the way down here, and found that they were all very good, but we'd especially liked a quiet classical trio, whose delicate balance of violin, cello and flute was both light and yet profoundly moving, with just the right appeal to mind and heart. Now, imagining where the trio would sit, I could almost hear their music for the ceremony, resonating in the beautiful drawing room.

As I went back inside, I contemplated the wedding procession. Some latent feminist instinct had prompted me to decide against being handed off from one man (my father) to another (my husband), so we'd agreed that, while our parents would all participate in the procession, I would walk down the aisle after them, alone.

Following the ceremony, there would be champagne cocktails and the wedding feast at tables in the garden if the weather was fine (and why shouldn't it be?), and then Erik and Tim had agreed to take charge of Jeremy's "playlist" of recorded music for people to dance to. Finally, Jeremy and I would depart for our honeymoon on *Penelope's Dream*. Suddenly, for the very first time, I could picture the entire wedding, from start to finish. It was a thrilling moment.

I went into the drawing room quietly, with a light tread so as not to wake any late sleepers, and I traced the path of the bridal procession, walking straight up to where Jeremy and I would take our vows before the tapestry. But the wall between the big windows was empty. Someone had taken down the tapestry overnight.

I frowned. David had carefully surveyed this location, and advised Leonora that it would be perfectly okay to leave the tapestry hanging here, with the drapes drawn to darken the room, until the wedding day, rather than carry the tapestry back to the château where it would have to be re-hung, only to return it here again in just a few weeks. Leonora, still looking slightly dubious, agreed to leave it behind, but she'd stipulated that she wanted to come back here this morning to check on it once more, just to make sure that not a single shaft of summer sun would fall across it and fade it.

I guessed that she must have shown up early today, been somehow displeased, and decided against letting even a speck of salty air land on it. I could picture her, fussily insisting on taking the tapestry home after all. Perhaps Leonora instinctively hadn't trusted Erik, Tim and Celeste not to touch it. This could be the first little ripple of trouble, but I resolved not to get sucked back into the flurry of clashing egos over wedding minutiae.

"Delegate, delegate," I muttered to myself, repeating Erik's advice like a mantra, determined to let Honorine handle the details.

My thoughts were interrupted by a chorus of French voices at the front door, as Celeste greeted Honorine's family and ushered them into the dining room for breakfast. I heard Honorine asking for me, and then, a few moments later, she came into the drawing room, smiling broadly.

"David and my mother are here; thank you so much for the lovely breakfast." She paused. "Did you take down the tapestry already? *Maman* will not be pleased, you know. There is a special way to roll it and store it . . ." Her face puckered in worry at the thought of a needless kerfuffle with her mother.

"But I didn't," I said. "I assumed that David came here early and took it back. You've just arrived now?" She nodded. "Maybe Erik or Celeste took it down, so we could clean up without disturbing it?" I suggested. But I knew perfectly well that they'd never do that without consulting me.

"No, no, I told them that you and I were going to look at it today, to compare and coordinate the swatches for the table setting with the colors on the tapestry," Honorine said, confused.

Jeremy entered the room now. "Margery, Giles and Hilary are still upstairs, they're just waking up now," he told us. Then he saw the looks on our faces. "What's the matter?" he asked.

"Jeremy, did anybody tell you they were going to take down the tapestry last night?" I asked idiotically but hopefully. It took him a second to register what I was really asking. His gaze travelled to the empty wall between the windows.

"Of course not," he said.

I went to the table and picked up my mobile phone, which was lying there recharging. I think I woke Erik. He and Tim had gone to visit some friends in Saint-Tropez. I asked if he could shed any light on this, but he said, "No, darling, it was still hanging there when I left, and nobody said anything to me about taking it down for safekeeping."

Another car had pulled into the drive. It was Aunt Sheila and Guy, as promised, here to see if we needed anything. Guy, apparently not a man to ever hold back his thoughts, said as he entered the drawing room, "Gracious, you all look stunned. Say, where's the tapestry gone to?"

I had been feeling slightly anaesthetized by my fear, but now, hearing the word "gone" aloud simply forced my mind to abandon the woolly feeling that was cushioning me from the truth. My heart began to beat rapidly with mounting panic. Still, I found myself pulling open closet doors and peering inside, in the desperate hope that someone had seen fit to put the tapestry away somewhere.

I could hear David and Leonora greeting Uncle Giles in the dining room. A few moments later, I heard French voices coming our way. David entered the room first, followed by a brisk and efficient Tante Leonora. Mercifully, Oncle Philippe had remained behind at the château.

The pleasant smiles on their faces pierced my heart, especially when they faded slightly at the sight of the empty wall. "Oh!" said Leonora. "I thought we made it clear that you should call on us to take down the tapestry properly, if that is what you have decided to do . . ."

For a moment, nobody had the heart to speak.

"Where is it?" David asked in a resigned tone, knowing that his mother would make him inspect it carefully before they carried it home. Another silence.

"It's gone!" Honorine cried, unable to hold back. Leonora's slightly reproving look changed to puzzlement, then deep concern, as if we were speaking a language whose nuances escaped her.

"You don't mean to say . . . someone *took* it?" David said, with a quick intake of breath.

"Aaaaaugh!" Leonora let out a scream that echoed in the room, igniting my frayed nerves.

Jeremy and David had a brief pow-wow, and then the house was searched from top to bottom. I couldn't even hear what they said, because I felt as if my blood was draining out of my head and I was actually on the verge of konking out. I sat down quickly to steady myself, while, all around me, rapid footsteps and excited voices went to and fro.

Then, the house became ghastly quiet. At last, Jeremy came back into the drawing room, from which I had not budged. He spoke to me gently, as if dealing with a mental patient who might go off the deep end at the slightest nudge.

"Penny," he said quietly, "I think we'd better call the police."

Chapter Twenty-five

A nightmare. That's what it was. A nightmare. First, we called Thierry, who, technically, was a marine gendarme with the harbor police in Nice, so his jurisdiction was boats and sea troubles. But we knew and trusted him, because of what happened last year with the yacht. He, in turn, called a cop friend of his at the proper police department, and the cop came over quickly, accompanied by an Inspector who would be in charge of the investigation.

They arrived dramatically in a car with flashing lights, but parked on the road below us, so that they could come up the driveway slowly, on foot, searching for clues along the way. It was hard to learn anything from the tire tracks, though, since we'd had so many visitors with cars criss-crossing over one another's path in the gravel driveway.

The Inspector was a short, elegant yet tough-looking man, with a bald head and very pale blue eyes set off by his suntanned face. He had a penetrating, no-nonsense stare that was a bit unnerving, as if experience had taught him to trust absolutely nobody. He was a proud dresser, right down to his gold watch and a gold chain around his neck. He gave short, sharp orders in rapid French that

I couldn't make out; but the young cop, who had big ears like a sugar bowl, sprang into action, checking windows and doors for signs of forced entry, looking for footprints inside and outside of the house.

Then they methodically began combing the first floor rooms for any other telltale traces of the thief. Whenever we asked a question, the Inspector was brief and brusque, and once he even held up his hand as if we were interrupting his thoughts and therefore jeopardizing the investigation.

"Later, we will talk," he said.

I wasn't in any particular mood to chat. My normal Girl Detective instincts had completely deserted me. Instead, whenever I passed by the drawing room, I kept staring at the wall where the tapestry had hung only a few hours ago, and I seemed to be trying, by sheer force of will, to make it materialize again.

I even found myself once more peering into closets and cupboards, harboring the wild, ridiculous hope that some well-meaning member of the group had put it there and forgotten about it. I had turned into an automaton, and I didn't care if anything I did made sense or not. So it fell on Jeremy and Honorine to manage the police and our guests. At one point, though, Jeremy must have seen me walking about with my vacant gaze, and he took me aside.

"The police think they've figured out where someone may have entered the villa last night," he reported. "One of the French doors in the dining room. The lock isn't broken, exactly, but it looks as though it was tricked open. Possibly the thieves had cased it out earlier, and set it up for re-entry later at night. They could have put something in the door—a stick or even a piece of cardboard—to prevent it from locking properly, yet making the door appear locked. They might have been watching the house ahead of the theft for such an opportunity, say, if one of the doors was left open when Celeste was airing out the room. It's a fairly sophisticated way to break in, probably done by a professional."

"Oh," was all I could manage.

"The Inspector has radioed his headquarters, to get the cops out looking for suspicious people, or odd work vans in the area," Jeremy said consolingly.

At this point, the cop and the Inspector, who'd been murmuring in French to each other, turned their attention to us. "I must have the names of everyone who was a guest in this house last night," the Inspector said curtly.

Without thinking, Honorine said, "Most of them are here, right now."

The Inspector raised an eyebrow. "*Ah, oui*? Then I must ask them to all remain here until I have a chance to find out what, if anything, they know that will help."

At this moment, Margery, indignant at being left alone to have her breakfast, and horrified by the presence of police, swept into the drawing room to investigate, demanding, "What on earth is going on here?" Uncle Giles trailed behind her, still munching a brioche.

"Who are you, madame?" the Inspector inquired.

"Who are *you*?" Margery demanded.

"I will ask the questions," the Inspector said sharply. "Starting with you, madame."

It took hours. The Inspector was very thorough; he sat right there in the drawing room, and one by one we all had to take turns being questioned alone, as he asked for a full accounting of how long we had been here, and what we had observed. After your turn was up, you had to leave the room but remain on the premises, in case he wanted to call someone back in.

The Inspector tactfully continued to behave as if we were all witnesses, not suspects; but his stern demeanor gave us the jitters. He asked Celeste and the gardener to provide a list of all the relatives they'd hired to help out, even though none of the extra help had been on the premises the day the tapestry arrived for viewing. Celeste swore that she had not even told any of them about the tapestry.

After Margery had her turn, she went out into the garden to smoke a cigarette, conversing in a low, complaining murmur to Uncle Giles. They were soon joined by Hilary, who was the last to come downstairs, still looking sleepy. The three of them commiserated about whether or not they'd be able to catch their plane back to London, which Penny-dear was now screwing up. I overheard this tidbit when I came out on the patio. Giles quickly put on a more tolerant face, and nodded with forced patience; but as soon as I turned away, they continued murmuring. I tried not to think about what they were saying.

David was extremely calm and coolheaded, in a role he was accustomed to, that of representing his family. I would like to say that my dear French aunt handled it well. But, she didn't. I couldn't blame Leonora for being upset, but her voice, so high-pitched to begin with, was now shrill and nervous, affecting me like fingernails running down a chalkboard. David steered her into the dining room.

"This is what comes of unconventional weddings!" Tante Leonora said, looking at me somewhat accusingly. "There are reasons to do things the correct way. Your father was the same—no regard for tradition unless it suited him!"

"Don't say such things to Penny!" Honorine argued, leaping to my defense. "This whole affair was your idea, she didn't ask you to help with her wedding."

"Enough!" David said sternly. "Not another word out of either of you."

I knew that they'd telephoned Philippe, but no one had conveyed any messages from him, and I found it all the more horrifying to imagine what he must be thinking and feeling now. I spent most of the morning fighting back tears, compounded by my own little bride-nerves, so newly acquired, and so easily plucked, like strings on a harp.

"Penny, sit down and rest. They'll find it," Jeremy consoled me.

"No, they won't," I said in a low voice. "It's probably out of the country by now."

"Let the police do their job," he said.

But finally, when the Inspector rose and thanked us all for our help, he did not exactly hold out much hope. He merely said he'd be in touch. David would have to go to the police headquarters to fill out some paperwork. As they drove away with a certain aura of finality, my heart sank.

Uncle Giles came over to me now, saying gently, "Penny, it looks as if we're not going to make our flight back to London, so I must get Mum settled into that lovely hotel you told us about."

"I am so sorry," I said.

"Not at all. Please don't hesitate to call on us if we can be of any help."

I nodded mutely, not trusting myself to speak. Uncle Giles glanced sympathetically at Jeremy, who said, "Thanks, Giles. I'll let you know if we hear any news."

As my guests filed out, Honorine, looking distressed, said, "Penny, I need to take my mother home. Papa has sent another car for us, because David had to go in his car to the police station."

"Of course," I said. I couldn't find the words in English to express my apologies, but I found them in French, saying, "*Je suis désolée*." Yes, desolate. That's exactly how I felt. The ultimate expression of regret.

Tante Leonora was passing by me then, and she heard my last remark. "Don't be sad!" she said pragmatically, but still with that new edge to her voice. "Just find it!"

She went outside and climbed into the back seat of the town car that Oncle Philippe had used to take me to the perfume factory, with the same driver at the wheel. Honorine hopped in beside her mother, and they drove away, the tires kicking up gravel and dust behind them.

"Whew!" Jeremy said. He looked at me. "My poor Penny. Leonora didn't mean to be sharp with you. You have to cut them some slack."

"Oh, Jeremy," I said in a choked voice, "what are we going to do?"

"We're going to let the police handle it," Jeremy said firmly. "Come inside. You look exhausted."

"What a horrible day," I said dully. I let him lead me upstairs, where he tucked me into bed and brought me a cup of herb tea, as if I were an invalid. I certainly felt sick at heart. I wanted desperately to sleep, to blot out the whole thing, and then awaken the next morning to find that it had been only a bad dream. The emptiness I felt was about much more than simply the material loss of the tapestry, beyond the value of its gold and silver and silken threads. I'd only just begun to hear the tapestry's message, yet it had somehow guided me out of the labyrinth of wedding plans to a measure of success.

So now, to have it wrenched away at this critical juncture was not only painful, but seemed like a bad omen that I didn't even want to contemplate. I sighed and closed my eyes, trying to conjure its return, as if I were calling on more benevolent spirits to make restitution for the evil forces that had spirited it away.

In the next few days, things didn't get any better. Honorine stayed with her parents in Mougins for a while, mostly to calm down her mother. Their servants had been questioned, and this disrupted their normally trusting, serene household. But Honorine was still conscientious about her job as our assistant, so she telephoned periodically to convey updates on the wedding plans. Meanwhile, David had informed us that the police were definitely on the case, checking out the usual suspects and places where such skanky business might be conducted, including ports and docks and other more nefarious spots. We had managed, for now, to keep it out of the newspapers, for fear of sensationalizing the theft of the tapestry and exaggerating its monetary value. But it would be listed with Interpol, to alert honest collectors so that they would know it was a "hot" item.

"What about dishonest collectors?" I said glumly to Jeremy.

Then, just as I was getting accustomed to this horrible state of affairs, I had to tell my parents about it, and I re-lived it all over again. My folks had been planning on coming to France shortly before the wedding, but now they offered to come sooner if I needed them. Morosely, I told them that there really wasn't anything they could do, so they might as well stick with their original plans.

For a brief spell we all waited for good news, believing that the first few days were the most likely ones when the tapestry might be recovered. I harbored the intense hope that the thieves would come to their senses, realize it would be too hard to sell, and leave it on a museum doorstep like an orphan. But no such luck.

I sat there in the drawing room, which was utterly silent except for the ticking of Guy's clock and its chimes announcing the quarters of each passing hour that the tapestry was still gone. One day, as I listened to the wistful chimes, I came out of my stupor long enough to have a sudden realization.

I turned to Jeremy and said, "I don't believe it was a regular burglary at all. Look at all the beautiful stuff that was in this room that night! The clock, for one thing. And the silverware, which would be much easier to carry out. Nope, this was a planned job to specifically take that tapestry."

"Yes, I know," Jeremy said gently. "The police think so, too."

I studied him miserably. "You didn't tell me that," I said. "What else did they say?"

"Not much," Jeremy admitted. "Thierry is keeping tabs on it for us."

We heard a put-put-putting sound outside. I glanced up listlessly. Honorine had borrowed Charles' Vespa. Soon we heard her light, quick footsteps as she hurried up to the front door. Jeremy let her in. "Any news from the police?" he asked. She shook her head.

"But, I have a message to you from my father," she said, sitting down breathlessly in the chair opposite me. Her large dark eyes were filled with warm sympathy as she gazed at us. I braced myself, expecting to hear that Philippe wanted to officially drum me out of the family.

"Penny," Honorine said, "Papa told me that he has little faith that the police will recover the tapestry." She paused, and the silence made this awful prospect sink into me in a way that I found physically painful, as if a member of the family had been kidnapped, but no ransom could bring it back.

"And so," she added, still rather breathlessly, "he wonders if he might impose on you, to request that you and Jeremy look into this matter personally. He says he has far more confidence in you two than the police. And he hopes that you will handle it very delicately," she added imploringly.

Before I could speak, Jeremy said rather quickly, "Of course we will do everything we can to help out. But let Penny and me talk this over alone so that we can figure out what would be the wisest course of action in a case like this."

Honorine took this to mean an affirmation of her father's request, so she smiled happily. Jeremy added gently, "It may be better if we call on someone outside of the family, but I'll let you know. Say nothing just yet, all right? Shall I give Oncle Philippe a call later today?"

Honorine nodded vigorously, then asked if there was anything she could do for us. I told her that if she wanted to continue to stay with her folks a little longer, it was fine with us.

After she'd left, I turned to Jeremy and said, "What's all this about calling on someone 'outside of the family'?"

"I don't want to see you turned into a scapegoat for this whole affair," Jeremy said firmly. "Suppose—and we have to consider this—suppose the tapestry is never recovered?"

"Oh, Jeremy! Are you kidding?" I cried. "Don't even say that."

"If someone actually hired professionals to take it, then the thieves don't need to seek a buyer," he pointed out. "We must face this, and I don't want your relatives blaming you from now to eternity."

"They'll do exactly that if we don't lift a finger to help!" I cried. "If ever there was a case for the firm of Nichols & Laidley, this is it. And now it's an official assignment."

"Yes, but I am thinking that we should sub-contract it," Jeremy explained. "Hire a private investigator who will make regular reports to us and to Philippe. We can help, but we don't need to be in charge. Thierry made exactly the same suggestion. He recommends a man who works the Côte d'Azur. A former police detective from this area, so he knows his way around, and has connections. Let him do the legwork."

"And the dirty work, you mean," I said darkly. "Like, telling them it's gone forever."

"You must listen to me on this, Penny. I want to protect your relationship with your French family," Jeremy explained.

"Fine. Get somebody to help us," I agreed. "Only make sure you let him know that failure is not an option. We *have* to find that tapestry. And, we've got a deadline. Our wedding day!"

Chapter Twenty-six

Well. You can't make an omelette without breaking a few eggs. And boy, was I walking on eggshells now. If you ever want to alienate every single person on your wedding list, just invite them to be suspects in a police investigation. Trust me, that'll do it. Overnight I'd managed to become *persona non grata* with both the English and the French side of the family. They now took the attitude that, had I not been such a stubborn little bride, so hell-bent on doing her wedding in her own independent and eccentric way, somehow this never would have happened.

I suppose it began innocently enough, with a fellow named Monsieur Felix. I don't know what I expected a French private investigator to look like, but this guy totally surprised me.

For starters, he was very tall and hulking, looking more like a boxer or a football player, with broad shoulders, and a straight nose on a face that reminded me of a granite monument to some medieval king. He walked with the slight, hunched stoop of a man who is always taller than everyone else, and therefore must accommodate them by bending a bit to their smaller status. Also, he had long, floppy brown hair, bushy eyebrows, and big hands and feet.

And, like an athlete, he wore a suit that seemed to have been specially made for his hulking frame because nothing else would fit him. But, being French, he had a way of wearing his jacket open, and his shirt without a tie, in an impeccable-but-casual, naturally debonair way.

Monsieur Felix came over to the villa and listened intently to everything we told him, while his dark eyes registered the quick intelligence of a man who comprehended the heart of a matter instantly. His gaze was very focused, yet there was an undercurrent of restlessness, like a horse who was snorting to get going. He conducted a thorough inspection of the villa, having already gone over the police report before he arrived. But he made his own list of everyone who'd been at the villa that weekend, and anyone who could have possibly known that the tapestry was going to be there that night.

"*Bon*," Monsieur Felix said shortly when we were done telling him everything we could think of that might help. "I will do what I can, and let you know what I find out."

"Wow," I said to Jeremy after he'd gone. "He seems pretty good."

"Thierry says he's the best around," Jeremy assured me. I actually began to feel my spirits rise. Maybe there was some hope, after all.

A few days later, our phone began to ring. And ring and ring. However, it was not Monsieur Felix who called, not once. It was everybody else. And if a telephone could ring angrily, this one did.

"Penny!" Erik said furiously. "I just found out from *my* sources that *your* sources have been investigating me and Tim. And just let me set you straight, little girl. Neither one of us would even *think* of taking your tapestry, and it is absolutely *nobody's* business about our little personal histories, so you tell your investigator to put *that* in his pipe and smoke it!" he said hotly.

"Erik!" I shouted. "We didn't ask him to do that. Calm down and tell me what happened."

"Just because Tim once got arrested for trying to—carry—an artifact out of Greece, which he tells me he *absolutely* paid for . . . to a man with a van who didn't give receipts . . . Timmy was young then, and didn't know how to do things yet . . . I *totally* believe him," Erik said stoutly. But even I could hear just the tiniest bit of surprise in his voice at this discovery.

I heard Tim murmuring in the background, and Erik added, "Yes, and you may as well hear it from me that once I had a terrible lover who took me to small claims court over the division of property. All because of an eighteenth century commode with gilt marquetry. I hope he gets buried in it." I couldn't resist a grin.

"Poor Erik," I said soothingly. "If it's any consolation, it really isn't personal. I guess it's what these guys do as a matter of routine. He has to check out everybody who was at the house that night."

"Oh, really?" Erik said. "Everyone? Then what, pray tell, did he find about you and Jeremy?"

I paused. "Gee," I said. "I don't know."

Tim must have gone out of the room then, because Erik said in a low voice, "Take it from me, when it comes to ferreting out your beloved's little secrets, you *don't* want to know. At least . . . not until after the wedding."

"Thanks," I said. "I'll take that under advisement."

I returned to Jeremy and reported this. "Monsieur Felix is snooping around all our friends and relatives," I announced. "Erik says we're on the verge of discovering each other's deepest, darkest sins."

Jeremy grinned. "I have no big secrets, I assure you," he said, then waggled his eyebrows at me.

"Nor I," I replied. "Except that I've gone around taking tons of pictures of the tapestry. Someone's bound to think it's mighty suspicious behavior."

"It is, come to that," Jeremy agreed. I told him about Erik and Tim's little past transgressions.

"So it would appear that whenever you put anybody under a microscope, even the innocent look flawed," Jeremy said.

"Like gems," I said. "Everybody's 'Very Slightly Included'," I joked, thinking of the diamond and gemstone clarity ratings for flaws.

But then I reflected on this more soberly, thinking of one nagging question Monsieur Felix had asked. *Was there any public announcement that the tapestry would be in this house? Who, beyond your guests and servants, knew that you were bringing it here?*

And the answer, of course, was, nobody. Not another soul knew that we were transporting the tapestry here. Just Celeste, the gardener . . . and my relatives and friends.

That afternoon, the phone rang again.

"Penny!" Honorine cried in great distress. "That man who works for you, do you know what he's been up to? He's going around poking his big nose in everybody's business! He's checked into bank records, taxes, everything. He's even been to visit poor Tante Venetia. She says he nearly scared her half to death, showing up on her doorstep and asking all sorts of questions!"

"Oh, dear. Could you just explain to her that he's simply trying to collect as much information as possible about the tapestry, in order to figure out every angle?" I explained apologetically.

"He has too many angles!" Honorine exclaimed. "It is too personal. Please tell him to stop, it is quite indiscreet."

"Yes, of course," I said hastily, ringing off.

I told this to Jeremy, and he muttered, "All right, we'd better give Felix a call. But I'm not the least bit surprised that he felt he had to check out the owner's family."

I stared at him in disbelief. "You mean you knew he'd do this?" I demanded.

"No, of course not," Jeremy said. "He probably just wants to make sure they're not scamming."

"What's that supposed to mean?" I demanded.

"In case they 'arranged' the theft, and are now trying to collect on the insurance," he explained.

I paused. "What?" said Jeremy, observing my expression.

"Nothing," I muttered.

"Spill it," Jeremy advised.

"I don't want to tell Monsieur Felix," I said, flushed with guilt. "Because I could be wrong. I wish I didn't even know."

Jeremy had to prod me again before I finally told him that I believed I'd overheard Leonora, only a few weeks ago, upping the insurance premium on the tapestry. "But I'm sure it's just a coincidence," I said stoutly. "She got all excited, thinking that I might find out it was worth more, that's all. And it's a good thing she did increase the premium, too, because while nothing can compensate them for the sentimental value of the tapestry, at least they're not out of luck completely."

Jeremy said, "Yes, well, let's hope they didn't just decide they wanted money *and* a tapestry."

I was still shocked by that suggestion. "Leonora would never do that!" I exclaimed, but as soon as I said it I thought guiltily, *Would she?* I rapidly went over all her words and gestures of late, and I saw how easy it was to construe them this way, once cast in the ugly green glare of suspicion.

"When people get desperate enough, they do unwise things," Jeremy said gently. "You did say that Leonora has been wanting to sell that tapestry for years, but Philippe wouldn't permit it."

For the first time, I felt truly irritated with Oncle Philippe. Why was he so willing to allow his beloved daughter to be married off into a loveless union with that boy Charles, just to protect his business interests, before he'd even think of selling that precious tapestry? And now, he may have caused his wife to take an extremely foolish risk.

"I may as well tell you," Jeremy said, "I did notice that Honorine has been acting a little funny, so I asked her if she told any of her friends about the tapestry."

"You didn't!" I exclaimed.

"Hang on! For weeks she's been skulking about with her mobile phone clapped to her ear, and every time I walk into the room, she quickly signs off. Very guiltily, it would seem," Jeremy explained. "I wouldn't have made an issue of it, but when this happened, I had to ask her, right to her face."

"Good God," I said. "Girls are always skulking around talking to their friends on the telephone. What's the matter with you?"

"Well, she insists she told no one about the tapestry," Jeremy said. "I believe her. I guess."

"Oh, stop it!" I cried. "We can't go around squinting suspiciously at everybody we know."

"All right," Jeremy said. "I'll ask Monsieur Felix to give us an update on what he's got."

Monsieur Felix responded to the call by saying that he had planned to stop by anyway. He arrived in a battered black Renault. Once inside, he accepted the coffee I offered him, then consulted a long, old-fashioned notepad where he'd collected his facts.

"I know that we have ruffled some feathers with your family," he said, nodding to me, yet without looking the least bit apologetic. "But, I assure you it was necessary. A mere formality, but we could not proceed without it. I thought you would wish to hear what I know."

I saw him eyeing the croissants on the table rather hungrily, so I gestured toward them. He smiled, slightly embarrassed at being caught, then nodded appreciatively and picked up one in his big paw, wolfing it down in two or three bites, almost furtively, and following it with quick, deep gulps of coffee. I noted sympathetically that he was clearly a man who functioned "on the go". I could picture him on a stakeout with his meals confined to a brown-bag, Hoover-it-in-quick status.

"Go on," Jeremy said to him.

"I will begin with the person who appears the least suspicious," Monsieur Felix said. "This ballet woman in Paris. Venetia. She has plenty of money in the bank, and no debts. I cannot find a single thing to link her to any such theft, since she is not the owner of the tapestry, and in fact gave it away, so there does not appear to be a sentimental value that would drive her to such an act. Shall I continue?"

"Please do," said Jeremy.

Monsieur Felix went on to confirm that David and Philippe were in important negotiations for a merger of their perfume company with Charles' father's big pharmaceutical business. "Philippe wants his family to retain control of the management of the perfume company, so, naturally, he and his son David would not wish for their family's difficult financial situation to be brought to light."

"Is it very bad?" Jeremy asked quietly.

"Oh, not so different from others like him," Monsieur Felix said. "Cash-flow problems. However, their personal finances are also quite tight." He flipped a page over and said, "For instance, the son." He went on to explain that, as it turned out, the solid, upright David had made some high-risk investments that tanked, and forced him to "borrow" company money to cover the losses. He, er, just recently repaid it, depleting his personal savings. His wife Auguste did not know this . . . until now.

"Holy cow," I said, awed.

"One has to consider that he might have 'arranged' the disappearance of the tapestry, as a way to sell it against his father's wishes," Monsieur Felix explained. "As for Madame Leonora, apparently she had already raised the value of the insurance premium. This may be significant. It may not."

I was just relieved that he'd found this out on his own, and I didn't have to "rat out" my own relative. He consulted his pad again. "There remain the other dinner guests at the château on the night when you say you were first shown the tapestry, and Madame Leonora offered you the loan of it for your wedding day."

As he reeled them off, my mind flashed back to that lovely weekend at Honorine's house, when her family arranged that special dinner to introduce us to their friends and neighbors. The mayor, the general, the professor, and all their wives . . . surely not. Although, that professor has come very close to the tapestry to examine it, as if he knew its value. At this thought, I began to wriggle again worriedly. I didn't want to finger anyone. This was a terrible job when it involved people you knew.

"I cannot say that there is any evidence against any of these individuals," said Monsieur Felix. "Nor anybody's servants, whom the police have thoroughly investigated. But I felt you would want a full accounting, in case what I have uncovered reminds you of something you would wish me to know. No one looks likely. But, for every thief, there is always a first time."

"Yes, of course, go on," Jeremy said, a little impatiently now, as if he wished to be done with it.

"Well, your English guests have their problems, too," Monsieur Felix said bluntly.

There was a long pause as Jeremy eyed him indignantly. I just stared at Jeremy as if to say, *Huh, how do you like having YOUR family investigated, eh?* Jeremy caught my look, and allowed a wry smile.

"Your Uncle Giles is a man with many household expenses," Monsieur Felix said, "which are normal enough—except that a real estate portfolio he owns has sharply decreased in value, so he has quite a bit of negative equity; and, of late, he's had to borrow a substantial amount to cover this."

"Good God," Jeremy said, looking truly surprised. I was, too, even though I knew that many families went into debt trying to keep up with the Joneses. Nobody was more conscious of suburban status symbols than Giles and Amelia, but evidently it was a complicated matter.

"And then of course there is your grandmother's decorator," said Monsieur Felix. "Hilary once had a client who accused him of selling fake antiques. Took him to court but failed to prove it." Monsieur Felix wetted the tip of his finger on his tongue, in order to turn the next page.

"Now, about this man Rollo," he said. "I did not see his name on the Inspector's report. He was at the villa when you decorated it, you say. Yet, he did not stay over that night, or return to the villa the next day, when you discovered the theft. Instead, he flew home to London that very evening?"

"Correct," Jeremy said shortly. I knew what he was thinking. The night of the theft, Rollo didn't even stay in his usual Riviera hotel. Didn't even stop to gamble at the casino, or flirt with the girls at the clubs. He e-mailed me to tell me he went straight back to London, knowing that I'd be pleased that he was doing as I asked and staying out of trouble.

I now pictured him, back home with his mum, Great-Aunt Dorothy, who, of all these people, I trusted the least. Dorothy still feels that somehow Jeremy and I had gotten more than our fair share of Great-Aunt Penelope's inheritance . . . simply because Dorothy can't bear to think of anyone else having money that she and Rollo might have gotten their hands on first. She never does her own dirty work, either. If she couldn't get lawyers to do whatever she wanted, the odds were that she'd assign it to Rollo. Yes, she could have pressured him to steal the tapestry to cover his ever-recurring gambling debts.

Still, I didn't believe that Rollo did it . . . not really . . . simply out of sheer practicality. Rollo likes to travel light. A great big tapestry wasn't his style. Unless . . . he was in cahoots with some pro who'd done the deed, sold it to a greedy collector, and given him a cut of the action . . .

Jeremy must have been pondering just that, because we'd both fallen silent. Monsieur Felix said rather alertly, "Is there something you wish to tell me about this man?"

"Only that a file on Rollo could end up being hundreds of pages," Jeremy said dryly.

"It very nearly is," Monsieur Felix said, with a shadow of a smile. "Various brushes with the law, but very petty incidents. A few unsavory connections. Yet, he does not strike me as a mastermind."

"No," Jeremy agreed. "And he's rather fond of Penny. I don't see this as one of his operations."

"*En fin*, there is this person who sells the clocks," Monsieur Felix said, about Aunt Sheila's beau.

"Yes?" Jeremy looked up sharply, a bit too ready, I thought, to hear something damning about Guy Ansley.

"It seems he once had a business partner who sued him for not properly distributing the profits," Felix said bluntly. "They settled out of court. This proves nothing, really." He closed his notebook. "That is the entire extent of it—except, of course, that we must note that Guy Ansley deals in antiques, and has a demanding clientele."

I said dolefully, "Monsieur Felix, if you keep this up, nobody will want to come to my wedding."

He gave me a glance of sympathy. "*Oui, je comprends*," he said. "It had to be done. So, we continue to search for the thief. And now, the real work begins."

In the late afternoon, Aunt Sheila stopped by before she left for London. She accepted the cup of tea I offered her. Guy was waiting back at the hotel, at her request, she said. At first, this struck me as odd, until she got around to telling us why she'd really come.

"So sorry to disturb," she said, "but, well, all this investigating has gotten Margery upset."

Oh, hell, I thought wearily. I was getting a little fed up with Margery and her high-handed attitude. This wasn't, after all, her drama.

"What's up?" Jeremy asked, sounding a bit irritated, too.

"Well, darling, it's like this," Aunt Sheila drawled, her green eyes bright with surprise. "Your grandmother doesn't want an investigation of our family to go any further, because she's petrified that that little man of yours will turn up something she *really* doesn't want put out there for public consumption. At first she merely hinted at it, and I couldn't imagine what this could be, until finally she told me something that happened to her, many years ago, which, quite frankly, I was gobsmacked by."

There was a silence. What could Margery possibly have done? Robbed a bank in her youth? Stolen a pearl necklace from a sorority sister? Forged a check at Harrods?

"It seems," Aunt Sheila said, as if she still could not quite believe it herself, "that Mum was once married to another man, before she married my dad."

Not only could you have heard a pin drop. You could have heard a pin drop a thousand miles away; it got that quiet. "*What?*" Jeremy finally said, in a low voice.

Aunt Sheila flushed. "It's true. When she was only seventeen, Mum was very briefly married to someone else," Aunt Sheila repeated, still incredulous that, all these years, Margery had managed to keep it a secret from her own children and grandchildren.

"It was a shotgun wedding, you see, to a boyfriend who'd 'compromised' her reputation by keeping her out late on a date," she said delicately. "So, her family forced the man to marry her. But apparently, he thought that ought to be all that was required of him, because he sneaked out of the hotel room on their honeymoon night before they—"

"Don't say it," Jeremy interrupted sharply. "Please God, don't. I get the picture."

"Whew! What a bounder," I breathed. "What became of him?"

"He ran off to Australia; so, Mum's father got the marriage annulled." Aunt Sheila turned to Jeremy, and said, "Fortunately, the gossip died down before your grandfather returned from military duty. He courted Margery, they got married, and nobody ever mentioned her first brief marriage again."

"Well, so what? What's *that* got to do with the price of tea in

China, or, for that matter, the tapestry?" Jeremy said incredulously. "Why is she telling us this now?"

"It's nothing to do with the tapestry at all," Aunt Sheila said calmly. "But since it's her deepest, darkest secret, your grandmother is terrified that somehow it will all come out again."

I tried to picture the cool, aloof Margery, with her cigarette and her reserved attitude, and all her posh social connections, nevertheless still highly—and secretly—emotional over an event that had traumatized her so many years ago. I felt a stab of sympathy for her, finding it touching that she should think of this long-ago guilty secret as something so dark that it bordered on criminal.

"Ohhh," I said softly, temporarily forgetting about the tapestry as I comprehended something.

"What?" Jeremy said crossly.

"Well, *that's* why your grandmother is so freaky about doing things 'right'," I said. "Imagine how she must feel, after causing a big scandal that made her family ashamed of her. Maybe that's why she's been so severe with you and your mom about—" I stopped.

"Morality," Aunt Sheila said dryly. "Only insofar as the perceived lack of it might stain the family's reputation. Well, it's true that her parents made her feel like quite the fallen woman. They saw to it that the world forgot about it, but they never let *her* forget it."

"How did you get her to tell you all this?" I asked. "Truth serum?"

"In a way, yes. Seeing that she was over-reacting to your detective's investigations, I knew there must be more to it. So I sat her down and she told me, over a bottle of wine," Aunt Sheila replied, smiling because I'd guessed correctly.

"Sorry you all had to go through this," I offered.

"Not your fault, darling!" Aunt Sheila replied. Jeremy shook his head in disbelief.

"Tell Grandmother not to worry. We've called off the dogs, where family is concerned," he said.

Aunt Sheila said, "Glad to hear it. I told her I was fairly certain you'd say that, and her secret would be safe—as long as she didn't give you and Penny any more trouble about the wedding."

Startled, Jeremy asked, "You mean you bullied her into cooperating with our wedding plans?"

Aunt Sheila's eyes sparkled mischievously as she said, "I think you'll find your grandmother fairly cooperative now." She rose. "Well, I must dash," she said.

Jeremy walked her out to the car. I sat very quietly, still reeling from it all. Apparently everyone toddles through life with guilty secrets and quiet shame, fearing that if the truth comes to light, we might not be forgiven, much less understood. While I was still pondering this, Jeremy returned and said, very soberly, "Penny, I feel terrible about the tapestry being stolen. It's really my fault."

"How d'ya figure?" I asked, astonished.

"If it weren't for *my* impossible relations—my pain-in-the-ass grandmother—we never would have taken it out of the château before the ceremony. There would have been no need for the inspection tour, and, possibly, no theft."

"Nobody's to blame," I said briskly. "Margery, in her own funny way, wanted to be involved in our wedding, and I'm glad." I paused. "Felix didn't exactly say he had any prime suspects, did he?"

"No, he did not," Jeremy agreed.

The tea tray was still sitting before us, so Jeremy poured himself another cup. I leaned across the table. "Jeremy," I said. "I've been thinking. There's got to be more to this tapestry than everybody realizes. I felt so, ever since I saw it, but I thought it was just, you know, an emotional thing. Now I'm totally convinced that there's some secret about it that we've got to figure out."

I expected him to chide me about going off on a tear that could make things worse, but to my surprise he said simply, "I agree. Let's have another look at those photographs you took. I think we should lay them out on the dining room table. Let's go through them one by one. Tell me everything you see, and what you think it means. There must be some clue that's been overlooked."

Chapter Twenty-seven

But as it turned out, it was Monsieur Felix who made the first real breakthrough. He stopped by the villa, totally unannounced, arriving in a green car that was different from the one he'd driven before, and dressed in dark glasses and a hat, like a man in disguise. Furthermore, he made us go out in the garden to talk to him. Mystified, we complied, and he made his announcement.

"Mademoiselle, you are being followed!" he declared.

"Me?" I echoed.

"Yes, you," he replied.

"By whom?" I asked.

"A professional! I've been watching for just this sort of thing," he said with satisfaction, "and yesterday, at last, I spotted him, following you around the market. I was able to track the man back, I think, to the person he reports to, in Monte Carlo. A very rich and powerful man, who is, one might say, *très formidable.*"

"For God's sake, who is it?" Jeremy demanded.

Felix was watching the two of us closely, and it suddenly occurred to me that if he'd spotted a man following my trail, then Felix himself must have been shadowing me and Jeremy. Which would mean that we were suspects, too. I felt a hot guilty flush, even though I knew I'd done nothing wrong.

"Do you know a man named Parker Drake?" Monsieur Felix asked, still eyeing us carefully.

"Drake!" Jeremy exclaimed.

"Why should he follow us around?" I said rather fecklessly. "He's not even taking your phone calls anymore."

Jeremy glowered at me. I forgot how men are, about keeping their own counsel about perfectly ordinary things, like losing a client, or a pending deal. As a single girl, I'd never minded blurting out my business woes (plentiful in the past), my financial status (historically pathetic) and my health issues (occasional allergies). Women routinely discuss their problems. Men are a bit more reluctant.

"Oh? Have you had business dealings with Parker Drake?" Monsieur Felix asked sharply.

Jeremy had to admit we'd been dancing around with Drake, then were inexplicably abandoned by him. "We had a few conversations. My understanding was that we were on the verge of being invited to some big event of his in Switzerland, and then, suddenly nothing," Jeremy said, still a trifle defensive.

"Think carefully," Monsieur Felix said. "Can you remember exactly when you stopped hearing from this man?" Jeremy and I just looked at each other.

"Right around the time the tapestry was taken," Jeremy said. "But that doesn't really prove much, does it?"

Monsieur Felix shook his head.

"Are Jeremy and I both being followed?" I asked, confused.

"At first, I thought so," said Felix. "You are together quite often. But this morning, when Monsieur Jeremy went down to the harbor to speak to your yacht captain, and you, mademoiselle, took the car to go to the market, alone, I saw that it was *you* that he was after."

He looked at me deeply, with utter seriousness in his hound dog face. He said, "Think back, mademoiselle, try to remember anything you can that seemed unusual . . . out of the ordinary . . ."

I was silent. Pretty much everything that had been happening to me lately was out of the ordinary. I was getting married, for heaven's sake. I'd been to all sorts of places where I normally would not go. And because I'd been finding the whole upheaval so unsettling and disruptive of my usual daily routines, I hadn't stopped to think about each and every thing that was bothering me.

But now, as I cast my thoughts back over all of it, my mind landed on the incident at the Train Bleu restaurant, when a man had smacked into me like a berserk buffalo on the loose, sending me sprawling on the floor. And, how another stranger had picked up my purse and handed it to me.

When I told Monsieur Felix about this incident, he said abruptly, "Do you have that handbag here in the house, now? Please bring it here, and dump everything in it on the table—but do so without a word. Say nothing, not even you, monsieur," he said to Jeremy.

I went inside and fetched the bag, then returned and did exactly as he said, spilling its contents onto the table, and both men peered intently at each item. Now, ya know. A woman's purse is . . . well. It's filled with lots of things. Stuff that men don't really fathom, all mixed in with the wallet, keys, lipstick, tissue pack, pens, organizers, medicinal items . . .

So. You can imagine how long it took to examine it all. While the guys were doing so, I was still shaking out the purse, which had a lot of small handy-dandy pockets for things like mobile phone, sunglasses, nail file, et cetera. I stuck my finger in each little pocket, and dug out every hairpin and coin and scrunched-up tissue that got stuck in the seams . . .

And then, out it came. A little chip of a thing, smaller than a fingernail, that made a tiny clatter as it hit the surface of the table.

We all stared at it. Then, Monsieur Felix picked it up and examined it closely, recognized what it was, and began to nod vigorously. "Ah, yes," he said. "Le Bug."

"A tracking device?" Jeremy demanded.

"Yes. Very 'quiet', that is, lightweight and not noticeable. No microphone on this type. It's a very common model. Used in business espionage quite often." He paused. "You say this man was investigating you as a potential business associate?"

"Sure, but why did he bug Penny?" Jeremy demanded.

"A good question. But you did tell him that you are a husband-and-wife team, that is, you work together, yes?" Felix asked. "You see, a man changes his suit often, but a woman always has a favorite handbag." Jeremy swore to himself, but Felix continued, "Such powerful men as Drake can be very—what you might say, paranoid—about new people. Security is everything to them, because they are often approached by very odd people indeed."

"We didn't approach him," Jeremy objected. "I mean, sure, my old firm was courting him for years. But he made the initial contact with me, right out of the blue. I didn't go after him."

He paused, recollecting, "But in Paris, his P.R. man *did* ask me about my personal life. I didn't find anything unusual in that; it's common for clients to want to be assured that you're a family man—so they'll know you're dependable. He apparently heard about our upcoming wedding in the press, anyway. I told him that my wife was visiting relatives in France, and we might have the wedding here."

"Ah," said Monsieur Felix thoughtfully. "Mademoiselle, try, if you can, to retrace your steps after this incident at Le Train Bleu," Felix said.

"We came down here, to Antibes," I said. "We hung around the villa with Rollo. Then I went out to Leonora's house to photograph the tapestry."

"May I ask, why did you take so many pictures?" Felix asked.

"I wanted to understand what all those images meant," I said. "The stories in the tapestry. I didn't want it in my wedding ceremony if it was full of omens of something unhappy."

"I see," said Felix, with a small smile of comprehension.

"Does Drake collect tapestries?" I asked incredulously. "I never saw that in our research."

Monsieur Felix shrugged. "Anything is possible," he said.

"But if he wanted the tapestry, why didn't he steal it from Philippe's château?" Jeremy asked. "It's the first place you went, Penny, when we came down here . . . after he bugged you."

"Because," I said slowly, "I changed pocketbooks that day. I wanted to wear something a little more elegant. So I left my usual bag here in the villa, and took another one out to Mougins."

"Ah!" said Felix. "Then you accidentally succeeded in throwing him off the scent!"

Now, no gal snoop wants to be told she's done her best work unwittingly. But, there it was.

Felix continued, "I would not necessarily assume that this man has anything to do with the disappearance of the tapestry. It could be that he simply spied on you to make sure that you are people he wants to do business with. So, I suggest that you continue to carry Le Bug around, except do *not* carry it when you go to the château. I will keep watching, and see where this leads us."

He paused, glancing back at the villa, then added, "May I also suggest that we have some associates of mine go through this house for any listening devices? We should do a clean sweep, to see if anything else turns up."

The next day he sent a team of two men, whom he'd assured us were trustworthy. They were respectful and careful, but they really turned the place inside out, although they did their best to replace everything when they were done. Felix told us that the villa was "clean", but he said, "One can never be a hundred per cent certain."

After they left, Jeremy was quiet for a while. Finally he said to me, "The hell with this. If Drake is having us followed, I want to know why."

"What are you going to do?" I asked. "You won't actually accuse him, right?"

"No," Jeremy said. "But I can get a closer look at him."

"How?" I asked. "He's not taking our calls anymore."

"Do stop saying that to all and sundry," Jeremy said, sounding irritated. "What's this damned party we were supposed to go to?" he demanded. "Can we get into that somehow?"

"Fat chance," I said. "It's an impossible invitation to wangle on your own. You know how many women would kill for that?"

"Women?" Jeremy echoed. "So, it's like a hostess thing?"

"Yes," I said. "And I'm sorry to say that my social connections aren't that good." I paused. "We could ask your mom. She offered to help."

"I'll do it," Jeremy said. "I want to make sure she understands that this has to be done discreetly." He paused. "And if Mum can't help," he said slowly, "I know someone who's social connections are even better than hers. Someone who, frankly, owes us big-time."

"Oh, God," I said. "Not your grand-mum."

"The one and only Margery," Jeremy replied.

Part Seven

Chapter Twenty-eight

"Absolutely not," Grandmother Margery said emphatically, when we returned to London. "I've asked all my best contacts, and it's unanimous. There isn't a prayer of a chance of getting an invitation to that party at this eleventh hour. Every table is full, every seat is taken."

We'd made this special trip back to London to plead our case in person. Margery was having tea with Uncle Giles' wife, Amelia, who'd come into town for her once-a-week shopping before scooting back to the suburbs. Margery's attitude toward Jeremy and me was polite, serene, but slightly wary, as if we were two little sticks of dynamite that could blow up in her face if she so much as struck a match.

"Surely someone might cancel out at the last minute," Jeremy protested.

Margery and Amelia hooted at that. "No one can beg, borrow or bribe their way into one of Tina Drake's costume balls," Amelia said smugly. "People have offered me hundreds for our tickets."

"You mean you're going?" Jeremy asked, forgetting not to look astonished. Naturally, Amelia took this as an insult.

"Certainly! We got three invitations to the masquerade ball: for

Giles, me and our oldest daughter. Your Uncle Giles is a very important person," she said huffily. "You two aren't the only ones who are getting to be well-known on the international scene."

This struck me as a perfect opening. I decided to play a hunch I'd had about Amelia ever since Margery's cocktail party. "Well," I said in a low, confiding tone, "we weren't going to tell you this, but actually, we're on a case, and that's why we need to get into that party."

Jeremy shot me a *Now-what-are-you-on-about?* look.

"Is it about the stolen tapestry?" Amelia cried, looking utterly intrigued.

"You must absolutely swear to tell no one," I warned. "It goes no further than this room. I mean it. Right, Jeremy?"

Jeremy caught on, and said very soberly, "If there's a leak, we'll know it came from here."

"What is it?" Margery asked eagerly.

"We think the thief is going to be a guest at that party," Jeremy fibbed. "We're on the trail, and we need to be in disguise to flush him out."

"Oh!" Amelia breathed in admiration.

"We could sure use some help, though," I said, glancing at Jeremy, who shook his head.

"You can't ask Amelia to take this on," he said, pretending to object.

"Take *what* on?" Amelia pressed.

Acting inspired, I opened my purse, and said, "See, this would be the plan. I would take your place at the party, but the only way it would work would be if you, Amelia, took my place. You would simply go about your usual business, but . . . you'd be carrying this."

Very gingerly, with exaggerated care, I laid "Le Bug" on the table.

"What on earth is that?" Margery demanded.

"It's a tracking device," I said in a low tone. "It's how the thief is keeping tabs on me. Or so he thinks! But if Amelia takes over for me, and carries this around, she'll lead him astray and throw him off the scent. She would act as a decoy . . ."

"You want to pull a switch!" Amelia cried. "I would be *you*, and you would be me."

I beamed at her. "Exactly," I said.

Then Margery, without knowing it, put the hook in. "But won't that be very dangerous?" she asked doubtfully. No one could miss the thrilled gleam in Amelia's eyes now.

"To a degree," said Jeremy. "But we'll have the P.I. keep an eye on Amelia, and anyone who follows her. We did this with Penny, and it was very successful. I'd like to take Giles' place at the party. If you help us out, Amelia, it could mean a big breakthrough with the case."

Amelia rose briskly. "You'll need to borrow our costumes," she said. "The theme is Versailles this year. I'll show you. I just picked them up today. You might need a few alterations, especially for Jeremy. He's slimmer than Giles."

But I was surprised to discover that I had yet another hurdle to gaining entrance to the Drakes' masked ball—first, I had to talk Jeremy and Honorine into those costumes. Drake's wife had schemed up something new this year: all the female guests must wear a Marie Antoinette style of dress, replete with big wide skirt and white powdered wig with ringlets—plus, we all had to have the same white eye-mask with white feathers. The men were required to dress like the French king, with powdered wig and all; and their identical eye-masks were black. The guests would dance away the evening at the Drakes' fancy-pants chalet in Switzerland; and, at the stroke of midnight, everyone would unmask, and find out who they'd been dancing with all night.

"This is quite perverse," Honorine muttered as she tried on her dress and mask. "And this dress is absurd! A low neckline, yet the bodice flattens one's breasts, too. Really, what can they have been thinking in those days?"

"You are supposed to be Amelia's daughter," I told her. "Which means you'll have to keep your mouth shut, so nobody will hear those dulcet French vowels of yours." I was still struggling with the funny little buckled shoes of the period.

From the next room Jeremy said, "I have to wear *stockings* and these weird pants that only come down to below the knee? You didn't tell me that." As Amelia had predicted, his outfit had to be altered to fit him, but it was all done now.

"Those stockings are called 'nether-hose', and those pants are knee-breeches," I informed him. "And if it was good enough for Ben Franklin and John Adams when they visited Paris, then it's good enough for you."

"You seem to have forgotten that I am English," Jeremy called out. "Your founding fathers were the enemy. We prefer not to speak of them in polite company."

"Hey. Don't forget to wear those gloves," I told him. "Otherwise Drake will see the ring I gave you, with the crest from the tapestry."

"Right. Gloves. Mercifully, they're not perfumed," Jeremy muttered. Then I heard him laugh to himself.

"Now what?" I asked.

"Oh, I was just thinking about poor Monsieur Felix," he said. "Since he's keeping an eye on Amelia, to see if anyone follows her, that means he's going to have a pretty exhausting day, running from car pool, to yoga class, to tennis lessons, and the hair salon, and the dog's veterinarian, and the kids' soccer club . . . that ought to teach Drake a lesson about shadowing a man's wife."

"I think Amelia's going to be one of our best agents," I said. "You'll see."

"She actually told me that she thinks I look like Giles," Jeremy scoffed. "Can you believe that?"

I was silent. Jeremy is a highly intelligent man, so it didn't take him long to figure out why.

"Good Lord," he said. "Say it isn't so."

"Only around the mouth," I said. "Not around the waistline and hairline." Honorine, seeing my expression, giggled.

Afterwards, when we'd all dressed normally again, and Honorine was busy packing up our costumes for the trip to Switzerland, I asked Jeremy, "So, what's the plan for this party? Do we have to impersonate Giles and Amelia all night?"

"Not necessarily," Jeremy said. "We pretend we're them just long enough to get in the door and size up Drake's operation. We should keep up the disguise as long as we can, but eventually he may figure out who we are, and I don't really care. Sooner or later I'll have to have a little talk with him, eye to eye, and find out why he's spying on us."

Jeremy held out something for me to see. It was made of plastic, but looked like an old-fashioned black-and-gold key. It even had a bar code on it.

"Apparently it's my ticket into his card game," Jeremy said. "Let's just hope he doesn't play with a stacked deck."

Chapter Twenty-nine

Lake Geneva is shaped like a crouching squirrel, with his nose to the eastern Mittelland Alps, and his tail hanging down in the west between the Jura mountains, and the Savoy—the highest peaks of Europe. It's the largest lake in the Alps, and it belongs to two countries. Nowadays, since they are both fairly civilized nations, this is a rather manageable situation. Basically, the northern shores are Swiss, and the southern are French. However, the city of Geneva has always been in a fairly defiant position, for it technically sits in the midst of French territory, yet it is one of Switzerland's most thriving and influential cities. And, to further complicate matters, the French actually call this lake "Lac Léman".

Honorine peered excitedly out of the car window at our first glimpse of the city of Geneva, for it was the birthplace of her favorite philosopher, Jean Jacques Rousseau, the son of a clockmaker. There was a statue of him on the Ile Rousseau, an islet in the river that divided the city, reachable by a narrow causeway. Jeremy obligingly detoured there so she could see it. Honorine told us all about how the city authorities of his time, as she put it, "Freaked out when Rousseau published his cutting-edge ideas about tolerance, education and freedom." So the Geneva bigwigs unceremoniously burned his books, and ran him out of town.

Nearly sixty years after Rousseau's death, the city fathers, still ambivalent about honoring their native son, placed their statue of him amidst such thick trees that he could not be seen from the city shores. And there he sits, to this day, in semi-exile, gazing out thoughtfully at the descendants of the grim old Calvinists who threw him out. Honorine blew him a kiss when it was time to go.

As we drove away from the city, I said a trifle apprehensively, "Hey. Are we anywhere near that weird underground nuclear laboratory full of subatomic particles zipping around in tunnels like race cars until they smash into one another, and either reveal the secrets of the universe . . . or blow us all to smithereens?"

"The particle collider. It's in the other direction, away from the city and the lake," Jeremy assured me. Nevertheless, we all cocked our heads for a moment, listening for any warning rumblings that might set off a tsunami in the lake. All was quiet, and life above ground continued undisturbed.

And so it was here—in a country known for discreet banks, assemblies of diplomats, excellent clock-making, beloved chocolate, fine skiing, and somewhat kitschy decor—that Parker Drake chose to be domiciled. We had booked into one of several hotels suggested in the invitation, so that we could stay overnight after the party.

As we drove farther along Lake Geneva's northern coast, I gazed at the rippling water that reflected a bright blue sky and towering mountains, as far as the eye could see. Nestled into sloping valleys were adorable old churches and little storybook farmhouses with steep triangular tiled roofs.

We settled into a cute, country-style hotel—with rustic wood beams painted in bright primary colors of blue and yellow and red, and decorated with childlike images of Alpine cows, sheep and flowers—not far from Drake's stomping grounds. If I'd had time, I would have gone out into the hills and yodeled and gathered edelweiss. But there was no time to lose. We got into our costumes and masks, then piled back into the fairly stodgy but expensive rental car that Jeremy believed Uncle Giles would have chosen to ferry his family to a masked ball.

According to the e-mailed directions, Parker Drake's secluded chalet was between Nyon and Allaman, along the "Route du Vignoble" in the wine-growing region of Lake Geneva. The high road where we were now driving, which also overlooked rolling fields of yellow and red flowers, afforded a splendid view of the famed terraced vineyards of the area, stretching from the steep hills right down to the shores of a dreamy blue Lake Geneva. When the sun was setting across the lake, as it was now, it turned the fields and hills to the color of pure gold.

But Drake's chalet was not visible from the road. Passing through wide vistas of farmland, we almost missed the driveway. It was Honorine who spotted the entrance, somewhat recessed from the road and flanked by thickets of pine. We turned in, and faced an enormous metal gate, painted to look as if it were made of logs from bluish-silver-grey beech trees.

The gate was dramatic yet rustic-looking, and, despite this Alpine setting, it reminded me of cattle ranches in American Western movies. As we got closer, I saw that the "logs" actually spelled out in gigantic letters: *CHALET DE DRAKE*.

"Geez," I said. "Somehow it looks like 'the von Trapp family meets Bonanza'."

We paused there uncertainly, until a voice from out of nowhere demanded, "Please announce the number on your invitation." A moment later the directive was repeated in French, then German.

Startled, I dug out the card from my purse, and handed it to Jeremy, who recited the code to whoever, "P3JQ5RL7."

I still don't know where that intercom was hidden. After a momentary silence, the gate creaked open, and we motored on. Drake's driveway continued for a long, long way. The whole time, all we could see were fields, blue sky with big white puffy clouds, prodigious evergreen, and towering Alps.

But just as I was getting lulled hypnotically by the sameness of this terrain, we were unexpectedly confronted with a barricade of dense shrubs, completely blocking the road. For one terrifying moment, it looked as if we were about to crash headlong into this wall of evergreen. But before Jeremy could jam on the brakes, the entire row of shrubs automatically swung open—as one, joined unit—for it was actually a secret gate.

"Good God," Jeremy muttered. "Who does he think he is, James Bond?"

"Perhaps," I suggested, "Bond is trying to be *him*."

At last, the way was clear, and the chalet now loomed into view, set against a backdrop of big, beautiful leafy trees of deep green and maroon. "Chalet" was a word entirely too modest for these digs, which was actually a compound of structures surrounding one majestic main building. The whole thing was situated behind a large man-made pond, or what the French call a *miroir d'eau*, architecturally designed to provide a perfect, stunning mirror of the chalet. We entered a big, circular driveway that slowly took us around this fancy pond.

We had caught up to a caravan of cars ahead of us, bearing other guests, all snaking around the large circle. This part of the driveway was flanked by tall, strange pine topiary, sculpted into severe, imposing, narrow triangles—seven on the right of the chalet, and seven on the left. As we approached, something about these towering, forbidding sentinels looked spooky, as if they were giant, other-worldly guards on the lookout for, well, interlopers like us. Beyond them loomed the big chalet.

"I am not exactly certain I like this place," Honorine said in a gloomy voice from the back seat.

I knew what she meant. There was a hint of the dungeon about the chalet, with its predominantly austere violet-grey color. High, narrow, rounded four-story turrets stood up on both sides like tall pencils, with peaked, pointy roofs that resembled upside-down funnels. The main building was four stories high, dominated by a low-hanging, steeply-pitched, sloping roof of an even deeper plum grey color. As our car crept closer to the front of the chalet, I saw that the front door was flanked by two white pillars, approached by a flight of stone steps.

The cars ahead of us took turns pausing to deposit their passengers, before being speedily driven away by valets. "Wow," I said, fascinated. "Lots of people here tonight!"

We watched the arriving guests as they approached the open front door. Because everyone was dressed in period costumes nearly identical to ours, with white wigs and masks, their appearance contributed to the odd impression that we had discovered a phantom party attended by ghosts of France's *ancien régime.*

"The guests are wearing masks," Honorine commented. "But not the servants!"

Jeremy pointed out Drake's P.R. man, who wore a suit and no mask, and he didn't engage with the guests at all, but hovered about, directing the servants. The guy was very tall, thin, with sandy hair cut close to his scalp; and he seemed to be looking over everyone's heads while he assessed the situation.

We were now "up at bat" as we reached the front steps. Jeremy stopped the car, and several footmen in livery snapped into action, opening the passenger doors for me and Honorine, and taking the keys from Jeremy as he got out, so that the young parking attendants could abscond with the car. As we ascended the stone steps and reached the arched front door, one of the footmen asked for our invitation, which I silently handed to him. He placed it under something that looked like a lamp, but was actually a scanner that picked up a computer code. He nodded to us, and we walked inside.

The huge entry hall resembled a fancy hunting lodge, with rustic beamed ceilings and oak panelled walls. A very wide, steep staircase was to our right. To our left, where all the servants were ushering the throng of visitors, was an enormous medieval dining hall. The room was already filling up with guests, who were chattering so loudly that their voices filled the air with a strange, reverberating hum of such explosive power that it made me think of the underground nuclear science lab full of subatomic particles racing about in a massive burst of energy.

The dining hall had rows of long tables made of rough thick wood, all set with candelabras, goblets, cutlery and plates—silver for the men, gold for the women. Butlers directed us to our places; Jeremy was put opposite me, and Honorine was seated alongside me. We were midway down the table.

Even if Jeremy had wanted to talk to me—which he didn't, since he'd sworn the three of us to silence, to avoid being caught—it would have been impossible to hear him, because of the cacophony of excited voices all around us. I watched in amusement as one waiter swooped down on us to fill our goblets with the choice of wine or diet cola; while another went up and down the table, placing big fondue pots with little fire burners underneath; and a third server set platters of caviar, and salad with shavings of black-and-white truffles; and another waiter offered bread, fruit, and a vegan health platter. Something for every appetite. Meanwhile, female servers descended on us, carrying silver trays with silver tongs, which they used to deposit small round items on each plate.

When I peered at my plate, I saw what they were. Miniature hamburgers. They were clearly designed to please the men in the party, because, while the women were given one each, most men accepted three or four of these on their plates, and it was apparently as satisfying as eating a big steak.

I looked at my cutlery, and saw that many guests were happily picking up their long pronged fondue forks to spear chunks of bread that they dipped into their cheese fondue. I laughed out loud. All this hoopla, and all this expense and exclusivity, and in the end, what the masters of the universe apparently wanted to eat at a charity gala . . . was fondue, burgers, and caviar.

Jeremy grinned at me, but poor Honorine looked utterly baffled at this culinary mixed-bag, especially when she bit into a hamburger and discovered a soft center of foie gras. If someone had served this eclectic dinner to a Frenchman, I suppose it might have been tantamount to a declaration of war.

Afterwards, dessert arrived—ice cream sundaes atop brownies. Throughout the entire dinner, there was absolutely no sign of the hosts. Now fully sated, the guests began to make their way out the back door of the dining hall, and into a grand ballroom.

This was a salon done entirely in gold and silver, except for the floor, which was made of alternating black and white diamond-shapes of marble. The walls were covered with gold-framed mirrors, gold light sconces, and gold-and-silver wallpapers of eighteenth century courtiers. Directly in the center of the room was a large white marble sculpture of the Three Graces, poised in their tunics over a circular base, with sculpted fish and turtles at their feet.

It was really quite an astounding spectacle, because, under the twinkling chandeliers, a throng of masked women, all dressed alike, began dancing with a matching throng of men who all resembled one another. And because the room was mirrored, the images swirling around were doubled and trebled and quadrupled, until you really didn't know if you were about to walk up to a real person, or run smack into a mirror. Somehow, the guests managed to keep dancing round and round and round, giddily following the dizzying path of the music, which at this moment was a Strauss waltz.

"What do we do now?" Honorine whispered to me. But a young masked man was already approaching to claim her as his partner, and he danced her away.

Jeremy took my hand and led me to the ballroom floor. We'd gotten only halfway across the room when the band stopped playing in mid-crescendo, and everyone fell silent, coming to an abrupt halt. A moment later, we heard loud, clanging bells from the chalet's tower, making the kind of racket that is usually reserved for the birth of a king or the crowning of a pope. As it turned out, it was Drake and his wife, who were now making their grand entrance.

Parker Drake's costume bore some resemblance to the other men's, except that his black coat appeared to be made of silk and leather. He stood erect and rigid, his forearm held out for his wife's gloved hand to rest lightly upon. Tina's dress was sort of like ours, except that hers was entirely of gold silk satin. They both wore elaborate powdered wigs, but her eye-mask was gold, not white like the other ladies'; and Drake's mask was silver, not black like the men's. So, evidently, the black-and-white rule for masks didn't apply to our hosts, as if these two gods were not required to play by rules that they themselves had designed for mere mortals.

Butlers now scurried around with trays of empty champagne glasses, shaped in the old-fashioned way, with wide, shallow cups (which some glassware historians claim were designed to resemble Marie Antoinette's breasts). When we were all clasping an empty glass, Drake raised one hand in a brief, dramatic signal.

The ballroom lights were dimmed, and the sculpted fountain in the center of the room was suddenly illuminated by lighting at its base. A split second later, the fountain's jets went on, spouting not water, but some leaping golden liquid that splayed out in several arcs and descended into a foaming, bubbling pool below.

"Champagne for everyone!" Tina Drake cried out, and the guests all laughingly rushed over to fill their glasses at the fountain. The butler had already filled two glasses, which he now carried ceremoniously to Drake and his wife.

One of the masked men, surely on cue, shouted out, "A toast to the host!" and everyone repeated, "To the host!" and then, like crashing cymbals, everyone clinked glasses and drank. After Drake had drained his glass, he actually tossed it up into the air, and his serving men scrambled to catch it before it fell and broke. The whole thing looked completely orchestrated, yet the crowd applauded as one of the servers caught the glass.

The music resumed, and Jeremy steered me across the floor, propelling us closer to the Drakes, so that we could get a better look. Drake and his wife were chatting to some of the guests, who clustered adoringly around the couple, jockeying for position and hanging on his every word, laughing hard at the smallest joke he made, as if they hoped some of his magic for amassing money would spill onto them. And these, I might add, were people that the rest of the world would consider already very rich indeed. I thought of all the other "important" people who had been ogling for an invitation and hadn't gotten one.

Now here we were, face to face. Er, well, mask to mask. Even with this subterfuge, I could see that Drake was undeniably a charming, compelling man, with a South African-accented voice that was cheerfully aggressive, and a deceptively boyish attitude.

As we sidled closer, I observed that he had one of those year-round suntans on his leathery face and sinewy neck. I knew from Honorine's research that he was in his mid-sixties, yet he appeared extremely fit and athletic, as if determined to be taken for a thirty-year-old. So his talk was mainly about his physical exploits of competitive sailing, mountain climbing, hang-gliding and car racing. I recalled that he was known to be an adventurer and supreme risk-taker, speeding his souped-up cars across treacherous desert tracks.

At the moment, he was talking, rather loudly, about having just survived a dangerous storm at sea in a sailing race around the world. As he described, with relish, his daring brushes with death, his enthralled audience "*ooh'd*" and "*ahh'd*" at each key moment.

"That was when we saw the sharks," he was saying, pausing for effect, and when everyone gasped, he flashed a smile of blindingly white teeth, continuing his narrative, while his audience listened, spellbound. He spoke in short, simple sentences, which somehow increased his conversational power, as if he were bestowing the gift of his words like a king's largesse.

Yet, with all this testosterone-fueled talk, I thought there seemed to be a trace of something geeky and awkward underneath. From photos I'd seen of him, I knew that his face was not conventionally handsome, that his skin was even a bit scarred. Without his mystique, perhaps he might not have been the sort of man that people were magnetically attracted to.

Drake's monologue was occasionally punctuated by a bolstering comment from his wife, who would enhance the anecdote with quick bits like, "Yes, the Sultan of Brunei *still* wants to buy your Lamborghini."

Tina Drake was blonde and statuesque, with large breasts that were displayed quite prominently. Her gown had a spectacularly long train that swept the ground like a peacock's tail feathers, and around her wrist she carried an ivory fan with a silk cord. She was the kind of celebrity who seems to effortlessly strike poses, yet behaves as if completely unaware of possessing such stunning looks. Her English accent was carefully poshified, but betrayed occasional wisps of working-class tones.

"Arm candy," someone muttered. "She used to be a fashion model, you know."

When the music stopped again, Drake turned to his wife, making a big show of adoring her, kissing her hand as if she were one of those mountains he'd climbed and conquered. Then he walked out the door.

A moment later, one of the servants banged a Chinese gong. It must have been out in the hallway, but the sound echoed everywhere. It was a signal, because immediately, some of the men also began to leave the room. The young fellow who'd been dancing with Honorine said enviously, "It's the card game. I hear you have to have a special pass to get in." He turned to Honorine. "More champagne?" he asked. She nodded, and he headed toward the flowing fountain.

Jeremy glanced at me and said, "Let the games begin. Will you be okay?"

"Sure," I said.

"You know what I mean. Don't do anything heroic," he said meaningfully.

"The same to you," I said. Jeremy grinned, and followed the other men.

Honorine, still eyeing her dancing partner, complained, "That boy cannot dance, he has stepped all over my shoes. And, he talked nonstop about how rich Mr. Drake is," she added under her breath. "You don't need to worry that he noticed my accent, because he has no interest in hearing my opinion!"

A pair of masked men were approaching us, and we soon discovered that the masks evidently gave some guests the permission they craved to be more daring and frisky; as if somehow the disguise also cloaked their less appealing attributes of stature (short), girth (fat) or other more ordinary features (baldness or big nose). If you said you wanted to sit it out, many of these men assumed it meant that you wanted to disappear into a dark corner with them. Under such circumstances, the safest thing to do was to keep dancing.

So, Honorine and I danced, and danced, and danced. Finally, when we'd simply had enough, we met up again by the doorway and slowly sipped champagne together.

"*La-la!*" Honorine cried. "It's all just too much!"

"Cheesit! Here comes our hostess," I warned, seeing the golden figure approaching us. Tina Drake had been working her way through the crowd, and now, as she drew nearer, she gave us a generic smile of pleasure at our company.

"Hi, I'm Tina . . . Parker's wife," she said in a disarmingly plain, frank welcome. "How are you ladies tonight? Don't you just hate masquerade balls? But my husband *adores* them!"

She was older than the two of us, but much younger than Drake. She was so refreshingly blunt and cheerful, and seemed to be a genuinely friendly creature.

"Marvellous," I said, doing my best to sound like Amelia.

"Anyway," Tina went on, "we've already raised half a million euros for the little orphan kids."

She now glanced encouragingly at Honorine. But Honorine appeared lost in thought, gazing off in the distance, not even responding with a smile for Tina, just seemingly submerged in her own world, contemplating . . . what?

I nudged her. Honorine nodded faintly and dutifully at Tina, not at all convincing, like a bad student who doesn't even try to listen in class. Tina smiled indulgently at Honorine's apparent youthful boredom, and was ready to move on, but then, totally inexplicably, Honorine suddenly said, with as little of her accent as she could manage, "I just love your perfume, where can I buy it?"

I sucked in my breath in dismay. Tina smiled patronizingly and answered, "Oh, sweetie, my husband had it specially made for me, with a secret formula so that no other woman in the world could have it." She glanced at me in amusement and said, "Excuse me, I must see to my other guests."

As soon as she was gone I turned to Honorine and said, "What on earth—?"

"That woman," Honorine said urgently, "I have seen her before. I mean, I have *smelled* her before."

"Honorine," I hissed, "*what* are you talking about?"

Undaunted, Honorine continued, "Didn't you smell that perfume of hers?"

"No," I said. "I didn't. And I don't see how you could have, either, with all these Marie Antoinettes dancing around, drenched in competing scent—"

"But I did," Honorine said calmly, "because Madame Drake's fragrance is one that my poor nostrils could not possibly forget. And you know where I first smelled it? In your offices, when you were away. Remember I told you that a woman came to deliver your gift for Jeremy from the jeweler? And I had to open all the windows, all over the house, to make that heavy, horrible fragrance go away? *Alors!* It's her."

"This is one of the richest women in the world, she doesn't work in a jewelry store," I objected.

"*Exactement*," Honorine said triumphantly. "Yet, she was wearing this awful perfume on that day, and she is wearing it now. She is absolutely the same woman who came into our office to deliver the ring. But how is that possible?"

Mindful of Jeremy's admonishment, I thought about how he always avoided leaping to conclusions. I said carefully, "I suppose two different women could have the same perfume. People steal formulas all the time, don't they? Maybe someone who worked in the factory sold it to a competitor . . ."

"*Impossible*," Honorine said emphatically. "You heard her. No little delivery girl could get hold of such a closely guarded, private perfume formula."

I got that prickly feeling on the back of my neck when I instinctively know that something is true, no matter how improbable. What this actually proved I couldn't say, but now all my bloodhound instincts were aroused. We had moved out of the ballroom for privacy, wandering down the hall and approaching the foot of the big staircase.

"Honorine," I said in a low tone, "stay right here and stand guard for me. If somebody's on their way up the stairs, cough loudly, so I'll know they're coming."

"What are you going to do?" she asked, looking a little scared, as if she'd caused this.

"Snoop around!" I said.

I suppose, on some level, I thought I might actually find the tapestry hanging on a wall like a captured moose head. But I think I just wanted to prove to myself that it wasn't there, and that there was nothing really amiss with the Drakes; that they were simply powerful people who inhabited a universe where paranoia was unfortunately not misplaced, and, as Monsieur Felix had suggested, Drake was only carefully vetting us before allowing us into their inner circle. However, I was no longer entirely sure that I wanted to have anything to do with these strange people, so, suddenly, there seemed a lot less at stake on that score.

I scampered up the staircase to an interim landing, then hesitated. It was dark, with only a life-sized painted portrait of a young woman in a Napoleonic "empire" dress and bonnet. I continued up the next staircase, which led to the second level; but when I reached it, I discovered a creepy butler posted there, dressed in a weird costume that made him look like a medieval executioner.

Very purposefully, he stepped in my path, and said loftily, "No women allowed on this level. Sorry. The powder room is down on the main level." I realized that this must be where the men had gone to Drake's private game room to play cards.

I nodded compliantly, feeling somewhat protected by my eyemask, so that the guy wouldn't really be able to identify me. I went back down to the little interim landing where I'd just been, and I ducked out of his sight, hiding in the shadows, my back pressing against the wall. And while I stood there trying to figure out my next move, I saw something very odd: the "painting" moved.

Drake's P.R. man stepped out from behind it, barking orders at someone into a cell phone. So, it was a secret door! I shrank tighter into the shadows, trying not to breathe. When he went past me I heard him say distinctly, "Well, she's around here somewhere, dammit, so find her." He closed the door, and moved on downstairs.

My heart pounding, I waited till his footsteps died away. Once I was certain that he was gone, I returned to the painting, searching for the hidden spring. Sure enough, behind the right side of the frame was a little metal square button. I pressed it, and the door opened obligingly. I stepped inside.

There was a private staircase, lit only by strips of small lights on the floor, along both sides of the stairs. Should I go up or down? In the dim lighting I peered down, and surmised that the stairs eventually led outside, judging by the grassy footprints that the P.R. man must have left behind. So I opted to go up. It was a longer climb than I expected, which indicated to me that I was bypassing the second level with the executioner-butler, and climbing to a higher floor.

I had reached a small, unassuming door, but it opened into an elaborate private suite with a personalized gym and massage table, small kitchen, refrigerator and bar, a bathroom, a steam room and a sizeable bedroom.

Beyond all this was an enormous office. Everywhere were photographs of Drake in all his exploits—sailing, climbing, flying a small plane, and big-game hunting. There were also tons of trophies and awards, for everything from these athletic competitions, to recognition of his charitable impact. The world had given him the keys to their kingdoms, and every conceivable token of their admiration, yet here was a man who apparently needed to be reminded of these things at every turn.

I'd instinctively gravitated to his office, with its massive desk and a computer connected to a huge flat screen. The entire wall behind the computer desk looked like one big glass bookshelf. As I approached, I saw that it was actually a very elaborate display case, locked, and filled with gleaming objects.

I drew nearer . . . and gazed at row after row after row of coins . . . rare coins that he'd amassed, illuminated within their case. Every one of them was fastidiously labelled, with the country of origin and the time period. Each sat upon its own little velvet throne, like a jewel. Roman coins. French coins. German, Iberian, Swiss, Austrian, Byzantine, medieval European, Indo-Greek, Caribbean, Scottish; and coins from Paraguay and Singapore and Bulgaria and the American colonies. Money, money, money. As far as the eye could see.

In a strange way, it made sense that coin collecting would be one of Drake's hobbies, perhaps even his secret favorite. For I could well imagine him in his geeky adolescence—an awkward teenage boy hoarding his best ones, and haunting the coin swaps. As I peered closer, I saw from their labels that they were very rare coins indeed. My researcher's "nose" was captivated by their historical value.

Then I reminded myself that I was not in a museum and should not be lingering like this. One thing I had certainly not seen was a tapestry, not a single one; and if Drake was interested in them, I'd surely have found a whole collection. I considered that I was probably wasting my time, but I should check out the rest of this suite, and then sneak back downstairs before I was discovered and accused of trying to steal something.

I was very careful, moving as quietly as possible. But when I pussyfooted past the sleeping computer, my motion made the computer "wake" and the screen went on with a soft, obliging groan. The screen now displayed several open files, with various photographs of rare old coins; so many that I didn't know what to look at first.

But then my eye was caught by an enlarged drawing of a coin that appeared startlingly familiar. As I drew closer, I gasped. I certainly recognized the "J.L." coat of arms and the half-moon behind it. It was absolutely the same insignia as the one on the tapestry. But what was it doing on this rare old coin? I squinted and leaned closer, trying to see what the text beneath it said, but . . .

Footsteps. Rapidly. Right outside, coming up the secret stairs, therefore evading Honorine's lookout post on the main staircase. I made the computer sleep once more, and I switched off the light, just as Parker Drake entered the room.

Chapter Thirty

"So. I knew you couldn't be trusted," he said, moving purposefully toward me. I thought, *Oh God, I'm going to end up a dead woman, floating around in Lake Geneva tonight.* And, by the time Jeremy figures out what happened, and dredges the lake for me, I'll already be one of those awful mysterious murders that go unresolved, forever.

"You just couldn't stay away, could you?" Drake said, close to me now.

I sensed that he was going to grab me, even before he reached out and clasped my arms in his aggressive grip. However, what I did not know was that he wasn't going to toss me out the window, but, instead, plant a big, wet kiss on me that lasted a lot longer than you might guess; or maybe it just felt interminable because of that suddenly awkward, overbearing tongue, which made it the kind of surprisingly bad kiss you'd get from a defensive, insecure date, prompting you to decide to never go out with him again. This guy may have kissed a lot of women in his day, but he'd apparently learned nothing from his experiences, possibly because he'd never had to. Eee-yuck. Not good.

"Mmm . . . you taste good tonight, new lipstick?" he murmured.

"Mmm . . ." I muttered noncommittally, in as low a voice as possible.

"Tina knows you're here," he said, running his hands over my bare shoulders. "She went and hired a private dick. He saw your car and plates. Very foolish of you, my sweet. I guess you just couldn't wait for daddy any longer?"

Now I really wanted to throw up. But of course I said nothing, banking on the dim lighting and my mask to keep up the charade. I managed to put my hand to his chest and push him away, and he assumed I was alarmed about his wife, because he said teasingly, "Don't worry. I'll protect you from Tina. Even if she does want to strangle you with her bare hands."

Just then, the Chinese gong downstairs sounded again. It made that sonorous *Bwoong!* that reverberated throughout the whole chalet. As if in echo, a ship's clock in the corner of the room began to count the hours with small pinging sounds. It was midnight.

"Ah," Drake said in an inviting tone. "Time for all good guests to unmask . . ."

He reached around to the back of my dress, searching for the zipper. I was still backing away, but not getting very far. And then I heard a voice, which, all things considered, sounded like an angel.

"Parker?" Tina's annoyed tone drifted from the main staircase and had an unexpected effect on Drake. For all his previous bravado, he suddenly straightened up, changed his relaxed tune and, very roughly, grabbed my arm and pushed me toward the door of the secret staircase, which he opened, shoving me down into it.

"Go!" he barked, as if accustomed to having his orders immediately obeyed. "Outside! Stay away from here tonight." Then he softened his tone and said insinuatingly, "I'll come to your place later."

Well, I didn't need an engraved invitation at this point. I was already scurrying down those steps as fast as my little feet could patter in those silly shoes with buckles. At the bottom of the staircase was a door that led straight outside, where the wind was whipping up off the lake. The night had become chilly, and as I stumbled across the lawn, my powdered wig kept getting caught on the darned shrubs and topiary, as if their brittle fingers were trying to pull off my disguise and expose me for the imposter I was. Breathlessly, I returned to the front door, went inside and hurried to the main staircase.

Honorine was waiting loyally at the foot of the stairs, peering out hopefully for any sign of me. Other guests were coming out of the ballroom and taking off their masks. Clearly the party was breaking up now. When Honorine spotted me she said, "Psst! Let's go into the ladies' room where we can talk!"

We ducked into the large powder room, tucked into an alcove just beyond the stairs. It was empty, but I knew it wouldn't be for long, with all those other guests milling around. We were still wearing our masks, for fear that Tina would walk in and discover us as not-Amelia and her not-daughter.

"*Mon dieu*, where have you been?" Honorine demanded. "Do you know how many of these masked beasts tried to pick me up all night? I am a sitting—how do you say—*canard* here—"

"Duck," I said automatically.

"*Oui*," she said, "and let me tell you, these disguises make the guests think they can do anything. A woman came over and kissed me on the lips . . . and she didn't even say hello first!"

"Never mind," I said hastily. "We've got to find Jeremy and get out of here, because everyone's taking off their masks."

"In those back rooms they're taking off plenty of other things, too," she informed me. I couldn't help smiling at her, recalling my student days when an alumna warned me that, after you graduate and join the wider world in your first job, the immediate, disillusioned question that occurs to you is, *Is this how grown-ups behave? Then what were all my studies and hard work and exams for?* Honorine had just that look of disillusioned disbelief on her face right now.

Since the ladies' room wasn't far from the stairs, we could hear the thundering herd of card-playing men as they came pounding down the steps. We tiptoed out cautiously. Jeremy spotted us immediately, and had already sized up that it was time to go. He wasn't wearing his mask, but carrying it, very calmly. When he saw us he warned, "You look more conspicuous with it on. The card game broke up before midnight, so Drake wasn't even in the room when the masks came off."

"No foolin'," I retorted. "I know exactly where he was at midnight. Let's get out of here before he figures out that I know what I know."

Jeremy shot me a quick look of comprehension, and shepherded us down a side corridor.

"Come on," he said, "let's mingle through that crowd."

We slipped past a throng of people who'd collected in the big front hall, and were now all kissing one another as if it were New Year's Eve. We weren't the only ones leaving; already, the valets were bringing the fancy cars around to the front, and people were piling into them, gaily going off to the next fun-seeking hot spot.

Now that this ball was winding down, I noticed that the estate was like an armed camp, with ominous-looking bodyguards, security men, and even toothy guard dogs accompanying them. A not too subtle signal that all good guests mustn't even think of skulking around, or staying overnight uninvited. The P.R. man was walking about with his walkie-talkie, and some other thuggy-looking guys doing the same. I wondered if they were looking for Drake's mistress . . . or me.

As soon as I saw our car being brought round, and the valets opening the doors for us, I scuttled gratefully into the passenger seat, and breathed a sigh of relief when we headed out to the main road.

"So how'd the game go?" I asked Jeremy immediately. "Did you lose your shirt?"

"Not quite," Jeremy admitted. "But being a loser was a better disguise than winning and drawing attention to myself. I was concentrating more on acting like Giles, while taking Drake's measure. We played poker, until it came down to a big pot with only two players. One of them was Drake, and they switched to piquet for the final round, just as Rollo said. I learned a lot—and not just about the game."

"What do you mean?" I asked, fascinated.

"Drake's a proposition-better," Jeremy replied. "I've met guys like him before."

"A compulsive gambler?" I said.

"No, it's different from regular gamblers. Guys like Drake don't do it for the money. They can afford to lose big sums. They just bet all the time, on everything and anything. I've had lunch with clients like that, and they bet on which waiter will get to the kitchen first; or how many cherries the bartender has in his jar behind the counter. Drake's like that. Once he gets going, he pushes it as far as he can. Plus, the guy is fiercely competitive anyway. He tries to act the good sport, but he loses his cool if the cards are against him. Still, he won pretty big tonight. He went out strutting like a rooster."

"You got that right," I said involuntarily, under my breath.

Jeremy gave me a suspicious look. "What do you mean?"

So, I told him the whole story. Yes, the whole one, although, initially, I wasn't sure how much detail to go into, what with Honorine in the back seat listening, wide-eyed, to every word. I told them about the computer and the coin collection. When I reached the part where Drake caught me in the room and mistook me for his mistress, I paused, but Jeremy said sharply, "What did he do to you?"

"Just kissed me," I assured him. "But believe me, that was bad enough."

"That bastard," Jeremy said darkly, and for a moment he looked as if he was ready to turn the car around, stomp into the chalet and slug the guy.

"He never knew it was me," I said helpfully, explaining how I got away.

We had reached the main gate, waiting for our turn to be waved through by men with lighted sticks. Jeremy stared straight ahead at the dark road through his windshield. Then he glanced at me accusingly and said, "Do you have any idea what kind of real trouble you could have gotten into?"

"Gosh, no, it never occurred to me," I replied dryly. Honorine giggled. Jeremy drove on.

When we got back the hotel, Honorine trotted off to her room, looking as if she was going to fall asleep as soon as she crawled into bed. So Jeremy and I continued to discuss the case in our room.

"If you ask me," I said, "Parker Drake, a.k.a. Mr. Genius Businessman, All-Round Adventurer and Charming Philanthropist, is also our Tapestry Thief!"

"Hang on," Jeremy cautioned. "Just because he seems interested in that 'J.L.' crest, does not prove that he's actually got the tapestry. At least, not in a court of law."

I snorted. "Obviously, we don't need a court to tell us he's got it," I said.

I was thinking of all the strange, inexplicable things that had happened to us lately. At the time, they'd seemed like isolated events. But now I reminded Jeremy about the night we'd gone to Margery's cocktail party. New connections occurred to me, as I spoke.

"Remember when we were parking outside your grand-mum's house?" I said. "You were annoyed because some guy was tailgating us. I wonder if we were being watched much earlier than we realized. Because, next thing you know, out of the blue, you got a phone call from Parker's P.R. guy, right there at the cocktail party."

I was retracing that whole evening now. "That was *also* the same night that Honorine chased a guy off our doorstep, right? We just thought it was another kook. But what if it was all connected to this?"

Jeremy gave this due consideration. "Even if what you say is true—that Drake was behind this from the get-go—what made him think we had any information about the tapestry in the first place?"

I was momentarily stumped. But Jeremy was gesturing as he spoke, and a gleam of gold caught my eye. "Oh, *no*!" I cried, aghast. "Is it possible that this whole thing got kicked into gear just because I went to the jeweler to have that signet ring made for you? I showed him the 'J.L.' insignia. And, the jeweler asked me about the source material. I said it came from a family heirloom!" I wailed in regret.

"Steady on," Jeremy counseled, reviewing this calmly. "True, there are plenty of unscrupulous dealers who, under cover of a legitimate business, scour the world for treasures that they know their illustrious clients would buy, no matter how it was obtained," he admitted. "I can certainly believe that Drake is one of those passionate collectors who will stop at nothing to get what he wants. If the jeweler is connected to Drake, and he alerted Drake when he saw the design—" He broke off, pondering this. "That would make our jeweler the missing link. No pun intended," he said, trying to lighten my gloom.

Then he continued more soberly, "But maybe it's *you* they're interested in. Miss Penny Nichols comes into the store with sketches of a rare antique design. They have your address, so they send a guy to our doorstep to snoop around. He sees our sign out in front, and learns that you work at a firm called Nichols & Laidley. Perhaps he even intended to break in, if Honorine hadn't startled him. Anyway, he reports back to Drake; and further investigation confirms that you're the well-known American heiress, famous for tracking down lost treasures."

This made me feel even worse. I don't quite see myself as others do these days—an heiress born under a lucky star. Frankly, I still feel like the same little unknown person I used to be, toddling around with her research and her bright ideas. But perhaps harboring an old image of myself was dangerous, or at least, careless. Now my French relatives were paying the price, with the loss of a beautiful tapestry.

Almost unwillingly, I found myself making sense of more odd occurrences. "This may explain Honorine's nose," I said glumly, telling him the story of the perfumed lady who came to our office. "Maybe, when the guy on the doorstep failed to get in, Drake sent his wife to snoop around. It sounds as if they do have a connection to the jeweler, so she makes the delivery for him, just to get inside."

Jeremy weighed this possibility. "Hmm. And what does Tina

Drake find? A ton of photos of a tapestry. If Penny Nichols is scrutinizing it so closely, it must be something worth having."

"And, you know what? Some of my photos of the tapestry disappeared from my office right after Miss Perfume showed up," I added. "Can that be mere coincidence? I think not!"

So, it was down to me again. One little innocent move on my part had apparently set off a whole landslide. Now I was utterly convinced that I had to recover that tapestry.

"Look," I said. "We've obviously just scratched the surface of this tapestry story. This guy Lunaire—Armand's patron. We've got to find out what he's all about."

The next morning, Monsieur Felix contacted Jeremy to report that nothing had come from following our decoy, Amelia—nothing except sore feet for the poor guy, who found the English homemaker's schedule exhausting, just as Jeremy had predicted. Monsieur Felix had not seen anyone following her, so he took Le Bug away from Amelia, and deposited it through our mail slot in London. He suggested we leave it there, since he believed Le Bug was *mort*.

"Sounds like he's hit a dead end," Jeremy told me. "But he'll keep trying. He's going back to France, where he'll keep an eye on the usual smugglers, criminals and shady characters on the Riviera. I told him about the coins you saw on Drake's computer, but he's never heard of them."

"Swell," I said. "Well, let him watch the ports and the crooks. Meanwhile, we need to trawl the old French law records of the trials of Lunaire and Armand. But my French isn't good enough for that."

"Neither is mine," Jeremy admitted. "We could have a colleague do it, but it will cost a lot."

"No, let's put Honorine on this!" I said, feeling suddenly inspired.

Jeremy agreed, so I went to Honorine's room to give her the new assignment. Her door was open, to allow the maid in. Honorine was out on the balcony, talking into her cell phone in a low voice, so she didn't see me come in, while she was gazing out at the view.

Lake Geneva was spectacular this morning, all blue sky and towering mountains and shimmering water. Little steamer ferries were plying their way across the lake, carrying visitors from one pretty town to another, where they would no doubt stop and sample the local cheeses and flinty white wines.

As I approached Honorine, something about her secretive tone made me pause, just in time to hear her say, "Oh, you know, lawyers aren't so bad, they can be quite useful. In fact, I have heard that *some* of them make excellent lovers!"

The next words she uttered really made me stop cold. "As a matter of a fact," she said in a wicked tone, as if confiding in a girlfriend, "I especially like English lawyers. Yes, one in particular. One I work with. That's right." Here she laughed lightly, with satisfaction and confidence. "Oh, he's very handsome, and he says he's 'wild about me'. Yes, it's true, he may already be spoken for, but what does that matter to a woman in love? I can surely beat out the competition, I'm younger than her, and anyway he says he's never met anyone as sexy as me."

I just froze right there on the spot. Not possible. Was it? Naw. But. "So, I will defeat my rival, and then I definitely see London in my future," Honorine was concluding. She hung up, and came bouncing away from the balcony, into her room, and straight toward me. I wasn't happy to see the surprised, stricken look on her face as soon as she caught sight of me.

"Oh!" she cried in dismay. "You are here!"

"Honorine," I said, ready to scratch her eyes out if necessary, "I'm sorry but I couldn't help overhearing. Who were you talking about?" I stared at her resolutely, just willing her to try to lie to me.

She stuck out her chin defiantly, then smiled in triumph. I think my heart skipped a beat. Then she admitted, "If you must know, I am in love. And nothing you say will make any difference. But Jeremy doesn't know for sure how I feel, although I think he suspects. Has he told you anything?"

I just stared at those big brown eyes that were looking so defiantly back at me. I couldn't believe it. I wouldn't believe it. "Jeremy?" I croaked in a dry, cracked voice. Honorine flushed bright red, and then began to stammer, in French, as if she were under such stress that her grasp of English had temporarily deserted her. "What about Jeremy?" I repeated.

"I would not want to be forced to choose between my job and the man I love, but I will if I must!" she finally managed to say. We stood there, staring at each other. Then she said pleadingly, "Surely you do not wish to cause trouble for Rupert."

"Rupert?" I repeated rather stupidly. "Rupert?" Then the light dawned. "Ohhh . . . *Rupert*. You're in love with Rupert?"

"For heaven's sake, you don't need to tell the whole hotel!" Honorine cried in dismay. "What if Jeremy should hear you? Please, don't make so much of it—and absolutely do not tell my parents!"

I couldn't help it. I started to snicker uncontrollably. Mainly from relief, and recognition of the absurdity of my response. At her indignant expression, I smothered my laughter as quickly as I could. But I was so relieved, I could practically sing with it.

"Okay, my lips are sealed," I gasped. Then I calmed down.

"Honorine," I said briskly, "*meanwhile*, how would you like to do some investigating? It may help us find the tapestry." She brightened, eager to contribute to solving this case.

I explained, "We need you to do some research in France. See if you can find out anything in the historical archives about Jean Lunaire."

I wrote down the name for her, and the relevant time period. "He's the wealthy patron of the tapestry-maker. Lunaire got arrested for trying to poison the king, and that's how Armand got into trouble. I'd like to know why Armand put his patron's initials and crest on a tapestry that was made for his own daughter, not for Lunaire. So, dig into the old French law libraries for records which may not be on computers."

We were heading downstairs now, with Honorine pulling her suitcase-on-wheels behind her. "Even if I did find such records, what good would it do, it's so old?" Honorine said doubtfully.

"Hey kid," I said firmly, with no time to mince words, "I've got a nose for this sort of thing. And *my* nose is telling me that we've got to go back in time and find out what happened. Not just Lunaire's trial, but you should also look into Armand's arrest. Remember, this is your family we're talking about. You never know what you might turn up, so do it carefully, and, um, please don't discuss what you find with your folks until you've spoken to me. All of this is top secret. Got it?"

Honorine, looking excited now, said, "I'll get right on it."

We had reached the hotel lobby. "Good," I said positively. "Do you have a credit card? Great, keep all your receipts, and make a record of where you go. Names, dates, addresses, notes."

"It will be done!" Honorine said respectfully. Jeremy was pacing around the lobby, waiting for us. Honorine went ahead to see that the bellhop put our bags into the trunk of the car.

Jeremy murmured to me, "Did I just hear you put Honorine on an expense account?"

"She can't pay for her expenses on the little salary she gets from us!" I exclaimed. "She'll be prudent, don't worry. And I want her to be businesslike, when she's on a case."

"Fine," Jeremy said. "Let's get out of here, and find out what Drake thinks we know."

Part Eight

Chapter Thirty-one

We didn't even bother to unpack when we arrived in London. The townhouse looked unmolested in our absence, since Monsieur Felix had been keeping an eye on it for us. We just deposited our luggage in the hallway; then we headed right back out the door, and made a raid on the jewelry store. The guy was in his shop, as usual, and he actually looked happy to see us when we entered.

"Either he's very good at faking it," Jeremy muttered, "or he's totally innocent and we're off our rockers."

Undaunted, I said to the man quite bluntly, "When I first brought you the designs for the crest I wanted to make, why did you ask me about the source material?"

"Why, to make certain it was done right," he said, surprised at my tone.

"Did you show it to anybody else?" Jeremy asked.

"Only the engravers," he said, but then a look of comprehension crossed his face. "Don't worry, they never make copies of designs that a customer has specially commissioned. You won't see that ring on anyone else."

"Oh, what a relief," I said, as if he'd guessed correctly. "But, just so I know, are you absolutely sure that nobody else saw it?"

"Certainly," the jeweler said, frowning.

"Don't you have any employees?" Jeremy asked.

"No. It's just me and my wife, who does the book-keeping," he said, nodding toward a framed photo on his desk behind the counter, along with another photo of two small kids and their dog. The wife was a plump, pleasant-faced woman who bore absolutely no resemblance to Drake's wife.

"But, we had a visit from a woman who said she worked for you, and she delivered the groom's gift," I said.

"A woman?" the man asked, puzzled. "I thought the engraver dropped it off to you. He said he would. I was in a hurry for a dental appointment that day, and when he came by to show it to me, he offered to take it to you himself. He and his brother have done this for me before, without any trouble."

The jeweler repeated what he'd told me on my previous visit, which was that the engraver and his brother worked together in the coin shop around the corner. But now, of course, the notion of rare coins rang a loud bell.

"What can you tell us about those two men?" Jeremy asked.

The jeweler shrugged. "They've been around for years, and I've always found them honest and dependable," he said. "I really think you can trust them not to reuse your design, but if it makes you feel better, you can tell them yourself." He wrote down their phone number and address on the back of one of his own cards.

"Think he's telling the truth?" I asked Jeremy, once we were out on the street.

"Probably," he said, "but just in case, we'd better hurry over there before he tips them off."

"Do *you* think we're on the wrong track?" I queried, peering at him.

"Nope," Jeremy said. "This is exactly the sort of peculiar spot you've dragged me into before. And, against all odds, logic and probability, you invariably are correct. Let's check it out."

When we reached the curving, narrow little cobbled street with all the hobby and antiques dealers, we quickly spotted the shop we'd seen before, with a sign that said, *Gifts and Engraving, We Buy and Sell Old Coins*. But as we drew closer, we discovered that the windows were completely empty now. Not only that, but the front door was locked, with the sign saying *Closed* hanging in the glass door, as if it would dangle there like that until the end of time.

When I peered inside, I saw that the contents of the entire shop had, for all intents and purposes, vanished. No more counters, chairs or displays. No cash register, and certainly, no coins. Just a couple of folding chairs and crumpled newspapers remained, and a bare light bulb hanging overhead, with its long pull-chain trailing forlornly. Even the window-blinds had been removed from their slots, and lay, instead, in an abandoned heap in the dusty window display.

"They're really gone!" I said in shock.

Jeremy consulted two nearby dealers, an antiquarian bookseller and a furniture man, who were standing outside their shops, commiserating. Both shook their heads, and said that early this morning, the engraver and his coin brother had simply packed up and vanished. No forwarding address or number, and they were in a great hurry. "They must have moved most of their stuff last night, because this morning they seemed to be finishing up their packing, and took off quickly," said the furniture guy.

"Easy come, easy go, I guess," agreed the bookseller. "They

didn't want to chat about it, either. We figured it must be tax or loan problems."

Then, without another word, the men turned and went back into their shops, suddenly busily rearranging their wares. It was a clear signal that they didn't care to jawbone any longer, so we left.

When we returned to our offices, Jeremy muttered, "Think I'll give Danny a call, to see if he can find out anything in his police files."

Later that afternoon Jeremy reported back to me. "Danny ran a check on his computer," he said. "Those coin blokes appear to be 'legit', as far as he can tell, with no police record, and nothing out of place in their drivers' licenses and normal business records."

He showed me his notes from the conversation. I kept staring thoughtfully at the men's surname. I said, "Why does that name sound vaguely familiar?"

I went to my computer and did a few searches. Then finally I found the significant match. I hurried over to the file cabinet Honorine kept for us, and pulled out the folder she'd made on Drake.

"Bingo! Jeremy, look at this," I cried. "Those coin guys have the same last name as Tina Drake's maiden name. Before she married Parker, see? There isn't any more info than that, but still . . . it can't be just a coincidence, can it?"

"I doubt it," Jeremy said thoughtfully. "We ought to talk to someone who's knowledgeable about old coins. Do you know anyone from your research work?"

"Not really," I said, "but it shouldn't be so hard to find."

By the next day, I'd located a man I thought would be helpful, and arranged a meeting with him. "He's a curator at a museum not far from here," I told Jeremy. "He specializes in French and European coins, and he's supposed to have a big collection. He said he thought he'd heard something about a coin with those initials on it, and he's going to see what he can find for us."

"Fine, let's go!" Jeremy said.

Chapter Thirty-two

The coin museum was in a section of London known simply as the City. It's where today's big banking and brokering gets done, but it's also where London pretty much began, with charmingly old-fashioned storybook names like Threadneedle Street and Cloak Lane and St. Swithin's. Some still call this area the "heart" of the city, although its very heartless, mechanized frenzy is supposedly what inspired the poet T.S. Eliot's grim appraisal of the modern world as a wasteland. Which gives you an idea of what transpires in all the mysterious trading offices around here.

The museum was not far from the Bank of England, and actually occupied an old defunct bank. It had beautiful high ceilings and skylights that let in good, natural light with which to view the vast array of coins sheltered in glass display cases, arranged upon original mahogany counters and oak tables, where, once upon a Dickensian time, clerks like Bob Cratchit counted out coins and bills while totting up the bosses' ledgers.

When we entered, our voices and footsteps echoed in the vast open space. The curator was patiently waiting for us at a desk behind the high, antique counters of bankers' windows. So, when he raised his head, I was startled into thinking that we'd stumbled upon some poor ancient ghost of a Victorian-era bank clerk that was stuck here waiting for depositors from past centuries to return. But it was only Mr. Marsh, a very slight, balding man, wearing black pants and vest, and a white shirt with sleeves rolled up to his elbows.

He now stepped out into the lobby, and turned on a few lights in the display cases that filled the room. As he peered into them, his round face became illuminated with an unearthly glow, making him look like the man in the moon.

"What an excellent collection!" I commented, gazing at the array of coins from ancient times to present day, exhibiting how mankind had found so many ways to barter, down through the ages. Some coins were no more than funny little slivers of metal, almost as thin as a sheet of paper; others had holes punched in the middle; a few even looked like square donuts. Many were so irregularly produced that they resembled little cookies with a bit nibbled off the edge, as if they'd been bitten by merchants trying to assess their true value. Some of their designs were simple and slightly crooked, like a child's drawing.

"Yes, we have some fine pieces," Mr. Marsh said, proud of his work. "This concave, dish-shaped coin is from the reign of Constantine."

He moved to another case. "I expect you're mainly concerned with the French ones. These, for instance, with warriors' shields on them, were made when France was known as Gaul to its Roman counterparts. The ones with the vine leaves are Celtic; and the big, thick fellows with crosses are medieval. Now, this silver coin, from the late 1800s, is a 'Marianne'—the image of Liberty for France—but it's not just her head, see? Here she is a complete figure, sowing seeds."

I peered at the accompanying display label for each item. There were so many words for making coins: they were minted, struck, cast, engraved. There were coins made of gold, silver, bronze, nickel . . .

The curator could not resist asking, "Is Penny Nichols actually your real name?"

"Trust me," I assured him, "I would never have made it up."

He smiled, and said, "French coins are a collector's delight, as they are quite artistic and complex in design. In medieval times the French towns and districts struck many coins of their own, until the Bourbon kings centralized French money. Here are coins from 1643, when the Sun King came to the throne as a child." He showed us a fairly sizeable coin, with the image of the new boy-king's head.

"But I don't see the one with the 'J.L.' insignia," Jeremy noted, peering intently into the case.

"Right," said the curator. "As far as I know, nobody has a single one. May I see your sketch?"

I showed it to him. He examined it closely, then murmured, "Yes, yes. That is indeed what was supposed to have been engraved on the Lunaire gold. But, you only have the 'obverse' side. You do not have the image that we think appears on the reverse side."

"If nobody has one, then how do we know what it looks like?" Jeremy asked.

"We don't know for sure," Mr. Marsh replied. He returned to his desk and picked up an accordion folder, which he brought to us. He spread its contents atop one of the glass counters. "I've heard of the Lunaire, but it doesn't much come up in conversation anymore."

He pointed to some tissue-paper tracings he'd copied from drawings in his coin books, to show me the best rendering he could find of the Lunaire. "Keep in mind that these may only be fanciful drawings. We're pretty sure about the 'J.L.' crest with *la lune* on the obverse, because the moon image appears on everything Lunaire owned. However, according to some accounts, the reverse side"—he pointed to a sun with a kingly face whose rays seemed like spikes of fire—"has this image of *le soleil*, representing the Sun King." I stared at the tracings, then copied them into my own notebook.

"Just who was this Lunaire guy?" Jeremy asked.

"He worked for King Louis XIV's treasury," said the curator, "and he managed to amass a great fortune for himself, thus becoming a great patron of the artisans he hired to turn his hunting lodge into a marvellous showplace. He had good taste, they say; he hired only the best architects, builders, landscape gardeners, et cetera, to build and decorate his country estate with impressive sculpture, fountains, gates and topiary; and the interior had exquisite marble baths, painted ceiling frescoes, and tapestries."

I nudged Jeremy at that last word. "But the guy wasn't a king, right?" Jeremy asked. "So how come there was a coin made with his insignia on it?"

"Because, I'm afraid that like Icarus, this man Lunaire flew too high, and one fateful day, at last, he went too far," Mr. Marsh answered.

"What did he do?" I asked, wide-eyed.

"It seems he threw himself a wild birthday party, inviting hundreds of guests to a feast prepared by his excellent personal chef. Among the many amusements, spectacles and games, Lunaire had a goldsmith make these tokens for his card-playing guests."

"He made his own currency?" Jeremy asked.

"They weren't actually coins. They were fancy gambling chips," Mr. Marsh corrected. "Their sole purpose was for that one night, when, supposedly, some fantastic games of cards were played.

Gambling was quite the rage then, and you'd be surprised at how high those stakes could get. The last hand played at Lunaire's birthday party was legendary. Various reports of the time say the pot of gold was heaped very high indeed."

"How many of these chips were in it?" Jeremy asked.

"Nobody can really say, because, just before the final cards were dealt, a mechanical fireworks display went awry, and burned practically everything to the ground."

"Oh, I've heard about such disasters!" I cried. "Kings in that era used to have very elaborate fireworks and complicated mechanical devices for staging dramatic entertainments for their guests. But sometimes if one malfunctioned, the poor worker who was operating the machine died."

"Well, this was a bad deal all round. The fireworks sparks landed where they shouldn't, and all the tents caught fire, causing a great panic. As the guests scrambled away for safety, and Lunaire's servants rushed to put out the fire, in all the fuss, the pot of gold vanished."

We all fell momentarily silent, imagining the scene. I could almost see the powdered wigs and elaborate costumes of the wealthy guests, with their fancy shoes and their great big hats; and all their jeweled snuffboxes, gilded perfume vials and lace handkerchiefs that they carried to keep the whiff of poverty and sickness at bay. I imagined lots of food, drink and hoopla. Not unlike Parker Drake's party, actually. In my vision of Lunaire's birthday jamboree, I saw the tents on fire, and all those revelers running wildly about in panic.

Mr. Marsh continued, "Later, when the king heard of Lunaire's birthday party and his audacious display of wealth—apparently, the king was shown one of the chips—he was jealous and displeased, to say the least. 'How dare anyone attempt to ascend higher than the king!' So, in short order, a conspiracy charge was trumped up, with envious men bearing false witness against him, and the unfortunate Lunaire was dragged off and thrown into prison. But they say it was really just an excuse to confiscate his property—and his gold."

"Did the king take the whole pot of Lunaire gold?" I asked.

"No. Apparently he found only some of the coins, even though he'd ordered his men to seize it all, to be melted down and deposited into the royal treasury. They never found the rest of it. The very day that Lunaire was arrested, the grounds of his grand estate were torn apart as the soldiers searched, in vain. Of course, it's possible that the whole thing was exaggerated, just to secure a conviction against a man with obviously high political ambitions. All we know for sure is that the man was arrested, tried and condemned to prison, where he died."

"Wow," I remarked. "What a story."

"Therefore, we can't be sure if any of the coins survived to the present day," Mr. Marsh concluded. "Still, among collectors, there are persistent rumors. People would forget about it and then, they say, one or two pieces of the Lunaire gold were supposedly sighted at coin swaps, down through the centuries, by credible people. Never for sale, just to show off, you understand. It has, however, been a long, long time since anyone has claimed to have seen one."

We'd been listening, spellbound. But now the curator closed his file. "That is all we know," he said. "I wish I could tell you more."

"Well," said Jeremy as we drove home, "it's obvious that, among coin fanatics, it would be a major coup to find some of that Lunaire gold."

"And I inadvertently woke up at least one lunatic," I said ruefully, "with my brilliant little design ideas. Those coin guys probably knew that Drake was numismatic."

"I beg your pardon? Is that anything like asthmatic?" Jeremy inquired.

"Hoo, hoo," I said. "You know perfectly well it means he fancies coins."

"A numismatic fanatic," Jeremy couldn't resist adding.

"Anyway, suppose the coin guys told Drake they had a hot tip?" I said. "It's not such a stretch, particularly if he's a top client, and if they are somehow connected to his wife."

"And if Drake heard that somebody like Nichols & Laidley were on the trail of these things," Jeremy agreed, "he'd definitely try to beat us to it. From what I've seen of him, he has to win at everything he does, and win big. Whether it's a sailing race or a business deal, or who's got the prettier wife—a guy like him will do whatever it takes to cross the finish line first."

My telephone rang. It was Honorine, calling from France. She was very excited.

"I found some things for you!" she exclaimed triumphantly. "Can you come to Mougins right away?"

Chapter Thirty-three

When we arrived in Mougins at the family château, we discovered that Honorine had enlisted the aid of her much-maligned suitor, Charles, the young French lawyer. Flattered to finally have Honorine's attention, he'd obligingly trawled the dusty vaults of France's arcane legal records for the trial of Jean Lunaire, patron of Armand the tapestry-maker. Honorine excitedly announced that they could shed more light on what happened to both men.

She ushered us into Philippe's library, a wonderful dark-panelled room, spacious and inviting, with numerous places to sit and read in any of its black leather-and-walnut chairs. The walls were lined with framed old maps of France as it had evolved over the centuries, and shelves full of books encased behind glass doors. The south wall of the library had tall windows instead of bookshelves, and looked out onto a small garden, with neat, precise square flowerbeds. The entire garden was enclosed by high stone walls with climbing roses and ivy, contributing to the cloistered, "secret garden" atmosphere.

In the center of the library was a big mahogany table with green-shaded lamps, where Charles had spread out all his notes. He shook hands with Jeremy, and shyly ducked his dark curly head as he gestured for us to be seated at the table. But when he began relaying the information, his voice took on a more authoritative, confident tone, which was a bit touching, as if he'd learned this tone from his schoolmasters.

"This Lunaire was quite a character," he explained. "For one thing, he didn't pay all his bills on time, and for that reason there were legal documents that may be useful. Trial and guild records show that he had many bills overdue . . . including those from his tapestry-maker, Armand."

Charles pulled out several handwritten pages he'd photocopied, mostly covered with numbers, and some French words in columns. "Apparently Armand made a great many tapestries for Lunaire, so Lunaire owed Armand a lot of money." He paused to emphasize the significance of this. "But all that debt didn't stop Lunaire from living high," Charles said, rather disapprovingly of such a patron. "There was a fantastic party . . ."

He shuffled through his notes, and, in effect, confirmed what the coin curator had told us about Lunaire's big birthday extravaganza that had sealed his fate. I examined the copies of old invoices, and although I couldn't make out the arcane French, I could imagine the gist of it as something along the lines of, *This bill is past due. Please make payment immediately!*

Charles continued his report, speaking in a careful, slightly punctilious way. "At Lunaire's trial, it would appear that people were tortured into incriminating him as conspiring to poison the king," he said. "Torture and poisoning, I regret to say, were not uncommon in those days. Lunaire denied the charges. But," he added, turning a page in his folder, with a frown of concentration, "all the same, he was sentenced to life in solitary confinement in prison, where he died."

Charles' tone was brisk and neutral, as he set aside one file and opened another. I glanced at Jeremy, who had been appreciatively observing Charles' earnest desire to appear professional.

"Go ahead," Jeremy said gently to him. "This is very good."

Both Charles and Honorine beamed with pride. "As to Honorine's ancestor, Armand, he was implicated in this plot against the king by a rival tapestry-maker, who accused Armand of procuring the poison for Lunaire during his frequent trips to Grasse," Charles reported.

"That tracks with what Venetia told us," I said to Honorine.

Charles continued, "Armand was in fact arrested in Grasse. But the king, who had already confiscated much of Lunaire's treasures (as well as hiring his gardener and chef), must have greatly admired Armand's tapestries, because he decreed that Armand's life be spared, and he was placed in house arrest, where, guild records show, the king had Armand supervise the training of apprentice *tapissiers*."

"Armand never left the house again," Honorine interjected, wide-eyed, as if she could never imagine surviving such a punishment.

"The apprentices were the only visitors that Armand could have, and he was heavily guarded at all times whenever he was in the company of others. Armand did manage to get permission to complete his wedding tapestry for his daughter, " Charles noted. "That is clear from Armand's ledger of expenses. He died shortly after finishing his daughter's tapestry. But, whether a patron or debt collector got his hands on it, we cannot say for sure. Apparently, as you know, someone must have taken the tapestry for himself, for it never reached Armand's daughter, and vanished into private collections, until it resurfaced at auction and Venetia got it."

"I wonder if the king himself took it?" I said.

"Who can say?" Charles answered. "Anything is possible, although I would think that if the king got it, somehow it would have shown up in the tally of royal possessions. I would wager that one of Armand's suppliers—say, a cloth merchant—took it for himself." Charles sat back in his chair, closing his file with a flourish.

"Well done," Jeremy said, which apparently was exactly what Charles wanted to hear, because he smiled happily for a moment, then lifted his chin and tried to play it cool.

"*Oui, merci beaucoup*, Charles," Honorine said.

Charles looked at his rather impressive steel watch. "I must go," he said, rising. "I hope this helps."

"I will see you out," Honorine said, following him. When he was gone, Honorine returned to the library and said to us, "You must stay to lunch as my guests."

It never occurred to me to wonder if Honorine had consulted her mother before inviting us to dine with her parents. Leonora seemed wary of our presence, but interested. Very politely and conversationally over the soup, she asked, "Anything new on the tapestry?"

Honorine answered before I could. "You bet!" she said enthusiastically, with a defiant gleam in her eye. "It turns out that one of our *vénérable* ancestors got into serious trouble with the law! Charles says that Armand the *tapissier* was accused of procuring poison from Rinaldo the *parfumeur*, and giving it to a nobleman named Jean Lunaire, who conspired to kill the Sun King!"

Leonora gasped, and all the soup spoons stopped.

"Honorine," Leonora said severely, "do you mean to say that Charles has gone home to his family to tell them that our ancestor was a traitor to France?"

Aw, geez, I thought, looking in consternation at Jeremy. Of course, a compliant son like Charles wouldn't be able to resist blabbing to his parents about Honorine's family's possible "criminal" past. It had happened ages ago, but clearly Leonora didn't like the idea of potential in-laws and business partners having anything at all to hold over her head, such as the disgrace of a treasonable ancestor.

"Why not, if it's the truth?" Honorine declared recklessly. I now suspected that she might be using this situation to blow her chances of marrying Charles sky-high, regardless of whether it meant she'd kill the merger deal as well.

Leonora was absolutely livid. "Honorine!" she said sharply, in a tone that even scared me. She waited for the serving woman who'd come out of the kitchen to collect the plates on a tray. Sensing that there was something troublesome hanging in the air, the woman hurriedly did her work, then retreated into the kitchen. Jeremy, watchful of it all, appeared as if he were weighing whether his intervention would do more harm than good.

Honorine had blushed beet red, and put her head down, but said nothing.

Leonora turned to me now, looking more than a little accusatory. "This has gone much too far!" she proclaimed severely, and I felt my own face go flushed and hot. "It is bad enough that the tapestry was stolen—a family heirloom which cannot be replaced, and which has somehow managed to survive all these centuries, until *now*," she said rather pointedly. "But then to dredge up old gossip and baseless scandals, which can only cast mud on Philippe's ancestors and good name! Well, it simply cannot continue. No, this digging must stop immediately."

I could see what she meant; their tapestry had survived kings, a revolution, Napoleon, two world wars—but not the wedding of their luckless American relative, Penny Nichols. I felt terrible, and I recalled my father's warning about how formidable Leonora could be. I'd never seen her really angry before. Phew, it was tough, being under that glare. I felt as if I'd been scalded with hot coffee, and, like a meek little mouse, I wanted only to disappear into a crack in the woodwork.

"*Arrete!*" came a strong male voice. It was Philippe, who'd been listening in silence all along. "*Au contraire*," he told his wife, "I believe the digging has only now just begun."

She gazed at him in astonishment. "You and Honorine are both willing to destroy the future of this family!" she cried.

"*Non*," he said in a soothing tone, but one that was filled with calm authority. "I believe that I, too, know part of the story, and I will give you my little piece of the puzzle. It was told to me as a boy, so it seemed like a fairy tale, and I thought nothing of it until now."

Honorine looked vastly relieved. "Please tell us, Papa," she cried.

"It is only this: Armand was in Grasse when he was arrested, because he'd come to see his daughter Eleanore. She had been staying down here for months, with her future in-laws, who lived in the old town of Grasse," Philippe explained. "You see, Eleanore's mother had died long ago, when the girl was only a baby, and so the young bride needed her mother-in-law's help to prepare for the wedding. Eleanore spent many months here, busy decorating and furnishing her new house, which the groom's father, Rinaldo the *gantier parfumeur*, built for the newlyweds. Rinaldo's son, Edouard, was working with him as a glove-maker, and would eventually inherit the business. The newlyweds' house stood at the edge of the flower fields."

"Where the gazebo is now," I said, recalling our visit there. I thought of the house in the lower corner of the tapestry, whose images were suddenly coming alive for me in a totally new way, as if Philippe himself was spinning out the story, like some enchanted weaver in a Greek myth.

"Now, here is something else you do not know," Philippe continued. "Armand's visit was very important because he was supposed to bring his daughter's dowry to Grasse. He wrote this in a letter to Eleanore, which *my* mother claims to have seen when she was a girl, although she said she did not know what became of it.

"In his letter, Armand told his daughter that he was owed a great deal of money and intended to collect it, so that he would have a sizeable dowry for her. He assured Eleanore that he would bring it before the wedding. He did not specify how much. But the king's soldiers arrested him on the road just as he reached the flower fields, before he could see his daughter—and she never saw him again. We always assumed that the soldiers took the dowry money away from him; we even wondered if he'd bartered for his life with it, somehow, so that he could continue to live in exile."

I looked at Jeremy, and he looked at me. We both knew what the other was thinking.

"It's possible," Jeremy said cautiously, "that this is all starting to add up."

Honorine looked baffled. "What do you mean?"

"We now know that Armand intended to collect on a debt," I began. "And we also know that Lunaire was his patron. Plus, Charles told us that Lunaire didn't pay his bills, and therefore owed Armand money." I paused. I figured I'd have to tread carefully here, considering Leonora's previous outburst. I glanced pleadingly at Jeremy, and he heroically allowed me to pass the baton to him.

"Suppose," Jeremy said, "that Armand went to Lunaire to demand payment for the tapestries he'd made for him. Like most men dodging their creditors, Lunaire probably claimed that he was short of funds, and would pay them later, as soon as he was able. But then, perhaps, Armand heard of this great big birthday bash that Lunaire was throwing for himself, sparing absolutely no expense."

"Bash?" Leonora repeated, sounding perplexed.

"Oh, *Maman*!" Honorine cried in exasperation. "He means a party!"

"A coin curator told us about a wild party at Lunaire's estate, where he had a goldsmith create golden coins as gambling chips," Jeremy continued. "There was an accident and a fire broke out, disrupting the games, and the entire pot of chips vanished. That much we know as fact. Now, however, Armand's letter raises a rather intriguing possibility."

I had been watching my French relatives' faces, and it was quite clear that they had not heard of the Lunaire gold. Jeremy looked at me questioningly, as if to ask if I wanted him to pursue this line with my relatives. Oncle Philippe, seeing this exchange, said encouragingly, "What do you think happened at this party, *chère* Penny?"

"Well, just suppose," I responded, practically seeing the scene unfurling in front of my very eyes, "that Armand showed up the night of the big party, and was even more stunned by all the extravagance he saw all around him. Food, fireworks, champagne flowing, reckless gambling. It must have infuriated him. Maybe he tried to have it out with Lunaire, who might have arrogantly told him to go away and come back another day. Or maybe Lunaire even refused to see him; maybe Armand had to talk to a secretary or something, to no avail.

"But then, the fireworks went astray, creating total pandemonium, with everyone running this way and that, servants trying to put out the fire, guests fleeing for their lives. And Armand starts to run, too . . . but then, he sees the table of gambling chips, just lying there."

I was picturing a table heaped with the Lunaire gold, and a gloved hand reaching out, sweeping it all into a sack. I got goosebumps, just imagining the smoky, chaotic scene. And if Armand took the gold gambling chips as payment for all the tapestries he'd made for Lunaire, who could blame him?

Honorine was practically jumping out of her seat now. "And then," she cried, "Armand takes the gold, saying to himself, 'If Lunaire won't pay what he owes me, then I shall do it for him!' And he grabs it, and runs away. That must be what he meant when he said he'd soon arrive with a dowry of the money owed to him!"

Leonora looked shocked, unbelieving, and still indignant. "Why is it that no matter what fanciful story anyone comes up with, it always ends with your ancestor being a thief?" she demanded.

"Not a thief, exactly," Philippe chuckled, as if this were a sort of parlor game, speculating about one's forebears. "But, perhaps, a man who had a sense of justice. Perhaps he did not intend to run away, not at first. He may have taken the gold to hold, to force Lunaire to pay his bills."

"But later," I suggested, "when he heard of the trouble that Lunaire had gotten himself into, and while the soldiers were busy digging up Lunaire's estate outside Paris, maybe Armand panicked and escaped to Grasse." Everyone fell silent for a moment, pondering this. It was Honorine who spoke first.

"Then, it's gone?" she said, crestfallen. "The soldiers took the dowry?"

"On the other hand," said Jeremy, "Maybe not. It raises quite another interesting theory." Everyone turned to him attentively.

"Suppose that, when the soldiers caught up with Armand on the road, he hadn't just arrived in Grasse? What if he'd found out, moments earlier, that the soldiers were in town looking for him, so he hurriedly hid his treasure somewhere? If so, he could have been on his way to his daughter's house to tell her, *after* he'd done the deed."

"So when the soldiers found him, he didn't have the gold on him! That would mean," I said, "it's been here somewhere, right under everyone's noses, for years and years . . . maybe even . . . in those flower fields!"

I immediately thought of the tapestry, with its dramatic sequences laid out like a movie storyboard. Now, in my mind, it seemed as if each image was passing over the light of a film projector, becoming illuminated and springing to life like a moving picture. And at this moment, I was seeing a close-up—of that circlet with Lunaire's insignia.

"Didn't Charles say that Armand got permission to *complete* his daughter's wedding tapestry while he was under house arrest?" Jeremy was saying. "And since Armand wasn't allowed to receive visitors or even letters . . . well, the only way he could possibly communicate with his daughter to tell her where he'd hidden her dowry was . . ."

"The tapestry," I squeaked.

"Which we no longer have," Leonora said meaningfully.

"Absent the tapestry, Penny's photos are all we have to go on," Jeremy remarked.

"Those 'J.L.' initials on the tapestry have always bothered me," I exclaimed. "I mean, why would Armand put his patron's insignia on a tapestry that was never intended for Lunaire? It *has* to be about the gold."

Honorine looked astonished. "What, you mean that old tapestry could be a treasure map . . . of the flower fields?"

"It's a long shot," Jeremy cautioned. "But, perhaps, one worth checking out."

Now it really was deadly quiet, as Philippe and Leonora exchanged glances of alarm and distress, which I did not comprehend at first. "But David is out there right now!" cried Leonora. "He is about to make a deal, to sell the fields to a real-estate developer who wants to make condominiums . . ."

"Holy cow, you gotta stop him!" I cried involuntarily.

"Easy, girl," Jeremy cautioned. "If we're wrong and you queer this deal . . ."

"Gee whiz, you can always find people who want to build condos!" I cried. "But how often do you get a chance to . . ." I didn't have to complete that sentence. Everyone was thinking the same thing.

Philippe nodded to Honorine. Leonora exclaimed, "Honorine, *vite!* Get David on the phone and tell him to wait!" The three of them jumped up and went into the library to make the call.

"You do realize," Jeremy said to me in a low tone, under all the excitement, "that we can't exactly go there and dig up the entire field, to figure out if they're sitting on a cache of Lunaire gold."

"No, we certainly can't destroy those priceless flowers—they've been growing for centuries to make some of the world's finest perfume," I agreed. "How are we ever going to figure out where Armand hid them?"

Chapter Thirty-four

David was supremely irritated by the wild phone call he got from Honorine, telling him to delay the deal that he'd been working on for nearly a year, which would have netted him a tidy sum. His wife Auguste was none too happy about it, either. But Philippe serenely believed that his illustrious American relative (alias, moi) would come up with the goods, and, after all, this was basically what Leonora had been hoping for all along, one way or another. So they said they'd hold off the deal . . .

"But hurry!" Honorine advised me.

Jeremy and I went back to the villa, to pore over my photographic jigsaw puzzle of the tapestry. It still had plenty of missing pieces, but I hoped to find some clue we'd overlooked. We spread them out, end to end, across the dining room table, and we kept scrutinizing them until I was bug-eyed.

"I knew it, I just knew that Armand was trying to tell his daughter something," I muttered.

"I wonder," Jeremy mused, "if Armand realized that he was about to be implicated in the poisoning plot. Perhaps not. Possibly he just knew he had to hide the gold for safekeeping. I imagine he believed that his hiding place would be temporary. And, when the soldiers came to arrest him, I'll bet he thought it was simply for the theft of the gold. Imagine his surprise to learn of the more serious charge against him, for conspiracy! Next thing he knew, he was stuck in his house up there around Paris."

"Yeah, that must have been so frustrating, being locked up far away from here, knowing that the gold was just sitting out in the fields," I agreed. "Until he thought of using the existing wedding tapestry to communicate. He'd have to be clever, and come up with a coded message that his daughter could figure out, all mixed in there with his nice wedding stories about marriage. But it would be tricky business, because he wouldn't want anyone else to decode the clues."

"Keep in mind that this is only a theory," Jeremy cautioned.

"Phooey," I said stoutly. I got up from my chair, and went scampering over to a closet. I came back dragging a funny old machine of mine, left over from my earlier research days. Jeremy stared at it.

"What the bloody hell is that?" he demanded, looking bemused.

"Just clear away those lamps from that wall, my good man," I said, pointing. "I need a nice, big drive-in-movie-sized empty space. This is how we researchers project photographs to make them bigger than life. Which is exactly what we need right now."

"Ah," he said. "Foolish of me to forget that I am in the hands of a pro."

We projected some images, examining their enlarged details. The entire house got so quiet that we could hear Guy's clock in the nearby drawing room, ticking away the minutes so audibly that Jeremy muttered, "I can't think straight with that damned thing going like a metronome in my skull."

"Focus, willya? This would be a lot easier if we had that tapestry," I groused. "It certainly gives Drake the advantage. He's probably staring at it right now, trying to beat us to it."

"Chances are, he doesn't know where the fields are," Jeremy reminded me. "So, focus yourself. I do think theses pieces are going to add up to something."

I kept staring, and zooming in, then stepping back and trying to get some perspective. There was so much to look at it, and it was all too easy to get lost in all the images. But finally, I saw something I'd barely noticed before.

"Hey," I said, peering at the enlarged photo of the central, bottom section of the tapestry. "Look at that little cartouche, right in the middle of the lower border."

"What's a cartouche?" Jeremy asked, intrigued.

I pointed to a small ornate rectangle. It resembled a miniature work of needlepoint on a cream-colored fabric, that was "mounted" in a brown frame. The "frame" was woven to look as if it was made of decorative ribbons that were tied into two bows, one at the top, and one at the bottom. This frame overlapped beyond the inside edge of the border, right into the body of the tapestry.

Inside the frame was embroided, elegant lettering that appeared to be a Latin proverb, written in black and gold, with violet flowers and silver-green leaves twining around its letters like a vine.

To me, the whole thing was like a tiny, fancy, ancient version of a framed "Home Sweet Home" or "Bless This House" that a lady might stitch and then frame and hang in her living room. This little framed picture in the border was flanked on each side by white swans and cupidlike figures known as putti. These decorations also overlapped beyond the border's edge, into the main body of the tapestry.

I peered closer to scrutinize the Latin lettering. Usually such inscriptions are archaic admonitions on the order of *A stitch in time saves nine* or *Gather ye rosebuds while ye may*. The sort of advice that makes you feel somewhat doomed anyway. I carefully copied down the Latin words that were inside the cartouche. Here is what it said:

BIBE PROFUNDE EX CISTERNA VITAE,
COLE CONJUGALEM UXOREM.

"You studied classics, didn't you?" I asked, pointing.

Jeremy squinted at it, then re-copied it on another piece of paper. "Hmmm. Hmm. That's the verb 'drink', I think . . . hmm . . . don't know what this word is, but . . . it's about a 'wife' . . ." He glanced up at me. "Have a drink with your wife?" he suggested facetiously.

"Surely you can do better than that, Mister," I said.

"Wish I had my old Latin schoolbook around," he muttered. "Wait a minute." He went over to the computer and did some rapid searching and clacking. Every now and then he'd stop and jot down a few words on his paper. Finally he came sauntering over to me, and slapped down his translation on the table. It said:

Drink deep from the well of life,
And treasure a faithful wife.

"I made it rhyme," Jeremy said modestly. "If I had been literal about it, that last line would have been on the order of, 'A faithful wife be your treasure'."

"That figures," I said, temporarily distracted. "Just once I'd like to see a work of art exhorting *men* to be faithful."

"Let's concentrate. Look up here, in the main part of the tapestry. On the bedspread where the flower fields are," Jeremy said, pointing to one of the oval insets on the left. "There's a water-well, see?"

I peered at it. Yes indeed, it was the scenario with the young man and woman carrying a bucket of water to the well, like an elegant Jack and Jill.

"You get it?" Jeremy said triumphantly. "*Drink deep from the well of life.* With so little time to act, Armand may have just thrown his treasure down that old well—"

"Of course!" I cried. "Armand could be saying, 'Drink deep and find the *treasure* of your faithful wife's dowry.' It makes sense, because a well is the perfect place to chuck your valuables, if you've got the king's soldiers on your trail, and no time to spare! Why, they used to do that back home in Connecticut, you know; the American colonists would throw the family silver and jewels down the well so the rotten Redcoats wouldn't be able to steal it." I paused. "Whoops," I said. "My apologies, but you must admit you Brits behaved very badly indeed in our Revolution."

"On the contrary," Jeremy said. "We English, in the end, simply decided to let you rowdy colonists go free, because Americans are clearly a far too troublesome lot."

"While we are arguing about history," I suggested, "Parker Drake is out there stealing Honorine's dowry. Let's go find out if there really is an old well in those fields!"

"I think we ought to have Monsieur Felix with us," said Jeremy, "so he can watch out for trouble and make sure we're not followed."

When Jeremy called him, Monsieur Felix quickly cautioned against saying anything on the telephone, just in case. He drove over, but met up with us out on the road, and he followed us at a slight distance. As we reached the turnoff for Mougins, he flashed his lights to signal that we weren't being followed, and it was okay to proceed.

We drove on to the château, with Felix still not far behind us. Jeremy warned me, "If this well really existed, it would have been centuries ago, so remember to tell Leonora that it's just a guess on our part, nothing definite."

I tried to be mindful of his caveat, but when Honorine came to the door, I figured there was no time to waste on social niceties. So I blurted out, "Honorine, we've got to see if there's an old water well out in the flower fields in Grasse. Armand may have hidden his treasure in it!"

She let us in, and brought us to see Philippe and David in the library. They looked mildly surprised to have us pop in on them unexpectedly, even though we were working on their case. Honorine spoke to them in rapid-fire French, to which they responded just as quickly, and I couldn't keep up. There was a long pause as she listened to them; then Philippe glanced up and realized that I couldn't make out his answer, so he translated, with an amused gleam in his eye.

"Yes, there was an old well, out in the fields," he said slowly. "I remember playing there, and stumbling on it when I was a boy. My governess scolded me for going too close to it, and nearly falling in; so, after that, it was boarded up."

He turned to David, and said, "Get the map of the fields, and I will show you. Then, we go and dig for buried treasure, *oui*?"

Chapter Thirty-five

When we arrived at the flower fields in Grasse, it was late afternoon, and most of the field workers had gone home. David rounded up a few of the remaining men, and, without explanation, he told them we needed to do some work on an old well. They armed themselves with shovels, spades and other equipment, then followed David, Jeremy, Honorine and me, with Philippe leading the way. Monsieur Felix remained by the gate, so he could keep an eye out for any unwanted newcomers.

Philippe headed down the main path, then crossed the fields with a purposeful stride, as if, even at his age, the boyhood memory of discovering the old well was seared into his mind. The earth was still warm from the day's sunbath, and the plants still plump from their irrigation in a land where water—and soil—is a precious commodity. The heady, mingled floral and herbal fragrances were mesmerizing; in particular, the lavender was so soothing that the act of marching across it became almost hypnotic.

As we veered off toward the western side of the field, Philippe came to an abrupt halt, and pointed at an area which received partial shade from ancient nearby trees. The rows of plantings simply ran right by and around the area, as if detouring around a boulder.

I gazed at where Philippe was gesturing and I could see a low, circular stone wall, topped by splintered wooden planks. As we came closer, I realized that the wall was actually an extension of the well itself, the very top of the stone cylinder. Some of the wood planks that covered it appeared to have fallen into the well. The earth directly around the well seemed to be turned over, raked up, occasionally clumped in mounds here and there; and some of the plantings nearby were a bit flattened, as if they'd been stepped on or rolled over by a vehicle.

"Has this ground been disturbed?" I asked.

Philippe shrugged. "Perhaps. But that is not unusual. Workers come and go here, and sometimes the earth is dug for use elsewhere."

"What about the planks?" Jeremy asked. "Have they been broken into?"

David examined them, then said, "Hard to say. They could just as well have deteriorated and fallen in on their own."

Under his direction, the workmen began to tear aside the remaining planks. Philippe's men assessed the well to be about thirty-two inches across and about twelve feet deep. One of the men, wearing a helmet with a light on its front, tossed in a rope ladder and hooked it over the top, then began to lower himself into the well, all the way down to the bottom.

"These old wells were originally dug by hand," Philippe told us, peering in.

"Is there any water still in there?" Jeremy asked, fascinated.

The man in the well said something in French that I couldn't hear. Philippe smiled and said, "He says there are tree roots pushing into it, but it's pretty much intact. A little water, yes, but not much."

One of the other workers handed a shovel to the fellow inside the well, who dug and explored for a while, while the rest of us waited to hear any news. The sound of his spade echoed back up to us. *Chip, chip, chip.* Honorine and I spread out a blanket that Leonora had given us, and we sat there, waiting. Philippe pulled a pipe out of his pocket, and stood apart from us, smoking thoughtfully, gazing out across the fields.

Jeremy was seeing these fields for the first time, so he went hiking around, pausing every now and then to gaze about, taking it all in. David, obviously a city boy at heart, paced along the path restlessly, then pulled out his mobile phone for messages, sending a few.

"My brother is a desk man, who must fill every moment with activity," Honorine murmured while watching him, not without affection. "How often I have heard him say that it bores him to do 'nothing'. Whereas Papa says 'doing nothing is one of life's sweetest joys'."

I glanced back at Philippe, who had closed his eyes and turned his face to the sun, like a flower.

"The way he does it," I said, "it's not 'nothing'."

Finally, the man in the well stopped digging. He called up to the other men, but he couldn't have said anything exciting, because nobody summoned David back. The guy only handed the shovel to his coworkers, and then climbed out, looking a little muddy. Philippe walked toward him, asking him something in French. The man shook his head. Then I heard him say a word I recognized.

"*Rien*," he said, shrugging. "*Rien.*"

"Nothing?" I said in huge disappointment. "At all?"

"What if it was buried *around* the well, not in it?" Philippe suggested to us. So, the other workers, under Philippe's orders, began to dig around the well's immediate circumference. Honorine and I eventually had to move to get out of their way as they dug closer.

But when they were done with this, the answer was the same. "*Rien.*"

They had made lots of holes. Everyone was very careful, but it was simply inevitable that we had uprooted a number of precious plantings. It did not escape my notice that David, who'd come back to survey and inspect the damage, was now glowering at Jeremy and me with undisguised disapproval. Jeremy pointedly ignored him, but I could feel myself blushing apologetically.

I turned my attention to some of the sketches and pictures which I'd brought with me. The tapestry borders and cartouche were decorated with a flower pattern that was very pretty—a bright, violet-colored bloom comprised of four separate petals, that were as delicate-looking as those of a sweet pea. The leaves, which looked like oval pods, were a silvery green color.

"What is that?" Honorine asked, peering over my shoulder.

"Moonwort," I said. "It was all over the tapestry. I looked it up before we came here. It was considered a 'magic herb' that protects against evil spirits, and enhances memory, so that a person can 'recover that which is lost'."

Glancing meaningfully at Jeremy, I added, "Moonwort also stands for honesty, integrity . . . and money and prosperity. It's known by lots of other names, too: silver bloom, silver dollar, 'two-pennies-in-a-purse' . . . and penny-flower."

Jeremy said affectionately, "Penny-flower? So you have a flower named after you, for honesty and prosperity. Not bad."

"Well, I was just thinking," I said. "*Moon*wort. The Latin name for it in the flower books is *Lunaria annua*. See? Like Lunaire. If we found it growing here, that might mean something."

"You won't find any moonwort here," David said crossly. "It's not the sort of thing we'd ever grow for perfume!"

"Not ever?" I persisted. "Even in Armand's time?" But by now even the kindly Philippe shook his head and was looking a bit exasperated. After all, we'd dug up his expensive flowers, and for what?

I simply couldn't believe it. Had the path gone cold? Was the whole thing a wild figment of my fevered imagination, while I was lost in the cryptic world of the tapestry? Its images surely would have been instantly recognizable metaphors to the people of its day, but perhaps the meanings were now lost forever to a modern world that has long forgotten what such symbols once meant.

Jeremy was thinking along more practical and possibly diabolical lines. "It's possible that Armand hid his treasure here. But I wonder if, centuries ago, somebody else got here first, and dug it up!"

"Ah! Anything is possible," Philippe agreed.

Disappointed, we all tromped back across the fields to the gate by the side of the road, where Monsieur Felix was calmly waiting for us. Jeremy had a brief chat with him; then, everyone headed for home—Honorine and her family to Mougins, and Jeremy and I to Antibes.

It was only when we were pulling into the driveway of our villa that Jeremy told me another possibility he'd been considering in private. "Someone may have gotten there first, all right," he said darkly, "but maybe not so many centuries ago. Suppose it was Parker Drake who somehow figured it out and beat us to it?"

I said worriedly, "The ground around the well *was* a bit disturbed, and it may or may not have been field workers who did that."

"We'll know soon enough," Jeremy said ruefully. "If Drake has found it, he won't be able to resist blowing his trumpet and letting the whole world know. So, all we can do is proceed as if he hasn't found the gold," he concluded. "And keep moving full speed ahead, to get there first."

Chapter Thirty-six

When we entered the villa, we were both so exhausted that we went right to bed, and slept the deep slumber of little kids who've been outdoors playing—or digging—all day. The next morning, I awoke thoroughly refreshed, and ready to do battle again. Jeremy was sleeping soundly, so I crept downstairs, made coffee and then went to take another look at the photographs still spread out on the dining table.

Later, when Jeremy came searching for me, I was still peering through the magnifier, examining two photographs in particular, very closely. "What's up?" he asked. "Find anything?"

"Take a look," I said, passing the magnifier to him. "Something doesn't match up here."

"What do you mean?" Jeremy asked, peering at it.

"This is the photo we saw yesterday, the one of the cartouche, in the bottom border of the tapestry," I told him.

"The cartouche," Jeremy muttered. "Oh, right, that tiny framed picture with the Latin on it," he said, staring at it.

"Notice how most of the cartouche sits inside the lower border," I said. "But, the little bow-ties at the top of the picture frame overlap into the main body of the tapestry."

"Right," Jeremy said, staring at it. "The top loops of the bows. So?"

"And the stuff on either side of the cartouche—the head of the swan, and the wings of the cupids—they also overlap beyond the border, into the main part, too, right?" I continued.

"Yes," he replied.

"Okay," I said excitedly. "Now, take a look at *this* photo of the *top* border of the tapestry." I slid the other photo over to him, and he moved the magnifier there. "See where the inside line of the border meets the top section of the main body of the tapestry?"

"Yeah?"

"What's the first thing you see, beneath the top border?" I demanded.

"Looks like some curlicues, and some bunches of white grapes, and maybe some white feathers," Jeremy reported, squinting hard now.

"But—I think all that stuff is actually the bottom edging of another cartouche!" I said triumphantly. "See? What you describe as 'curlicues' could be part of a bow-tie on a cartouche. And, the white feathers could be swans' wings. And as for the 'white grapes', why, those aren't grapes at all, those could very well be the little toes of the cupids."

"Let me see yesterday's picture of the bottom cartouche again," Jeremy said, sounding excited. I shoved it back to him. He scrutinized it, then went back and forth between the two photos. "You know, you're right," he said slowly. "It's as if there was once a matching cartouche on the top border of the tapestry, but most of it got chopped off, leaving only the bottom part of it—these snippets that overlapped into the main body of the tapestry." He looked up at me now. "But where's the rest of it? Maybe Armand started out making a matching cartouche for the top, then, what, he changed his mind?"

"Or," I said triumphantly, "he *did* put a matching cartouche on the top border. But this isn't the *original* top border!" I waited a moment for the significance of this to sink in. Then I said, "Suppose *somebody replaced the original top border with a new one*?"

Jeremy looked up at me and said nothing, at first. Then, when he spoke, it was in a low, quiet tone—because Jeremy is the exact opposite of me, and when he's on the scent of something important, he doesn't jump up and down about it, he just gets very, very quiet.

"Can they do that?" he said. "Can they replace one border with another?"

"Sure," I said. "There were weavers who specialized in only making borders. Because some tapestry patterns, like the ones based on Greek myths or Bible stories, were used again and again, sold to different clients, only with customized borders. You know, you could have your own family crest or coat of arms put onto the borders of a tapestry, to make it more personalized. Besides, borders sometimes wear out, from hanging on nails and poles, with the whole weight of the tapestry pulling on them. They can be repaired . . . or sometimes, replaced."

"So, if the top border, which is now on the tapestry, is merely a replacement," Jeremy said, "then maybe the guy who made the new border didn't bother to duplicate all of the original, complicated artwork from the old one?"

"Exactly," I said. "From what I can see in these photos, the current top border is a lot simpler—and probably cheaper—than the bottom one. I don't see any gilt, for instance, and there's plenty of gilt on the bottom. In fact, the existing top border bears more resemblance to the *side* borders than the bottom one."

"Couldn't Armand just have run out of the good thread?" Jeremy asked. "He was in a bit of a hurry, you know."

"I don't believe it," I said. "This is a wedding tapestry. Why would he spoil it at the very top, with chopped-off pictures and all?"

"Well, now you say so, I must admit it does look as if there's something amuck with the top of this thing," Jeremy agreed.

"Which might indicate that the replacement border was made in a totally different workshop," I said excitedly. "Possibly even in a completely different time period! After all, the tapestry was missing for centuries. Who knows which owners might have done the deed, all those years before—"

I stopped. Then I said briskly, "Well. I'd say it's time we paid another little call on Venetia."

"It's a long way to go if she's not home," Jeremy warned. "What if she's, say, on vacation?"

"Honorine says she never goes away," I said. "The element of surprise is essential. I want to look her in the eye when we ask her. How soon can we get to Paris?"

Part Nine

Chapter Thirty-seven

When we rang the buzzer, Venetia's husky voice cried, "Come in, Justine!" and she buzzed us in.

"I'll bet Justine is one of her ballet students," I whispered to Jeremy. I felt a trifle guilty, but not enough to resist taking advantage of the situation, and we sneaked right in.

The maid must have been out doing the day's marketing, because Venetia herself came to the door, leaning on a straight cane like an old-fashioned ballet master. She glanced up expectantly, then saw who it was, and her face changed. She looked fearful, apprehensive, but not angry.

"I am expecting a student at any minute," she said defensively. "You really should have called ahead. I will be happy to see you, but some other time . . ."

I began talking in halting French. She listened attentively, not, I think, because of what I was saying, but more out of the fascinated horror of listening to French being spoken by someone with an Anglo-American accent and cadence. Nevertheless, I ploughed on, having composed this little speech on the way over. Basically, the gist of what I said was, "I am so sorry about the theft of the tapestry. I feel responsible, and wish to make amends. We think we may have some hope of recovering the tapestry, but we really need your help."

"Oh, *mon dieu!*" she cried, with theatrically exaggerated despair. "Haven't I done enough, putting up with that awful big ape of a man you sent to investigate me, asking his policeman questions, as if it were I who were the thief? Believe me, I told him everything I know. If it's gone, it's gone, there's nothing more I can say or do to bring it back."

"If you answer our questions, there won't be any need for Monsieur Felix to come back and bother you," Jeremy said, in that lawyerlike way that is ostensibly reassuring but is also is a threat.

Venetia eyed him cunningly, then sighed, and allowed us to follow her into the back room, where she enthroned herself again on her satin daybed. She closed her eyes as if prepared to endure the unendurable. "Make it quick," she advised.

"We need to know," I said simply, "if the tapestry was ever changed or remade."

Jeremy was watching her carefully. She opened her eyes slowly, and said, as if stalling for time, "What do you mean? Can I be expected to know its entire history, when I only owned it a short time?"

I laid out a few photos on the low table in front of her. "You see," I said helpfully, "here are pictures of the tapestry's border when it hung in Oncle Philippe's house. Take a good look, especially at the top border. I hope that these pictures will help you to remember, because we think it's important."

At first, she almost refused to look at the photos. She waved her hand and said airily, "It was so long ago. What possible difference can it make now?"

"Did you change the border?" I asked eagerly. Venetia glanced at Jeremy, perhaps mindful of his warning. She studied me carefully, then made an elaborate ritual of reaching for her eyeglass case, and adjusting her reading glasses, and peering at each photo, one by one. She was silent the whole time, and there was a long pause when, at last, she had examined each one. Then she looked up at me imploringly. I gave her my most encouraging, sympathetic smile.

"Ah," she said finally; then she coughed, somewhat guiltily. "Now that you mention it . . . I suppose . . . yes . . . I would say . . . come to think of it . . . of course, it was so very long ago . . ."

Her voice trailed off. I tried not to pounce. "There *was* a different border, then?" I asked. She nodded. "Why was it changed?" I persisted.

"Oh, I suppose we wanted to tidy it up for Philippe and Leonora's wedding," Venetia said vaguely, hoping she could get away with only that much. "It was worn out and in need of repair."

"But it wasn't just repaired, it was replaced, right?" Jeremy asked. She nodded.

It was obvious to all and sundry that Venetia was hedging. But why? On a hunch, I asked, "Did something unusual happen to the tapestry?" I held my breath, knowing that, at any moment, her door buzzer might ring again, and if the student came up, then Venetia would seize on the distraction; and this opportunity for a confession might never come again.

Venetia looked at Jeremy, embarrassed. Then she stuck that pointy little chin defiantly in the air. "Well, if you must know, I'd caused it some . . . damage."

"What did you to do it?" I asked, fascinated.

"I shot it!" she cried.

"Why did you shoot it?" I asked calmly, as if I were asking why she'd gotten a haircut.

"Well, I didn't do it on purpose!" she exclaimed. "I meant to shoot my husband!"

"Good Lord," Jeremy marvelled.

"I had no intention of killing my new bridegroom," she assured us. "I only wanted to scare him." She looked at me conspiratorially. "Sometimes," she said, "a man has to know that you mean what you say, when you tell him that there are certain things you will not tolerate."

"Another woman?" I guessed.

"Not just any woman," she snorted. "Do you think I would bother over just any other woman? *Mais non*, this little upstart was another ballerina in *my* company! This I could not overlook!"

"When did it happen?" I asked.

"Only a month after our wedding!" Venetia said. "I couldn't stand for it. Would you?"

"Certainly not," I said stoutly. We both looked at Jeremy, as if to say *J'accuse!* to his entire wayward lot of males, from the beginning until the end of time.

"Ah," said Jeremy, not to be outdone. "*Un crime de passion.*"

Venetia shook her head. "No, not quite," she said. "If it were passion, then I *would* have killed him. This was merely a warning. As it was, I simply aimed for the bottle of champagne, which my husband and that *chatte* had been drinking." Even after all these years, she could still picture it, and her eyes flashed with fury at the image of the other female who had dared to trespass.

"As I am by nature a woman of peace," she continued, totally seriously, "I was not accustomed to shooting. So, I shot the tapestry instead. As soon as I touched it, the gun went off three times—*tac-tac-tac!*—before I even realized. Which, as it turns out, made the point very well." She sighed and bowed her head dramatically, as if she'd just confessed to an actual murder.

"Did your husband stop seeing the other woman?" I couldn't resist asking.

"*Absolutement!* But more importantly, my rival believed I was quite mad, and she did not wish to test her luck with me again, nor make a permanent enemy of me," Venetia said, still relishing the successful vanquishing of a professional rival as well as a competitor for her husband's affections.

"Then I'd say you hit the target right in the bull's-eye," I said. She stared for a moment, then burst into an appreciative, deep-throated laughter.

"You women are amazing," Jeremy muttered.

"I think it's amazing that she stayed married to the guy," I said out of the corner of my mouth.

Venetia heard this, but shrugged. "*L'amour*," she said cheerfully. "So, now you know all I can tell you about the tapestry," she added sheepishly. "You can see why I had to replace it quickly, so that there would be no evidence of any 'assault', which my rival could claim I'd attempted. That is why the new border was so much simpler, and less costly. And as I said, the old one was all worn out anyway," she added reasonably. "It was time to replace the *selvage*."

"Is there any record of the tapestry's original border? Paintings, sketches, photographs?" I said.

"*Non, non*," Venetia replied, "nobody, not even the auction house, could come up with any other records, no modello or cartoon, there was nothing, because Armand made it for his daughter, not for a client. Whatever sketches or plans he'd had, he must have destroyed, so that no one could copy it."

Or find the treasure, I thought. Then I added, "I meant, do you have any pictures of your wedding with the tapestry in it?"

She shook her head. "Not of the wedding, because we were married in a church, and we took no pictures of the religious ceremony. Ah, but wait!" she cried, reaching out to grasp my hand in hers, which had those chunky rings, and long nails painted blood-red. "There *was* a replica of the border pattern—painted right into my private wedding car on the *train bleu*!"

"What?!" I nearly shouted.

"Oh, yes," Venetia recalled. "When my husband bought the private train car, it was very luxurious, but the walls were simple and austere; too much like a businessman's wife's idea of luxury—so, so, so very provincial. Therefore, my husband hired my artist friends who had painted all the wonderful stage sets in my ballets! Ah, they made my private car *très, très bon* for my wedding."

The dreaded buzzer now rang, and Justine the ballet student had arrived. Venetia distractedly told her to come up. Then she directed Jeremy to go to the chest of drawers in the corner, and open the middle drawer, and get the red scrapbook—no, not *that* red one, the other one—and bring it to her.

"What about the artists?" I prodded. Venetia explained that her pals at the ballet theatre replicated the motif of the original tapestry border, all along the interior wall moulding of her wedding car on the train. Excited now, she thumbed through the scrapbook that Jeremy had deposited into those red-taloned hands, and she became so engrossed that, when Justine popped in, apologizing profusely for being late, Venetia said, without looking up, "Yes, yes, go do your warm-ups and we'll start soon . . ."

Justine glanced at us, grateful that we'd managed to distract and entertain Venetia so that she hadn't bothered to scold the student for being late. Obediently, Justine trotted off to the far side of the enormous room, deposited her dance sack on the floor against the wall, peeled off her sweat-jacket, and began to do her limbering work at the ballet barre.

"Ah!" Venetia cried suddenly. "I have it!" She plucked out a black-and-white photo that had been stuck in a pocket with other photos. She leaned over to the lamp next to her, and squinted at it. "*Quel dommage!* It is not a very good picture," she admitted. "But at least it is something."

I wanted to snatch it out of her hands, but I waited until she passed it to me.

"Oh, it's the interior of the car!" I said eagerly, leaning under the lamp myself now.

"It's hard to make out, but I assure you the car's marquetry is Art Deco," Venetia said. "And, see the pretty mirrors, made of pale blue glass, etched with opaque figures of dancers in the classical manner, like Isadora Duncan? And see the bed? The very finest linen, embroidered by Spanish nuns."

It was dazzling, but I did not want to be distracted by the other decor. All I cared about now was the strip of painted border on the walls. I stared at the blurry image where, tantalizingly, I could just about make out some swirling, artistic designs on a painted strip running along the moulding atop all four walls of the carriage. But it was too blurry to discern anything like a cartouche or a Latin inscription. It was frustrating, to be so close to seeing the pattern. I wished the photographer had focused on the walls in the background—instead of the bride and groom, damn it.

Jeremy peered at the photo, then said to Venetia, "And what has become of this great wedding railroad car?"

"Ah well, during the second World War, the military took over the railways, too," Venetia said mournfully. "That war was the end of an entire world. Many friends gone, and never again such luxury and beauty like we had in the old days." A more serious, meditative look came over her face. "So, the army commandeered many of the private railcars and refitted them to suit their purposes; and eventually the old cars were retired or destroyed. I lost track of it long ago, I do not know what became of it."

She fell silent again, then glanced at her student while saying to us, "If you need the picture, you may keep it a while. But, when you are done, I would like to have it back."

In the cab returning to the airport, my telephone rang. It was my father.

"*Bonjour, ma petite fille*," he said affectionately, but with a slightly scolding tone. "I know that you are on an important case, but someone has to worry about what we're going to feed your wedding guests, and I could not wait for a girl with stars in her eyes to give me the go-ahead. So, I have decided to take charge." He pronounced that last word as *shcharzge*.

"Thanks, Dad," I said meekly.

"I have, already, several recipes to tell you about," he continued. "So if you have any special requests, now is the time, because soon the menu will be engraved in stone." I smiled, picturing him seated at the kitchen table, poring over all his fabulous recipes from his days as a gourmet chef. Food was sacred to him, and to our French guests, too. So I pondered this very seriously.

"Everything all right?" Jeremy asked, seeing my frown of concentration, as I listened.

"It's my dad. He's planning the wedding food. Anything special you want?"

"Everything he cooks is fantastic to me," Jeremy said fervently; then suggested, "langoustines."

"Dad, Jeremy would like langoustines," I reported. "And, I noticed that in France they have something wonderful called blue lobster. It's not really blue on the plate, of course, but it's so delicate."

"Ah, yes," he said, and I heard him mutter the notes he was jotting down. "Shrimp, lobster . . ."

"Just don't pick any fish that's going extinct or is cruelly fished," I warned, "or my Women4Water gals will be after me."

"Leave it to me," my father said. "I will put the rest of my ideas on ze e-mail to you. You let me know *tout de suite* if there is anything you want to change."

"Thanks, Dad, you're a peach!" I cried.

"Peach, yes, well, that reminds me, dessert," he replied. "The cake. Do you want a layer cake or the *croquembouche*?"

"Oooh," I said, visualizing the French wedding dessert that is made of small, ball-shaped cream-filled puffs or profiteroles, stacked high in a narrow, triangular shape like a little Christmas tree, and all "glued" together by caramel, which crunches delightfully when you eat it; hence the name *croquembouche*, or "crunch in the mouth".

Of course, on the other hand, I've always adored authentic Victorian layer cakes . . .

"I could do some-zing like a combination," my father offered, having guessed at my conundrum. "I'd make a white cake, lots of pretty layers going from larger-to-smaller, in the American wedding style; with buttercream frosting and flowers, and a bit of crushed hazelnut or pistachio. And on top, instead of little bride-and-groom figures, I could put two *croquembouche* ornaments . . . of doves, or swans . . ."

"Yes, swans!" I cried, thinking of Jeremy's research on happy couples. "And, can the frosting flowers be the color of the burgundy roses I'm carrying for my bouquet?"

"*Très bien!* Now you're talking!" Dad chuckled. "What kind of ganache do you want between the cake layers—coffee, raspberry, apricot, chocolate?"

"Can we get some chocolate on this cake?" Jeremy was already asking me. "Dark, of course."

"Dark chocolate ganache filling, Dad," I said. "Honorine is coordinating all the wedding details," I added, "so if you need anything at all, just let her know."

"*Bon*," said my father approvingly, and we rang off.

"Gosh," I said to Jeremy, "we really are getting married, aren't we?"

He kissed me. "Looks that way," he agreed, holding my hand in his.

"Think it'll change us?" I asked with a grin.

"Only for the better," he promised.

"I'm marrying you for your finesse and diplomatic skills, naturally," I responded.

"Naturally," he replied.

"I wish we could solve this case before the wedding," I added fretfully.

Jeremy suggested, "Let's see if Monsieur Felix can use his connections to track down Venetia's private wedding car on the *train bleu*."

He telephoned Monsieur Felix, who apparently had something to tell him, too. Jeremy listened intently without saying a word, until finally he said, "Okay, good idea," and ended the call. He turned to me, saying, "Felix wants to meet with us at the airport. He thinks there's someone skulking around the villa, looking to start tailing us again."

"I left Le Bug at the townhouse in London, just as he suggested," I objected.

"Yes, well, perhaps they've got wise to that," Jeremy said. "But, this is actually good news."

"How d'ya figure?" I asked.

Jeremy said, "It means Drake hasn't found the coins. Yet."

Chapter Thirty-eight

When we arrived at the airport in Nice, I immediately began glancing over my shoulder for signs of the man who was tailing us, whom I christened The Follower. I soon began imagining that everyone I saw was a suspicious candidate. At the terminal, I thought one particular scruffy, bearded guy was especially shady-looking, leaning against a wall beside our gate, in a manner that struck me as creepily aimless—but it soon became obvious that the poor guy was merely waiting for his wife and little kid to come out of the ladies' room.

Meanwhile, Monsieur Felix was lurking nearby, too, in his own spy-versus-spy mode. With his great hulking, bearish frame and long floppy hair, you'd think he'd always be utterly conspicuous. Yet, somehow, even out in broad daylight, he managed to become invisible when he was in public on a job. So, neither Jeremy nor I spotted him, until he stepped out of the shadows, at which point I nearly jumped out of my skin.

"I have a car, come with me," Monsieur Felix said. As he drove away from the airport, he took his own mysterious circular route—just in case—even though he was confident that The Follower hadn't cottoned on to our arrival yet.

"Shall I drive you to the villa?" he inquired. Jeremy told him that we needed to stop by our yacht and speak to the captain, so Monsieur Felix headed toward the harbor in Nice. The summer surge of tourists was evident in the heavy traffic on the Promenade des Anglais and along the pebbled beaches, where throngs of vacationers lay under umbrellas, on chairs and blankets, gazing at the shimmering Mediterranean Sea.

As Monsieur Felix expertly steered his way around clogged traffic lanes, he explained that he believed Drake might be getting antsy over our absence. "Perhaps he is afraid that you have already beaten him to the treasure," he said.

"But we haven't!" I exclaimed in exasperation. "We are no closer to finding that tapestry *or* the coins. And now we can't make a move, for fear that Drake's going to figure out what we're up to."

"Maybe it's *not* so terrible," Jeremy said thoughtfully. "I've got an idea."

"I'm listening," I said.

"Drake will keep looking for the Lunaire gold until somebody finds it," Jeremy said logically. "The only thing that will *stop* him from looking, is if either *a)* he finds it first, or *b)* we do." He grinned. "If he thinks we've snaffled it already, he will stop looking."

"You mean, like, we fake that we found it?" I said, catching on.

"Correct," Jeremy replied. "Now—how would you and I behave if we'd found a pot of gold?"

"We'd be thrilled," I said, picturing it. "We'd probably want to stash it away somewhere safe, while we were contemplating our next move. Some place where nobody else could steal it."

"Right," Jeremy said. "We might, for instance, put it in a bank vault. And then walk around acting miserly and smug."

"That would make you a most sensible couple," Monsieur Felix commented. "Many people in this part of the world would want to flaunt what they had."

"Either way, it would make Drake think he'd lost the contest," Jeremy said. "There would be no need for him to have his man tail us anymore. Which would buy us some more time."

"Unless, of course, in a fit of fury, Drake just decides to, you know, kill us or something," I said.

"Then," said Felix, "I will shoot *him.*" I actually couldn't tell if he was serious or not.

"No, Drake will keep his powder dry," Jeremy said. "I am willing to bet that he'll at least try to meet with us, and pretend he wants to do business, while he's trying to figure out the best way to get his hands on the Lunaire gold. So, all we need now is to put on a little drama, to convince the guy who's tailing us that we've got the goods."

"*Excellent*," Monsieur Felix approved. "I will send you the *Go!* message when the fish bites the hook. Then you will know that it is time to make your move."

"Meanwhile," Jeremy said, "we need your help in tracking down an old railroad car from the *train bleu.*" He repeated what Venetia had told us.

Monsieur Felix listened, then nodded vigorously. "Let me see what I can find."

We'd reached the harbor, a horseshoe-shaped affair with three-story buildings ringing the road around it. The shops and bistros were doing a bustling business, their doors flung open to entice the Riviera's visitors. Here and there an aproned waiter lounged outside, resting against the doorway, surveying the scene. At the harbor, the boats were lined up in neat rows; and out at sea, splendid sailboats and big yachts passed to and fro. Overhead, the seagulls swooped in joyous arcs.

Monsieur Felix parked several yards away from where *Penelope's Dream* was berthed, and he instructed us to wait in the car while he scoped out the harbor for any signs of The Follower. Jeremy and I sat back, gazing out at the small waves splashing against the boats, and the occasional duck bobbing on the water's gentle ups and downs, and the sun brilliantly glittering on all the polished decks, and the sea itself, which looked as if somebody had scattered sapphires into it. We watched idly as other boaters were chummily calling out to one another while hosing their decks and loading supplies.

"Can't wait to put out to sea again," Jeremy murmured, inhaling the salty, invigorating air.

"Let's just go straight to the honeymoon, and worry about the wedding later," I joked in agreement. "Just float away, all by ourselves."

"Know what?" Jeremy said. "There's nobody on earth I'd rather be stranded with on a desert island than you."

"Same here," I agreed. "But, must we get stranded? Let's just find a secret cove to call our own."

"Okay," Jeremy said. "Can we still be primitives? I want to score you a fish with my bare hands."

"Sure," I said, feeling pleasantly lazy already.

Monsieur Felix returned to us now, and he reported that The Follower wasn't hanging around our yacht. "However, that fellow Rollo awaits you there," Monsieur Felix said, nodding toward a man standing on the sidewalk in front of *Penelope's Dream*.

"That figures," Jeremy said. "What could he want now, do you suppose?"

"Well, I told him to check in with me whenever he's back in town," I explained. "I'm trying to keep tabs on him while he's at the Riviera."

Monsieur Felix said he'd go ahead to Antibes to check out our villa, to see if The Follower was lurking there. We got out of the car, and he drove away. As we walked toward the yacht, I said to Jeremy, "I've been thinking about what Monsieur Felix said. You know, about flaunting the gold."

"Yes?" Jeremy inquired.

"Well, if I actually had some of those great old coins, I could make a fantastic charm bracelet."

"Fine," Jeremy said. "When we get our hands on them, you've got dibs."

"I'd need about five of them," I continued, as we approached the yacht. "And since no one in recent memory knows *exactly* what they looked like . . ."

"Ahh!" Jeremy exclaimed, catching on. "We flaunt a couple of fakes, so Drake's man is convinced that we beat him to it. Beautiful. It's about time that we 'up the ante'. But, this will require the help of a good forger."

We were now only a few feet away from Rollo, who always manages to feel right at home on our yacht. He stood on the pavement near the passerelle, leisurely smoking a cigarette.

"Perhaps we should consult our trusty guide to the underworld," Jeremy observed. "Let me deal with the yacht first; then we'll see if Rollo's up for it."

Rollo saw us now. "Ahoy, mates!" he cried. In his light-colored linen suit, expensive leather boat shoes, Panama hat, sunglasses, and casual attitude, he looked as if he were the yacht's owner. I was surprised that he wasn't on board already, lounging in a deck chair, until he explained.

"Your captain wouldn't allow me to smoke on deck," Rollo complained mildly. "Made me walk the gang-plank." He took one last puff, then dropped the cigarette on the ground and stepped it out with the toe of his shoe.

"You *did* instruct me to look you up when I'm back in town," he reminded me, with a sidelong glance at Jeremy.

"Yes, I did," I agreed. "Come on up."

Penelope's Dream was sitting pretty in her berth, getting all spiffed up by the crew for our big honeymoon voyage. The yacht was built in the 1920s, just perfect for old-fashioned romantics like me and Jeremy. Her burnished wood flooring, brass rails, mahogany panelling and cabinetry, and teak steamer chairs with striped cushions, all contributed to her jaunty, cozy aura, as if we could float off not merely to sea, but to an elegant yesteryear. Her furnishings and fittings were old-fashioned and sometimes eccentric, with inviting salons and decks to lounge about in; yet Jeremy and the crew had carefully updated her engine and equipment, so that she could part the waves with the best of them.

There's always a wonderful first moment, when you walk up the passerelle and are momentarily suspended between land and sea. Then a quick hop, and you're on deck. The crew greeted us with their usual formal pleasantries, and after ensuring that we were comfortable, they discreetly left us and went on with their work. Rollo and I ensconced ourselves on the steamer chairs on the aft deck, while Jeremy went up to see Claude in the pilot house at the topmost level, to go over the final details of plotting our honeymoon course.

"I wouldn't say no to a whiskey," Rollo called out to Jeremy, who answered that he'd bring it over on his way back.

"Rollo, how's your mum?" I asked. Dorothy is such a tough, imperious, unpleasant old woman, who sees all other human beings as potential enemies, so it's hard to imagine her ever being human enough to be ailing. But I asked solicitously, mostly for Rollo's sake, and to size up how he was faring.

"She's actually much better, thank you," he said as he sat down comfortably with a grunt. I regaled him with a few details about the wedding, which he listened to in amusement. When Jeremy rejoined us, he looked purposeful and businesslike.

"Rollo, it seems we may need your expertise again," Jeremy said, handing him his glass of whiskey, with the ice clinking gently.

Rollo gave Jeremy an appraising grin. "Oh? Well, I certainly hope this assignment is easier than the last one you put me on, in Corsica."

"Hopefully, yes. We need fake antique coins," Jeremy said. "They'd have to be first-rate, to confound the experts. And, there must be no loose lips to sink ships. Can it be done?"

Rollo raised his eyebrows. "Will these coins be used as, er, counterfeit currency? In other words, are we bucking the law here?"

"No," said Jeremy. "It's to trap a rat."

"Well, that's all right, then," Rollo said. I told him the time period of the Lunaire coins, and I showed him my copy of sketches we'd gotten from the coin gallery curator. Rollo studied them closely, and asked for a few more practical details, but only what he needed to do the job; he never once asked any nosey questions about what we were really up to. I made a duplicate of my sketches for him while he and Jeremy worked out an estimate of the cost of the pieces. Jeremy told him it must be made of real, solid gold, properly "antiqued", and that we needed only a few pieces, rimmed by a setting with a loop on top, so that they could be easily slipped on to any charm bracelet.

"Yes, I see, charm bracelet, right," Rollo said. Thoughtfully he added, "You going to wear this, Penny? Ah, then, you'll be wanting a man who's more on the honest end of the spectrum, not someone who'll double-cross you and start minting some of these for himself. I think I know just the man. French. Artist type, craftsman.

Could use the money. I'll tell him it's for a birthday gift. He'll be fine. And he's fast, very fast. I'll get on it right away."

"Great!" I said enthusiastically.

"Of course, we haven't calculated a fee for yours truly," Rollo noted. He glanced slyly at Jeremy. "This Lunaire gold. Any chance of the real McCoy turning up on this case?"

Jeremy said, "Possibly, but it's quite a long shot."

"Ah," said Rollo with satisfaction. "Well, if so, I wouldn't mind trousering one."

"Even if they did turn up, we'd have to consult the owner," Jeremy said. "But I think he'd be amenable. Can't promise."

"Fine," Rollo said. "In the event of failure, you can buy me dinner at the restaurant of my choosing."

"Deal," Jeremy agreed.

I grinned. Rollo is the sort of man who lounges about indolently for long periods of time, punctuated by sudden, excited bursts of energetic activity. This, I surmised, was why he was prone to gambling. He was easily bored, and needed a high degree of stimulus to get him going. It made him more open to risk than most people. Add that to his love of antiques, and he was what you might call a natural for the occasional odd job for the firm of Nichols & Laidley.

"Have you eaten today?" Jeremy asked him, rather unexpectedly.

Rollo looked surprised, then said appreciatively, "Yes I have, thanks." He began punching a number into his new phone. A moment later he said briefly, "Hullo, Luc? Got a little job for you. Care to talk about it? How long will you be there? Fine, I'm on my way."

All business now, he finished his drink with evident enjoyment, then stood up briskly. "I'd better get a move on," he said, but paused to caution me, "Do be careful, Penny dear. People in this neck of the woods play for high stakes." Then he quickly adopted a lighter attitude, and, tipping his hat, he added, "But I am on BlackBerry if you need me." And with that, he sauntered down the passerelle and headed for his parked car.

Jeremy looked at me suspiciously. "Rollo is 'on BlackBerry'?" he queried. "Since when?"

"Since last time we saw him. I suggested it," I confessed. "To keep an eye on him. He checks it regularly, and he likes to send me funny e-mails."

Jeremy shook his head reproachfully. "One of these days," he predicted, "we'll get an e-mail from him saying, *Took off with your yacht. Must dash. See you whenever.* Just don't say you weren't warned."

His telephone rang. It was Monsieur Felix. Jeremy listened to the brief update, then hung up and told me, "Felix spotted The Follower driving past our villa, but then the guy headed onto the highway back to Monte Carlo. So for now, the coast is clear in Antibes. Felix says he'll let us know when the guy is tailing us again. Now all we need is a little luck."

Chapter Thirty-nine

Rollo came up with the goods quite quickly, just as he'd promised. Nevertheless, we had a fairly nerve-wracking spell of waiting, because The Follower took a brief hiatus. It was like watching for a shark to return to take the bait. Finally, Felix sent us a signal. *Go!* It was time to put our plan into action.

I let Jeremy drive my blue Dragonetta, so I could concentrate on my little starring role in this caper. As we headed for Nice, Jeremy glanced up in the rearview mirror and announced, "Red alert. The Follower is now on our tail, travelling in a white Peugeot at six o'clock."

"Why can't you just say he's right behind us?" I inquired.

"Less fun," Jeremy answered. "Hah. There's Felix, coupla cars behind at nine o'clock."

Left lane, I surmised. But once we swung onto the main road beside the Promenade des Anglais, it was harder to keep track of who-was-where in all the dense summer traffic. Jeremy just concentrated on driving, which was dicey enough, even with the aid of white-gloved policemen who were sternly, vigorously directing traffic, to impose order over potential chaos. At one point, when all the cars slowed to a crawl and then came to a dead stop all around us, I thought I would go mad with suspense.

Finally we inched our way off the Promenade, onto a smaller street with a parking lot. Jeremy parked the car. The Follower parked his a few feet away to the left. And Monsieur Felix parked his a few feet away to the right. All the chess pieces were now in place.

"Okay, it's showtime," Jeremy muttered. He got out of the car and came around with a flourish of courtesy as he opened my door. I stepped out and looked about, with exaggerated caution, clutching my handbag as if it contained the Hope Diamond, with a smug little smile on my Sarah Bernhardt face. We headed toward a shopping area tucked behind the big hotels and apartment buildings. No traffic was allowed here. There was a wide pedestrian walkway, flanked on both sides by rows of shops and restaurants that are popular among summer visitors.

Jeremy and I slipped into a posh little jewelry store where we had to be buzzed in to gain entry. Once inside, we walked right up to a display case that contained women's gold bracelets. The Follower got himself buzzed in a moment later, pretending to look at cuff links. Monsieur Felix waited outside, ever watchful.

"*Bonjour!*" sang out a saleswoman as she swooped down on us eagerly. She was dressed in a tightly fitted red suit that revealed just a bit of her cleavage.

"Here it is, darling," I said to Jeremy, loudly enough for The Follower to hear every word I uttered. "These are solid gold charm bracelets. Aren't they adorable?" The saleswoman took a bracelet out of the case, and spread it out on a black velvet mat so that we could admire it.

"See, honey?" I said to Jeremy. "The links open and close manually, so I can slip a charm anywhere I want, instead of having to get a jeweler to solder it on every time I get a new piece. It's just *perfect* for these." I opened my handbag and pulled out a black felt sack with a drawstring. The saleswoman watched as I opened the bag and carefully laid out five fake Lunaire coins on the mat.

"How pretty!" she exclaimed, turning them over to admire them. "They're coins, aren't they? Are they all the same? Yes, they are."

"They're antique coins," I said with housewifely pride.

"How nice!" she said. "I don't believe I've ever seen anything like them before."

"These are the only ones in the world," Jeremy announced broadly, acting like a boastful hubbie. "Been in my fiancée's family for years. There used to be more, a long time ago, but her ancestors melted the rest of 'em down for the gold. Yessir, these are the only ones in existence now."

"They're a wedding present," I announced brightly. "We're getting married soon."

"Oh, congratulations!" the saleswoman cried. "Why don't you try them on with the bracelet?" she said encouragingly. I attached all five. Then she helped me hook the bracelet on my wrist. With a great flourish, I held it up to the light, angling this way and that, so everyone could see the dangling, gleaming charms. I didn't dare look directly at The Follower, but I could feel I'd gotten his attention.

"Perfect!" the saleswoman said encouragingly.

"I agree!" I proclaimed.

"We'll take it," Jeremy said, handing the saleswoman his credit card. She went off to ring up the sale. When she returned, she handed me a velvet box for the bracelet. I dropped the empty box in my purse, saying, "I'll wear the bracelet. Thanks."

We had chosen this shop not only for the bracelet, but because, right around the corner, there was a small, discreet, venerable old bank that Jeremy had already scoped out a few days ago. We quickly ducked inside, with me glancing around appraisingly, like a housewife who wants to make sure that she approves of the vault that her husband has picked out for them.

The Follower remained on the pavement, staring at us through the glass window. I got a better glimpse of him now—he was a man in his early thirties, thin, in a nondescript suit. There was something hard in his expression, something tough and distinctly at variance with his casual pose. When I glanced up, he quickly turned his face away, and lit a cigarette. Across the walkway, Monsieur Felix established himself on a park bench, pulling a sandwich out of his pocket, like any guy in the crowd.

It was cool and quiet in the bank, where a manager, who was expecting us, now greeted us. I guess The Follower assumed that we were properly distracted, so he slipped into the bank and quickly went over to the counter where the deposit slips and pens are, and he pretended to fill out a form.

"I don't see why I can't wear my nice bracelet now," I said very audibly, with a fake little pout.

Jeremy replied with a rehearsed, scolding tone, "Now, darling, you promised to wait until the wedding to wear it. It will be much safer in here."

Feigning reluctant acquiescence, I allowed Jeremy to unclasp the bracelet, with its charms attached, so that I could put it in the velvet box that the jewelry saleswoman had just given me. The bank manager, who'd momentarily stepped out to check on the vault, returned and escorted Jeremy and me into the room where all the private safe-deposit boxes are kept under double lock-and-key.

Now that we were out of sight, I took the bracelet out of the box, and slipped it in my purse; then Jeremy locked the empty jewelry box in our allotted slot, and locked it. When we returned to the lobby, The Follower was still there, waiting for us, now actually reduced to pretending to be tying his shoelace as he spied on us.

We left the bank and returned to our parked car, with the broad smiles of two people who've suddenly and unexpectedly fallen into clover. We even hugged and kissed, and practically dusted off our hands as if to say, *There! That's a job well done*.

We drove away with the wind in our hair and The Follower on our tail. But, The Follower didn't track us all the way back to the villa; he turned off in another direction. Apparently his boss was the sort of man who wanted to hear bad news right away. Our little performance seemed to have worked.

"Felix is gone, too," Jeremy reported, eyeing the rearview mirror.

"The whole thing is too creepy for words," I said.

"Now," said Jeremy, "we wait for Drake to make the next move."

Monsieur Felix contacted us a few days later. He pulled up in his battered black Renault, and came loping purposefully up to us. We all agreed that none of us had seen The Follower, and hopefully this meant that Drake had called him off the surveillance. But, since The Follower had vanished once before and then resurfaced, we couldn't be sure.

"Meanwhile," Monsieur Felix triumphantly announced, "I am happy to report that we caught a lucky break. I have found Madame Venetia's wedding car."

"You did! Where is it?" I squealed.

"Well, like many of the cars, it was taken out of rail service in the second World War and kept in a rail yard. *Évidemment*, it did a brief stint as a bordello in occupied Paris, until the Americans arrived and used it for a hospital." He paused. "Overflow, you know, because of the war. Anyway, when the war ended, some of the cars were auctioned, and Madame Venetia's was sold to a wealthy eccentric, who kept it in his backyard for many years, *until* . . ." Here Monsieur Felix's voice became rich with pride, "A chef from Provence bought it, and turned it into a restaurant."

"Does the restaurant still exist?" Jeremy asked hopefully.

"*Bien sûr!* Not only does it exist, it recently earned another gold star. It is in Vence. A village up in the hills above Nice."

"I know where Vence is," I cried. "It's a pretty place where Matisse made his great stained-glass window for the church." Monsieur Felix gave us the address and telephone number of the restaurant.

"Jeremy, we have to book a table there right now!" I said. "The only question is—will it still have the original border pattern?"

"Only one way to find out," he said. "Provided that Monsieur Felix tells us the coast is clear."

Monsieur Felix smiled. "I will continue to signal you via e-mail. As long as you're not being followed, I will keep reporting that everything is *OK!*"

Chapter Forty

The old town of Vence sits amid the hills of Provence, looking down from its ramparts onto the other little villages below. The market square, with its beautiful fountain, was once a Roman forum. Our restaurant was farther into the countryside, considerably off the beaten path, down an old dirt road. Just when I was beginning to think we'd taken a wrong turn, we came upon a sign, painted and lettered like a vintage Orient Express poster.

We turned into the driveway, which led to a sudden clearing, where we saw what appeared to be a magical train, several cars long, that seemed as if it had somehow jumped off its coastal track, and miraculously, madly climbed up into the hills, then arrived at a dead halt. It looked exactly like its name, *Le Train du Temps Perdu*.

"A train from a lost time!" I marvelled.

We parked, as other diners had, in a small round parking lot encircled with white rocks. The entrance path to the restaurant was flanked by two sets of "ecologically correct" imitation railroad tracks, which ran through a front yard that was actually a wonderful herb garden. The herbs were whimsically allowed to grow between these wooden ties, as if they were weeds that had sprung up along an old, disused train track. Weeds, indeed! They were delightfully fragrant cooking herbs: thyme, basil, oregano, marjoram, borage, parsley, lavender, fennel . . . all the sunshine herbs of Provence and Liguria. There were also patches of bright-faced, edible flowers. The man who'd taken our reservation on the phone had told us that the entire menu was organic, even the wine.

The restaurant itself was composed of vintage railcars cobbled together from various old train lines and time periods, but somehow it all worked. The maitre d', an attentive, smiling middle-aged man in a sleek dark suit, greeted us as we stepped into the first car. It was a cute old smoker with an instantly clubby atmosphere that immediately evoked the world pictured in a framed vintage black-and-white photograph near the door, featuring turn-of-the-twentieth-century men with jowly faces and curling moustaches, seated in leather chairs with their cigars and brandy glasses in hand. Nowadays, nobody was allowed to smoke here; nevertheless, it was still filled with convivial patrons drinking cognac while playing at the antique chess tables. I was struck by how narrow and low-ceilinged the cars were, making the atmosphere cozy and intimate, but definitely out of time.

Jeremy glanced at the chess tables and said longingly, "Wouldn't mind playing a game."

"Keep moving, buddy," I murmured. "We're on a mission."

We were led through a Bar Car from an old train that once picked up travellers from transatlantic ocean liners docking in Cherbourg; and where, right now, a few nicely dressed young couples were happily clustered around an antique bar with a frosted glass mirror, decorated with needle-etched tulip designs. Next was the Kitchen Car, redone with black and red lacquer panels and abstract geometric artwork, where patrons dined on casual fare served to them at vintage kitchen tables. This was followed by a First Class Sleeper, decorated with tiger-lilies, whose bed had been replaced by one very long table for large dining parties like the family now seated there. We moved on to a big, fancy Pullman dining car, lined with forest-green leather banquettes, crimson curtains in the windows, and adorable Orient Express lamps; it was occupied by serious French diners, and a few English and American tourists who had clearly made a reverent pilgrimage here.

While we walked through all this, my historian's nose quivered delightedly at the stunning decor and antiques, but I soon felt rising trepidation as I realized that these cars had all been overhauled, repainted and refurbished. Each bore a framed black-and-white photograph of what the original car had looked like. I held my breath as we reached the very last car on the "train", afraid of what I might find.

The quiet, private Bridal Car had its door open, revealing that it overlooked a larger kitchen garden with rows of vegetables, salad greens and fruit trees. This car had only four tables, each seating just two people, so it was meant to be a romantic place for couples. I noticed two slender, elegant pairs of French diners in their forties and fifties, and a young couple, shyly absorbed in each other, probably honeymooners. All the napkins on theses tables had bridal white lace edging, and the plates were a soft rose color. White roses and velvety violets stood in silver vases.

Jeremy and I were seated at a nice booth tucked in a corner, with blue leather chairs and a white marble tabletop. Ordinarily, this would be a great table, so very private. It was not, however, an ideal spot for two decor-spies like us.

A waiter quickly appeared, handing us menus of a normal amount of offerings, which were nevertheless printed on the most enormous-sized menu folder that I have ever seen. He said he would return shortly to tell us the specials of the day.

"Psst," Jeremy said from behind his leather wine list, "I didn't see any framed photo of this original car, did you?"

"Nope," I replied.

"Did you bring Venetia's photograph?" he asked.

"Yes," I whispered, ducking behind my gigantic menu, surreptitiously comparing her photo to the patterns on the walls all around us.

We were definitely in the right place. Just as Venetia had said, two of the walls were covered with pretty mirrors made of pale blue glass, decorated with opaque figures of barefoot dancers in Isadora Duncan-style tunics, holding bunches of purple grapes beneath bowers of flowers. This motif was echoed on the other two walls, which were covered with wallpaper friezes of similar dancing figures in white and blue. The marquetry was indeed Art Deco. Atop each wall was a continuous strip of painted woodwork, just beneath the moulding, running all around the Bridal Car. I squinted, trying to make out their design . . .

"Cocktail?" asked the waiter, reappearing. "We are featuring a lovely rosé champagne today by the glass. May I suggest that for your pleasure?"

"Sounds good," Jeremy agreed hurriedly, and the waiter smiled and went away. I guess he thought that Jeremy was smitten with my charms and eager to be alone with me, like the other diners who were intent on their own private conversations, murmuring quietly. I tried peering into the mirrors to see if the wall patterns were reflected there.

Within a few minutes, I whispered, "Jeremy! Is that a cartouche over the doorway?"

"Do you think I have eyes in the back of my head?" Jeremy inquired, since he was facing one of the walls without mirrors.

"And the flowers," I continued in a low voice. "They *could* be the purple moonwort."

"Are you sure?" Jeremy asked. Then he glanced up and said, "Here comes that waiter. Better take a look at the menu and pick something to eat."

"How can you think of food at a time like this?" I demanded.

He scanned his menu and said appreciatively, "All in the line of duty. Wow, this is excellent *gastronomie*. Might as well enjoy ourselves."

So, when the waiter returned with our cocktails, we ordered the day's special. He suggested a particularly fine red Sancerre wine to accompany it. All the while that Jeremy was handling the ordering, I kept surreptitiously trying to figure out the wall patterns.

I thought we were playing it very cool, acting like everybody else around us, but the waiter evidently noticed my eager gaze, because after he took our order, he smiled at me and said proudly, "Perhaps you've heard of the decor of this carriage? They say it was made for a bride. It was painted by Cocteau, in the 1930s, so the artwork has been carefully preserved just as it was."

"Lovely," I breathed, not allowing myself to catch Jeremy's eye until the waiter had departed.

"Just like Venetia to fail to mention that her little artist friend was Cocteau!" Jeremy said. He reached into his pocket, pulled out something and handed it to me, under the table. It was my camera.

Startled, I took it. "Go ahead, shoot the cartouche," he said.

"Are you mad? We'll look like a couple of awful tourists and they'll throw us out," I hissed.

"You want to crack this case or not?" Jeremy asked. "Just do it fast. I'll go stand under the doorway, and you pretend you adore me and want a photo, and you can shoot the cartouche."

"I do adore you," I said distractedly, "but . . ."

Jeremy got up, went to the door, turned round and smiled sheepishly at me. A few other diners looked up momentarily, then chose to ignore such gauche creatures as us. I snapped away, but my lens couldn't pull that darned cartouche into a close-up. So, I had to get up from the table, and move closer.

The waiter returned, sized up the situation and, as if hoping to put an end to it, said, "Shall I take a picture of you together?" I had no choice but to hand him my camera, and go pose foolishly alongside Jeremy, while the waiter wasted the last precious bit of my camera's battery power on us two dopes.

"Swell," I muttered when I returned to the table. "I guess we're insulting the chef."

"Quiet," Jeremy said. "I memorized it. Give me something to write on."

I quickly tore a sheet from my notepad and handed it to him. Meanwhile, I sketched the other designs I'd seen all around the room, which I now identified as swans, putti and moonwort. So, when the waiter arrived with our food, there we were, like two kids, earnestly doing art class.

Well, *you* try to surreptitiously copy a whole four walls of pattern, whilst dining on an incredible meal. Somehow, we managed to get one wall after the *amuse bouche* of lightly breaded and baked oysters with a lemon and caper sauce; then we copied the second wall while devouring a fish course of turbot baked with fennel and black olives, served with just-plucked-from-the-garden skinny French string beans; and we got the third wall while feasting on delicate roasted hen, with potato croquette and a garden salad of greens topped by tiny pink, blue, purple and yellow edible flowers;

and the fourth wall while nibbling on a dessert of fresh fig tarte with lavender honey and caramel ice cream. It was the kind of meal which, as my father says, "One remembers forever, into one's dotage, when you have no teeth left, and you're nodding by the fireplace in your robe and slippers."

By the time the check arrived, I was fully sated, and I had all those images and Latin lettering swirling in my head. I only hoped our notes would make sense when we got home. We rose, thanked our gracious hosts, and marched down the front walk, past its railroad ties and fragrant garden.

"Wow," I said as we climbed into the car. "If that's how they ate on the *train bleu*, why on earth did they ever invent airplanes?"

"A meal like this should be followed by a nice nap in the garden," Jeremy observed sleepily. He checked his mobile to see if the coast was clear. The message from Monsieur Felix was the same. *OK!*

Chapter Forty-one

When we returned to the villa, we printed out the new photos and notes, and added them to the other ones on the dining-table jigsaw-puzzle of clues.

"You were right about the old top border," Jeremy said, impressed. "There's the cartouche, the swans, the cupids, and the moonwort. Look. It matches up perfectly with the cut-off bits in the main body of the tapestry. Here's the Latin from the new cartouche."

He consulted his notes:

Sequere Virum Quem In Matrimonium Locavisti,
Domus Post Te, Via Pro Te.

"Let's see if I can get that into English," Jeremy muttered, scribbling.

When he was done, however, he still looked puzzled. "You're not going to like it, because it's just more of that obedient wife stuff."

He showed me his translation:

Follow the man that you have wed,
Your home behind, your path ahead.

"That's not so bad. It sounds like those Bible passages, about a woman leaving her family and her childhood village behind, to follow the man she marries," I observed. "But, that can't be all there is to it. Does it mean something more when you put it together with the bottom one?"

We looked at the two of them, one under the other:

Follow the man that you have wed,
Your home behind, your path ahead.
Drink deep from the well of life,
And treasure a faithful wife.

"Well, it would seem that the top cartouche of the tapestry is advice to the bride, and the bottom is advice to the groom," Jeremy noted. "Makes sense, but it doesn't shout 'buried treasure'."

Hugely frustrated now, I exclaimed, "Somehow, in spite of all our pictures and notes, there *must* still be something in the actual tapestry that we're missing in these photos, something we need in order to solve it. Oh, Jeremy, we've just got to get the tapestry back!"

The telephone rang. It was Honorine, with one of her wedding-plan updates. She was happy to report that the decor for our wedding train carriages, and the donations to Women4Water, were, she said, "pouring in". Even Margery and Amelia were quite pleased.

"Great," I said. "Anything else?"

Honorine scanned her list. "Jeremy's clothes are ready. Rupert will pick them up. I must hang up now, because your mother is scheduled to call me from America, so we can go over all the RSVPs."

We rang off, but a few minutes later a telephone shrilled again. I thought it was Honorine calling me back about the guest list. Then I saw that it was Jeremy's mobile ringing. He picked it up.

It was Drake's P.R. man. Jeremy held the phone between the two of us so that I could hear. At first, it sounded like the usual business B.S., in which he smoothly explained that Parker Drake had been *incredibly* busy with his breakneck schedule, but he's been *really* wanting to meet you and your lovely fiancée. I listened, barely breathing, as the guy invited the two of us to a "small party" on Drake's yacht in Monte Carlo this weekend.

"And Mr. Drake would *personally* like to invite you to join his regular card game," the P.R. man said silkily, as if he were offering Jeremy a private audience with the Pope.

I must say that Jeremy handled it beautifully, acting like a guy who was eager for a new client, and was properly impressed at the right moments. Then the call ended.

"Now what?" I asked.

Jeremy grinned. "Looks like Drake bought our little performance in the jewelry shop! He must think we've got the only remaining Lunaire coins in existence. You know, for the first time, I really do believe that he stole that tapestry."

"But he's not just going to just hand it over," I objected.

"No, which is why we have to keep up the bluff," Jeremy said. "Until we can figure out for sure what his game is."

Part Ten

Chapter Forty-two

The principality of Monaco seems like an improbable little country that somehow managed to survive in the shadows of two powerhouses, Italy and France. You would never guess that, once upon a time, Monaco's ruling dynasty was a formidable big noise along the Riviera coast, bossing around the nearby towns and collecting taxes on their prized lemon and olive harvests. The Grimaldi dynasty's stronghold here began in the 1200s, when a family member who belonged to a political party from Genoa—and was known as Francesco the Spiteful—disguised himself as a monk, and, in the dead of night, simply knocked on the door of a fortress in Monaco. Having gained entrance, he started knifing the guards; then let in his lurking team of warriors, who stormed the place and took over—and Monaco has belonged to the Grimaldi dynasty ever since.

However, by the 1800s they fell short of funds, until Monaco's ruler at the time, one Prince Carlo III, decided to build a casino on a rocky promontory. In no time at all, it became a popular winter resort. They named it after the rock it stood on, and the prince who built it—Monte Carlo.

Today, Monte Carlo is still a magnet for gamblers, but summer is the big season, and it kicks off with the Grand Prix. Top race car drivers go zipping around its streets, roaring past its hotels, shops, and the pricey apartments, which the world's richest-of-the-rich claim as their primary residence, in a land that doesn't charge income tax. About fifty banks do a bustling business sheltering hotshot money, and security is so high that it's said the whole town can be "locked down" at a moment's notice.

But Monsieur Felix had an investigator's particular take on the place. "It is totally bugged," he proclaimed. "Yes, everywhere you go, there is ze camera on the streets. And in ze restaurants, hidden in the floral arrangements, you find ze microphone."

I couldn't tell if he was joking or not; he seemed serious, especially when he added, "Do not say or do anything in public in Monte Carlo that you would not want the whole world to see and hear."

Monsieur Felix apologetically informed us that he had a previous commitment, which required him to go to Paris on the night of Drake's card party. But he assured us that he would be "on call", and if we needed immediate help, he could alert the police and "other associates" on the Côte d'Azur. I felt a little uneasy at his absence, but Jeremy assured me it would be okay.

Meanwhile, Rollo stopped by the villa to teach Jeremy how to spot a marked deck of cards. As we were leaving for the party, something compelled me to say, "Rollo, could you stay on call tonight?" I'm not sure whether I said this because I wanted him to keep out of trouble, or if I simply felt that we could use all hands on deck.

"Be happy to, my dear," Rollo said agreeably.

Jeremy and I set off in his modern green Dragonetta, which our friend Denby, who restores and services "collectible" autos, had driven down here from London for us, so we'd have it available for the wedding. We took the *Moyenne Corniche* road, that runs along the middle level of the cliffs above the Mediterranean. Soon Monte Carlo appeared below, like a great enchanted rock sticking up out of the sea. As we wound our way down the curving road, I tried not to think of Princess Grace meeting her untimely end on these hairpin turns. Round and round we went, circling down in the seashell-shaped spiral that took us finally to the harbor. There, at one side stood the famed Casino and the Hotel de Paris; and on the other side, a majestic castle, the official residence of the Prince of Monaco.

We had reached the "Port of Hercules", filled with yachts of all shapes and sizes, its quay dotted with trees and flower boxes. Old pastel-colored buildings with balustrades and balconies overlooked the boats. Behind the harbor were stacks of pricey apartment houses and, rising beyond them, the verdant green hills of Monaco, high and sheltering. We parked the car, and headed for Drake's party.

Now, the funny thing about people with money is that they never seem to think they've got enough. In fact, if you ask them how rich they are, they will object and say, "*I'm* not rich. But So-and-So, *he's* rich." And So-and-So obligingly proves it, by having the biggest yacht in the sea. Except that in this neck of the woods, there are about a dozen So-and-So's, who are all competing to be the biggest Big Shot, as, over the years, the yachts keep getting bigger and bigger. In Monte Carlo's harbor, gigantic yachts are allowed to dock right alongside their tinier counterparts, and the view from above makes them look like great big whales snuggled up with little minnows.

Drake's tub sat there dwarfing all the other yachts around it. He had named his monster *The Jackpot*. It was three hundred forty feet long, made of steel, with two diesel engines, and could run a speed of twenty knots. The lettering of the boat's name and its escutcheon (shaped like a medieval shield with the letters "P.D.") were carved in twenty-four-carat gold. There was an on-board helicopter, and I noticed that the boat was registered in the Bahamas. It was rumored that Drake had paid two hundred million dollars for it.

The steward who helped us aboard informed us that tonight's cardplayers were a specially handpicked group of men from which the lesser players had been "winnowed out". With that sort of announcement, I expected the whole place to smell of brandy, beer and cigars.

But as we traversed *The Jackpot*'s gangway, the first and overriding smell to hit my nostrils was not cigars, nor cooking, nor the salty sea. It was a huge wave of perfume-mingled-with-shampoo, emanating from the Wives-and-Girlfriends who "belonged" to the cardplayers. All those gals had sprayed, spritzed and glazed themselves with cosmetics and fragrance, as if the men were great big honey bees buzzing around for the prettiest blossom.

Even Jeremy noticed the cologne. "Wow," he said, "that's enough to knock out an entire city."

When my feet touched the deck, one of the serving crew looked at my soft white flats, and he hesitated, glancing at a neat, orderly row of high heels, which apparently the other female guests had deposited there. Then he gave me the go-ahead, so I didn't have to remove my little boat slippers.

We were escorted to the big aft deck, under the shade of a black-and-red canopy with a picture of a gold octopus on it. There was an enormous round table, the likes of which would have made King Arthur fierce with envy. Seated around the table were about a dozen men, all playing poker. They were dressed in deceptively casual attire—shorts, T-shirts, sunglasses and baseball hats—as they played their ferociously competitive card game while drinking beer.

Despite their unassuming clothes, I could recognize a few celebrity guests. A champion race car driver here, an Irish politician there, a topnotch soccer player, a British TV host, a French rock star, a German car magnate. And, of course, Parker Drake himself, in white shorts, with his suntanned, muscular arms sticking out of a bright red T-shirt.

There was a throng of other guests who were not cardplayers, but seemed happy to either watch or lie about in lounge chairs on other decks, drinks in hand. Startled by the scale of both the boat and the guest list, I glanced at Jeremy. He was accustomed to dealing with bigwig clients, so he took it all in stride. As we stood there, I noticed that in the center of the card table was a pile of chips, which the men were betting with. These were Drake's own special gambling chips—black with red letters, "P.D."

In a flash, I knew that Jeremy had been right. Drake surely craved the Lunaire coins. That simply had to be the reason for this particular invitation.

"Perhaps you'd care to join the ladies?" a steward asked me, and I allowed myself to be directed to the upper deck. I saw Jeremy watching to see where I landed, because he was appraising where he should sit at the card table, so that he'd always be in full view of me if I peered over the rail from above. We'd devised a signal of patting the top of one's head if we wanted the other's help.

When I reached the upper deck, it looked to me, at first, as if it were covered in porpoises. But, as it turned out, these well-oiled creatures lolling about were not mermaids but simply sunbathing female guests, sprawled out on blankets—poolside—lying on their stomachs with their gleaming backs exposed to the sun. Only female crew members were allowed up here to tend them. I felt I'd entered a harem of some sort. I had a bathing suit tucked in my bag, but the sun was hot, and I'm a redhead. I was in no hurry to lie down and bake.

Then I spotted Tina Drake, fully dressed, sitting on a lounge chair under a white awning, at a big table with other women, who were drinking chilled white wine, and nibbling on salmon and shrimp hors d'oeuvres. I realized that, even up here, the guests had been divided up further—the Wives congregated at the more prestigious seats, near Tina, from where they could assess how much trouble the sunbathing, unmarried Girlfriends might pose.

So, where did a bride-to-be belong—with the Wives or Girlfriends? One foot here, one foot there? Tina resolved this for me, by waving to me to join her. I accepted a glass of wine, and sat down in the shade, where a nice sea breeze kept me cool.

I would like to say that the conversation was absolutely scintillating, but it wasn't. These fabulously rich women, with all the time and access that money can buy, spent the afternoon flipping through a nearby pile of the very same fashion and entertainment magazines that the whole rest of the world reads, and dishing about famous actresses, singers, models, and wives of powerful men—some they knew, and some they didn't—as if the celebrities were schoolmates to be either enviously worshipped or jealously despised.

The only time my shipboard companions appeared sympathetic with the subjects of their gossip was if the celeb had been through a terrible divorce. This was, apparently, a woman's biggest gamble, and the sisterhood rose up in righteous indignation if they believed a woman had gotten shafted in an alimony settlement; but they chortled with appreciative glee if someone reported, "*She* took him for half of what he had, and honey, you know what that adds up to!" This apparently was a subject quite dear to the hearts of all the ladies on deck, transcending the rivalry of Wives versus Girlfriends.

Such chatter made it easy for me to just sit there and cluck agreeably at the right moments. The other women, having initially sized me up, decided that, while Tina was friendly to me, and a few of them had vaguely heard of me, I was not yet what they would consider a Famous Wife. So their attitude was a slightly condescending tolerance.

That was fine, because it allowed me to close my eyes and listen to the sea, as the boat ploughed out into deeper waters, reached a fairly private cove, and dropped anchor. The ladies' voices drifted into the background, as they do when you're at a beach, and an occasional phrase emerges from the blur of distant murmuring. As the sun began to slip down lower in the sky, some of the suntanning Girlfriends rose, pulled on a blouse or caftan, and went into a dressing room to shower and get ready for dinner.

Periodically I got up and wandered about, casually peering down at the card game on the deck below, to see if Jeremy was trying to signal me. From what I could tell, he was doing rather well. Several men had "folded", tossing in their cards, and they rose from the table, stretching, to wander off and sit at smaller tables, where they could indulge in the food and drink that was constantly being offered by various serving crew.

"You guys are really in love, aren't you?"

It was Tina, who'd suddenly appeared alongside me at the deck railing. Up close, I saw that her beauty was like a beacon; the kind of dazzling good looks that can't be ignored, which often invokes uninvited male fantasies, and female jealousy, thus isolating the beautiful one from the herd. She had that slightly wistful quality that beautiful women can have, when plain old friendship eludes them.

Tina had come to check on me, in that good-hostess way of hers, but she was now smiling in amusement. I realized that she'd caught me gazing at Jeremy, and she probably thought I was pining away for my fiancé. I blushed.

"I've heard that you two are a good team," she continued, in a light, offhanded, but curious tone. "I guess you really must like each other's company, if you work together all day long."

I smiled warily, wondering if she was somehow onto us. But then, after a moment's hesitation, she divulged what was really on her mind. "What's your secret?" she asked, attempting to sound casual.

I felt momentary panic. I didn't have a secret. I gazed down at the top of Jeremy's head, and felt the usual surge of warmth and delight at the mere sight of him. I recalled all that we'd been through together, and the patience and good humor and thoughtfulness with which he'd handled it. But I couldn't just say, as the song goes, that I'm "mad about the boy".

"I have no idea, Tina. It just happened," I admitted.

"You know what I mean," Tina said a trifle impatiently, as if she suspected that I was deliberately holding out on her. "A guy is always great when he's chasing you. But how do you know that this one's the real thing?" she demanded. She was, after all, a very rich gal, quite used to getting what she asked for, and being told what she wanted to hear. I wondered if, perhaps, she asked every woman what their secret recipe for love was; in which case I shouldn't be so serious about it.

But then she said in a low tone, so that the others wouldn't overhear, "You guys seem different from a lot of couples I know."

There was something sincere here, beneath her offhanded veneer. So I thought about it carefully, wanting to be utterly honest with her. "I guess it's down to trust, like knowing you can count on each other when the chips are down," I said, feeling a bit shy.

This seemed to satisfy her. "Right," she said, nodding sagely, in a triumphant tone, as if I'd just validated her own wise opinion. "Trust is everything," she agreed, more lightly now, brushing away a stray lock of blonde hair that the wind had blown across her cheek. Some of the other wives called out to her, and she waved back, excusing herself and rejoining them.

There was a sudden roar of male voices from below. I peered over the railing again. Drake was aggressively upping the ante with bigger and bigger bets, effectively forcing the players to give up all their chips or quit. I watched as the number of players dwindled . . . smaller, smaller, smaller . . . until it was down to three players, and Jeremy was among them.

The crowd of onlookers was growing bigger, as some of the Wives-and-Girlfriends went down to watch the men play; and now and then, one of the crew would pause in his duties, assessing the progress of the game. There were also some security-type men, looking a bit incongruous in dark suits and reflecting sunglasses, whom I hadn't noticed earlier. As I watched, the third player dropped out.

And then, a few moments later, I saw Jeremy, very casually, reach up and pat the top of his head. Or, he was just smoothing his hair. To tell you the truth, I couldn't be sure, but I thought I'd better get down there, just in case.

When I reached the main deck, it was so quiet that whenever someone in the crowd made a distracting sound, they were very quickly silenced by glares from other onlookers. Meanwhile, the kind of people who can't stand suspense now walked away to the fore-deck, for drinks and chatter. At the table, it was still just Drake and Jeremy, mano-a-mano, as Rollo had said. And the game was piquet.

The change in attitude was palpable now, tense and sharp, and the playing took on a dramatic quality that was almost dizzying. I watched as Drake dealt out twelve cards each, with the remaining stack face-down in the middle. Then he shoved in a big stack of chips, and Jeremy matched it, and raised it. After that, the game moved even faster, with Jeremy and Drake exchanging terse calls like "trio", "good", "no good" and "*septieme*" as cards were thrown down, and points tallied along the way. The pot continued to build.

Now Tina Drake and more of her female guests appeared, and they all clustered closer, as people in casinos do when the stakes get really high, and everyone wants to be there for the big moment. It became so quiet that I could hear the slightest accidental sound, like ice clinking in somebody's drink.

Then Jeremy glanced up at me, and I saw in his eyes that it was time to play our ace-in-the-hole.

Me. And my charms.

I slipped off my light little navy cotton cardigan and tied it round my shoulders, so that my bare arms were visible in the sleeveless, navy-and-white dress I wore. I reached out for a glass of champagne from the tray of a passing server, deliberately causing my bracelet—and its five bright charms—to clatter a little on my wrist, visibly dangling where they could catch the light of the setting sun, which struck them with the fiery orange rays of summer. The gold responded and twinkled with a fire of its own.

Jeremy smiled at me broadly, playing the man who's proud of his little fiancée, intentionally prompting Drake to glance up in my direction. I sipped my champagne in order to raise my wrist higher . . . and the gold flashed again. Five little charms, dancing on their golden chain, like brilliant bait on the end of a hook dropped right in front of a big fat fish.

From my many visits to antiques shops and museums, I can recognize the smitten look a collector gets, when, no matter what the price, he *has* to have it. Drake had exactly that obsessive look on his face right now as he stared at the charms. It was his turn to raise the stakes—or not. Distractedly, with a red flush beneath his tanned face, he pushed forward all his chips. The crowd said, "Whoo-oo!"

Drake ignored this, and said calmly, "What say we make it a little more interesting?" He glanced at his wife. "Let's have that necklace, babe," he commanded shortly.

There was a brief, communal gasp among the Wives-and-Girlfriends. Having just hung out with them, I knew that jewelry was like insurance, for "walking away" money. Besides, it was such a pretty necklace, of golden seashells interspersed with luminous pearls.

However, that wasn't nearly as disturbing as the look on Tina's face. Her expression was not simply that of a woman who doesn't want to part with her favorite trinket or her insurance. Hers was a shocked, suddenly naked, wounded look, indicating that this necklace had far greater sentimental value because, perhaps, it symbolized something good that had once been between them. I saw quite plainly that Drake could have asked her to pitch in anything else—a ring, an earring—but he'd chosen the necklace. Why? Because it was so visibly stunning? Or was it to prove something more? It made his offhanded, imperious, *I-don't-care-I'm-so-rich* gesture seem particularly vicious to me, and I, too, felt a surge of indignation.

But Tina quickly recovered, and assumed a defiant, *Then-I-don't-give-a-damn-either* look as she reached up and unclasped the necklace from her suntanned throat; and then, out of habit, she clasped it closed again, as if in consideration for anyone who won it. She handed it over to Drake with a look that—well, if it could kill, he'd be more than dead. He'd be bled, dead and retread.

Jeremy glanced at the necklace, glittering atop the pot of chips. Then he said to Drake, "Ah, well, I don't quite know how to match that, I'm afraid."

Drake said, "Oh, I think you can."

Jeremy pretended to be baffled. Drake, looking impatient, said, "What about your girl's bracelet?"

All eyes were on me. Acting startled, I held up my arm and looked at the golden charms myself. A convenient little murmur of expectation and awe ran through the crowd, allowing Jeremy to act like a man who's got his—ego—on the line now. He nodded to me, and I unhooked the bracelet with a regretful sigh. I saw Drake's gaze locked on the fake Lunaire coins as I handed them to Jeremy, who held the bracelet a moment, then put it reverently atop the heap, along with the rest of his chips.

The crowd allowed itself to gasp. But I was not prepared for Drake's next move. He turned to his wife and ordered, "Check it out."

Obediently, Tina opened her purse and took out something wrapped in a bundle of black velvet. She laid it on the table, and peeled back the velvet from the object. I saw that it was one of those magnifiers that jewelers use.

"I never shop in Monte Carlo without this!" she told the crowd, who laughed nervously.

Drake looked from me to Jeremy, and smiled his reptilian smile. "My wife, like her brothers, is a coin expert," he said.

Jeremy raised an eyebrow. "I didn't find it necessary to verify your wife's jewelry," he pointed out, stalling for time. The crowd laughed, as if Tina's jewelry collection was so well-known that only an outsider would question it.

Drake shrugged and said, in that challenging-but-affable way of his, "Humor me, okay?"

My heart was pounding like a train now. Jeremy had warned me that Drake might wish to scrutinize the coins, but since they were real gold and a first-rate job, we were willing to risk it. Rare antiques are not always easy to authenticate, even for experts, who have been known to argue for centuries over whether a particular painting is a genuine Michelangelo or a Rembrandt. And since no contemporary expert had actually seen a Lunaire coin, I figured we had some leeway. But I hadn't banked on Drake's "trophy wife" being an actual coin expert, just like her brothers.

Tina's hand was poised over the bracelet, but before picking it up, she asked Jeremy, "May I?"

Jeremy acted as if he couldn't refuse such a pretty request. "Certainly," he said confidently. Tina took the bracelet, laid it out on the velvet, and began to peer at each coin, one by one.

I held my breath as she peered through her magnifier to examine the first coin. She turned it over, scrutinizing both sides, then moved on. By the time Tina got to the second coin, I wanted to scream. When she continued on to the third, I thought I'd faint dead away. As she reached the fourth, I'd already decided that it was a shame I'd never written out a last will and testament. And at the fifth, I was ready to leap over the railing and take my chances of swimming to shore.

Finally, at long last, Tina looked up at her husband.

"Well?" Drake demanded.

"Yes," Tina said, without hesitation. "They're the real thing."

Parker Drake's eyes absolutely glittered, but he recovered and moved quickly, as if he wanted to act fast, before Jeremy or I had a change of heart. "My apologies," he said with a conciliatory grin. "The bet is accepted. Assuming you accept mine?"

Jeremy nodded with his best upper-crust attitude, as if he considered it all too beneath him to argue further.

Now all eyes were on the cards. Piquet, I knew from Rollo's tutelage, is a subtle game of strategy. The skill in the play comes not only from building the strongest possible hand, given the cards you've been dealt, but also from closely observing the cards your opponent has chosen to throw away . . . and those he chooses to play. In piquet, even a relatively weak hand can be a winner, if the cards are played just right.

Drake, of course, was a master piquet player. He was watching Jeremy closely now, with an air of supreme confidence. But then Jeremy did something that seemed to rattle Drake—he led with the Nine of Clubs. Drake checked his hand again, then took a nervous look at his discards. Staring intently at Jeremy, Drake threw down the only card he could . . . the Ace of Clubs.

Even with my limited knowledge of the game, I knew what this meant. Drake may have won the "trick", but he was now clearly out of clubs, or he would never have thrown down such a high card to beat out a lowly Nine. It also meant that Jeremy was probably "holding Clubs"—a risky maneuver that Drake hadn't counted on. If Drake was to lose the next trick, Jeremy could take control, and sweep the rest of the tricks by leading with his Clubs, thereby scoring enough points to win the entire pot.

My head was spinning as I recalled Rollo's admonition, now ringing in my mind. *Smarts, skill . . . and luck.*

Drake hesitated. He glanced up at the sky, then, in a quick single motion, he slapped down the Queen of Diamonds. It was the wrong choice. Jeremy had the King of Diamonds.

Now Jeremy took the remaining series of tricks with a succession of clubs that Drake could not beat. All the cards had been played. It was over.

At first, nobody moved. Nobody even breathed. So I wasn't even sure I could believe my own eyes. But then, Drake's P.R. man quickly signalled the steward, who expertly and rapidly scooped the entire pot of winnings into a black bag with a drawstring cord, as if to get them out of Drake's sight before he decided to eat them or something.

Drake's face was dark as a thundercloud, his eyes like angry slits, his seething breath pushing his tanned, yacht-racing chest up and down in fast waves, as if it was about to blow his head right off his neck. But, with forced control, he turned to his wife and said in a low voice, "See to it that our guests dine at the club tonight."

"Dinner in Monte Carlo tonight, folks!" Tina announced quickly, taking her cue. "In the V.I.P. room. All ashore that's going ashore."

Her guests, eager to be considered V.I.P.'s, and glad to be released from the tension of the game, now broke into happy, relieved chatter as they dispersed, gathering their belongings, and clambering into the speedboats that would take them back to shore. Apparently they were so accustomed to Drake throwing money around that they didn't think the loss would resonate with him, since in these circles it's important to look as if your disposable income is, well, disposable. I could see that this game would be forgotten by his male guests tomorrow. The women, however, might hesitate to ever again wear good jewelry to a card game.

As Tina moved to accompany her guests on the speedboats heading back to shore, Drake barked at her to stay aboard. "But darling, our guests," she reproached mildly.

"You can catch up with them later," he said tersely. "We're having Penny and Jeremy for dinner tonight."

Honestly, that's just the way he said it, as if we were the entrée, you know, roast leg of Penny-and-Jeremy. Fricasséed friends.

Tina looked at us and said, "You heard him. The master 'asks' that you stay aboard."

I felt a stab of alarm, watching the vanishing speedboats bearing everybody else away to safety. For, underneath all this was the implicit threat that Jeremy and I were not ever going to get off this boat until Drake bloody well said so. I wondered if he was going to conk us on the head, steal the charms, and feed us to the sharks. Oddly enough, such headlines in this rarefied stratosphere didn't seem that far-fetched. I'd seen typical stories as, *Swiss banker found dead in his Monte Carlo apartment after being seen in clubs with airline hostess. British bigwig caught on tape in S&M tryst with hooker. French broker found in apparent suicide on eve of his approaching testimony to investigative committee.* We'd fit right in. *Heiress and fiancé vanish in the Mediterranean; last seen at private card game aboard yacht of zillionaire coin collector.*

Drake's P.R. man was saying, "Your winnings, Mr. Laidley. We cashed the chips for you. It's all here." He handed Jeremy a leather pouch with a zipper, which to my mind looked like a man's shaving kit. Jeremy glanced inside, examined it briefly, and seemed satisfied. He extracted the charm bracelet, and handed it back to me. As I hooked it on my wrist, I saw Drake watching this little move.

"Well, then, we're squared," Drake said, a bit too heartily. He put one of his leathery hands on Jeremy's shoulder, and Tina led us into the big dining salon, whose glass walls were really sliding doors that could be opened partially or completely, to allow an unobstructed view of the sea, and the sun's long, glittering trail across it, like a highway line leading right up to the sky. The sparkling water seemed to be teasing Drake with silver and gold reflections that made rippling light patterns on the ceiling, and bounced off the dangling charms on my bracelet.

"Fascinating," he said, gazing at the coins, as if mesmerized. "I'd like to hear more about them. I'm an avid coin collector myself." Tina was watching us all silently.

"Not much to tell, really," Jeremy said carelessly as we paused for drinks at a black-and-white bar. "Penny's family has a tradition of passing them down to the new bride as a wedding gift."

"Got any more of those coins, do they?" Drake asked.

Jeremy shook his head. "Oh, no. These are the very last of their kind."

"Indeed." I was surprised by how badly Drake was controlling his expression of utter desire. This was a man who made mega-deals before breakfast. And I'd seen him play cards, so I knew he was perfectly capable of self-discipline. Except not now. He wanted it that badly.

"Have you heard of the Lunaire gold? There's actually a very interesting story behind them," Jeremy said maddeningly, and launched into a brief history of the famed birthday-party card game, which Drake obviously knew about, but was now being forced to endure while he pretended to be hearing it for the first time. He kept nodding his head mechanically, but was still quite fidgety. By the time Jeremy finished, Drake was practically panting for them.

"How much do you want for them?" he asked with a toothy grin, as if half in jest.

"I really had no business betting them in the first place," Jeremy said. "Got swept up in the heat of the moment, I suppose." He shook his head ruefully.

Undaunted, Drake persisted. "Come now. Let's play for them. Just tell me what you think they're worth," he said challengingly, "and I'll match the bet."

To my utter admiration, Jeremy went for broke, looking him straight in the eye and saying, "The fact is, Penny's family is so distracted by the recent theft of their tapestry that we can't even think of risking the loss of a single coin. Surely at least not before the tapestry is recovered and restored to them," he declared.

Tina made a little gasp, and Drake raised his head sharply. Until now I'd been watching Drake closely, thinking to myself, *Does-he-or-doesn't-he have it*? Now I was thinking, *You rat, you've got it!*

But Drake only said smoothly, "Oh? Yes, I think I read something about that in the newspapers. Well, perhaps I can help. I have excellent contacts who are experts at—recovering things." He smiled his crocodile smile. "What's the tapestry worth?"

Jeremy said calmly, "Quite frankly, since it's now on Interpol's list of stolen goods, it won't fetch a farthing for the guy who actually has it."

Well, of course, now everybody knew what everybody was talking about, even though Drake had not once admitted outright that he was the sticky-fingers behind the theft. But it was clear that we were looking Beelzebub right in the face, and he was about to name his price.

"If my man can locate it for you, then how about it? The tapestry for those coins," Drake said.

"One coin," Jeremy said swiftly.

Drake laughed as if he'd been insulted. "Four," he said in a retaliatory way.

Jeremy shook his head. "Two."

"Three," Drake said with a smirk, as if this was where he'd expected it to land.

Jeremy and I looked at each other and pretended to hesitate. Jeremy was so convincing, he made it easy for me to follow his lead; so, acting like I was being a big, brave girl, I nodded.

"At least," I said, "we'd still have a couple of coins in the family, for future generations."

Jeremy pretended to be slightly pissed off as he turned to Drake and said, "Show me the tapestry. Then it will be done."

Drake didn't wait another instant. He rose and went out on deck, walking far enough away so we couldn't hear him. I saw that he'd pulled out his mobile phone. He seemed to say very little, then paused briefly. Soon he put his phone away and returned, looking much more relaxed now.

Smiling winningly, as if he'd finally trumped Jeremy, he said, "I expect to hear from my 'friend' within the hour. Meanwhile, I insist that my honored guests now join me for dinner. You've surely heard of my chef. I took him away from the royal family."

I had no idea which bereft monarch he was talking about, but Tina, who'd been silent as a stone throughout this, now took her seat at the far end of the table. Drake sat at the other end. There was nothing for it, but to take the side chairs that a steward was pulling out for us. I shot Jeremy an imploring look, but he gave me a *Brace up, darling* nod, as other stewards appeared, bearing wine.

"We're dining on ostrich steaks tonight," Drake said as he unfolded his napkin. "I have them flown in." He did not appear to be joking.

I have no real control over my mind, which was now picturing a big, long-legged ostrich running and running. I have heard that they are, actually, quite speedy creatures. So, I was wondering why this particular ostrich hadn't run fast enough, to spare me from being faced with him on my plate. Perhaps he had stuck his head in the sand—always a bad idea, but one which I was contemplating doing now.

"Oh, for God's sake, Parker," Tina said in exasperation, seeing my aghast look. She turned to me and asked rather mechanically, as if this wasn't the first time she'd clashed with her husband like this, "Do you eat beefsteak?"

"Yes," I said gratefully. She signalled a passing steward. "Got any?" she inquired, indicating that she clearly would accept only an affirmative reply.

The man nodded, and hurried off to inform the chef; but Parker caught his arm on the way out and ordered, "Barbecued."

The stewards moved swiftly, as if they were feeding a lion that would devour them if he was made to wait for his food. They soon returned, bearing silver trays with enormous silver domes over them. The head steward deposited a platter heaped with ostrich steaks in front of Parker. On the other end of the table, in front of Tina, another server placed the beef. So, when Jeremy and I were politely asked by a waiter what our preference was, it was like choosing up teams in this marital boxing ring.

Nobody chose Parker. He didn't seem to mind in the least. As for the beefsteak, it was top quality, quite tender, perfectly cooked . . . and slathered in barbecue sauce. Tina calmly picked up her knife, with its enormous ivory handle, which had probably been yanked off some poor unsuspecting elephant's tusk, and she scraped most of the sauce off to the side of her plate, then calmly ate.

So, we all ate, drank and waited. The beefsteak came with baked potato and asparagus, and a good red wine from Drake's costly cellar, much of which, I knew, he'd won at auction amid great public fanfare. But I must say that Drake was not exactly conducive to good digestion. The stewards looked extremely nervous whenever they brought something to him, always serving him first, so that he could inspect it, appraise it, then taste it, and accept or reject it. This was interspersed with rather incongruously ordinary dinner conversation that was mainly about sports, chiefly boating.

Each time the servers brought Drake a new platter to approve, he peered at the food, still chewing the previous, with a suspicious attitude; and the momentary tension was so thick that you could have cut it with a machete. By now the staff practically tiptoed around him, for his every directive was barked like a military order. Throughout the meal, Tina just sat there and ate, and drank plenty of wine.

Only once did Drake outright reject what he was served. It was the coffee, which he thought was too weak. Now, a man is entitled to a decent cup of coffee. However, I was truly taken aback when he expressed his displeasure thusly: "Tell that fucking sous chef I'll tear his heart out of his chest and eat it while he watches, if he ever serves me another cup of coffee like this again."

It was at this pleasant juncture that Drake got the return call we'd all been waiting for. He opened his platinum, diamond-encrusted phone, and listened, then snapped it closed, turned to Jeremy and said triumphantly, "It's done."

He actually smirked at my astonishment, since this whole action was, after all, designed to impress. Then he turned to Jeremy and said, with a broad sweep of his hand, "Call one of your servants at your villa, and tell them to look on your patio."

Whoa. This was more than creepy. Oddly enough, all I could think to say to Jeremy was, "It's Celeste's day off. But Rollo's on standby."

"Call him," Jeremy said quickly.

I did. Rollo landed on the phone like a duck on a junebug. He'd taken his on-call situation very seriously. From the background noise, it sounded as if he were in his hotel bar, watching a ball game on TV. I said, "Rollo, could you go over to the villa and look out on the patio? I am told that our tapestry has been found and returned."

Rollo didn't ask if I'd lost my mind. He just said quickly, "I'm on my way."

There was another spot of waiting, during which time Drake showed Jeremy his sailing trophies in a locked cupboard over the bar in the salon. Tina, having evidently heard these anecdotes umpteen times before, was flirting with the barman, who trotted back and forth restocking the bar. Drake did not seem to notice or care.

I spent the time gazing out at the moon, which had just risen in a darkening blue sky over the sea, and I pretended to be utterly transported by the vista, while secretly plotting about how Jeremy and I might jump ship if this little scam of ours blew up in our face. *Let's see*, I was thinking, *there's a lifeboat right out on this deck, but that will take too long, so maybe we should just grab a couple of life jackets and dog-paddle out to that yacht over there, but then what if the owner is a friend of Drake's? Hmmm . . .*

When my phone rang, I jumped on it gratefully.

"The deed is done," Rollo said dramatically.

"Rollo, is the tapestry there?" I asked.

"It most certainly is."

"And is it the right one?"

"Seems to be. I dragged it inside and unrolled it, and I'm looking at it right now."

I told Rollo a few identifying features of the tapestry, to be as sure as I could. Rollo, being a fanatic collector of fine antiques himself, examined it carefully as we spoke, finally convincing me that it was the real deal. "Okay," I said. We hung up.

I nodded to Jeremy, and, acting somewhat sorrowful, allowed him to remove three of the fake coins from my bracelet, which he then handed to Drake. The moment the coins landed in Drake's palm, his fingers closed on them in a fist; and he actually waved his fist in the air, like a soccer player congratulating himself on a score. Then he put the coins right into his pocket.

But there was still something in his smile that chilled my blood. He was staring at the remaining two coins on my bracelet.

"What a shame to break up the set," Drake said. "I really should have all five of them."

I felt the pit of my stomach go cold. Drake's tone had a new menacing quality that I didn't care for. Furthermore, he must have pressed a button somewhere under the bar or table, because suddenly, four very thuggy-looking guys appeared on deck. From their thick, muscular bodies, pugnacious stance and tough faces, I knew perfectly well why they'd been summoned. I stifled a gasp when I saw that, under their jackets, each man wore a holster with a scary-looking gun. I mean, they were carrying *firearms*, for God's sake. I felt suddenly paralyzed with terror, and, for the first time, I really believed that this night could end badly.

But I have no idea what Drake actually meant to do, because, at this fortuitous moment, I heard a distant bell. Actually, it was not so distant. It was quite close, coming from a boat that was bearing down on us. It rang its bell again, and this time, we all went out on deck.

"Who the hell is that?" Drake demanded.

I felt a surge of relief, and wondered if I was seeing a mirage. Yet, there it was, with its name clearly visible. *Penelope's Dream*. And there was our captain Claude, waving at us. And, zipping ahead of it, I now saw, was our little motorized lifeboat, chugging determinedly toward us with all good speed, piloted by Gerald, a member of our crew.

Drake's men moved forward, as if ready to spring into anti-pirate action, but Jeremy said, loudly and commandingly, "Hold it! Those men are with me."

As the launch came pulling up alongside us, Gerard beamed a searchlight our way, and called out loudly and briskly, "Mr. Laidley, sir. You and Miss Nichols are late for your engagement tonight."

Gerard is a big beefy Welshman with numerous tattoos on his enormous arms. You don't mess with a fellow like him. Meanwhile, the rest of our crew stood on the deck of our yacht, watching closely. One of them had a pair of binoculars trained on us. The tense, alert body language of our crew indicated that they'd be happy to fire cannons if necessary. Not that we had one. A cannon, I mean.

So, for a moment, we were all at an impasse. Drake and Jeremy were staring at each other, and everyone else watched and waited. Drake's men glanced at him uncomfortably, as if awaiting his orders. Drake, still in the glare of Gerald's spotlight, seemed to recognize his conspicuous position. He turned to Jeremy, with that gambler's gleam in his eye.

"My three against your two. High card takes all," Drake said challengingly. He signalled a steward. "Get a fresh deck," he ordered, and the guy hopped-to.

I couldn't believe it. Here was a master of the universe, standing on the deck of the biggest yacht in Monte Carlo, with the world at his command, and a stash that would make King Midas weep—and yet, at that moment, he seemed completely blind to everything that he had. All he could see were the two coins that I possessed, and he didn't; and he was acting like a man who felt really, truly poor and deprived. Apparently nothing would console him, until he got his hands on those remaining two coins. His face was calm enough, but I could see the veins in his neck standing out.

So, when his steward appeared with a brand-new deck sealed in cellophane, and broke it open, and laid it on a small table, Drake gestured toward Jeremy to cut the deck. Jeremy glanced down at it, feigned hesitation, then reached for the cards, and cut them to reveal the Jack of Hearts. Drake sprang forward, cut the remaining cards, and drew the Ace of Spades.

He stared triumphantly at Jeremy, who looked furious but trapped, like a guy who can't renege on a bet in front of all the other guys. I must say that Jeremy's acting was superb. Because, as he later told me, thanks to Rollo's coaching, Jeremy had spotted that the so-called "fresh" deck of cards was a marked deck. So he knew that Drake couldn't lose. But of course, it was all part of the game.

Drake held out his hand to me. I took the last two coins off the bracelet, and dropped them in his eager palm. "Let's go," Jeremy said shortly. Gratefully, I scampered over to where Gerald was waiting, his hand extended to help me down into our little launch. Jeremy was right behind me.

"Wait, Penny," said a female voice unexpectedly. I looked back, and saw a figure move behind Drake. It was Tina. She had drunk quite a lot today, and it hadn't made her tipsy, exactly, but she seemed to take a defiant pose. She was holding her pashmina shawl and a purse. "Can you drop me ashore?" she asked. She turned to Parker. "I have guests waiting for me," she said casually.

Drake glanced at her, then shrugged indifferently. So Tina climbed in, and Gerard expertly turned the launch around and headed away from Drake's *Jackpot*.

"Where to, sir?" Gerard asked Jeremy.

"Drop us ashore in Monte Carlo so I can pick up the car. It'll be faster," Jeremy replied.

Tina took out a tiny gold phone decorated with silver starfish, and I heard her telling her chauffeur to be ready for her. Under the noise of the motor, I whispered to Jeremy, "How did Claude happen to—?"

"I told him to bring the yacht to Monaco, stay close enough, and await my instructions," Jeremy explained. "Then, I sent him an e-mail—*Go!*—as soon as Drake returned the tapestry."

The rest of the ride to shore was utterly speechless, until the little motorboat slowed as it pulled into the harbor, reached the dock and we began to disembark. I had been studying Tina through lowered lashes so she wouldn't notice, and I was wondering just one thing: Had she actually been fooled by the fake Lunaire charms?

Tina spotted her waiting limousine, but then she turned to me, as if she'd read my thoughts. With a gleam of satisfaction in her eye, she said in an amused, knowing way, "So Parker has the Lunaire coins, huh? Or does he?"

All I could say was, "Why—?"

"I wasn't sure if they were real," she replied. "But after Parker gambled away my necklace, well, that was the last straw. It means he's done with me. So, for once I felt like watching somebody else cheat him." As I digested this bit of news, she smiled. "Besides," she said daringly, "I'll soon need all the friends I can get. I'm betting you'd make a good one."

Jeremy had come to my side. "Wait," I said to Tina. I turned to Jeremy, and said to him, "Please let's give Tina back her necklace."

Jeremy reached into the pouch, pulled it out and handed it to her.

"Thanks," she said casually, as if I'd just handed her a favorite candy bar.

And away went Tina, in a cloud of memorable perfume.

Chapter Forty-three

"Thank heaven it's you!" Rollo exclaimed, pointing his flashlight at us when we entered the darkened dining room where the tapestry was laid out on the floor. Rollo was sitting beside it in the shadows, like a loyal guard dog. He had helped himself to Jeremy's favorite cognac; the bottle stood on a small side table, and was considerably depleted. Rollo held a big snifter in one hand, and a large, heavy flashlight in the other, brandishing it like a weapon.

"When I heard the car, I doused the lights and feared the worst," Rollo explained, as Jeremy switched on the overhead light. "Thought old Drake had sent someone to dispense with me and the damned rug. Drink, old boy?" Jeremy nodded.

Rollo grinned, handed Jeremy a snifter, then said affably, "Care for a drop, Penny dear?"

"Sure," I said, feeling suddenly weak-kneed. I sat down and sighed in relief. But every time a twig snapped outside or an owl hooted, I jumped. I actually shivered when I said, "I can't believe the thuggy way Drake delivered it."

"Never mind," Jeremy said. "We've got to move fast now. Let's examine every stitch of this tapestry."

First, I checked on its condition. Mercifully, it did not appear damaged by the theft, although it was a little dustier. I was hugely relieved, as if a long-lost friend had been rescued from ransom. This mysterious gift had taken me on quite a bumpy ride, as if Jeremy and I had endured some mythological "trial" to test our love. We must have come through it somehow, for now, gazing at its images, I experienced a strong, authentic kinship.

"Come on, fellas," I said briskly, emerging from the spell. "Let's find out what this tapestry wants us to know." I shuffled through my notes.

I'd always been bothered by the fact that the groom was marching ahead, without so much as a backward glance to his bride. It reminded me of myths of doom and superstition that I didn't want to have on my wedding tapestry, so I had averted my eyes without even realizing it. Now I gave it all a good, hard look.

"*Drink deep from the well of life*," I murmured, looking at the lower cartouche. I handed Rollo the translation of the Latin that Jeremy had made, so that Rollo could keep up with us, as I studied it anew.

"Strange," I said. "While that Latin proverb on the bottom certainly seems like advice to the groom, he actually isn't on the same horizontal layer as the water-well. The well is in the line above him, so maybe he's on his way there."

"*And treasure a faithful wife*," Rollo read aloud.

"Treasure," I repeated. "Dowry, from a faithful wife."

"Well, one thing we *do* know is that the Lunaire gold isn't in the well," Jeremy noted wryly. "So why did Armand even bother to mention the well in the Latin proverb?" He was gazing at our notes and pictures from the Bridal Car in the restaurant, with the design of the original top border of the tapestry. "What's my translation of the Latin in the top cartouche, Rollo?" he asked.

"*Follow the man that you have wed,*" Rollo continued reading aloud.

I stared at the young groom, and I followed the gesture of his outstretched arm. He was scattering some sort of petals on the ground, as if to perfume and soften the path that his bride would follow. This was something new to me, because I had not been able to see these delicate petals in my photos. With all the other insets and images on the tapestry to distract the eye, the scattered petals looked no more significant than fallen leaves.

But now, gazing at the fine detailing in the actual tapestry, I noticed that these flower petals were violet, with green leaves, all flecked with gold and silver thread, resembling the petals of the violet-and-green moonwort in the borders.

Even more interesting, the petals were not simply scattered in the same straight line as the groom's horizontal row of the procession. Instead, as I traced the petals, I realized that they fell on a diagonal line that cut across all the other horizontal rows stacked beneath. Starting from the lower right corner of the tapestry—where the newlyweds' house was—the petals traced a path climbing upward diagonally to the left, crossing into the bride's layer, at her feet, continuing upward to the groom's layer above her, where he was slightly to the left, scattering them. If you extended the diagonal line beyond the petals, it led you to the well, where the groom was presumably heading. But why?

"Petals," I said, pointing. "On the ground. See? It's moonwort. Going on a diagonal line from the lower right to the upper left." Jeremy peered at it.

"*Your home behind, your path ahead,*" Rollo continued.

"Aha!" Jeremy exclaimed.

"What—what?" I cried.

"*Your home behind*—didn't you say the gazebo is now standing where the newlyweds' house once was?" he demanded.

"Yes," I answered.

"It's directions," Jeremy said triumphantly. "There's the *home*—the house—and it's below, therefore *behind* them, they've passed it. The tapestry-maker is giving his daughter the *path* to follow."

"But if all it does is lead to the well, it's a dead end, right?" I asked.

"Wrong," Jeremy said excitedly, "because '*drink deep from the well of life*'—only tells you which *direction* to strike out in. It's not the final destination. Don't you see, he's saying, if you stand with your back to the house, and you aim yourself in the direction of the well, and go *ahead* of it—because of 'the *path* ahead'—that's where they will find the *treasure*! If you extend the diagonal line beyond the well, look where it lands." He traced it with his finger—and stopped at the "J.L." circlet of the Lunaire gold.

"Ohmigosh!" I cried. I had goose-bumps now.

"But how far ahead of the well?" Rollo asked pragmatically. "We need feet or yards, man!"

"True," Jeremy admitted. "It's a big field. And there are absolutely no numbers on this thing."

Yes, there was still something crucial that we were missing, we all knew this. But what? It had to be right under our eyes, a number, a direction, something . . . I could feel it. Like the game we played when we were kids, searching for hidden treasure; the person who'd hidden it would only say, "You're warm" if you were near, or, "You're cold" if you were too far away. We were burning hot, I just knew it.

Then, at that moment, away in the drawing room, Guy's clock began to chime the hours, beautifully, softly but resonantly, like a far-off bell from the past. Midnight. When I was a teenager, my father used to call it "the hour of charm", a paternal caveat, which meant that if I wasn't home before the clock struck twelve, the charm of the evening would wear off—my coach might become a pumpkin, my escort might be too drunk to drive, and other creatures of the night would become more aggressive and dangerous.

Ten, eleven, twelve . . . The lovely, silken sound echoed sonorously in the silent house, weaving its way into my thoughts, counting the passing hours . . . and telling me something more. I suddenly raised my head alertly. I was experiencing one of those Proustian moments . . . only, in audio. I remembered how, that night in his shop, Guy had explained to me the way the clock mechanism worked, and I'd asked him about the year that the clock had been made . . . and he'd tried to show me how he could tell the exact year. But there had been a distraction that night—Jeremy knocked something over. Then, later, just before Margery came to inspect the villa, Guy had been telling Erik about it, too . . . the day the tapestry was stolen.

I picked up the telephone and started dialing. "Who are you calling?" Jeremy asked. "It's late."

"Your mum. I have to speak to Guy Ansley," I said. "It's only eleven o'clock in London."

Aunt Sheila did not sound sleepy, and I heard music in the background. I apologized for calling late, explaining that I didn't have Guy's home number.

"No bother. We were just finishing a late supper. He's right here," she said.

He came to the phone, jovial as ever. I said, "Guy, please tell me how you were able to figure out the exact date that the clock was made? Did it have something to do with the Latin inscription?"

"Ah, yes, it's a chronogram," he said easily.

"A chronogram?" I repeated. "What's that?"

He told me, very patiently and carefully. "It's like a riddle, a game. You see, certain letters in the Latin alphabet also represent numbers. Roman numerals, that is. The letter *I* equals the number one; the letter *V* equals five, and *X* is ten, and *L* is fifty, while *C* is a hundred, *D* is five hundred, and *M* is a thousand. Anyway, you pull out only the letters that represent numbers. It was easy to do in your clock, because the Latin proverb was inscribed in gold—*except* for the number-letters, which were in silver. That's how I was able to pull them out so quickly. And when I added them all up, it came out to 1725."

"Letters! Latin! Look!!" I spluttered to Jeremy and Rollo, who appeared utterly baffled. I hastily babbled into the phone, "Thanks a lot, Guy! You've been more help than you know. Talk to you soon," and I rang off. Then I quickly explained the concept to Jeremy and Rollo.

"Ah, I see," Rollo exclaimed, going to examine the actual Latin on the tapestry and photos:

SEQUERE VIRUM QUEM IN MATRIMONIUM LOCAVISTI,
DOMUS POST TE, VIA PRO TE.
BIBE PROFUNDE EX CISTERNA VITAE,
COLE CONJUGALEM UXOREM.

But then Rollo's brow furrowed. "There are an awful lot of *D*'s and *M*'s among those letters that represent numbers," he commented. "If we added them all up, we'd have a number totalling in the thousands. I can't imagine what that would mean."

"Wait a minute," Jeremy said, staring at the tapestry and the photos. "Only a few of these number-letters have the moonwort twining around them. See?"

I stared, and saw that indeed, only certain letters were decorated with moonwort, and were set off with gold and silver thread. Now that I was aware of it, they gleamed and practically popped out at me.

"Quick, let's add them up!" I cried.

"Okay," said Jeremy. He called out the letters:

V + I + I + V + X + V + I + X = ?

Then we converted them into Arabic numbers, and added them up:

5 + 1 + 1 + 5 + 10 + 5 + 1 + 10 = 38

"Total of thirty-eight," I said. There was a silence.

"Great," Jeremy commented. "Thirty-eight whats? Feet, hectares, horse heads?"

"Paces," I said firmly. "'Your *path* ahead', right? It's footsteps."

"That's as good a theory as any," Rollo agreed.

Jeremy muttered, "So, let's get this straight: Armand is telling his daughter that she must stand with her back to the house—leave it behind—and go in the direction of the well—that is, follow the husband's path of the moonwort—and *then*, maintaining that direction, you must march thirty-eight paces beyond the well . . ." He raised his head. "Well, we might as well try it. Sooner than later."

"I say, old man," Rollo said mildly. "It's past midnight. And it's dark out there. Could be wolves."

"There's a full moon," I reminded them. "That should help light our way."

"Time is of the essence," Jeremy proclaimed, "because Parker Drake might just find out that the coins he's got are fakes."

"We'd have to convince David to rip up those fields again," I reminded. "He already thinks we're crazy. So this time, we'd better be right."

"Wake up the whole bloody house if you have to," Jeremy said. "Tell them that at the very least, we've already recovered their tapestry. And we may find much, much more. So I should think they can humor us, one last time."

Chapter Forty-four

Well, we did. Wake up the whole house, I mean. By the time we arrived at the château, every light was on, and the house itself looked fairly alarmed, its windows ablaze, like eyes flung open wide in shock. We must have looked fairly comical, trundling in, carrying that heavy rolled tapestry, with me on the front end, and Jeremy in the middle doing most of the heavy lifting, and Rollo bringing up the rear.

When we got inside, my French relatives, overjoyed to get their tapestry back, helped us set it down and unroll it, and they squealed with delight at the sight of it again. We all agreed that it would remain here with them until the wedding.

"What a great detective *chère* Penn-ee is, to recover the tapestry!" Leonora cried. I was just glad I was her "dear" Penny again, after being Little Miss Trouble-Maker for so long.

"Never mind the tapestry!" Honorine exclaimed. "We're going digging for buried treasure!"

She was already dressed for a hike, with fancy boots and jeans and jacket. Charles was with her, too, wearing his hunting clothes, appearing ready to shoot a moose. David looked as if, against his better judgment, he was prepared to follow the firm instructions to cooperate that he'd gotten from Philippe, who stood by watching us, silently smoking his pipe. Philippe and Leonora remained at the château. Honorine jumped on the back of Charles' Vespa, while the rest of us piled into cars with electric lanterns, spades and shovels, setting out for the flower fields in Grasse. From the back seat, Rollo kept a sharp lookout, reporting that nobody was following us, so far.

When we arrived, it was very spooky, crossing the fields at night. There was that bright, full moon, which made the terrain appear eerily alight, even whitened, looking almost as if the fields were covered with snow. Far off, I heard weird animal or bird cries, I couldn't tell which. So, you can bet that I had no problem taking the advice from the tapestry, about letting the groom go first.

As we reached the gazebo, Jeremy explained our idea of how to proceed, and everybody participated. Honorine and Charles aligned themselves with their backs to the gazebo, where once the honeymooners' house had stood. David and Rollo went out and parked themselves where the old well was, beaming their flashlights back at us, so that Honorine and Charles could aim in that direction and then march toward the well. Jeremy and I tracked them from the sides, to make sure they were aiming correctly. When Honorine and Charles reached the well, still pointed in the proper direction, Jeremy took over, to pace out the thirty-eight steps beyond the well.

"But, how do we know how big Armand's stride was?" I wondered. "Or, his daughter's."

"Fine, you march on a parallel track to me, but do your own counting," Jeremy said. "Your thirty-eight paces will be shorter than mine. We'll get a wider area to dig, but we'll cover all bases."

And away we went, marching alongside each other, with Jeremy slightly ahead, on account of his big feet. We counted and paced.

Thirty-six, thirty-seven, thirty-eight . . . Then we came to a dead halt.

"Here," Jeremy said finally.

"I'm here," I said, a few feet back.

"I say," Rollo observed, huffing and puffing alongside us excitedly, "if this field were the tapestry, surely we are now right where the 'J.L.' crest was."

"Good. So we should dig out a square area between Penny's spot and mine," Jeremy said.

"All of it?" David demanded. "Are you quite sure this time?"

"Be quiet and start digging!" Honorine cried.

So Rollo, Jeremy, Charles and David began the Big Dig. Honorine and I kept watch, and told them when they were getting too far afield. The clank of spades and the *Sift-sift* of earth was a tantalizing sound, until we heard a *Thunk!* whenever one of them hit something. This happened a couple of times, and all the digging immediately ceased. But each time, it was only rocks.

"I should think it wouldn't be buried terribly deep," Rollo observed.

"Bear in mind, that the ground shifts over time," Jeremy reminded them. "So it may have sunk lower than its original position."

On they went. *Shump, shump, shump*. They kept digging. Then Jeremy hit something so hard, it sounded like pay-dirt to all of us. The men dropped their shovels and ran over to him. Honorine and I leaped forward, shining our flashlights into the hole they'd dug.

Jeremy was brushing the loose earth off it, to get a better look. We all peered in, and Honorine and David bumped heads. "There's something shiny there!" Honorine exclaimed.

"It looks like a box," David reported. This awakened my research mode.

"Don't drag it up!" I cried. "If it was made of wood, it might be disintegrating. Dig all around it, loosen the earth, until you can get something flat under it, and lift it like a pancake."

David looked at Honorine in confusion. "*Qu'est-ce que c'est 'pancake'?*" he inquired.

"*Une crêpe*," she said briefly. The men carefully cleared away the ground at all four sides. Then they slid one of the flatter shovels under it, and heave'd and ho'd until they managed to loosen the whole box from the ground beneath it. Finally, they were able to lift the box up, up, up—just like a pastry chef with a wooden paddle hoisting a loaf of bread out of the oven—and deposited the earth-smeared item on a big white cloth that Leonora had thoughtfully provided us.

"Whuf! It's heavy!" Rollo exclaimed. Everyone turned and looked at me expectantly.

The box was about nine inches by twelve, and eight inches high. Very gingerly, I brushed off the dirt with a soft cloth. As I did, it began to gleam more brightly, and I saw that it was a cedar-and-brass chest with gold-tooled leather. Its outer walls had been painted, and were faded now, but I thought I could make out the gold, silver, violet and green colors of moonwort.

"Oh!" I said with a gasp. "It's a good, solid box, see, the gilt brass fittings? I bet it has . . ."

I explored it gingerly with my fingers, searching for a special trick lock, which such antique coffers often had. I felt along until I reached a moveable panel at the back of the lock, that, when touched, might release the hidden mechanism.

"Here it is," I breathed. I tried it, but it wouldn't give. I peered closer, and realized that dirt had accumulated underneath the latch, preventing it from releasing. David handed me a small screwdriver, which I used to carefully scrape out the dirt. When I tried it again, this time, at my touch, the lock sprung open. Everyone aimed their flashlights at it now, as I lifted the lid. We all peered inside.

Moonlight made the contents gleam and glint and practically wink at us. A heap of golden coins. I reached in carefully, and picked up one, then another, and another. I handed a few of them around, and we all examined the dazzling coins in the palms of our grubby little earth-covered hands. They were heavier and thicker than I'd expected, with a weight that felt serious and good in my fingers.

"There's Lunaire's initials and moon crest on the obverse side," I breathed, pointing. Then I turned it over, so I could see the reverse. The coin curator was right; it was an image of the sun. But it didn't look exactly like his sketches. It was more dramatic, with fierce eyes; and the fiery rays were not spiky, they were more like curling waves of flames. That face, yes, that was different, too. It was more of a Zeus-like face, just like the sun in the pie-shaped window on Armand's tapestry. It didn't resemble Louis XIV, the Sun King. Perhaps this had annoyed the proud king.

The men were busy doing what men instinctively do . . . counting them.

"Twenty-one, twenty-two . . ." they were chanting.

"Hey, guys!" I cried. "Dontcha think we should get this baby to the château and count 'em up there at our leisure? Anything can happen out here in the middle of this field!"

"She is right," David said briskly. "Close it and bring it home."

I thought I heard a rooster crow, by the time we got back to the château. The sky had gone from charcoal-colored, to milky white, to a violet-blue-grey with streaks of lemonade-pink. Leonora watched in astonishment as the men hurried inside, carrying the chest of gold into the library. They flung back the lid, and began arranging the coins in stacks on the big table, counting as they went.

I stood back, watching my French relatives lay out the Lunaire gold in neat, orderly rows, stopping now and then to exclaim and examine a coin or two closely, as if they could not believe their own eyes. I was suddenly exhausted, and I sat down gratefully in a nice, comfy leather chair.

I realized that I was still clutching one of the coins. Lying there in the palm of my hand, the Lunaire gold seemed to be a repository of its own history, giving off a palpable vibe of mingled valor, risk, vanity, and playfulness. I gazed at the haughty expression on the face on that aristocratic moon, wondering about Jean Lunaire, who had ascended high, higher, higher on the ladder of success, only to have it all go up in sparks and flames . . . and, even worse, invoking the wrath of a king who envied him for having too much ambition—and, perhaps most unforgiveable of all—superior good taste.

Then my thoughts turned to the hardworking Armand, who made such beautiful tapestries, for idle rich people who felt entitled to—well, have their cake and eat it, too—until one day their carelessness brought on the revolution that proved their historic undoing.

But most of all, I found myself contemplating the life of Armand's daughter, Eleanore. I guess I felt a special kinship with a long-ago bride. She had been waiting for a dowry—and a father—that never arrived. She must have been so baffled and distraught by the strange fate that had befallen her father; and afterwards, she'd spent the rest of her life unknowingly close to the treasure he'd meant her to have.

Oncle Philippe came over now, to sit in the chair beside me. Occasionally he chuckled at the sight of his family happily counting their good luck. Here, at last, was the secret dowry of their ancestor's . . . only a mere handful of centuries later. I felt that somehow, it had always been destined for Honorine, so I found a rather satisfying symmetry in all this.

"Looks like the circle's been completed," I commented. Oncle Philippe's eyes twinkled. Then I asked, "What became of Eleanore, after she got married?"

He smiled. "I am told that Eleanore was especially bright—she was very good with numbers, and could add up long, three-digit columns in her head, without aid of paper or pen. By all accounts she was an excellent businesswoman, having had the experience, in her girlhood, of working with her father. So, she worked with her husband to build up their company. They had many children, and both Edouard and Eleanore lived to a ripe, old age."

I gazed at Honorine, her face alight with excitement as she watched the treasure being arranged in stacks, before her very eyes. David now announced the final number of coins. "Five hundred twenty coins," he proclaimed.

I called out, "I have one more here!" and I rose to go and add it to the stacks, but Oncle Philippe stopped me. He opened his palm, where he was holding four pieces of Lunaire gold that he'd picked up to examine; but, instead of adding them to the final tally, he insisted, over my protests, on adding them to the one that I'd been holding in my hand. Then he pushed my hand closed over them.

"*Alors*," he said. "*Now* the circle is complete."

Part Eleven

Chapter Forty-five

"Far be it from me to tell you what to do with your life," I said to Jeremy. "But I'd just like to point out that if it weren't for Aunt Sheila's horologist, we never would have found the Lunaire gold."

It had been two weeks since we dug up those gold coins, and now our wedding was only a week away. We'd spent the day sorting out final wedding preparations, and packing up for our honey-moon. In the late afternoon, we managed to steal a little quiet time for just the two of us, drinking glasses of iced tea while sitting on the wrought-iron chairs on the patio, overlooking the sparkling swimming pool.

"True," Jeremy allowed. "I admit that it can, at times, be useful to have a clock-man about the place. You never know when you're going to need another chronogram decoded."

"He's a nice guy, and you were a pain in the ass," I reminded. Jeremy smiled ruefully.

"Well?" I said.

"What?" he asked, his eyes narrowing.

"Don't you think it's high time that you extended a personal wedding invitation to Guy Ansley?" I demanded. "I sent him an official one, but your mom told me that the poor fellow actually volunteered to stay away from the wedding if his presence would cause a rift between you and your grandmother."

"Very sporting of him," Jeremy said, pretending to consider Guy's sacrificial offer. I lifted my tea spoon menacingly over his knuckles. Jeremy said quietly, "Yes, I'll give Guy a call."

"Good," I said. "And make sure you mean it."

"You are becoming a bit of a bossy-boots yourself," Jeremy remarked.

"Humph," I said. "When you're done, let me talk to Guy. I'd like to ask him if he'll transport that lovely clock he gave us back to London, after the wedding. When we return from our honeymoon, I want to walk into the townhouse and see that beauty, right there on the mantel, waiting for us."

"You won't walk," Jeremy said gallantly. "I shall carry you over the threshold."

He picked up the day's newspaper from London, which had been lying on the table untouched, as we'd both been too busy to even glance at it. "Wow," he said, "you don't have to worry about seeing Parker Drake behind every tree and shrub. Looks like his lucky streak is at an end."

He held the paper aloft, so that I could see a headline:

MULTI-BILLIONAIRE ADVENTURER UNDER INVESTIGATION FOR TAX FRAUD

"Drake appears to be in serious trouble," Jeremy said, scanning the article rapidly. "Among other things, he has secret bank accounts in tax-dodging havens," he reported. "Not so secret anymore. Apparently he's been moving money all over the world. This is a big deal." Jeremy looked up and said, "Well, he made one big mistake."

"Tangling with the firm of Nichols & Laidley?" I suggested.

"True enough," Jeremy grinned. "But I was referring to his divorce. Tina's suing him, so he tried to pretend he had less money in his personal holdings, to shaft her on the alimony. That was stupid. He should have given her what she wanted, just to keep her quiet."

"What did she want?" I asked.

"Among other things, the yacht," Jeremy said. "She knew where to sock it to him. He cried poverty, as only a billionaire can, and this infuriated her. You know what they say: 'Hell hath no fury . . .'"

"Like a woman who's had her favorite necklace bandied about in a card game," I concluded.

Jeremy looked up, then said thoughtfully, "You know what this means? Drake won't be able to bid on the Lunaire gold at auction."

Oncle Philippe was selling some, but not all, of the coins. The experts had already assessed the Lunaire gold to be worth nearly $500,000 per coin . . . and it was expected to go even higher at auction. "It is definitely *not* a good time for Drake to conspicuously throw money around," Jeremy explained. "So I guess that means the museums and his rival collectors will get the lot."

"You forgot Rollo," I reminded him. "I thought it was sweet of Oncle Philippe to let Rollo have one."

"Yes, it was," Jeremy chuckled. "It seems right, somehow, that there won't be just one person hoarding all those coins. You know, I believe that's what Drake really craved—the glory of being the guy who discovered—and was the sole owner—of the Lunaire gold."

I thought about Drake and his painstakingly labelled coin collection in his office at the chalet in Geneva. "I actually almost feel sorry for him," I said, shaking my head.

"I don't," Jeremy responded. "That jerk nearly ruined our relations with your relations."

"Drake spurred us on to find that dowry," I reminded him. I couldn't help seeing everything in mythological terms now, where even ogres have a valuable role to play in the hero's adventure. "You might say it's thanks to Drake that Philippe doesn't have to sell off his flower fields," I pointed out.

"No, it's thanks to you," Jeremy said. "And Honorine doesn't have to get rushed into marriage. She's got plenty of time to fall in love now."

"Er, slight new development on that horizon," I said. Jeremy raised his eyebrows. "It would seem," I said, "that Honorine is faced with a dilemma. She has two suitors. And both are lawyers. She told me this morning."

"Two?" Jeremy said, puzzled.

"One is Charles. Apparently, he's redeemed himself—somewhat—by having been so willing to help her do all that Lunaire research. She now admits that he may have 'potential'."

"So, who's the other lawyer?" Jeremy asked, amused.

"Rupert," I replied.

"Rupert? Why, that little snake in the grass!" Jeremy exclaimed. He mulled this over. "I had no idea an office romance was in the making, did you?"

I smiled wisely. "So," I said, "when I asked her which guy she favored, she gave me one of those shrugs, and said, 'Well, of course, I like both Charles and Rupert. It's *très difficile*. I can't quite decide'."

"You sound just like her," Jeremy said.

And at that moment, Honorine came driving up in Jeremy's car, for she had gone to the airport to pick up my folks, who'd just arrived from the States. I heard their excited voices as they came in the front door. Minutes later, Honorine appeared at the patio doorway.

"Your parents are here!" she exclaimed breathlessly. "Your father went straight into the kitchen, because he has a whole suitcase full of cookbooks and recipes for the wedding!"

"I'd better go see him," I said, but before I could rise, Honorine put her hand on my arm to detain me a moment. She sat down with us, and took a deep breath, as if bucking up her courage.

"Something on your mind?" Jeremy inquired.

"*Chère* Penny and Jeremy, I hope you will not be offended by what I have to say," she announced worriedly.

"What?" I asked.

She paused, then took the plunge. "I must say—I quit!" Another pause, and then, very excited now, she blurted out, "Because, you see, I am going to perfume school."

"Wow!" I said. "Does that mean you passed that fragrance test?" She nodded. "Great!" I said. "Hey, maybe you'll turn out to be a real Nose."

"I'm willing to bet on that one," Jeremy commented.

"Who knows?" Honorine said. "But anyway, I had a long talk with Papa, and I might want to participate in running the family perfume business," she said, very correct and formally; but then she added, rather slyly, "I could still travel all around the world, looking for new scents! I may even someday start my own line for the company."

"Ah," said Jeremy, and we both suppressed a smile, imagining that David would be getting quite a bit more help than he'd ever imagined. Honorine, as if reading our thoughts, giggled.

"I've been doing some research of my own, just like you do," she confided. "I believe the wave of the future is to start a high-end boutique line that specializes in being green, *au naturel*, herbal, organic, and made of local, heirloom ingredients with handmade, traditional methods. Papa is of course delighted, but first I will learn not only about scent, but to make a business plan for my 'experiment'."

"Oh, that sounds wonderful!" I exclaimed.

"Now, I must ask you some-zing," she said, her brow puckered with genuine concern. "And please answer me truthfully. Will you and Jeremy be able to manage without me this winter?"

I tried not to breathe a sigh of relief. "Honorine," I said, "there's one thing I've learned. Never fight with destiny. You must follow your star."

We all went into the kitchen, where my father was already on the telephone, talking rapidly in French to the chefs at the restaurant of the pretty hotel where our guests would be staying. One of these chefs was a pal from Dad's cooking days. Dad would supervise all the food preparation, and the cake.

"Darling!" my mother cried as I kissed her cheek, "your father has absolutely exhausted me with this wedding-feast talk, all the way over on the plane. I am in *desperate* need of a nice gin-and-tonic!"

"Right away," Jeremy promised. My father hung up, beaming, and I hugged him.

"The chefs are sending someone over here with samples of the appetizer," my father announced. "We must all taste them, so don't anybody budge from this house!"

Honorine gazed at my parents with frank fascination, and now she grinned at me, as if to say, *Well, this explains you!*

My mother wandered out into the drawing room, drink in hand, and stood in front of the tapestry, which had been re-hung there, only just today. I followed her.

"Now I understand all the fuss," she said enigmatically to me. "It looks just like you."

"It scared me, at first," I admitted.

"Why, naturally, darling," she said. "If it were easy, anyone could do it."

"Do what?" I asked. "Get married? Everyone *does* do it."

"Not the way a serious girl like you does," she said, with that mysterious knowing attitude that mothers have.

"Mom," I said. "This is it. If you've got any advice for your little bride-daughter, do it now."

I expected one of her vague, airy responses that she gives whenever things get too personal for her. But she turned to me, her eyes suspiciously bright, and said, "Oh, sweetheart, I always knew you'd be just fine. But, remember that *how* you speak to a man is as important as what you actually say. Take some breaks during the day so that you're not overtired and cranky when you see each other. And always let him know, with your voice, that you love him. And darling, if ever something happens that seems too much to bear, to either one of you, then see that you come home to us and take some shelter. Both of you. Don't be afraid to ask for help. Your father told me to tell you this."

I had tears welling up in my eyes that now spilled over, down my cheeks. My mother handed me her handkerchief. "Well," she said briskly, resuming her usual aplomb, "I'd better go and unpack, before I fall asleep standing up."

When Honorine found me later, I was still sniffling a bit. She looked slightly alarmed.

"It's okay," I said. "Everything's fine."

"It better be," she said. "Otherwise *Maman* will tell me it's all my fault."

At my puzzled look she said, "Oh, yes, you know, when the tapestry disappeared and everyone was yelling at you, and it nearly ruined your wedding, she said to me, 'This is what comes of you showing up on her doorstep and making trouble for her.' So, you see, I *had* to make sure you made it to the altar."

"Well, you *were* kind of like a little rabbit who led us down the rabbit hole," I teased her.

Honorine smiled, then showed me why she had been looking for me. "Tante Venetia sent this, so you would have 'something blue'," she whispered, handing me a satin-covered box. "She regrets that she cannot travel these days."

Inside the box was a blue silk garter, studded with pink satin hearts that had little pink and blue gems twinkling in them. "They're sapphires," Honorine told me. "They are quite good, but honestly, you don't have to wear it, if you don't want to."

"Are you kidding?" I said. "Pass up a magic charm for my wedding day? Not a chance."

Chapter Forty-six

After weeks of stifling hot weather, Nature saw fit to send us a storm of near hurricane force. The power blew out for a couple of hours, but, mercifully, the generators kicked in. We were on a countdown of mere days before the wedding, and everyone was running about in a state of high-strung nervous excitement. Celeste arrived each morning, glaring at the sky, announcing that the weather had come from some other, ill-bred country—Spain or Russia, for instance. Each day she did her chores and then, in the afternoon, when ready to depart, she cast another baleful look at the sky, as if to warn it against further disruptions. Day after day, however, we faced more wind and rain; and one day, the airport at Nice was closed, with traffic redirected to Paris.

"Trust in Nature, eh?" I wailed to Honorine. "You and your Rousseau!"

"Never mind," my father assured me. "It can't last, and when it's done, the air will be more pure and clean that you ever saw. It will help you keep your head when you take your vows."

I thought he was just trying to keep me from throwing a full-scale bridal fit, but as it turned out, Dad was right. The day before the wedding, the sky and sea were suddenly becalmed, and the air was fresh and invigorating. The sun had not yet peeped out, but I saw patches of blue breaking up the layer of cloud cover. Here's what a newspaper reported about that day:

TRAIN BLEU REVIVED AS AMERICAN HEIRESS WEDS ENGLISH LAWYER

International guests climb aboard private train for pre-wedding gala

Destination French Riviera

THE PRE-CEREMONY FESTIVITIES for the wedding of multi-millionairess Miss Penny Nichols to Mr. Jeremy Laidley commenced in London this morning, as English guests of the happy couple boarded the high-speed Eurostar train at St. Pancras Station in London. We zipped across the English Channel at a hundred eighty-six miles per hour, while enjoying a spectacular brunch hosted by the groom's grandmother. And was the champagne flowing!

It was Paris by midday, where another high-speed choo-choo awaited us at the Gare de Lyon, this one dubbed the "Nichols-Laidley Express". Here the English guests were joined by the French and American friends and family of the bride and groom. All were escorted onto specially commissioned private cars, decked out with vintage accoutrements from the old Orient Express, Pullman and Train Bleu collections, which, to this reporter's mind, were so authentic that it made one want to light up a pipe, and solve a mystery!

I did do a bit of sleuthing, and discovered that all the exquisite silverware, delicate linen tablecloths, fringed lamps, and period artwork were, in fact, donated by the guests themselves, in lieu of wedding presents. What a great idea! All such furnishings will be donated to Women4Water, the bride's favorite charity. Will the bride set a trend among the socially conscious well-heeled? Quite possibly, since the president of Women4Water has reported that the charity's phone and e-mail lines have been jammed with offers of donations, from more folks who wish to participate in this excellent international drive to restore clean drinking water to all the world's children, and to promote healthy seas for the planet.

Now, I don't have to tell you which direction this new incarnation of the old train bleu was pointed—south, south, South of France. As the train pulled away from Paris, the party was already in full swing. Guests were fêted with fine sauvignon blanc wine and a sumptuous luncheon of roast quail on a bed of delicate herb-infused rice, with hearts of palm. Mmmm!

And, oh that scenery! A casual look out the window revealed a panorama of changing vistas across the lush and verdant French countryside, with its ancient castles, rolling farms, stunning forests, breathtaking mountains, and the gorges and rivers that the train traversed on magnificent viaducts spanning the sky . . . Ah, a feast for all the senses.

And, the band played on! Somewhere south of Lyon, the singing began, with an impromptu Cole Porter duet by American guests "Erik and Tim". Not to be outdone, this was answered with a Noel Coward ditty by the groom's mother's English beau—one Guy Ansley. Spontaneous applause ensued for all performers. After that, it was fun, fun, fun to the strains of music spanning the entire twentieth and twenty-first centuries.

Arriving in Cannes at 6:45 P.M.*, the last wedding guests boarded the train, these being the French family of the bride . . . Fourteen minutes later, the train pulled into the station at Antibes, where guests were brought to a luxury boutique hotel on the gorgeous Côte d'Azur, for a supper under the stars, poolside.*

Tomorrow, the nuptials take place at noon, at the private Riviera villa of the happy couple. But keep an eye out for the young bride and groom, because, word is that they will be sneaking off for the honeymoon aboard their vintage yacht known as "Penelope's Dream", which will bear them away to . . . where? Glamorous "parts unknown" . . .

I put the clipping in my wedding scrapbook. By all accounts, this dispatch from the bridal train was fairly accurate, for many of our guests later confided to Jeremy and me that the party atmosphere on the gussied-up train was elegant and irresistible, and that even the haughty Margery joined in the singing and dancing. I kept a pair of dinner plates from the event. They say, *Nichols-Laidley Express* on them, with the letters shaped to resemble a cute little train, roaring down the track along the coastline.

Chapter Forty-seven

Penny Nichols
and
Jeremy Laidley
request the pleasure of your company
on their wedding day . . .

The morning dawned sunny and crystal clear, as if someone had taken a chamois cloth and polished the sea and sky, specially for us. I woke early, with the soft sunlight streaming into the room, gently nudging me to rise; yet Jeremy, apparently, had awakened even ahead of me. He was not in the room when I first stirred, but soon there was a knock at the door. When I opened it, he entered with a formal attitude, carrying a breakfast tray.

"Hi," Jeremy whispered, setting the tray on the bed. "Nobody else is up yet. Just us. I made breakfast," he said, lifting a cover off a plate. "Now, your father told me that you love scrambled eggs. He also says that 'Anybody can cook gourmet, but only a real chef can scramble an egg'. We shall see."

Jeremy scooped up a little on a fork, and carried it to my lips. I tasted it, as he waited.

"Mmmm . . . *Parfait*," I said softly. He opened a bottle of chilled champagne he'd stolen from the cellar. Then he poured it into two little glasses, and sat beside me, and we drank a toast to the day.

For a while, we just sat there, leaning against the pillows, gazing out the open window, watching the sun rising, listening to the birds singing about the day.

Then he turned to me and said softly, "So. Feel like getting married today?"

"Actually, yes," I said, a bit shyly, but without an ounce of hesitation. "Yes, I certainly do."

"Good," he said with a smile.

"And you?" I teased. "How do you feel about it?"

"I feel fine," he said tenderly. "You see, right from the beginning, I somehow always knew that we belonged together. I believe you'll find it quite convenient. I'll be here to kiss you every day . . . catch you if you stumble—as you are wont to do occasionally, when you're off on one of your mad assignments—and, I can also offer a shoulder to cry on . . . a hug to protect you from the rain . . . that sort of thing. In short, to be here on call, at all times . . . just in case you need me."

"Oh, but I do," I said. "I need you always. I need you to stick around for a long, long time."

"Excellent," he said, as we finished our little glasses of champagne. "Then I'd say, it just so happens to be a wonderful day for a wedding."

And, as beautiful as the rest of the day became, I must say that my most vital memory, the one I cherish above all, is that sweet little moment alone that we had together, just the two of us, eating our breakfast, quietly listening to the others as they stirred and rose, and the house came to life. It is truly lovely to watch a day gently unfold, a perfect new beginning, every morning.

* * *

When it was time to dress, we parted ways. After my bath, I spritzed myself with the cologne that Oncle Philippe had made just for me. Jeremy had been whisked off to one of the guest rooms to dress. That left me alone in the big bedroom, but not for long. I was standing there in my new satin lingerie, when Honorine, Aunt Sheila, Tante Leonora and my mother trooped in, chattering excitedly, to fuss over me. They were carrying my gown, which had awaited me overnight in the closet of the small guest room we called the Renaissance Room.

The ladies all looked so pretty in their gowns. Honorine was in violet silk, Aunt Sheila in light yellow satin, Tante Leonora in a silvery pale green chiffon, and Mom in a dusty rose taffeta. They were like a bouquet of flowers, fragrant and bright-faced.

Honorine had given me a customized box of cosmetics that looked like a painter's palette, and now she helped me with my makeup, while the others carefully unwrapped the dress. Then they lifted it over my head, letting it descend all around me like a lovely white mist, its flowerlike folds drifting down to settle softly upon me. Aunt Sheila fussed with my hair a bit, getting it just right before my mother placed the cap-and-veil ensemble on my head, like a crown.

"*Regarde!*" Honorine exclaimed, steering me toward the mirror.

There was something very startling and dramatic, yet at the same time, natural, about seeing the dress in my own mirror, in my own home. While I stood there, my mother gave me the gift of a pearl necklace, from her and Dad. Then I stepped into the white satin shoes with gold heels.

When I was all dressed and ready, everyone else stood back respectfully, as Tante Leonora moved forward to take a final look at the full ensemble. She did a few lightening-quick adjustments—a tug here, a flick with her hand there, a pinch of a seam, a fluffing of the skirt, a smoothing of the train . . . then she, too, stood back and surveyed it all. I still don't know exactly what she did, but it made a visible, subtle improvement.

"Someday, Tante Leonora," I said, "you must tell me how you French women do it."

"One day quite soon," she replied, "you will realize that you already know."

And then, as suddenly as the ladies had arrived, they all scurried away. I had that strange moment which many brides do, when everyone else was so busy getting ready that they left me entirely alone, and nobody seemed aware of this. So I stood there, listening attentively, as cars pulled into the driveway, and doors slammed, and there were footsteps everywhere—on the gravel path, in the hallways, out on the patio—and the musicians began tuning up, while the hum of voices downstairs grew louder and more excited, with the arrivals of more and more guests. I heard the classical trio playing a Beatles tune, *In my life, I love you more . . .*

"Wow," I said to myself. "That's one big party going on down there."

Knowing I'd caused all this, I got a little scared. There was a knock at my door, and then my father came in. He was wearing his super-best suit, the kind that makes a man look seriously great, the one he uses only for extremely special occasions. This, too, thrilled me. It meant that my wedding really was a great big grown-up sophisticated deal.

"How are you, Penn-ee?" he inquired. He squeezed my hand.

"Fine," I said, still standing, so I wouldn't crumple my dress.

"Is everything okay?" he asked calmly, sitting down at the end of the bed, as if we had all the time in the world. At first I didn't catch on. I was so accustomed to him telling me that Jeremy was a fine boy, so I was a bit surprised and amused by his next comment.

"Are you sure this is what you want?" he said neutrally, as if it would be completely okay if I told him I'd changed my mind and wanted to fly the coop. If I'd said so, he probably would have serenely taken me for a long walk on the beach, and bought me an ice cream cone.

I smiled. "Yes, Dad, everything's okay." Then I added, "But thanks for asking."

"A father must, you know," he replied.

There was another knock at the door. Honorine came rushing in, with a big, shiny white box.

"Your flowers have arrived," she said breathlessly. She put it down on the top of the chest of drawers. When she opened it, the scent of freshly cut roses filled the air. My bouquet had come from Philippe's flower fields, arranged by a local florist. The roses were, just as I'd requested, a burgundy-red, with velvety green leaves, and little sprigs of white baby's breath here and there. They were bound in gold and white ribbons, with white streamers edged in gold.

"Your mother says be sure to hold it up, not down," Honorine said with a smile, then went out.

My father and I looked at each other. "Typical Mom," I said.

There was another quiet moment, during which a cool breeze came off the Mediterranean Sea, pirouetted across the lawn, twirled a little jasmine in its fingers, and then tripped lightly into the room, where it settled, warm and soft and caressing, like a veil across my skin. Someone knocked at the door, but did not enter. My father seemed to know what it meant.

"It's the message from downstairs. It's time," he said. He opened the door, stepped into the hall, and waited out there, leaving the door ajar for me.

I took one last look at the room, for no reason whatsoever, except that, well, yes, I would be coming back . . . But I would return as a married woman. I wondered how it would feel. I felt a surge of anticipation now, a kind of flow of courage, you know, the courage that comes from moments when you feel you're truly alive.

I picked up the bouquet, and went out to the landing. My bridal party was standing there, poised as if on the brink of something very serious. No one spoke now. Honorine came over to carry the train of my dress for me, and she and I descended the left staircase—slowly, slowly, slowly—while everyone else went down the other staircase, on the right. I saw my old boss, Bruce, at the foot of the stairs. He was not only quietly "directing" my wedding video, but, with his camera on a tripod, he was shooting this part of the opus himself, covering the procession, as the bridal party gathered in the circular foyer. Bruce had discreetly placed two other cameramen in the corners of the drawing room.

Honorine fluffed out the train of my dress again, and made a careful, last-minute check, in that earnest way she has of taking her assignments very seriously. Then, she went to the open door at the back of the drawing room, and nodded to the musicians, who began to play Handel's *Water Music*. Honorine tilted her chin up, poised like a pearl diver about to leap, and then off she went, starting the bridal procession. She moved down the center aisle, very slowly, scattering pink and white rose petals along the way. When she reached the first row, she took her seat beside her family.

Aunt Sheila was next. She was standing near Jeremy, and gave his cheek a light kiss. Then she turned and blew me a kiss, and went to the drawing room door. As she did, a very elegant-looking silver-haired Italian gentleman rose from a chair in a back row. Jeremy's Grandfather Domenico had arrived from Italy, with a few of his relatives who were seated nearby, watching with delighted smiles.

He wore a smart grey suit and vest, with a yellow flower in his buttonhole, and now, he stepped into the aisle, and offered his arm to Aunt Sheila, who took it gracefully. Together they went down the aisle, until they reached the front row, where they found their seats across the aisle from Honorine's family.

From the foyer, Jeremy moved forward. In his pocket he wore a silk handkerchief of the same burgundy color as the roses in my bouquet. Now he looked at me intently as he passed by, and I got a brief, reassuring whiff of the cologne he'd gotten as a gift from Oncle Philippe. I smiled at Jeremy, and I saw, reflected in his smile, that he had seen what I wanted him to see. He turned, very serious, and went through the doorway, into the drawing room, then, slowly, went down the aisle alone. When he reached the end, where the tapestry was, he turned, faced the crowd, and waited.

My mother took my hand in hers, squeezed it, then released it. My father offered her his arm, and the two of them went down the aisle, walking in perfect time with each other, until they reached the aisle seats in the front row on the bride's side.

So, then it was just me. I stepped forward, pausing at the threshold of the room.

The music changed. You know what it was. The pretty little classical trio played it very sweet and light, and the charming melody wafted across the room to me, as if it were beckoning me to come.

La-la-la-LA,

La-LA-la-la . . .

Suddenly I felt myself floating forward, gently, on the balls of my feet, as if I were propelled by a puff of air, like a sailboat, now drifting down the aisle, past all those familiar faces to my right and to my left, which were so startling to see, after the heightened moment of solitude I'd just experienced. It was like watching my past life go by, as I spotted my girlfriends from the States, smiling at me with excitement, and Jodi from the charity group, who gave me a conspiratorial wink; and then I saw Diamanta's face in the crowd, having come over from Corsica. The Count von Norbert and his son Kurt were there, too. And sweet Simon Thorne, looking dapper as ever—I think that Great-Aunt Penelope surely liked having her old dancing partner here again. Then there was Thierry and Monsieur Felix, looking spiffy in suits; and Charles and Rupert, apparently each unaware of the other's significance to Honorine . . . and Harold, Jeremy's old boss from his law office.

It seemed as if they were drifting past me faster now, but they were all there . . . Erik and Tim, looking so proud, as if they might bust their buttons; and Tante Leonora, Oncle Philippe, David and Auguste, making such a beautiful row of family with Honorine; and Guy and Rollo, and even, by God, there was Great-Aunt Dorothy, appearing so impressed that she looked like a canary who'd swallowed a cat.

I saw, across the aisle, Uncle Giles and Amelia beaming at me from their seats alongside Grandmother Margery, who appeared rather pleased and proud; possibly because Clive, the English photographer who'd photographed the Beethoven Lion, had been aboard the Wedding Train, snapping away madly, taking shots of all the guests on the train, whose faces then appeared in the newspapers' society columns . . .

But while I was moving past them all, there was one face that was like a bright, guiding light throughout, steering me across the gulf . . . Jeremy, waiting for me there, standing before the tapestry. Next to Jeremy was our captain, Claude, who stood ready to perform the ceremony. I came floating up and took my place beside Jeremy, landing as softly as a feather, borne on a breeze. The music stopped, and I heard our words reverberating in that lovely room.

I, Jeremy, take thee, Penny, to be my wife and partner in life . . .
Jeremy, with this ring, I thee wed . . .

"And now," said Claude, "you may kiss the bride."

Chapter Forty-eight

Penelope's Dream pulled away from the harbor, leaving a trail of flowers in its wake. Our voyage began just cruising along the French and Italian Riviera, finding secret, private little coves where we could row ashore for romantic picnics. For a charming while we turned off all the phones and radios, allowing ourselves to just be lovers alone and away from the cares of the world. Well, not quite alone. There were ducks that swam beside us for awhile, and real swans, too . . . then gulls swooping overhead.

One afternoon, we were lying on our backs in the steamer chairs, gazing idly at the sky, watching the clouds to see what pictures we saw in them.

"Hello, wife," Jeremy said, as we lay there sipping our drinks, inhaling the fresh salty air.

"Hello, husband," I responded, feeling more contented than even I had ever dreamed possible. (And ya know I do like to dream big.)

"Well?" he joked. "Has marriage changed us?"

"Too early to tell," I replied playfully.

"Perhaps now we can finally settle into some quiet domestic bliss?" Jeremy murmured.

"For years and years," I agreed.

"Let's make some ground rules for the future," Jeremy offered. "One, no more cases involving relatives."

"I agree!" I said wholeheartedly. "Two," I contributed slyly, "no more weird 'invitations' for awhile from the big movers-and-shakers of the world."

"Deal," he said. "Maybe we should try a little gentleman farming."

"Yes," I sighed happily. "Gardening is good for the soul."

Well. Little did we know, of course, as we lay there watching the sunset and making our best-laid plans, that even as we spoke, back in London, a letter was being slipped through the mail slot of the firm of Nichols & Laidley. It dropped on the floor with a conspicuous clack. Honorine wasn't there anymore, so the letter lay there for some time, awaiting our return. This one was on very fancy, official stationery—a heavy cream-colored vellum, embossed with initials: "H.R.H."

We would like to engage you on a matter of great importance to us, which also concerns a relative of yours . . .

The clock on the mantel chimed knowingly. Well, so much for ground rules. Life is what happens to you when you're making them. But after all, I never expected to go through my days without breaking a few. Now and again. Very soon indeed.

THE END

A Rather Charming Invitation

C.A. Belmond

This Conversation Guide is intended to enrich the individual reading experience, as well as encourage us to explore these topics together—because books, and life, are meant for sharing.

A CONVERSATION WITH C.A. BELMOND

Q. This is the third book in your "Rather" series, which began with "A Rather Lovely Inheritance" and its sequel, "A Rather Curious Engagement". What's it like to follow your main characters through three novels? Did you plan this to be a series at the onset?

When I began writing *A Rather Lovely Inheritance,* I was completely focused on telling the story of an American girl who unexpectedly inherits a windfall that requires her to go to Europe, prompting a personal journey as well. I loved the idea of a modern-day girl taking a "Grand Tour" abroad, while delving into her family's history in London, France and Italy. Once she accomplished her mission at the novel's end, well, there was still so much for Penny to do, see, and experience, that it seemed as if her story was really just beginning. To my surprise, the same thing happened at the end of the sequel, and at the end of this book, too! I just follow the trail, as Penny and Jeremy do whenever they are on a "case", yet, at the same time, each novel feels like its own complete and unique world to me.

Q. Throughout this novel, "A Rather Charming Invitation", there are various examples of very different marriages and couples. Was this deliberate?

Oh, yes. I had great fun with Penny behaving as a "bridal anthropologist", that is, allowing her to "research" marriage by taking a closer look at the other couples she meets, while she's trying to figure out if a wedding will be a good thing for her relationship with Jeremy. I think most brides go through this at some point; they suddenly become more acutely aware of how other marriages seem to be working . . . or not working. So, in her *Charming* adventure, Penny is introduced to marriage in all its permutations: arranged marriage, shotgun weddings, unfaithful spouses, marriage of convenience, marrying-for-money . . . and, the dearest of all: marriage of mutual love, passion, respect and companionship. Penny is an observant but nonjudgmental woman, so she notices the wistful, touching aspects of humanity as well as the hilarious. And of course she uses it all as a way of puzzling out what she wants for her own marriage. Or, as Penny herself defines the task: "How to tie the knot . . . without unravelling the unique love that brought us together in the first place."

Q. How does it feel for you as the author to have your main characters, Penny and Jeremy, get married? What was it like to write about their wedding?

Very satisfying, actually. When I set out, I knew one thing for sure: Penny and Jeremy would have to find their own unique way to marry, in a style that suits their newfound, jaunty life. Penny is such an earnest "seeker" that she would naturally resist anything about a wedding that's inauthentic, superficial, egotistical or grimly dutiful. Also, I wanted to indicate that marriage wasn't going to spoil their fun. So I especially enjoyed having Penny and Jeremy attempt to plan a wedding smack-dab in the midst of one of their typical adventures. It's my way of saying that life goes on even while you're on the road to taking this big step, and the wedding can be part of the pleasure of moving forward together.

Q. In the earlier novels, Penny's English side of the family dominates. Now, in this novel, Penny gets an unexpected visit from a French cousin, which sets the whole romp in motion. What prompted you to write a novel about the French family connection now?

Penny's French father and his family were always there in the background, so I wanted to find out more about them. The cousin who entices Penny into this world, Honorine, is someone who Penny compares to the rabbit that led Alice in Wonderland on all her adventures. Since Penny hasn't really known these relatives until now, they represent a "buried treasure", in other words, an aspect of herself that she has always wished to explore but didn't dare. It's as if she's giving herself permission to be sensual, sophisticated, and natural.

Q. Penny's French relatives are at odds with Jeremy's English family, in a struggle about which country the wedding will be held in. Is there something inevitable about a tug-of-war over weddings where families are involved?

It would seem so. Jeremy observes that they are in peril of re-igniting the Hundred Years' War between France and England! No matter how amicable a couple is, they're not immune from the pressures that families invariably exert. So, in dealing with these warring factions, Penny and Jeremy find themselves bickering as they try to work out their differences. But even when they argue, there's a fondness and intelligence between them, underneath the strain. Ultimately, they genuinely like, and prefer, each other's company, so they are willing to put their loyalty to each other first.

Q. What made you use an ancient tapestry as a linchpin of the story?

I found that a tapestry is a very enjoyable and useful way to illustrate the complexity of customs and emotions that surround weddings. I had great fun with the notion of golden threads, loose ends, knots and entanglements. Historically, weddings evoke various traditions, and not all of them are so great for women, what with bartered brides and other such arrangements. For today's brides, these can be confusing metaphors, resulting in a patchwork of values which often contradict one another. Are love and passion essential to marriage? Is it necessary to declare one's intentions to the world? Is a wedding a ceremony for parents, or for the people who are marrying? Every bride must sort out this puzzle for herself, but it helps to look at history, and why these traditions began. Penny isn't interested in displaying her wealth, nor are her parents trying to marry her off to make some social or political connection; so she must reject a few of the old rituals. At the same time, she is bemused and confused by some of our narcissistic, vainglorious twenty-first century trends. But if a betrothed couple takes the time to sort out what matters to them, they just might find the thread that leads them out of the labyrinth, and they can emerge even stronger.

Q. As they ascend higher in society, Penny and Jeremy encounter some very powerful, sometimes strange movers-and-shakers in Geneva and Monte Carlo. At the same time, Penny must research her family's French ancestors, which leads her to the rarefied world of artists and their rich patrons during the reign of the Sun King of France. There seem to be some parallels here—aren't there?—between the wealthy of today and the wealthy of the "ancien régime"?

Yes, indeed, although I must say that I did not set out to do that. It just evolved in the story; it was one of those serendipitous things that make writing such a pleasure. The card games, the ostentatious display of wealth and power, the peculiar inability to ever have enough. Humanity does seem to repeat itself in history. And, underneath it all lurk the same human fears, insecurities and lack of self-awareness, which do play out in the most astonishing ways.

Q. Trains "run through" this novel quite a bit. There's the legendary Train Bleu restaurant in Paris. And the character of Venetia, the aging ballerina, recalls the actual train bleu from the 1930s. Without giving away the rest of the story, let's just say that there are other fanciful occasions involving trains in the novel. Are these trains a symbol of Penny's journey?

Yes, because trains have traditionally been a meditative way to move forward, from which you can view not only where you're going, but where you've been. A train window is also a vista to parts of the country that you may not see from the road or the air. So, it's a way for Penny to find links not only between France and England, but also between her ancestral past and her own future.

Q. Clocks and time seem to have special significance in the novel. How did this come about?

This, too, was something that began in a small way but then took on more significance, quite naturally, as the story unfolded. And, like the tapestry, a clock can be much more than a mere decoration. I find that antique clocks are often very sweet, for they were handmade in an era when their creators were inspired by natural symbols of the passage of time—the stars, the planets, the tides. So, while such clocks measure the fleeting nature of life on Earth, they can sometimes capture that which is eternal.

QUESTIONS FOR DISCUSSION

1. As Penny is planning her wedding, she is introduced to all kinds of couples, both in her life and in her historical research. Discuss the various unions in the story. How do they differ? How do they influence Penny's decisions? Are there certain qualities that all couples have in common?

2. Why does Penny feel unsettled about getting married? What events increase her uncertainty? What is she trying to protect? How does the city of Paris affect her?

3. Jeremy is under pressure from his relatives to conform to what his family regards as a proper and conventional approach to the wedding. This causes conflict between him and Penny, until he has an insight which seems to suddenly clear the air. What was this important insight?

4. There are heroic images of knights, and "trials" and "triumphs" in the tapestry, as well as the image of a betrothed couple passing under an archway to test the sincerity of their love. What trials did

Penny and Jeremy have to go through in order to reach their wedding day in the spirit that they wanted?

5. What do you think was Honorine's role in the novel? What about Guy Ansley? What role does Parker Drake play? Tina Drake? Monsieur Felix? Do these people symbolize anything apart from their everyday aspect?

6. The antique clock in the story has symbolic significance, but also plays an unexpected, practical role in solving the mystery. Discuss the various scenes in which the clock appears and influences the action.

7. Penny sometimes finds the tapestry perplexing, sometimes inspiring and comforting, sometimes ominous and gloomy. What tempers her response to it? Can you think of particular scenes that were "turning points" in her feeling for the tapestry?

8. Perfume is a powerful element in the novel. The flower fields in Grasse, the old perfume factory, the masked ball in Geneva, and the women on the yacht in Monte Carlo—these scenes all pivot around scent. What is the significance of fragrance in each of these turning points?

9. Trains from the past and the present are a recurring theme throughout the novel. Discuss the novel's various journeys, departures, arrivals and destinations. How do they impact the ultimate resolution of the story?

10. There are many invitations in the novel. Is there any one that particularly stood out to you as the "charming" one?

11. Penny and Jeremy try to achieve a balance in their work and personal lives. Have you known couples who work together? What are the particular challenges, and what are the rewards?

12. In the weddings that you have seen and participated in, what conflicts arose? How did people resolve them? Did this affect the marriage afterwards?

ACKNOWLEDGMENTS

Heartfelt thanks to my husband Ray, for your intelligence, insights, and irresistible humor. Special thanks to Margaret Atwood, my Good Witch of the North, for your warmth and encouragement all along the way. And to my knights-in-shining-armor: Michael Carlisle, for your intuitive wisdom and elegant wit; and David Forrer, for your smart, considerate advice and unshakeable good humor. Many thanks to all the other wonderful folks at Inkwell Management. A double-thanks to the two Karas in my life: To Kara Cesare, because you've become so much more than an editor, you're a true and cherished friend; and to Kara Welsh, for your faith in me and your ever-inspiring support. Thanks also to the great team at Penguin, especially Rachel Kahan, Claire Zion, Craig Burke, Catherine Milne, Jesse Feldman, and the many talented people in the art, sales, marketing, copy, promotion and production departments. I'd also like to express my appreciation to Peter Struck at University of Pennsylvania, for helping me get beyond my high-school Latin for this book. And to Vivik Kaylan for your generous design assistance. Special thanks to Ginger Barber for always being there when I needed advice. Fond thanks to Elizabeth Corradino, for your good counsel and loyal friendship. And finally, my warmest regards to all my readers around the world—I deeply appreciate your "lovely, curious, charming" letters, as we travel together from one adventure to the next!

ABOUT THE AUTHOR

C.A. Belmond has published short fiction, poetry and humorous essays. She was awarded the Edward Albee Foundation Fellowship and was twice a Pushcart Press Editors' Book Award finalist. Belmond was a writer-in-residence at the Karolyi Foundation in the South of France, and her original screenplays were short-listed at Robert Redford's Sundance Institute and the Eugene O'Neill Playwrights Conference. She has written, directed and produced television drama and documentary, and has taught writing at New York University. Her debut novel, *A Rather Lovely Inheritance*, launched the original story of Penny and Jeremy. The second book in the series is *A Rather Curious Engagement*. And now, the third and newest novel is *A Rather Charming Invitation*. For news of upcoming works and events, visit the author at her Web site, www.cabelmond.com.